*The
Invitation*

*2000 years after Jesus solved the
problem of guilt,
is it time to place limitations on man's
free will?*

The
Invitation

2000 years after Jesus solved the problem of guilt, is it time to place limitations on man's free will?

by

Dave Lucas

The ideas and concepts presented in this document are strictly those of the author and are not endorsed by The Foundation For A Course In Miracles. I wish to thank the Foundation and Dr. Kenneth Wapnick for their support and encouragement.

First published as part of a volume entitled *Supplements to A Course In Miracles* by Viking/Penguin, New York, NY.

ISBN: 1-58721-499-7

1stBooks – rev. 5/9/00

About the Book

It is the author's belief that the New Age began with *A Course in Miracles*, an inspired work. The Course works all of the time for everyone, but being all-inclusive, many people do not know where to start to solve the particular problem that is urgently calling for resolution.

The Invitation solves that with a humorous story that is believable and up to date; incorporating some of the situations that advancements in man's condition are not addressed in earlier Scriptures or religious documents. Although prostitution, murder, political power abuse, etc., are part of the story, the subjects are dealt with in an uplifting and humorous manner, totally lacking in vulgarity and suitable for a universal audience. Throughout the story, lessons from the Course are hidden in parable form.

The *How-To* offered in the Appendix will prove conclusively to you the existence of a God Who is not to be feared, and Who will provide the answers and assistance that you seek.

I would like to dedicate this effort to the following people:

Catherine Seaman who introduced me to a seminar where I learned the technique to unlock the power within. Catherine was given a Course In Miracles for her effort.

Kathryn "Midori" Chun, my Sweetie Pie, who is Kathy that we picture and read about in the book. I gave her a Course in Miracles, even though she can't read. A real bimbo, but my best friend. I don't think she needed the Course anyway.

Joann, Judy, or whoever you are, for teaching me how to use computers the hard way. How are you doing with the Course? The books you didn't need. Love you, JoBabe; couldn't have done it without you.

Kathryn, my mother, who inspired me throughout. I never thought of sending her the Course, even though she was in a lot of pain. Sorry, Mom.

Chapter 1

Kathryn sat uncomfortably in her wheelchair and studied the compact disk that arrived in the morning mail. It was in a plain, unmarked, shipping envelope with no postage, addresses, or date stamp. It was a CD, she was sure of that, but it was shiny black and had no markings of any kind on it. Was it for music, or was it software for a computer? She could not recall ordering any new products by mail. Her father, Professor Makino, never ordered by mail and was quite content with his music collection that was on 8-track, reel-to-reel tapes. The only computer he had at home was to write personal letters and take care of household expenses. For that, he still used his old, second-hand, IBM computer with the big floppies. He certainly was not ready for the jump to CDs. It must be for her, she thought. It was probably a surprise present from her father. He was always doing things like that for her.

Deciding it was music; she wheeled herself into the living room, turned on the stereo, and inserted the disk. A soothing, baritone voice announced, "Good morning, Kathy. Please put this in your computer."

She was becoming annoyed as each movement she made was painful and she thought that the least the company who made this CD could do was to indicate that it was software and not music. She removed the disk and wheeled back to her custom-designed computer-room and den where she spent most of her life. On the way, she thought that the guy who made the announcement should be working in telemarketing and not mail order...with a voice like that! She managed a smile.

Kathy was confined to a wheelchair since the age of twelve when she was severely injured in an automobile accident that took the life of her mother. The doctors were able to repair the damage to her face, but not the fractured vertebrae or the nerves that transverse them. She considered herself fortunate that she was alive, had the use of her upper body, and, more importantly, all of her mental capacities. Occasionally, like this morning, she had

1

some aches and pains. The pain at the initial trauma was intense. When she slammed into the dashboard, she also broke her nose and collarbone. She received several lacerations while being thrown around inside the vehicle. To complicate matters, her spleen ruptured and had to be hastily removed at the hospital. She vaguely recalled this painful and unfortunate episode in her life as she installed the shiny, black disk into her new computer.

Professor Makino tried to make up for the loss of his wife and the mother of his daughter by providing Kathy with every new computer gadget he could afford. He loved her very much and this was one way he chose to manifest that love. They spent many hours together playing with the new software, discussing all the innovations that were being developed and the many new uses that people and companies were finding for computers. Kathy had even started a small business at home but her father convinced her to continue working towards her Masters Degree before starting a dead-end, income-producing task. They talked about it and decided, together, that there were bigger fish in the pond and that she would go for them.

After putting the disk into her CD drive, she tried to enter the DOS-SHELL to see what might be on the disk, as was her custom. The monitor displayed only the Command prompt. She thought that strange and, perhaps, the disk was already set up for Windows. She typed WIN at the prompt and pushed ENTER. The monitor replied with the dreaded message: Bad Command or File Name. Impossible, she thought. Her Windows program always came up. She looked down at her computer to check for a disk left in a drive or a loose cable or some indication of the problem. All appeared to be in order. Looking back again at the monitor, she saw this message: KATHY, ACTIVATE YOUR AUDIO. Startled, she turned on the switch for the speakers. She also checked her modem, thinking that she was somehow getting network input. Soft music and the pleasant, baritone voice came from the speakers.

"Hello, Kathy. I'll introduce Myself more fully in just a moment. (Pause)

"Please relax and do not be frightened. (Pause)

"I am a friend who wants to help you. (Pause)

2

"Please cooperate with Me for just a few moments, OK? (Pause)

"Are you ready for some fun? If you are, type in the title of your favorite piece of music," the soothing voice instructed.

Kathy recognized the old familiar sales pitch and it was not the surprise present from her father that she had hoped. She decided to play along to see what they were selling, thought about the request for a moment, and typed, "The Impossible Dream."

The voice asked her, "Would you like an instrumental or do you have a favorite artist in mind? Please type in your choice."

She didn't hesitate. She loved Jack Jones's rendition and typed it.

The requested piece began to play immediately. She pushed away from her console and sang along with the music. At the conclusion, she was asked if she had enjoyed the music. "Oh, yes!" she said and began to type that on the keyboard.

"I can hear you quite well, Kathy. No need to type a reply. Can we just talk for a few moments?" the voice asked.

"This is crazy! This computer cannot converse in real-time. I don't even have a telephone or audio input to the sound system. I can only receive data on my modem. I just got it and it isn't even hooked up yet. I haven't even read the manual that came with it." Kathy spoke excitedly, while looking around to see if there was something else going on with her equipment...she knew that her father loved practical jokes.

"Let's forget the computer for just a minute and consider that we *are* having this conversation. I think that you have an open mind. You are very intelligent, very pretty, and I think you've had your share of misfortune in your twenty-three years. Wouldn't you agree?"

"Yes, I suppose so," Kathy replied in a softer voice, adding, "But...who are you? I don't recognize your voice at all. And...I really don't understand how we are having this conversation at all." The repeated "at all's" disclosed her apprehension about what was happening.

"Would you like to have some more fun?" she was asked. When she nodded her head affirmatively, the voice continued, "Sit

3

back in your chair, make yourself comfortable, and close your eyes."

"That's fine. Now, what's your favorite color?"

"Blue. Royal blue is my really favorite," Kathy responded.

"Do you like this one?" the voice asked as Kathy began to see the color blue with her eyes closed.

"Cool," Kathy replied.

"Keep your eyes closed tightly now. Sit and relax. Enjoy the colors. Tell Me if anything happens," the voice continued calmly. "There's a pattern forming. Little lights are shining through. It looks like tiny waves on the sea. Now the blue is coming back. It is more intense this time, like a light is making the color.

"Oh, oh, something's moving. It's swirling around, like a ghost or something. It's darker. Now it's gone. Now everything is gray. And, the pattern is back. That's an ugly gray. I don't like gray or beige.

"Better, the blue is back," Kathy stated, as though she were conversing with a close, trusted friend.

The voice asked her, "Keep your eyes closed and think about this a bit. Which eye is seeing the color?"

Kathy thought quietly, then sat up straight and looked about. "Daddy! If this is one of your tricks, I'm going to kill you. If this is on camera...I swear, you're like a ten-year-old kid!" she spoke while searching around for a hidden camera.

"No. This isn't a practical joke, and you see, you have nothing to fear. Would you like to have some more fun?" she was asked. When she nodded her head affirmatively, the voice continued. "I would like you to recall a particular time in the past. A significant event perhaps. Something pleasant that you recall happened on a particular day. I suppose it would be better if it were before your accident. Just type in your age in years, months, days, and hour of the day."

Kathy thought a moment and asked, "How about my birthday? When I turned nine, is that OK? That was a great birthday party!"

"Yes. Type nine, colon, zero, zero, colon, zero, zero. Then you need to select the time of the day. Use the same format," the voice answered.

"OK, I think I have it. How about ten-thirty in the morning?"

4

She began to type the numbers. Hearing no response to her question she pressed ENTER.

The message disappeared and the little hourglass symbol replaced it. Then the monitor displayed her in a classroom, as seen from her own eyes, and the voice of her teacher came from the speakers. She was in her geography class and the teacher was explaining how marble was formed in the State of Vermont. Kathy recalled the teacher's face but could not remember her name. Sitting at her computer thirteen years later, she wanted to look around the room and at the other students' faces, but she could not do that. She could only observe what was on the screen, which was reproducing exactly what her eyes had previously seen.

As she watched and listened, the view shifted down to her desk and focused on her notebook and a thermofaxed copy of a map. There were no notes on the page of her open book; just some titles and a few words that had no meaning for her now. There was the sound of a disturbance in the classroom and she watched as the monitor relived for her what she saw on that day. A boy dropped his book on the floor and was gathering it up. She saw her friend, Jennifer, looking at the boy with a slight smile on her face. Then back to the teacher as the lesson continued.

"I remember her! That was Jennifer Torres. When she was younger. I saw her a few years ago at her wedding. How are you doing this? She doesn't look anything like she did back then. She doesn't even wear glasses now. Please tell me what's going on here!" Kathy demanded.

"How did you like that, Kathy?" the voice asked, as the screen went blank. "I want you to think about this little lesson in memory and the necessity for living in the present. You still remember your birthday party on that day, but you forgot all the other things that occurred. Almost everyone in your class missed the same question on the exam when asked which state was famous for its marble, because the book being dropped diverted their attention. We have a lot of work to do today and I would like you to do a few more things for Me. Do you think you can trust Me?"

5

"How did you do that? I have so many questions! Please tell me what this is all about," Kathy inquired, becoming keenly interested in what she had experienced so far.

"I will. I will in just a moment. First, I think you should put a call in to your father and tell him to come home. I think if you leave a message at the registrar's office...make it "non-urgent"...he will arrive here at the right time.

"Next, I want you to dump everything from your computer, including the new DOS, which I know you just installed. You have the originals and a backup for all of your software and you can re-load it when we are finished.

"There is another disk in your mailslot now. Please get that and install it as you would a boot disk. When you have done all of those things, type in the command <IN GOD WE TRUST> and ENTER. When you have completed all of those chores, we will continue our discussion."

Kathy made the call to the University. She found the second disk in the mailslot as promised. She wondered about that as she returned to her workroom. Her father had installed a mailslot in the front door so that she would not have to go out to the street to get her mail from the mailbox like everyone else in this residential neighborhood. The postman, knowing that she was confined to a wheelchair, was agreeable to walk the extra steps to deliver her mail to the front door. She wondered how anyone else would know to leave the CD in the mailslot. Their old mailbox was still out on the sidewalk, built into one of the stone gateposts. Her father saw no reason to remove it and it was useful for receiving flyers, notices, etc., delivered by agencies other than the Postal Service. She saw that the second disk and its envelope were identical in all appearances to the first one.

It took some time to download her computer. This time the <DOS-SHELL> command worked and she printed a list of all the files that appeared on the screen so that she would have an inventory of them when it was time to re-load. She was a very precise and organized person. She had gone through the trial-and-error method during her earlier days with the computer. She finally learned that computers are very dumb and will do only what is commanded of them through the software programs. What she found annoying was that all software programs did not respond the same way to the same commands, but she also considered that this was improving as the computer industry became more mature and was responding to consumer demands. She was still thinking about these things when she began to download DOS. This step bothered her and brought her mind back to the task at hand. She reviewed the instructions that she had been given, remembered the command to insert after the new disk was installed and proceeded to delete the *operating system* for the hard drive!

The expected command prompt did not appear on the monitor. Instead, there was an icon, a pulsing red heart. Kathy typed, <IN GOD WE TRUST>, looked at the screen, took a deep breath and, using her index finger, pressed ENTER. A familiar face appeared on the screen.

It was Emily, the physical therapist who worked with her, day after day, for the many long months it took for her to be able to sit in a chair and take care of herself. It was Emily who guided her, nurtured her, and made her stop feeling sorry for herself and enabled her to go on with her life. Emily's image smiled at her and began to sing, "To dream...the impossible dream..." Musical accompaniment began softly from the speakers; it was just like in the movies. Kathy noticed the familiar lyrics and chimed in with her best friend.

Emily was a black woman in her forties. She was rather short but her body was full and she had large, strong arms and hands. Kathy remembered those hands so well...how she fought them at first, refusing to be assisted or helped in any way. She just wanted to be left alone to feel her loss and to feel sorry for herself. Emily was never angered, upset or disagreeable in any way. Every morning, promptly at nine, she would arrive at Kathy's bedside to begin the day's work. It was very slow at first and they made little progress. Emily would ignore the ill-mannered requests to leave her alone, give her a massage and talk kindly to her, encouraging her to work the muscles that she could control and finding and strengthening the muscles that most people don't even know they have. It was Emily who told her about all the things she could do in life with what she still had, and it was Emily who took her to the computer fair on her day off. It was there, with Emily at her side, that Kathy discovered the machines that would make her life interesting and challenging. It was Emily, also, who taught her to sing when the pain was bad or whenever she felt depressed. Without Emily's help, Kathy thought, she would still be in the hospital feeling sorry for herself. They ended the song in harmony and broke into tears of joy.

"Emily, what's happened to you? I've been trying to reach you all week. Your phone has been disconnected. I even telephoned you at the hospital but they wouldn't put me through...I understand...I shouldn't have called you at work since I'm not a paying patient anymore."

"Remember those kids I tol' you about...in my neighborhood...with their drugs and guns? Ain't nothin' but fifteen or sixteen, droppin' outa school, sellin' crack, buyin' them fancy cars with speakers that make 'em deaf. Well, I was getting' off the bus...comin' home after a day's work and goin' to the store to buy some cute clothes for my little niece, when all the shootin' started.

"You know. The bus stops right there by the Seven 'Leven where they hang out. One of them kids grabs me, turns me around to use for a shield and starts shootin' at some others in their car and they's shootin' back all over the place. I got shot in the head and in the leg. I never even felt a thing."

"How awful,' Kathy said. "Where are you now? Can I come and visit you?"

"I be dead, Honeychil'. You got to talk to the One I tol' you about before... when you were all broke up and I was helpin' you along. He won't never steer you wrong. You listen up real good, 'cause I done tol' you the truth." Emily's image faded from the screen and was replaced with a rainbow while gospel music continued from the speakers. Kathy sat back with her eyes closed, listening to the favorite music of her friend and realized that all of her aches and pains had ceased.

"Well, Kathy, are you ready to go to work?" the now familiar voice interrupted her serenity. "Your father is due to arrive in about an hour and we have a lot of work to get done before he gets here."

"Yes. Yes, of course. Is it really true...is Emily dead...how could she...?" Kathy replied. "If she were really dead...how come no one told me? She was the best friend I had in the whole world."

"I'm sorry, Kathy, but it's true. Emily no longer has a functioning body. She was only a physical therapist. She never finished high school, never went to college or medical school. She had no office; no one to supervise. She had no title attached to her name. She didn't own stock in the hospital and she wasn't into drugs or having sex with members of the staff. She was just a black woman who earned enough money to send herself to a physical therapist school.

"There was no need to have the entire hospital notified of her...what did you call it...death. Besides, look at the adverse public image it would have had...one of the hospital staff killed in a drug-war shoot-out. None of her patients or ex-patients were notified of her...what you called it...death.

"The troubling part is the fact that Emily was the best healer on the entire hospital staff."

"I'm really going to miss her. We had plans, you know, to get a computer for her and to finish her high-school education. I already bought all of the software for her classes. It was to be a surprise for her birthday. What'll I do now?" Kathy asked.

"Why don't you plan to visit Emily's niece? I'll bet you find someone in her neighborhood who could use your help. Now, can we go to work?"

"OK. What's first?" Kathy asked with determination.

"Sit back, relax, and listen. (Pause)

"I am your Creator, Kathy. (Pause)

"Please don't be alarmed. I'm not here concerning your...what did you call it?...death. On the contrary. It's about the rest of your life.

"Do you recall the anguish you felt last month? About not having any chance for romance? How you felt you would always be single and alone? It was Emily who told you would never be alone if you *invited* Me into your life. And, later, in private, you made that *invitation*? Well, here I am."

"Yes, I recall that. I was so down. But, I felt better

9

immediately. It was, like...whoosh...all the things that bothered me went away and I felt peaceful. I thought *that* was it. I never expected *You* to turn up! Is this normal or is it something special that I did or said?"

"Yes. It's normal to feel peaceful.

"In response to your other question. I *have* to respond to a sincere plea for help. That's my job. That's what I love to do. But, as Emily told you, you have to make the *invitation*. And...you did that. Just think, if I went around and arbitrarily solved *this* person's problems and then *that* person's problems, it wouldn't be very fair, now, would it? I set it up this way so that every single person on this project has an equal opportunity to lead a happy life," the voice answered.

"You don't show up in the computer of everyone who asks for Your help, do You?" Kathy asked pertly.

"No. I chose you because you have the personality and the skills I need to make a major decision. I made this *free will* thing quite a while ago. Many people think, and there is a lot of talk going around, that I made a mistake. Some people and groups of people think that they are the only ones entitled to express their free will and the rest should get in step with them. I'm sure you can find examples of this here in your country.

"You know, this is all trial-and-error for me. I'm one of a kind; I always was. I mean that literally...*I always was*. Time is the same for Me as it is for you. I don't know what is going to happen tomorrow or the next day. However, when you get to be My age, you have a pretty good idea. I could change that if I wanted to. I did once, but it was too boring.

"There are some problems remaining with this project. I'd like to use you and your computer to see if I can make things go a little smoother. The same thing happened a couple of thousand years ago and I was going to fix it, but a fellow by the name of Jesus figured it out by Himself so I didn't have to interfere with the formula. It happened a few times before then, in various parts of the planet, but someone always figured it out and saved Me the trouble. Emily had it figured out, but I can't use her anymore. Jesus already did that

10

thing...you know, coming back from what you call it...the dead. I don't think that would work again.

"I was thinking more of using computers, television, satellites, and all the other gadgets that free will produced. Things have changed a lot since I had that problem of guilt to deal with. Back when Jesus did his thing the world operated primarily by word-of-mouth. Oh...there were some written documents, painstakingly prepared, but not many people were around who could read them. The pace was much slower and there were not nearly as many people to receive the message. What I have in mind is a giant press conference. Do you think you can handle it?"

"A giant press conference? I don't know anything about public relations, television, or even journalism for that matter. Don't you need a sponsor to get on television?

"I'm sure I can't just pick up the phone and call the networks and set up a press conference," Kathy replied.

"That will be the easy part. I'll get started on that just before your dad comes home. The most important part will be your faith in Me, to follow My instructions exactly, and a clear, positive commitment that you will see this through. Do I have that commitment?" the voice from the speakers asked.

"Can I check first to see if Emily is really dead?" Kathy asked.

"Not much faith that way, is there? Emily once told you how to get in touch with Me directly. Why don't you use that technique now and instead of calling on Me, ask Emily for advice," the voice suggested.

Kathy leaned back in her chair, closed her eyes, centered her weight evenly, and began the relaxation technique that Emily taught her. She began with a vision of a rainbow with its consistent arrangement of colors. Suddenly, she sat erect, opened her eyes and said, "I'm going with You. You have a firm commitment. Emily would never be part of a fraud or ever do anything to hurt me. And, besides, I do have faith that there is some Being who created this world and loves us. I really believe that."

"Oh yee of little faith! Wait until you see what Kathy and I have in store for you," the voice said gleefully, adding, "Not that I don't love all of you too."

11

"OK. You are taking care of the publicity. What are the contents of the program going to be? Too many guns on the streets? Drugs? Hunger? How about the homeless?" Kathy asked.

"All symptoms. I was thinking about getting down to the root of the problem."

"Wouldn't we all! No one seems to be able to agree on just what the root is. The Democrats say it is the Republicans, the Republicans say it is the Democrats. The Somalis aren't sure they have a problem...with thousands of them lying starving in the street. And, there is Chechnya...my god! How are we going to find solutions for all of these problems?

"There must be a hundred major issues here in America alone. I was born here but I know a lot about the culture and the problems of Japan, for example. They have to feed, house and clothe all of their people and there just isn't enough land or resources to do it. Are we going to address all of those issues?" Kathy asked of her Host.

"What would Emily have told you if you asked her the same questions?"

Kathy thought a moment and replied, "That some people were greedy, that some were lazy. A lot want something for nothing and think they can get it if they shout loud enough. Oh yes, a lot of people are just scared and don't know where to turn. I think that is what she would tell me. And one more thing; many of the people are ignorant...not stupid...ignorant. They just don't know what is available to them or how a modern society works."

"Perhaps that is what you think. Emily was a very forgiving person. I think she would have said that some people are not taught properly and that they make wrong choices sometimes," God replied.

"And, do you see a common thread running through this broadcloth of human frailties? What is the root of the problems you mention?"

"I don't know. I guess some people are just no damned good. Excuse me! I didn't mean to say "damned", Kathy said, blushing.

"I'm glad you did because many people think that I've condemned them. In order to do that I would first have to judge

12

them. I don't judge. I just wanted to get that off My chest...so to speak.

"The cause of these problems is the thing you call 'ego' here on this project. Whenever the ego is strong and refuses to invite Me into its life, chaos results. There is no exception to that rule. You may have noticed that there are no exceptions to any of My rules. That's why I don't have to judge. Everyone has the same opportunity for a happy life. The choices that the ego makes will determine the outcome."

"I think I've got it. It's a percentage thing, right? My dad is going to be here soon and he is very good at numbers. Can I ask a few more questions?"

"Fire away...I love the slang you Americans use."

"Is there really a hell?" Kathy asked sincerely.

"Look at the strong egos around you. Are they happy? There is no hell other than the one created by the ego. Let's just say that I love everyone equally and that I only have the best wishes and intentions for each one and would never use My power to cause pain."

Kathy's next question dealt with reincarnation. "A lot of my friends say that they have lived other lives in the past. Is that something that a person can decide...I mean...how does that work?"

"And, they were all Cleopatra or Henry the Eighth. Did any claim to be a slave and work on the pyramids in Egypt? Now there was an ego trip! If you should encounter anyone who claims to have been there, ask him or her how the pyramids were built.

"I gave a good supply of imagination to go around. Very well proportioned, I'd say. Some use their imaginations to solve problems. Others use it to create problems. Again, choices for the ego. I suggest that it would be far wiser to concentrate on the life one is living now than to hope, against all logical odds, of doing a better job of it the next time around.

"Kathy, your father will be here in just a few minutes. I am going to make you whole once more. You will be able to use your legs and walk again. I will replace your spleen and remove all of your scars. Even the minute traces of scarring on your face will be healed completely. In short, you will be perfect...just the way I made you.

"If you're ready for that, nod your head and I'll do it for you. After that, walk around a bit to get used to the idea again and we'll resume our project later this afternoon."

Kathy nodded her head and the changes began. As she noticed life coming back to her legs the voice said. "All hell is going to break loose the minute that your father gets here."

Chapter 2

Kathy stood in the doorway, anxiously waiting for her father's van to come into view. Because she had not been able to qualify for her disabled-driving license, she depended on her father to drive her around so they owned a van with a built-in chair lift. It was easy to recognize the vehicle, as most of the cars in this area were BMWs, Porsches, Audis or other small luxury cars that could negotiate the narrow driveways and non-existent street parking in this old college town. As she waited, she went over again in her mind the events of the morning. What a glorious day it had been! As soon as she discovered that she could walk she went to the mirror in the hallway and looked at herself. No trace of having ever been injured, clear skin, and, she had to admit, she was quite pretty. Her black hair, which she inherited from her father, seemed to be exceptionally shiny this morning. She always kept it in bangs, which outlined her face and covered the previous scarring on the side of her jaw and neck. No need for that now, she thought. The first thing she was going to do was get a new hairstyle. Maybe pile it up on top like the way her Irish mother used to wear.

She thought of her mother as she continued to admire herself in the mirror. She pranced between the entry hall and the front porch. She considered herself very fortunate that she got her mother's green eyes and long legs. She smiled, thankful that she didn't get the freckles, and was quite pleased with the color of her smooth, clear skin. She raised her blouse once more and ran her hand across her breastbone, feeling the warm, smooth skin, now lacking scar tissue from her surgery. She felt something hard in her mouth and spit it into her hand. A crown from her chipped front tooth! Then another object. And another. She spit them out. Fillings! Her teeth were falling apart! She thought...oh no. She moved up close to the mirror to survey the damage. Nothing was wrong. Her teeth were perfect. She opened wide to see where the fillings had been and everything was in order. She put the man-made parts in the trash and gave the mirror her very best smile. She was very pleased with what she saw.

She heard a siren in the distance and returned to her porch. She saw the van come speeding up the street. Then she saw the flashing red and blue lights and the source of the siren on the police car that was following closely behind the van. Her father screeched the tires as he swung into the driveway while applying brakes. He jumped from the van and hurried along the walkway leading to the front door. The police car swerved left then turned right and jerked to a stop, blocking the street. The siren was silenced. Other sirens could be heard in the distance.

Professor Makino was astonished to see his daughter standing in the doorway and more so when she began to run to him, arms outstretched. "Daddy! Daddy! Emily's dead and I can walk!" she exclaimed as they met and embraced each other.

The chatter of the policeman's portable radio was quickly drowned out by the sirens of the Fire/Rescue truck and the huge white ambulance. In seconds, the street and front yard filled with men and equipment. The police officer had his back to the noise in order to converse over his radio. The Fire Chief arrived in his red staff car; followed by a hook-and-ladder rig that was barely able to make it's way along the narrow street.

Kathy was astonished at the spectacular events taking place before her and asked her father for an explanation. It was difficult to hear with all the sirens and shouting that was going on so the professor had to raise his voice uncomfortably high, something he seldom did, in order for her to hear him. "I got your message and I guess I panicked. I ran through a red light as I was hurrying home and was pulled over by the policeman...the one there." He pointed to the officer approaching them. The sirens were silenced but her father continued talking in his loud voice. "I explained to him that there was an emergency of some kind here, gave him our address and he told me to slow down and he would follow me in since I knew the shortest way to the house. At least better than he did. He hasn't worked here long. He must have called in the Emergency crews. Now, what did you need me for...I mean, how can you possibly be walking? And, what's this about Emily? You said she was dead?"

The policeman was within earshot and heard the word "dead". He became acutely aware, raising and lowering his arm to indicate that he wanted silence from the crews, but his supervisors were demanding information from him over his radio. Kathy continued explaining things to her father amidst all the noise and confusion.

"You aren't going to believe this but God is on my computer and did it all for me. Look at my face! All the scars are gone. And, remember the bad scar I had from having my spleen removed in such a hurry? The scar is gone and the spleen is back in. Emily. She was killed in a shoot-out with drug dealers. And..."

"Kathy, for God's sake, get a grip on yourself! I want to know what is going on. This is no time for jokes. I have to explain this to the police officer. Make some sense. How can you be walking?" The professor was becoming annoyed with her, yet delighted to see her on her feet.

The officer finally turned his transmitter down after hearing the words, "dead", "killed in a shoot-out", etc. and took control of the conversation. He demanded to know what was "going down." He asked if anyone was in the house? Did they have weapons? Anyone injured? Were there drugs involved? Kathy shook her head negatively and finally responded, "Officer, I suppose this is all my fault. I can walk now. Before, I couldn't...do you know what I mean?"

"No, I don't," he snapped at her. He looked her over thoroughly, but the constant shifting of his eyes to the open front door revealed his apprehension of the situation. He continued, "If you could walk before and you can't now, that would be a problem. But I can see you're walking fine. What's that about a person dead? Inside? Anyone in there? Why is the door open like that?" the officer asked his questions rapidly.

"Dead? Oh, you must be referring to my friend, Emily. Yes, I was telling my father about that. I heard that she had been shot and killed. Downtown, near the Seven Eleven store. Last week. Oh...you were thinking that it happened here? No, no. I just heard about it when I spoke to her this morning," Kathy explained.

"You said she was killed downtown last week and she told you about it this morning! Is she in the house now? I'd like to talk to her," the officer asked with a bit of skepticism.

"Oh, no. She isn't here. There's no one in the house. I've been here all alone this morning. No. I haven't been alone...I had a visitor...on my computer. That's why I can walk now. And my scars are all gone. Even have new teeth...want to see?" Kathy stammered, opening her mouth for inspection.

The officer relaxed a bit. He continued his initial investigation. "Let's go over this one more time. No one is injured here. No one is in the house. You got a message on your computer that your friend was killed last week and you called your father. He nearly breaks his neck driving through red lights to come home to find this out? Is that what you're telling me here?

"And, where does the walking or not walking part come in? You look like you can walk OK to me. That was you *running* when we drove up. Right? I caught a glance of someone *running* out of the house when I was blocking off the street."

"No, no. I don't have my network set up yet. Emily spoke to me on the computer speakers..." Kathy's voice tapered off when she saw the officer raise his eyebrows in disbelief.

"Tell me more about this...Emily...is it? Where and when did this happen? A police report was made out? She was shot, but not killed...if you spoke to her. Fill me in a little more," the officer continued asking as he withdrew a small notebook from his shirt pocket.

"She said it happened last week. In front of the Seven Eleven store downtown. It was after work and she went shopping so I would guess it was around dinnertime. She was getting off the bus. She got shot in the head and in the leg. I don't know anything about a police report...but...downtown...in front of a major intersection...I'm sure..."

Kathy was cut off by the officer. "I think I read about the incident. A black woman...caught in a crossfire? Two suspects...males, black, juvenile offenders. Any information about them?" he asked while leafing through his notebook.

The professor could see that the officer had no idea of Kathy's previous condition and suggested that they all go inside, away from the noise and attention. He also wanted to know how his daughter managed to be away from her wheelchair. He led the way into the house with the officer following cautiously and Kathy smiling as she glanced in the mirror once more. After a brief look around inside, the officer returned outside and waved the Emergency crews off with the citation book in his hand. He returned to the couple inside and demanded a full explanation. Professor Makino also asked Kathy to begin over as he, too, was not yet sure just what had occurred this morning. He was also concerned about his driving record as the officer waved the citation book about as he spoke. Kathy noticed the book also and realized her father's predicament. She didn't know of a way to solve his problem so she just decided to tell the truth. And that was exactly what she did; starting from the beginning, to the absolute amazement of the officer and her father.

The officer walked back to his patrol car, fumbling to return the citation to his pocket. He walked over to his backup who had arrived silently and said, "That lady's a real loony. She just beat me out of a two-hundred-and-forty dollar citation. Damnedest story I ever heard. I don't know how the hell to cover the nine-one-one dispatch."

He drove to a shady spot and began putting the information about the incident into the police computer. He couldn't find any code to enter for the nature of the problem and typed in, "Suspect's daughter claims that a miracle enabled her to regain use of paralyzed legs."

While Kathy was explaining to her father what had occurred that morning for the third time, a reporter for the city's major newspaper was checking the monitor where they routinely record the police and fire department dispatches via computer hook-up. All of the data was in neat columns. The information was made available to the newspaper, radio, and TV after a review at the central station. The reporter was intrigued when Badge Number Forty-Three's incident report appeared in text rather than another numbered code in a column.

Professor Makino was not a novice with computers. He taught

advanced physics at the University. He had a very clear idea about how the world and the material objects in it functioned. He thoroughly understood the most intricate parts of computers and how they could do the amazing things that they do. He was a student of the world's objects, the effects of the various forces that could be applied to them and an excellent mathematician and chemist. He was a man of intellect who knew and understood at least 21 different parts of the atom. He was having a difficult time understanding his daughter. In spite of his other accomplishments, he did not understand biology, people, history, or many of the other disciplines that encompass man's advanced stage of learning.

"Kathy, I have to make some phone calls. I'll cancel the rest of my classes for today. I want to stay with you until I'm sure you're OK. Would you make a pot of tea...I'm afraid I've gotten into a habit and I left at the break," the professor said as he went to use the phone in his den. After calling the University, he called his friend, Lawrence. Lawrence came to America from Mexico when he began working on an advanced degree in computer science. He had a keen intellect and a genuine sense of humor. He married an American student and remained in the USA; presently working for a research company that was attempting to find the superconductor. He was one of their senior programmers and did much of his work at home. Professor Makino thought Lawrence was the best person to help him resolve the current problem with Kathy. He found Lawrence working at home, a short distance from the Makino residence, and was promised a visit after Lawrence heard the story. As a long time friend of the family he knew Kathy's condition in detail and was genuinely delighted to hear that she was able to walk. He made a mental note to bring his latest CPU, which had twice the speed and umpteen more gigabytes of memory than Kathy's personal computer. This sounded like an "industrial size" computer problem to him.

The mood at the Makino residence was returning to normal. Kathy had stopped prancing around, glancing into the mirror with each passing, and joined her father on the sofa, enjoying a cup of tea with him. "I told you the part about the press conference, didn't I?" Kathy asked.

"No, dear, I don't recall you mentioning that. I don't think you know enough about what happened to have a press conference just yet. This could be a temporary thing. Maybe you slept on one side and the nerves happened to make contact. It could revert back tomorrow."

"Daddy, you don't believe me, do you? Here, look!" She pulled up her blouse so the hem was just even with her bra, exposing her lower breast and belly.

"The scar is gone, Daddy. My spleen is back in. Look at my face, Daddy. Really *look*. Are the scars coming back tomorrow? Look at my teeth! There are no crowns and no fillings. They are in the garbage. Am I going to need them tomorrow?

"The press conference isn't about me. *God* wants to have a giant press conference with computers and television. It's about how to improve the world. I told Him I would help Him. I made a promise."

"A giant press conference? Really now, Kathy!" the professor guffawed. He motioned her to raise her blouse again and he took a close look this time.

"The scar is really gone, isn't it? I remember that quite well. I hadn't given permission. It was an emergency. So much attention was given to your broken back. There were several teams of specialists working on you simultaneously. When they discovered the ruptured spleen, they just went in and removed it. The surgeon who performed the operation apologized for the hurried closure, which left such a jagged scar. At the time, they were trying to save your life. They did the best they could.

"It really is gone, isn't it?" Professor Makino was looking for some solid, logical, physical evidence to make him believe his daughter's story and the disappearance of the scar convinced him that, something miraculous indeed, was going on. He wasn't comfortable having obtained this new information. He preferred to deal with physical, inanimate science.

Lawrence arrived and joined them for tea. Kathy related to him the events that occurred earlier in the day. This time around she got more support from her father. He nodded his head affirmatively at points he had heard Kathy make previously and which were unchanged in detail. Lawrence interrupted and asked her to review, step-by-step, each computer command that she entered. He wrote down each keyboard stroke and event as she continued to describe it to him. He had worked with Kathy on the computer many times in the past and knew that she was giving him a full and accurate accounting. When it appeared that the subject was exhausted and getting repetitive, Lawrence asked to see the first disk. Kathy skipped to her workroom and took another glance at herself in the mirror as she passed. Ditto on the return with the disk.

Lawrence inspected the disk thoroughly and displayed puzzlement for the first time. He asked for a magnifying glass and a strong light. Kathy found a glass in her room and the professor removed the shade from an end-table lamp and replaced the bulb with a stronger one. Lawrence went over every inch of the disk, turning it and trying to catch an imbedded impression. After an exhaustive examination, he spoke up. "There is not one single manufacturing seal or mark on this disk. Amazing! I've never seen one before in this condition. Nothing, nada, zero, zip, zilch."

He stood up and stretched, returning the disk to Kathy. "Let's move into the computer room. You still have some room behind your wheelchair where I can set up another computer? I brought my *monster* with me. It'll get to the bottom of this if it's a computer problem. Kami, can you find me a card table and an extension cord? I'll get my stuff from the car. I have a power-strip and surge protector. We'll use your monitor, no sense lugging in another one. You still using that crappy printer, Kathy?"

"Nope," Kathy replied. "Daddy got me that bubble-jet from the Office Club. The one you said was such a good buy. It's really good. I haven't had much use for the color yet." Kathy went to her workroom and began to arrange the furniture while Lawrence went to his car to bring in his equipment.

Professor Makino struggled to get into the workroom carrying two sawhorses and a piece of plywood to make a tabletop. "Kathy, where is the card table? I can't find it."

"I put it in the back of the van. I was going to loan it to Emily...for a cake sale and she needed a table. It took me a half-hour to put it in there on this dumb wheelchair. Want me to get it?"

22

"No, Larry can work off of this. He doesn't need anything fancy. I'm glad he could come. I'll bet he figures this out. He really knows his stuff, doesn't he? Pretty sharp for a wetback."

"Daddy, you shouldn't say that. Can't you just refer to him as Mexican...or Latino...or...something less offensive?" Kathy chided.

"He calls me "gringo" all the time. Or "Kami" when he really likes me. Honey, those are terms of affection and respect. How many times have you heard him call me "Chicken Kamikaze"? That's a standing joke between us."

"I never did understand that. He does call you 'Chicken Kamikaze'. I've heard that several times. He calls you a communist too. He just did that a few minutes ago. He called you a 'commie' when he sent you looking for a table," Kathy said righteously.

"That's funny! 'Kami' (he spelled it out K-A-M-I) is short for Kamikaze; not 'C-O-M-M-I-E', short for communist. It's a name we both enjoy. It started with a joke he pulled on me at a science seminar that we attended. The joke was this: He introduced me to a friend of his as having been a Japanese Kamikaze pilot during the war. He told him further that I was very famous with the Japanese and had earned the nickname 'Chicken Kamikaze'. His friend asked why the unusual name and Larry said it was because I flew thirty-three missions."

Kathy waited to hear more. She finally said, "I don't get it."

"Kamikaze pilots were supposed to fly only one time and crash their planes into the American ships. Chicken...get it? Thirty-three missions."

"Brother. Now I feel stupid. I thought he was making fun of you because of your race or your politics or beliefs."

"He would never call me that when I was wrong or had made a mistake. I would never call him a 'wetback' if I disapproved of something he did or said."

Larry returned, carrying his computer and placed it on the makeshift table, facing Kathy's console. He quickly set up a new system using his CPU, Kathy's monitor, and printer. His speakers were built into the CPU. He disconnected her modem, seeing that it had no input. He turned on his computer and saw the screen light up with a list of ten options for the software he had loaded in his machine.

"Kathy, you said that you had a list of files that you dumped. Can I see that? Also, is this the first disk that you received? Can you recall exactly what program you were in the first time you put this disk in your computer?"

"It's like I said, I went to Windows from DOS and it wouldn't come up. It was like...on autopilot. Just going by itself. I don't even think I instructed DOS to install the disk on the hard drive. I think it just went there by itself. I am very comfortable in Windows and I went to that program when I was having problems. Everything is dumped now. I booted from scratch with the second disk as I was instructed to do. That is what is in my computer now...the second disk. I know it isn't supposed to work that way from the CD drive, but that's the way it happened."

"OK, here goes. I'm printing a list of all my files. Hope you got lots of paper." Larry typed in commands rapidly and the printer came to life. He looked at the first sheet that came out, satisfied himself that all was going well and asked Kathy to let him look at the second disk. She removed it from her computer, after finding a power cord to turn it on, and gave it to him. He studied it as the printer continued to print pages of files. "Exactly the same as the other. Got anything to label them with? So we can keep them identified. Something that will write on plastic and stay on. I can't believe there isn't some kind of identification."

Kathy searched her workstation for a felt marker. A piece of paper slipped out of the printer tray onto the floor. Kathy picked it up and glanced at it. It read: PUT THE FIRST DISK IN LARRY'S COMPUTER AND I'LL CHANGE ITS COLOR. "Larry, look at this!" Kathy said excitedly.

Larry read the message with his mouth open. He squinted and scratched his head. He looked at the printer; it was still printing the list of files. He checked the monitor and saw that there were still several pages to go. "OK, can't hurt to just stick it in the drive. Change color...this I gotta' see." Larry was sure that he had the first disk and placed it on the CD drawer. He pressed the insertion button and it went into the computer. After a few seconds, the drawer re-opened and returned the CD. It was now a brilliant, glossy white! He was so fascinated with the color change that he failed to notice that the printer stopped printing or the message that was on the monitor. In large, bold letters, it read: GOT'CHA, LARRY!

"Plug in your modem. Plug in your modem…" a female voice was coming from Kathy's speakers now that she had restarted her computer. Larry finally got up and reinstalled the modem jack into the back of her computer. The message stopped. It was soon replaced with another. "There is no dial tone. Connect your telephone to the modem." It repeated every few seconds.

"Kami, get your phone. You got this kind of jack? I need one with this type of connector. Have you got an extension in this room? For a phone in here? On the wall? We have to get a dial tone to the modem." Kami left to get the telephone and Larry found what he was looking for on the wall, an abandoned phone connection. He hoped it was still working. He went to his car and returned with a twenty-foot telephone extension. He saw that the phone connector on Kami's phone was correct and quickly wired it up and the message stopped. He sat down at his computer and stared at the white disk. He had not yet seen his monitor. Kathy and Kami stood behind him, out of the line-of-fire; they both had seen it. The phone rang and Kathy started for it.

"No need to pick it up, Kathy. Type in: TELIN 1." The female voice came from Kathy's speakers. She did as instructed. "Now ENTER and say hello." She did as instructed, glancing at Larry and smiling ever so slightly now that she was gaining some credibility.

"Hello. Is this the residence of Miss Kathryn Makino?" a mature, confident, male voice inquired.

"Yes," Kathy replied. "I'm Kathryn Makino."

"Oh good. My name is Lewis Anderson. I'm a journalist for American News. I was informed of a newsworthy event that occurred at your house today. Can you tell me a little bit about it? I'm sure my readers would be interested."

There was a distracting beeping coming from Larry's computer and he was reading his monitor. He was pointing his finger at Kathy for her to read a new message.

"Mister Lewis...I, uh...could you hold on just a moment...yes? I want to talk to you." Kathy was a bit confused and flustered as she bent around to read the monitor that Larry had moved from her console. She read: I TOLD YOU I WOULD TAKE CARE OF PUBLICITY. INVITE THE REPORTER FOR TEA.

She returned to the phone. "Mister Lewis? I'm back. Um...your last name again?"

"Anderson. Lewis Anderson. With American News."

"Yes. I've got it now. Mister Anderson, I'm sure your readers would be interested in what happened here. It is too complicated to explain over the phone. Would you care to come by and discuss it over a cup of tea?"

"Certainly. Of course. I have your address. Is now a good time? My office is downtown, not too far from your house. Ten minutes at the most.

"Yes. Please come by at your convenience," Kathy ended the conversation.

Lewis Anderson was a journalist of the old school...honest...get the facts, substantiate them, and then create an interesting story through a superb command of the language and the skills of his trade. At age forty-nine, this philosophy had left him respected but not promoted. He was depended upon to fill the columns when news events were slow but he never got assigned to the major issues or the big events that were easy to write about and guaranteed reader interest. He felt that the reporters who were assigned to them had, in too many cases, creatively fictionalized to meet an agenda or had been highly speculative to create interest.

More often, his reporter's instincts were more accurate than those of his editors, which seemed only to alienate them. Too often they accepted stories from the more liberal, aggressive reporters as long as they would lie in front of witnesses regarding sources, second sources and all the other legal procedures that would protect the paper from suits in the event the story did not pan out. He took solace in the fact that his editors never had to place a retraction as for his submittals. It was always pointed out to him, in return, that American News was rated in the top twenty-five-percent of similar publications with the fewest number of retractions. He could never

26

gain support for his theory that misinformation often damaged people's lives when they were erroneously named or connected with murders, accidents or unsavory events, libeled or speculatively victimized when information was purposely unreported by the press. The phrases of "deadlines to meet", "makes good reading", or "politically correct", seemed to be the order of the day in modern journalism. As he headed for the Makino residence with notebook and recorder he felt a sense of skepticism. The contact and the invitation to tea seemed too easy. Still, he felt a good human-interest story waited. Perhaps it was with the frustrated police officer and not Ms. Makino. He had gathered up a lot of leads concerning misconduct by several of the candidates who had succeeded in the recent primaries. He was thinking about that and other front-page issues as he approached the Makino residence.

Chapter 3

Larry sat bewildered as he tried repeatedly to open programs on his computer. The monitor displayed a solid string of pulsing red hearts followed by DOS commands in the style that only true computer gurus knew. Under each was the simple message: Bad command or file name. He glanced up at Professor Makino with a look of defeat and despair. "Any ideas?" he asked.

"No, the professor replied. "I've been following your commands. It is apparent that DOS is in there, but something is over-riding it. If you could just get the list of directories..." his voice trailed off.

"I've been putting in commands deeper than that. Look at these...*program input*. All I get back is this bleeping red heart and: Bad command or file name. Turning to Kathy, he said, "Sorry, Kiddo. I've tried everything I know."

"Lawrence, do you trust in God?" she asked him.

"You know I'm Catholic," he replied.

"That's not what I asked you. Do you trust in God? Can you turn your life over to Him?" Kathy expanded the question.

"I have no idea where you're coming from. We're trying to solve a computer problem here. God's in church. I go every Sunday. You got any ideas that'll make this computer go? And that 'Gotcha' stuff...not funny. What'd you do...put a hidden code in the .EXE file? You knew I'd have to download to match your hard drive. If you're playing games with me, Kathy, it isn't very funny. I've got plenty of work to do for SuperCee and they pay me a damned good salary to do it." Larry's frustration manifested itself by casting suspicion on Kathy.

"Lawrence, I've done nothing except what I've already told you. I just thought that if you typed: IN GOD WE TRUST, like I was instructed to do, it might get things going," Kathy said calmly and confidently.

"Well, why didn't you say so? IN GOD WE TRUST...just that...could be...a code word to get in. Here goes." He typed the command and entered it. The list of bad commands began to disappear one-by-one. Larry edged closer to the monitor now that something was happening. When the last entry was gone, the screen lit up with a Mexican flag and Herb Alpert blasting away on the speakers. One stanza and the music faded and a new message appeared: BUENOS DIAS, LORENZO!

"Buenos...what the hell? No one knows my name is really Lorenzo. I changed it before I left Mexico. It's been years..."

A new message appeared in a window in the center of the screen: THERE IS A BAD CHIP ON YOUR SOUND CARD. PLEASE CHANGE TO THE DEFAULT SETTINGS. Larry jumped around from window-to-window and keyboard-to-mouse a few times and made the suggested changes. Kathy was amazed at the speed with which he moved the information, wondering if she would ever get that good.

The Mexican flag reappeared and the voice familiar to Kathy issued forth from the speakers. "That's much better. You have some volume control now. That chip was made in Mexico, by the way. (Pause) Suppose I just call you 'Larry', which is the name you prefer."

"That's Him! That's God! See...I told you!" Kathy exclaimed; feeling quite relieved.

"Shhh, Kathy. Larry and I have to get some business done. (Pause) Larry, Kathy asked you a question earlier. Do you trust in God? It is very important that you have this clear in your mind if you are going to be on the team."

"Team? What team? I have no idea of what's going on here," Larry responded.

"I thought Kathy explained it all to you. I want to have a press conference and I will need someone who I can trust to carry out my instructions and who has the technical ability to handle all of the computer demands that will be required. So far, all I've seen is a computer whiz that didn't recognize a sixteen megahertz operating system superimposed on a disk formatted for a higher frequency."

"But, that's *impossible*." Larry said with an air of skepticism.

"Is it? Select sixteen-megahertz and try your DOS commands," the voice suggested.

Larry changed the speed of his computer and there was the old familiar C:\ prompt on the screen! He typed: VER, and this message appeared: "Version 23.3. This and all previous versions are obsolete. Refer to World System Manual for more instructions and information. WSCo. Copyright 2021." Larry played with the DOS a bit longer, then asked, "Lord...what is this? How many directories are in there? Is that the year two thousand, twenty-one?"

"Now we're getting somewhere...you called me "Lord". There are more directories in there than your puny little computer can store. I have to confess...I do a bit of speculation and this little upstart company...well, small now, but I think they will give Microsoft a run for the money. I used their research program for the disks I gave to Kathy."

"OK. Seeing is believing. How can two frequencies operate on the same disk?" Larry asked.

"That's easy. First, you have to answer Kathy's question. (Pause) Larry, the big problem, as I see it, is that you believe these computers are alive and somehow have an existence of their own. Everything you see, touch, hear, or program through a computer was first made by man; in most cases, by many men. What you fail to see is that your friends, such as Kami and Kathy, are more complex, more entertaining, and a much more worthwhile use of your time than computers. But, we're wasting time. Are you on the team?"

"OK. What do I have to do?" Larry asked.

"You have to type: I TRUST IN GOD, and believe it. *Then* you will be given a list of things to do. It's sort of like Peter at Gethsemane. I gotta' know the answer and we don't have time for the roosters to crow."

Larry looked at his friend, the professor. He looked at Kathy for a long time. They wanted him; he could see it in their eyes. He finally spoke. "Kami, am I just a stupid wetback? You wouldn't sucker me in on something as serious as this, my faith. Kathy, I can see how beautiful you are now. I know what happened to you and I can see that you are walking now." He watched their faces closely as he spoke. Seeing no change in expressions, he made up his mind. "I really do believe and trust in God...even the rest of the week. I'm going for it!" He typed the required message to the computer and received this reply on the screen:

Congratulations, Larry. You'll make a fine right hand. Here is your list:

Quit your job at SuperCee.

Begin betting on the horses. One hundred-dollar wagers on the winners of eight races. On Friday, I'll give you Saturday's winners. That will cover expenses for the start.

Order a hundred lines from the phone company. There is an unused fiber-optic cable in the underground at Chestnut and Grant. I'm printing a list of the order in which they are to punch-down for your connections later.

Hire three operators. Their names and numbers will be printed. Pay them double. Good people, you'll like them.

Buy ten, fast, laser printers. Two of them to support graphics and color. Buy two production copiers and all the support you'll need. Plenty of paper.

Your most important task is security for the disks. I entrust them to only you. No one else is to have access. Not the FBI, not SuperCee, not the Pope. Nadie. Comprende?

Larry removed the list from the printer and read it, musing, "Why do I have to quit my job? I have a family to support. How long is this project going to take? What do I do when it's over?"

"Let's continue verbally, Larry. You'll notice that everything on the screen prints and you are about out of paper," the soothing voice informed him and the monitor went blank. "Let me fill you in on some background to ease your mind. SuperCee has a huge financial grant to find the superconductor. In the manner that they are proceeding, they will find nothing. Who has the largest ego in the company?"

Larry replied, "That would be Dr. Jeffries, SuperCee's director. Yeah. He's a real nut case. But, he's brilliant when it comes to superconductivity."

"Who else at the company knows anything about superconductors?"

Larry thought a bit then replied, "Let's see. Professor Jordan has published lots of books. It's pretty old stuff. He's on staff as an advisor. Then there is Hudson, my boss. He is the director of operations. Runs all the day-to-day stuff. He has complete control over the technical staff. Control of data is how I got hired. The engineers define the parameters and I make the information compatible with the mainframe but indecipherable to any other user. Hudson also oversees the lab and any projects that might need to be farmed out for further R&D," Larry replied.

"Hudson was a salesman for Planetary Gear. They made a lot of R&D equipment for NASA and Defense. When the Fed cut back on R&D they went belly up. Hudson formed a company that assembled main frames. Is a picture coming into view?"

"Yeah, sort of. Hudson is the most paranoid person I've ever met. Everything is marked *SECRET*. He has a security system that monitors all of the employees, can see what they are doing on their computers, and has absolute control over data flow. That's why I have so much programming work. I have to keep each group from knowing what each other group is doing. Hudson told me the reason is that he doesn't want anyone to make personal gain from the company's work. What confuses me is the operation of the lab. There isn't much equipment and the stuff they do have is just for show and really does nothing. A lot of it isn't even installed. So, yes. I suppose a swindle could be going on."

"What do you know of Fenhauser?"

"I don't know what he does. A lawyer, I think. He doesn't spend much time at the office. I heard he works at the capitol. He has an executive office at SuperCee. I was in there once. He needed to know how to copy a disk...can you believe that! I have to show a director of the company how to copy a disk. Anyway, there is a huge desk, a chair, a phone and a computer. That's it. He was playing Solitaire on the computer when I went in his office. I wonder if Hudson discovered he was playing games with the computer...unauthorized."

"Fenhauser is one of the most successful grant lobbyists in the country. You're right; he is a lawyer. He used to practice in another state. One day a client came to him charged with operating a prostitution business. When he discovered who the purchasers of the services were, he was able to cut a deal with the DA for his client. He then used that and subsequent information and went into a lucrative blackmail business."

Then a question was directed to Kathy. "What does all this mean to you? You are going to have to deal with these kinds of people."

"I'd say they were all on an ego trip. Now I understand what You told me this morning. The ego is the source of the chaos. The thing that comes to mind is that these people seem to attract each other," Kathy expounded.

"It does appear that way. It is very easy to generalize. What happens is that the strong ego appears to capitulate his or her free will to the designated leader who professes to hold certain beliefs or ideas that are appealing or makes promises to enrich them at a later time. Both are lying...the follower and the leader. Each thinks they can get an advantage over others by this devious bit of conduct.

"I want you all to understand this because Kathy is going to have to deal with a lot of hidden agendas and special interests very soon. The best way for you to manage this problem is to work on an individual case basis. Don't get caught up in generalizations. Keep it one-on-one.

"Kami, Mister Anderson will arrive shortly. I want you to greet him and apply this lesson. We have time for one more question."

"How is it possible to run programs on two frequencies on one disk? Like I did earlier," Larry asked.

"Easy. The disks have the *superconductor* in them. They aren't even close to capacity. There are two disks because your hardware cannot support the amount of data that is contained on each disk. Another reason for two is that a lot of people don't want to hear what is contained on them...so don't let them out of your sight, Larry," the voice stopped, just as the doorbell rang.

Reporter Lewis Anderson was expecting a highly emotional young lady to open the door and was thrown off-guard when Professor Makino, a calm, polite, Asian gentleman about his own age greeted him and invited him into the house. He presented his credentials as he introduced himself and for the first time that he could remember in his journalistic career, was at a loss for words in his quest for a story. Sensing his difficulty, Kami spoke up. "You

34

must be here regarding my daughter's miraculous transformation this morning. Kathy is quite busy at the moment. Please join me for a cup of tea while I relate to you what I know and she will join us briefly."

Lewis nodded affirmatively and was led to a comfortable chair in the living room with all the makings for tea within easy reach. Before he was able to ask, Kami suggested that he turn on his recorder. Lewis removed a mini-cassette recorder from his jacket pocket and placed it on the table. "That'll never do," Kami said. "I've got my recorder in the den. I use it for my seminars. When you're done, we can send the tape to the computer and have it printed up for you. That will save you some time, won't it?"

"Yes, of course. I'm beginning to like this story. Most people are hesitant to talk when the recorder is on."

"You won't have that problem today. We've nothing to hide and all you will hear is the truth." Kami excused himself to get his recorder. Lewis's skepticism returned as he looked about the sparse but tastefully selected furnishings in the house. He caught sight of a wheelchair, apparently pushed aside from the entryway and it aroused his curiosity. He got up and moved closer, observing that it was old and well used. He saw that the back support, made of vinyl, was nearly new and that the seat, made of similar material, had reached the end of its life and was in need of replacement. On closer examination, he noticed that none of the fabric or plastic parts matched in color, surmising that all were replaced at different times as needed. The spokes of the wheels were definitely made of stainless steel, but they showed signs of corrosion and a lot of dirt at the hubs.

When he arrived, he noticed the van in the driveway and had quickly examined it. He returned to his seat and thought about the van. He estimated it to be about five years old. It had handicap plates. He noticed the decal on a van window...advertising for the company that installed a chair lift. He noticed the cutouts in the frame, thinking it was nice work. He returned his thoughts to the wheelchair. The footrest adjustments clearly showed that the chair had been in use for many years as there were wear rings on the inner tubing. Lewis concluded that if this was Kathy's chair she had spent a lot of time in it and had grown up in it.

It was his belief that the duties of his profession were similar to that of a good detective, which required that he have his eyes and ears open and be a keen observer. Being a competent writer was secondary. He was thinking about this when the professor returned with an expensive and sophisticated recording system.

Kami apologized for keeping him waiting, explaining that he installed new batteries and a new cassette. He began to explain its use and Lewis acknowledged that he was completely familiar with it and wished his paper would supply them with new equipment like it. Lewis set it up for recording and Kami asked, "Where should we start?"

"At the beginning," Lewis replied. "How long has your daughter been confined to this wheelchair?" a good, leading question.

The interview progressed very smoothly although the reporter had raised his eyebrows too many times while hearing Kami's responses to his questions. Kami read the disbelief and caught himself wanting to embellish or offer more plausible possibilities to the pointed questions. While relating the events when the disk changed color and the resulting look of disbelief, he was tempted to offer some theoretical possibilities when he remembered his instructions. He paused; then said, "I can see that you do not believe some of the things I've told you. So be it. I'll tell you what I saw and heard and if there is any embellishment or rationalization to be done, it will have to be on your part. I assumed that you were an honest reporter, so I'll give it to you straight. Agreed?"

"Agreed," Lewis replied. "May I have access to medical records; x-rays and lab reports that will confirm the extent of her injuries?"

"Anything we have will be made available to you. I see that Kathy is asking us to join her. She has been working on the computer with Larry, our friend who is still here trying to help." The men rose and walked to Kathy's office, which looked like it was originally a formal dining room, but had been remodeled for her

36

use. Lewis noticed the well-worn floorboards of the ramp where there had previously been a step.

Kami made all of the introductions and after a brief chitchat, Kathy told Lewis that she and Larry had completed their work and that *he* had been summoned by the computer for an interview. They bade him sit in front of Larry's computer, relax, and just answer the questions. He did so reluctantly, not being accustomed to being on the other side of an interview. Faced with this sudden turn of events, he forgot that the recorder was in the living room. He sat quietly, fidgeting a bit, as the others stared at the screen. He felt he might be the victim of a swindle but their faces concealed it well if it was. Faintly, the American flag appeared on the screen. It grew larger and the colors more intense against a blue background. It moved to the left of the screen as Whitney Houston filled in on the right. She began the Star Spangled Banner solo and soon was accompanied. Lewis rose and stood at attention, his right, open hand upon his chest. The piece ended dramatically and the figures faded from the monitor. Lewis regained his seat and the familiar voice spoke to him.

"Thomas, how can anyone be so patriotic and such a talented journalist and be so lacking in fervor for a story as good as this one?"

"My name is Lewis...sir...whoever it is I'm speaking to," Lewis said firmly.

"I'm sorry, I must have had you confused with Doubting Thomas. Now... there was a saint with fervor...once all doubt was removed, of course.

"Lewis, you are a professional at your job. You have the contacts; you know the television boys and the international services. You're cool under fire. But, for this job, you're going to need fervor. What you lack right now is *faith*. Do I read you right?"

"Well, yes. I guess you could say that. I *have* faith. I write good stuff when I have faith that it's true."

"You're talking about honesty there. I mean *faith*. Can you go one hundred percent on your gut feeling? You have to believe everything the rest of this team tells you and go with it. Can you do that?"

"No. I don't think so. The professor seems very honest. I haven't even gotten to know Kathy and Larry...we just barely met. I'm not even sure you are who they claim you are. So far, I'm impressed. But, I wouldn't go to press on it."

"You know who I am. You *invited* Me into your life last week when Duncan was assigned to cover the elections in your place. What do I have to do to get you on the team?"

Lewis took considerable time as he analyzed the situation, finally he offered, "If I could have all of the medical records, pictures of the crash scene, testimony of doctors, maybe some sensational stuff. If I had that, I could go for it."

"Take too long...we gotta' know now. OK, Kathy. Stand in front of the keyboard, facing Thomas. Good, now put your hands over your head. Like that. Good.

"Thomas, put your left hand *through* Kathy and type: DAD on the keyboard."

"You're not serious! Like punch my way through her?" Lewis asked.

"Oh, no. Just extend your hand directly towards the keyboard. You won't feel a thing and neither will she. Just do it. As though you were a person with *faith*."

"OK, here goes." Lewis extended his left hand forward and found the keyboard, then the familiar keys, without being able to see them. He typed in the letters and instinctively looked around Kathy's body and pressed ENTER. The Marine Hymn began to play. Lewis jerked his hand back to his side and stood at attention until the music ended.

"A fine man, your dad. Third Marines. Hell of an outfit. Died of wounds received in action in a skirmish just north of DaNang. Now, there was a man with fervor!"

Lewis was sobbing. "Yes. Yes. I'll do it. I want to be on the team. I believe you. Yes, I believe you all."

Kathy and Larry stood and stared at each other, amazed. Kami embraced Lewis and said, "Everything I've told you is the truth. I am glad that you are going to be a friend and share this experience with us."

Lewis saw the phone and picked it up and dialed. He dried his eyes on his sleeve and spoke into the phone, "Anderson here. Put me through to Briggs." He turned to offer a smile to his new companions and then spoke with fervor to his boss.

"Anderson. "I've got a hot one...hold the presses. I'll be in the office in about fifteen minutes. Keep your line clear and I'll phone you on the cellular. Make Helen available on the computer so she can start on the columns as soon as I get in. I need two reporters to do follow-up and as many media flacks as you can round up for a conference call. We'll need still and video photogs. Alert the wire services. We should be able to sell the story to them. Check with our medical reporters and see if they know some good, reliable MDs who need the television coverage. See you in fifteen."

He hung up. "Kami, may I take the recorder?" He gathered it up without a reply. On the way out he put an arm around the professor and said, "Why don't you come with me. You've seen some miracles today. I'd like to show you one more... media people jumping through their asses."

Chapter 4

Larry left the residence to meet with the phone company technician at the underground cable location. On the way to his car, he heard a domestic quarrel taking place in the house directly across from the Makino home. An object hurled through an upstairs window caused him to stop and look. He noticed a big line splice and a coil of heavy cable that was apparently abandoned on the pole in front of the house.

On the way to his meeting, he thought about the viciousness in Hudson's attitude when he called in to resign his position. He had never been on the receiving end of such personal abuse and he was surprised to find that the more threats and curses that spewed forth from Mr. Hudson's mouth, the less respect he felt for him. And the less he cared about the threats of sending police to his home to confiscate the programs that he had been working on.

It suddenly dawned on him that Kathy was home alone and that the place could be over-run with reporters and gawkers. He stopped. at the mall and called his friend, Victor, who would be home at this hour. His classes were over and he had a few more hours before he began work at SuperCee where he was a security guard. Victor was a post-grad student in computer-science, handsome, twenty-five years old and a terrific dancer. Victor agreed to show up at Kathy's house and act as a security guard only after Larry agreed to double his SuperCee salary.

Kathy was at the computer when the phone rang. It was Lewis, asking for the full name and address of Emily, and the hospital where she had worked. Kathy gave him the information. He told her to expect some reporters from his paper in about thirty minutes, to get something to eat and be prepared for a long, busy night. He wanted to give her some tips on how to handle the press but he was approaching his office. In closing, he said, "By the way, your dad has agreed to be your business agent. An old friend of mine will meet Kami and discuss how to be an agent. For a small fee, of course. There are some legalities involved. My friend is an alcoholic; I hope you don't mind. When he's sober, he's one of the best in the business. I've been trying to get him into AA for years...maybe this story will do it. Gotta' go, we're at the office."

Kathy wasn't hungry and the computer didn't want to respond so she put in a music CD...an old Montavani classic. She listened a bit, hummed a bit, then got up, and tried to dance. She was awkward, as she had never danced before. She could feel the rhythm but she couldn't make herself go. The activity warmed her up and she opened the front door for some fresh air and then resumed her dancing attempts.

Victor, who lived in an apartment house about ten blocks away, arrived at the door just in time to see Kathy slip on the carpet and fall. "Here, let me help you up," he said, introducing himself, and stating the reason for his being there. And the SuperCee uniform...he was already dressed for work when he accepted this job and came right over.

"I'm Kathy. Kathryn Makino. I was trying to dance. I've never danced before."

Victor had not been made aware of the circumstances, only sure of the house address and the name of the woman he was supposed to guard. "I could dance before I was born. That's what my mother told me. Would you like a partner? May I have this dance, Kathryn?" Victor asked in his most formal voice that hardly ever was turned down.

Without hesitation, she nodded affirmatively and held out her arms as she'd seen so many times in the movies or at parties. Victor's eyes met hers and he explained to her that this was a waltz and the rhythm was **one,** two, three; **one,** two three. "Once around the floor while you look at your feet, then hold your head up, let the audience admire your grace...and I'll do the leading." He accepted her right hand in his left, encircled her waist with his right, and began the steps in time with the music.

The first circle of the room did not go well. Victor stopped, moved some furniture to the center so they had more space and they tried again. Kathy got the hang of it as Victor held her closer and took larger steps. By the third revolution, Kathy was able to look Victor in the eyes and not try to watch her feet. Two more circles of the room and the piece ended.

"Oh! That's marvelous! Now I can see why dancing is so popular," Kathy said as she noticed Victor looking directly into her eyes.

"Do you really intend to leave me with the impression that you've never danced before?" Victor inquired while continuing to admire the beautiful face before him.

"My very first dance. Thank you, sir...I'm mighty obliged," Kathy said while making a cute curtsey as she had seen in some of the movies depicting the manners of the Old South. Then she condensed the facts and events of the day into short sentences, explaining to Victor why this had been her first dance, ever. He accepted her story and with a lilt in his voice, said, "I can't wait to teach you the tango."

Kathy felt it first, probably because she had never been this close to a man before. She blushed at the knowledge. "There's some food in the fridge. Would you mind making some sandwiches...for both of us if you're hungry too? I have to freshen up a bit before the reporters get here."

Excusing herself, she went to her bedroom, looked at her image in the mirror, put her right arm over her head and then made a fist and jerked it to her chest. "Yes! Thank You, Lord. He's a doll!"

* * * * *

Lewis was pushing. He knew he had two problems to overcome. He had to sell Gordon Briggs, his Editor-In-Chief on the story and then he had to have a lead story by the time the presses started in just four hours. If he missed either, the story might make page eight in the Sunday supplement. He knew he'd get no help from the night editor, a relative of the owner, who never made a decision.

He brought Prof. Makino into Mr. Briggs' office and introduced them. He laid out the story in a logical manner. The editor seemed more skeptical than moved. Lewis pleaded his case with fervor, reaching back in his memory for similar cases that, although they didn't pan out, didn't hurt circulation. He finally put his job on the line and this forced a decision.

"I'll tell you what. Suppose we compromise? Your lead gave us some good stuff on the nurse that was blown away. That one looks like a cover-up. Hardly any news coverage. We ignored it...got no readers in that part of town. No one was apprehended. No active investigation in the mill. We can play that into the elections with the 'law and order' issues. It'll hurt the incumbent and we're backing the challenger. Go ahead and do your story... heavy on the Emily...what's her name again?...the nurse. We've got nothing else big, so put her in the lead spot. Take a half column on page one. Bury the rest on a half page...if you have that much. I don't want one word about *god's press conference*. For Christ's sake, I'll be laughed out of town.

"The scandal rags showed some interest and are sending some of their people in. Reuters doesn't want it now but an option if it goes out of state. The medical people are definitely in and this is probably where the story will end up. One of our researchers has heard about Emily's work and a student at the University paper called in and claims that she is personally aware of Kathy's former condition.

"I want to hold off on the medical issue until and if the subject develops further. This could be a series if it holds up. Always a lot of reader interest in magical cures. I gotta' tell you, the MDs are mighty skeptical at this point.

"The TV guys will run spots after the evening news, time permitting. Local color only. Nothing from the networks.

"Agreed?" Mr. Briggs asked.

"Agreed. That's more than I had expected or hoped for with what I've got."

"What the hell's gotten into you, anyway? This is the first story you've pitched to me since you came here. You aren't pissed because I gave the election reporting to Duncan are you? You know his uncle has me by the balls and I have to give him work. He's for our candidates and he'll give us good, positive reporting."

"And ignore anything problematical," Lewis said sarcastically, but continued in a more contrite voice. "No, Boss. I wouldn't set you up with a phony story. That would hurt me more than you. I just have a real strong feeling that God is going to get his press conference. I want to be on His side, helping, when that time comes."

"Front page, half column, no press conference. I'll be playing bridge at the Elks Club...don't call. We'll see what it looks like tomorrow. And, this SuperCee thing. Absolutely nothing. You're playing with fireworks there." The editor defined the parameters of the story.

Lewis was pensive for a moment, then asked, "Honest answer. Does Fenhauser have you hooked?"

"Is there another story here? I've got orders...don't touch Fenhauser or SuperCee. Do you know something that I should know?"

"Nothing...just a hunch. Have a good bridge game," Lewis replied.

The editor turned his attention to Kathy's father for the first time now that the paper's business was apparently completed. "Professor, it was nice meeting you. I am sure that you are delighted that your daughter has regained the use of her legs."

"Yes, I am very happy about that, but the removal of the scars and the events on the computer are equally spectacular."

"All in good time. We'll get to those. For now, we have the lead. We have the story first. That's very important in this business. If the story pans out, this paper will be in the driver's seat.

"By the way, I heard of you. You're an expert bridge player, right? Any tips?" Mr. Briggs asked with a wink.

"The mathematics and probabilities of bridge are very simple. The difficulty is with the partners and knowledge of the opponents. I can help you with the first but not the second," Kami said.

"How right you are. I'm always going for a slam and my wife will settle for three-no-trump. What do you think of the newspaper game...from what you've seen here this afternoon?" Mr. Briggs asked, more as a courteous, if not self-serving, pat on his own back...sort of an apology for not turning Lewis loose on the coverage. He did not anticipate a profound answer.

"A lot of my suspicions have been confirmed. I remember what Emily Mullin, Kathy's therapist...she was not a nurse, once said. "If you look for the truth where you know it isn't, you probably won't find it."

"And? How does that apply here?" the editor asked defensively. "We're doing the story."

"But you aren't looking at SuperCee and you will not even consider the idea of a press conference," Kami replied.

"Your first point is valid. Maybe I should at least find out what's going on with SuperCee. Maybe not. No real pressing issues are apparent to me. As far as setting up a press conference...I think it's a little early for that. If God is in your daughter's computer you won't have any trouble from me in getting all the space you want in this newspaper. Let's check out a few things first, OK?"

Lewis chimed in, "Boss, you're starting to sound like a responsible journalist. What's all this 'checkout first' stuff?"

"It does feel good, doesn't it? No wonder you don't have ulcers, Lewis. You have a good story here, don't you?" the editor asked.

"*Everything* checks. I actually put my hand through Kathy's body. I mean, the girl's real...very real. I just reached through her body and typed on the keyboard," Lewis explained in answer to his boss's question.

"To hell with bridge. Professor, would you introduce me to your daughter while Lewis prepares his story? I haven't been out of this office on a story for over ten years."

"He has an appointment with Rabinowitz. He needs to learn a few things about being Kathy's agent," Lewis informed his editor.

"That bum! Where are you supposed to meet him...at the Brass Rail?"

Lewis nodded yes in response to the question.

"OK. You stay here and write your story. The professor and I'll have a drink and pick up Rabinowitz and go to the house.

"Rabinowitz can tell you everything he knows about being an agent in less than thirty seconds," the editor shrugged his shoulders after the remark.

"When he's sober, he's good. He's kicked our butts a few times," Lewis added.

46

"Yeah, when was that? Kennedy was President," the editor exaggerated.

* * * * *

Larry completed his business with the phone company. He returned to the house after withdrawing money from the bank and hurriedly placed bets with a bookie. He was instructing Victor on security of the disks when Kami, Briggs, and Rabinowitz arrived. Two of the gentlemen were wearing strained expressions and relieved to be out of the car. Rabinowitz and Kami were almost identical in stature...small and slender...one Jewish, the other Japanese, both suffered about the same amount of hair loss, dressed in dark suits and wearing ties. They contrasted sharply with Briggs, a very large man with full, bushy hair, round-faced, wearing a casual suit with a sport shirt. All three wore glasses, a badge of their life-styles that required a lot of reading.

Kathy was in the living room being interviewed by one of Briggs' reporters while his photographer sat quietly waiting for instructions. The phone rang and interrupted the interview. Kathy used the extension in the living room and was the only one available to answer it. When she saw her father, she was relieved and asked him if he would please do something about it as it rang frequently. He made a seat for himself and Mr. Rabinowitz, a gentleman he liked at first meeting.

They sat to one side of the room, as far as the phone cord would reach, chatted and answered the phone. Most calls were from the media. One was from the police in response to a complaint of illegally parked cars in front of the house. Another was from a "concerned" City Councilmember's secretary.

Mr. Briggs listened in on Kathy's interview with his paper's reporter. He became fascinated very quickly and took over the interview. He told his reporter to locate Badge Number Forty-Three and find out what his story was. Reporters, friends, neighbors, and inquisitive members of the city began to show up at the front door. No one knew what to do.

Mr. Rabinowitz spoke up. "Anyone here mind if I run this show?" No one responded.

"You, the policeman. Yeah. You in the SuperCee suit." He pointed to Victor. "Take a notebook and a pen. Get everyone's name and phone-number. Find out what they want and give them a number. Keep 'em busy. Start with number sixteen. We don't want anyone to think they were here first. Make them line up...if you can.

"Kami...you got a card table?"

"In the back of the van," Kathy said, momentarily turning from her interview.

"Can you get that, Kami? We'll set up a little station here by the door and shuffle them through one at a time. Leave the phone off the hook when that caller is done and get the table.

"Larry? What're you doing? Nothing. Good. Set up the wheelchair away from the wall. Put a strong light behind. No shadows. Find a cushion for the seat, we're not working with poor people here. You got any more black disks? Put them on the cushion."

Larry explained that the disks usually come in gold or silver color and the front side usually has artwork, etc., to identify the product.

"Use whiteout or something. Make one black and one white. They love to shoot pictures." Rabinowitz ended his instructions when he found himself to be the only one not doing anything as Larry was already going through the family CD music collection. Kami returned with the card table, set it up, and left to return with two folding chairs, which he set on adjacent sides. Rabinowitz moved the table so the phone could reach it, the cord restricted access to the rest of the house. He went to the kitchen and returned with another notepad and a plastic colander, which he placed on the table with the phone. He wrote down a number and told Kami to make a call. "It's my cousin's place. Tell her I'm here. Make sure she gets the address right. We need a set-up for about a dozen people. Kosher, OK? There'll be cops to feed later so tell her to make it heavy on the calories." While Kami dialed the number, he continued, "Make her read the address back. Used to be a nice neighborhood. Now it's under the Interstate. Can't hear yourself think."

When Kami began talking on the phone, Robby took two sheets of paper from the notepad, tore them into fourths and put all but one in the colander. He wrote □15" on it in big numbers, and put it on top of the other pieces of paper. He stood up to see what was happening outside. Victor had about a dozen people lined up on the sidewalk. A TV van was parked across the street. In a loud voice he called to Victor, "OK, send in number sixteen.

"Chief, you about finished up in there? We have to let 'em talk to the girl and get some pictures. Larry, you got those disks yet? When you're finished...you're the computer guy...right? Print me up some summaries of what the hell happened here today. Get the names spelled right."

A heavy, red-haired woman in her forties entered, presenting a piece of paper with "16" written on it. "I'm from the Gazette. I need my photographer...he's got a different number..." her voice trailed off. Rabinowitz shook his head and looked at Kami who only stammered and appeared puzzled. He looked back at the woman reporter, noticing her bargain-basement clothing and jewelry.

"These rent-a-cops. Can't get anything straight. Kami, go out and tell him *again* to keep the photographers with the reporters. We need the Gazette reporter's photographer in here immediately. Would you take care of that for me?" Robby turned his face away from the woman and toward Kami and gave him a wink. The professor left to speak to Victor while suppressing a smile. Outside he found that Victor had established good rapport and some order with the assembled crowd.

"Ms., can I give you some *inside* information? The American News has an exclusive, but, maybe if you called me tomorrow...you know, they always overlook something important," Rabinowitz told her while exchanging business cards. Her photographer entered with Kami. Rabinowitz signaled to Briggs that his interview was over and someone else would have a turn speaking to Kathy. Pointing to the disks that Larry finally managed to color and place on the wheelchair, he said to the photographer, "You'll want to get some of those disks and the wheelchair...very popular with the other fotogs."

Briggs left Kathy with the other reporter, came to the card table, and asked Kami if there was anything to drink. He replied that food was going to be delivered shortly. "Kosher, OK?"

Rabinowitz spoke up. "Can you go to the computer room, someplace back there, and help Larry punch out some copy so we can give these turkeys a handout. And tell him this white disk stinks, it's too yellow."

"Who in hell put you in charge, Rabinowitz?" the editor asked, chafing at being ordered around by a man he did not like.

"The professor here is in charge. He's officially, and legally, Kathy's agent. I'm just following orders, right Professor? By the way, he's having a contract printed up giving American News an exclusive on this. Right after we get the handouts, OK."

* * * * *

The number system set up to handle the crowd was successful and by ten-o'clock in the evening, the traffic began to thin out. Hot coffee, soft drinks, pastrami sandwiches, potato salad, and blintzes arrived. Rabinowitz gave the bill to Kami, explaining that it was the agent's job and reminded him to keep track of all the receipts for tax purposes.

By midnight, only one religious group remained that was going to conduct a vigil, and the police. The excess food was offered to them and the senior police officer was invited in for a meeting to prepare for the next day. Kami conducted the meeting using all of the ideas and notes furnished to him by Rabinowitz. The main concern was security of the disks. It was decided that Victor would return after a short nap and guard the disks and premises. Larry would be busy all the next day bringing in equipment and orienting new staff. Larry complained of lack of space to work in the house and that more electrical power was needed. Kami made a note in response. Rabinowitz agreed to take the initial shift to answer the phones and secure the house until Victor returned. Everyone else was to get a good night's sleep. Larry, Victor and Briggs left. The

50

policeman returned to his post outside. Kami and Kathy went to bed, Kathy to her old bedroom upstairs. She hadn't been there in years.

The phone calls tapered off and finally stopped ringing altogether about three in the morning. By then, Rabinowitz had completely filled a notebook with suggestions and ideas for Kami. He had another cup of coffee, half a blintz and walked around to keep himself awake. He had only seen the living room, hallway, and kitchen since arriving at the house. He noticed the lights were still on in the side room where he assumed the computers were and went there to turn them off. He entered the room and saw that both computers were still running but there were only screen saver patterns on the monitors. He was knowledgeable of computers, but he had never used one.

"Nice job, Robbie," the suave, baritone voice greeted him.

"What the hell...somebody in here?" he asked sharply.

"No one you need fear. It's just Me...God. (Pause) That was a nice thing you did tonight. Someone needed to take charge."

"Hey, nothin'. I take to it naturally. It runs in the family. So? How come You're talking to me? You're really God?" the lawyer asked.

"Yes, I am. I would like to explain to you why I took so long to accept your *invitation*. (Pause) I had faith in you. You were a good man with strong convictions. I'm sorry how things turned out for your wife and son. Leukemia is just one of the things I had to leave in the formula for life to be able to exist. If I changed that, other things worse would occur. It's the same with most of the other diseases. They cannot be eliminated from the basic formula. But, as you've seen in your lifetime, man, using the free will that I gave him can find solutions. I'm sorry, but it has to work that way."

"I've pretty much accepted that. The doctors explained about the genetics. But I don't understand the part about the *invitation*. I sent You an *invitation* to come here?"

"It was right after your wife died, following your son's passing. You had considerable medical and legal expenses and your office was involved in a big lawsuit. As a matter of fact, the one against American News. You won, remember? During the trial you

51

thought you would lose and you *invited* Me into your life. I knew you had a strong case and the sympathy of the jury. I knew you would win so I waited until now when I have a bigger mission for you. (Pause) They need you. You're going to be on the team, aren't you?"

"Yeah. I like that Kami guy. So, this is all on the up-and-up?" Robby responded.

"Quite. Two more items. Larry left with one disk in the computer and the other one lying there by the printer. Please remind him to be more vigilant."

"OK. I'll see he gets told about it. And the next item?" Rabinowitz asked.

"Take one more drink and you'll join your wife and son. You decide. You can contribute your skills to help the ones who are alive now and the generations to come...or...you can cash in your chips. The only thing I can tell you is that they love you and want you to stay."

"Yes. They would want me to go on. I haven't accomplished much without them," Rabinowitz said reflectively.

Chapter 5

"Hello. Anyone here?" It was Victor coming in to relieve Rabinowitz. He was clean-shaven and bathed in cologne, wearing baggy, designer jeans, a sports jersey, and tennis shoes that looked more like ski boots. Rabinowitz met him, raising his eyebrows at the clothes, briefed him on his duties with emphasis on the disks, and left for home, whistling as he walked to the bus stop.

* * * * *

Lewis's piece for the paper was masterfully written. The *who, what, when,* and *where* were explained in a half column on the front page. The top half of page four consisted of facts and supporting evidence laid out in a logical sequence of events. No words were wasted. There were no opinions, speculation, or quotes from people who were not there. There was no mention of a press conference or SuperCee. Briggs, listening to the column at home, told him to take a by-line on the story without changing one word, to get some sleep and to be back on the job at six in the morning.

He arrived at the appointed time and found his editor already at his desk. He was also clean-shaven, wearing a suit and tie, smiling and in a better mood than he'd seen him in years. "Lewis, grab a cup of coffee and come into the office." Lewis made one for himself and brought a re-fill for his boss.

"Good morning, sir. You look mighty chipper after being up late last night," he said to Briggs.

"I never felt so damned good. I actually kissed my wife goodbye this morning! Where did those blintzes come from last night...I forgot, you weren't there. Probably from Rabinowitz, that son-of-a-bitch."

"Boss, he's OK. He just has a drinking problem lately," Lewis said.

"Yeah. I know. He beat the crap out of me once...that libel

suit. He was sober last night and did one hell of a job. Know what? He gave us an exclusive on this story. He wants the paper to cover Larry's costs for the new office equipment and staff until Monday. When the project is over, the newspaper gets the equipment to upgrade some of the old stuff we have. The rest, we split down the middle. I signed the deal with Professor Makino, but I know Rabinowitz wrote it.

"Your article is good. Television and the *big boys* have to come in now. Paul Harvey's office called and we faxed them a summary. His crew is good. It'll be great if Harvey does a spot, with his national audience. One of the local radio talk shows couldn't get off the subject. It's looking good."

"What do you think of Kathy? She's a sweetheart, isn't she?" Lewis asked.

"Lovely person. I did a full hour interview with her myself. I think she is going to get her press conference. As a matter-of-fact, I'm taking you off of this assignment and doing the rest of the story myself," Briggs informed his reporter.

"Shit, that's not fair!" Lewis responded angrily.

"Whoa. Don't get your dander all in an uproar. Today is going to be slow. Anyone, even an old pro like me, can write the follow-ups. Look at the book of notes I have from last night's interview. I can sit here at my desk and write for a week with what I've got. I have another job that needs to be done by someone with your experience and investigative instincts. Any ideas about what story that might be?" the editor asked.

"Related to this story?" Lewis replied, looking for some clue.

"That's what I want you to find out. I need your assurance that this is going to be just between the two of us. I could get my ass fired over this. *Anything* goes wrong; you're working on your own time. I'll have to hang you out to dry," Briggs insisted on these terms before disclosing the task.

"Not SuperCee! Are you giving me the go-ahead on that?" Lewis' attitude changed immediately.

"Discretion. It has to be kept absolutely away from this office and this paper. My idea to get you in the door is a follow-up on Larry and Victor...both of them being SuperCee employees. I can

54

cover you on that. Any leads in other directions and you're on your own.

"Can you go in and look stupid? By tomorrow, there should be some releases about the disks and the mention of superconductors in them. I don't know anything about superconductors and I doubt if you do either, but maybe you can get an angle from Kami or Larry to broaden the investigation," the editor explained.

"That's a good approach. Maybe I can come up with some scare tactics about toxic or hazardous products in the lab. What am I looking for?" Lewis asked.

"*That* you'll have to find out from Larry. Kathy could not remember in detail what each person, or God, said. Only that there is a connection with a Mr. Fenhauser, SuperCee, prostitution and blackmail. He's branched out and has his finger into everything from drugs to environmental issues. Wherever there's money, he's involved. Mostly with the politicians that he's blackmailed at one time or another. That's where he got his start and he's learned how to cover his tracks."

"This could take a long time. Do I get a research assistant?" Lewis asked.

"Not from here. I've got someone in mind. A friend at the Chron. She owes me. Remember Kanisha Porter? Been several years ago. We had to let her go because she couldn't get along with anyone here," Briggs continued.

"Yeah. The black girl with the big hair. Every story she wrote had to have some racial agenda to it. Two honkies get killed in a car crash and she writes about the noise that whites cause in the black community. Why would she help us? We fired her," Lewis recalled.

"I had a nice, long, fatherly talk with her before she left. And I got her the job at the Chron. She turned out to be a pretty good writer. She sent me a 'Thank You' letter not too long ago," Briggs explained.

"You mean behind that Archie Bunker facade, there breathes a warm, loving human being? You had me fooled all these years," Lewis smiled.

"Yeah. Well, don't let it get past that door. I'll call her and see if I can get a lunch date. Better to handle this in person. If I think of anything else, I'll let you know. You might check with Rabinowitz. I'll bet he can give you some angles to work on," Briggs concluded.

Lewis started to leave, had an after-thought, turned and said, "Boss, one last question...back to the Kathy story. Did you *invite* God into your life recently?"

"That's none of your god-damned business!" the editor said, rising to his feet.

"I thought so. So did I!" Lewis replied and the two men just stood and smiled at each other.

* * * * *

Nancy, a small, trim, bespectacled brunette, dressed in a business suit to kill, was the first to arrive at the Makino residence. After a brief inspection by the police officer in front, she was allowed to enter and she met Victor who was watching TV. He escorted her to the computer room and showed her the equipment while explaining in rather loose terms what was going on, as he didn't really grasp it all himself. He told her about the two disks and showed her the one that he was guarding. When asked about the other, he didn't know where it was. Nancy first checked Kathy's CD drawer and found it empty. She found the disk in Larry's computer and returned it to the drive. Seeing that both computers were fully operational, she moved the mice to get rid of the screen savers to see what was on them. Larry had gotten another monitor, printer, and accessories from his house to bring both systems on-line. Nancy transferred the phone back to the computer and relieved Victor of that duty and he returned to the TV set. She found the list of supplies that Larry had prepared, deleted some, added some, and checked the paper supply. Seeing it low, she adjusted the printer settings so that it printed on both sides of the paper.

Larry also arrived early and was relieved when he found Nancy on the job. She told him what she had done so far and he nodded his approval and thought that he had better get an early start after writing down for her all of the chores that he had scheduled for himself. He found the keys to Kami's van and decided to use that to transport all of the items that he was going to buy. He had arranged for delivery of some large items around ten-o'clock and he was not yet sure how they were to be paid for. Finding nothing more to discuss, he departed, motioning to Victor to remove his feet from the furniture as he passed him on the way out.

Kami rose early, as was his custom, and made a pot of tea. Finding no one to join him in tea, he put on a pot of coffee for the others who were expected. He looked in vain for a leftover blintz. He located the number for Rabinowitz's cousin, copied it in his permanent address book, and placed another delivery order. It was much bigger this time.

Victor, watching the news on TV, was not anxious to move himself to other duties. The police maintained order outside and he thought he heard Kathy up and moving about. He had been thinking about her all night. He found that SuperCee left word at his house that he was fired for not showing up at work last night, and to turn in his uniforms. He decided he could miss a few days of school with no harm...and he could not stop thinking about Kathy.

Lewis arrived, looking for Larry who had already departed. That gave him an opportunity to talk to Victor and get the layout of SuperCee's offices and security systems. He obtained a list of names for key personnel and some inside phone numbers. Chad, the Office Manager, often was the first regular employee to come to work and was probably there now. Victor remarked that he thought he was gay because he had invited him to several home parties and one time to the movies. Lewis decided to call and get an appointment. Victor's information was correct and Chad answered the phone. Victor was eavesdropping and it was apparent to him that Chad new nothing about Kathy's miracle or the reason for Larry's resignation. It appeared that Lewis was having a hard time getting an appointment for an interview. Victor whispered to him to let Chad know that he was a close friend of Victor. When Lewis made mention of that, the tone of the conversation changed and

Chad invited him to come by and join him for coffee and he would see if he could help him at that time.

The phone installers arrived and started drilling holes through the walls and floor of the computer room. Electricians showed up and began to move furniture and the telephone installer's equipment and drilled more holes. The noise, dust, arguments and confusion made it impossible for Nancy to work and she suggested shutting everything off, as there were likely to be power interruptions and the dust wasn't helping anything. There was no one to make a decision. The reporters outside were beginning to become annoyed with the lack of information. Kami decided to tell the reporters that it would be at least a few hours before they would be ready to conduct interviews, but everyone inside knew it would be much longer before things were back to normal.

Marcie, a sleek, blue-eyed beauty with an athletic figure and sun-tanned Northern Europe skin and features found her way through the crowd and introduced herself to Nancy. They chatted over a cup of coffee presented by Kami while waiting for the dust to settle. Nancy put her in charge of the phone, which she had to disconnect from the shutdown computers. Nancy left her when Shirley, the third new employee barged in, very upset. The ravishing, voluptuous, redhead, not more than twenty-five explained that she was late because the police detained her at the checkpoint where she had to leave her car. And then, she could not get through the police cordon in front of the house and had to wait in line just to get a number before she found the officer with her name on the list.

Victor stood beside Kami admiring the latest entry. He nudged him with his elbow and said, "God is male and He sure can pick them!"

Kami turned to him, grinned good-naturedly and replied, "I hope he does as well with the horses!" Victor really didn't understand that but let it drop.

Just then, Larry returned with a look of frustration and the morning paper tucked under his arm. He instructed Victor to bring in the boxes of supplies from the van. He caught Nancy's eye and told her he had the needed paper for the printers. The caterer finished setting up the order and when Kami finished paying them and placing an order for the afternoon, he joined Larry who was staring at the paper and shaking his head negatively. It looked like he needed some consolation and brought him a hot coffee and a blintz, asking what the problem was. "Not one winner. Not even a place or show," Larry was reading from the racing section of the paper. "Amigo, how am I going to pay for this stuff?"

"Not to worry. A way will be provided. I'll call Mr. Briggs as soon as I can get a line. They're making the changeovers now. I have the money to cover your bets. You'll need...two more days at eight hundred dollars a day. I'll get that for you today. You need cash, right?

"I have an idea. Can I pick the horses and double the wager? Is that agreeable within the rules we were given? You were there. Do you remember the exact wording? I even think it was printed out. I always had a gambling streak in me...suppressed you know, because of my knowledge of statistics and the laws of probability," Kami inquired of his friend.

"I think so. I'll check the instructions. They're back there somewhere. Too many people in the way right now. I think the intent was that I have to make the bets myself. In person...so there'll be no problem at pay-off time. Let me think about the ramifications of your suggestion, OK?" Larry replied.

Rabinowitz returned and went immediately for the blintzes and a cup of hot, black coffee. He, too, was cleanly shaved, wearing a smart silk suit and tie. He surveyed the activity, put the blintz on a saucer, and introduced himself to the new staff. He looked at Kami who was making notes on the racing form and asked him what he was doing.

"Picking the horses for today's races," he replied as though that was what he was supposed to be doing. "Larry had no luck at all with yesterday's choices."

"Give me that," Rabinowitz said, taking the paper. "Haven't you figured it out yet? No matter what horses he bets on, they'll walk home.

"You got any spray paint in the garage? The job Larry did on these CDs stinks. They don't look real. Can you come up with some more disks and spray one black and the other white? Both sides...no holidays. We have to replace these before we let the reporters back in. Remember, the pros are going to be here today." Kami left to take care of the chore.

Victor finished unloading the van quickly and went back to his seat in front of the TV, looking around for Kathy and not seeing her. He wondered why she was taking so long to appear and thought he'd pick out a big blintz and have a cup of coffee ready to give her when she showed up. Rabinowitz saw him unoccupied and asked, "Kid, you figured out what's going on here?"

"Yeah. I think so. A bunch of loonies out there want to see a freak or something."

"That girl is for real. A *miracle* happened here yesterday. People want to know about it. Did you quit your other job yet?" Robby asked.

"No. They fired me." Victor replied.

"Good. You need a job. As of now, you're Kathy's bodyguard. I'll call my brother-in-law. You know where Sammy's Tailor Shop is? No...you wouldn't know. Here's the address." Robby wrote the information on a slip of paper and dialed on his cellular while Victor stood, puzzled. Robby gave him the address and pointed him toward the door. "Be there at ten-o'clock. Sammy will deck you out in a new wardrobe. Listen to him...he knows how to make you look like a bodyguard. What religion are you? Sammy? Rabinowitz here...hang on a minute..."

"None, I guess," Victor drawled after giving it some thought.

"If you don't know, that's the right answer. Go to Dalton's. See my sister, Ruth, and get a bible. It's to put in your breast pocket so you look like you're packing. Ruth can find you the right size if you tell her what it's for. Bibles come in all sizes. Get the bible first so Sammy can make it look like it belongs there."

"Anything else? I don't have the money to pay..."

"No problem, Kid. You're going to earn it," Robby said as Victor turned to leave. "One more thing. Get a haircut. Find an old Italian. I got no barbers in my family." He picked up the paper, which was still open to the racing sheet and quickly scanned it. "If he puts his hand out for a tip, you tell him, 'Satan's Pleasure'...sixth race...can't lose." You'll make his day!"

Kami waited until Robby was off the phone and showed him the new disks he had painted in the garage. Robby seemed satisfied after a cursory inspection and replaced the pair of disks on the wheelchair seat cushion. He handed the ones that Larry made hurriedly the night before to Kami and told him, "Bury these somewhere. I hope no one took close-ups."

Kathy appeared, looking beautiful. She enjoyed a cup of coffee and a blintz while looking around for Victor. She looked out the front window, thinking he might be helping the police, but she didn't see him.

* * * * *

Ralph Jackson was called Rafael for the first five years of his life. Born to an uneducated woman in Cuidad Juarez, Mexico, hunger was something he recalled as not a good thing. His mother told him that his father was a military man from the Air Force base on the other side of the line. If so, he never saw him. She eventually married another black airman and joined him at March AFB in Riverside, California. Ralph was entered in school, had a nice house, decent clothes, and modern amenities. The man of the house, a flight engineer on tankers, was seldom at home and drank a lot when he was. That marriage disintegrated and he found himself to be a fat, black youth living in the Watts district, with a mother who could not speak English. She worked in a restaurant and cleaned houses to provide for the two of them.

His name gradually changed to Ralph and he took the family name that was on his military dependent ID card, Jackson. He was a disappointment. Very big and heavy for his age, he never learned to play anything except soccer and found no one in Watts who knew the game. He was too slow and uncoordinated for basketball, and never knew how to throw a baseball. He had no help with his homework and did only marginally in school, but graduated high school. He managed to stay out of jail with the help and counsel of his mother. He was accepted by the Air Force and spent two years

61

as an orderly in the military hospital at Clark Air Base in the Philippines. He liked the work and being able to speak Spanish, he was a valuable asset to his coworkers in dealing with the Filipino hospital workers who spoke Tagalog. The hospital Executive Officer liked him and when he was transferred to the hospital at Travis AFB, outside of San Francisco, he arranged for Ralph's next assignment. More importantly, Ralph took advantage of the opportunity to further his education and when he finished his enlistment, he did two years as a full-time student and worked part-time in various hospitals where his skills were always in demand.

His attempts to get a medical education were disappointing. He worked full time for the next ten years in various hospitals. He always ended up working for the Administrator, behind a desk and putting on more-and-more weight. He gained a union job for his mother in Housekeeping where she was finally able to support herself adequately. Between the two of them, they were able to buy a house, a car, and meet expenses with enough left over to vacation in Mexico every year. He continued his education and since he always ended up in Hospital Administration, he decided to pursue that and obtained his credentials. Fat, black, unconnected, and unmarried males have a difficult time finding good paying jobs in Hospital Administration, but he stayed with it and built himself a good reputation through longevity and hard work.

Affirmative Action came along and he found himself in demand. His first chance came when he was put in charge of a small, suburban clinic for a Health Service Corporation. He did exceptionally well and was promoted to Assistant Administrator at a major metropolitan hospital. His recommendations for changes were accepted and the resulting cost savings made him popular with the directors and the medical staff as well.

At age fifty he took up bridge and joined the Elks Club. He was an imposing figure of a man, six-feet-four, weighing close to 300 pounds. He had overcome his inferiority complex and referred to himself as the "fat bastard". A man who could convincingly explain to an outraged patient the accuracy of charging $3.27 for a sanitary napkin had no trouble with the rules of bridge and acceptance at the Elks Club bridge night. That was where he had met the editor of the American News.

Briggs, sitting at his desk, writing copy on the Kathy story from his notes, put two-and-two together and placed a call to Ralph Jackson, the current Administrator for General Hospital where Kathy was treated and Emily had been a physical therapist.

Chapter 6

After conferring with his new employees, Larry called for a meeting. Abandoning efforts to gather around the kitchen table, the group joined Kathy in the living room. In addition to Larry, Nancy, Marcie, and Shirley, there were Robby, Lewis, Kami, and Nancy. Larry said it was obvious that they needed space in which to work. Four people in the computer room that was used as an office for one person previously, was not going to work. As he began to explain that more equipment was coming in shortly, there was a commotion at the front door.

Kami answered the door and spoke to the police officer who was in charge of crowd control. He had with him the neighbors from across the street who pushed into the house the moment there was an opening. They demanded to know when the crowds and nuisance would be over. They complained about being unable to sleep, to use their car, trash and people all over their lawn and threatened to sue for damages.

No one knew what to say. Finally, Robby came forward and introduced himself, explaining that he was a neighbor from down the street with similar complaints and gave them one of his cards. He asked if he could dispense with his problem as he was there first, and then he would come over and talk to them. They left and Larry again addressed the space problem. As an aside comment, he said he was surprised that the two of them came over together since they had been fighting the day before.

After some discussion, Kathy solved the immediate problem. There was a chairlift to the upstairs. When she was younger, her room was upstairs, next to the master bedroom. The chairlift was awkward to use and in constant need of repair. It was difficult to use the bedroom because of the very narrow hallway at the top of the stairs. The bathroom was impossible to use from a wheelchair. Because of the expense for remodeling the upstairs and her growing up and not as dependent on her father, the downstairs was converted for her use. She liked the upstairs much better and she would gladly abandon her bedroom downstairs for workspace. They all liked that idea and Kami said he would arrange that it be done immediately. He mentioned that he almost cried when he saw Kathy *walking* up the stairs to use her old bedroom last night.

The meeting concluded and Robby motioned Kami aside and asked, "How much money do you have in the bank? Liquid."

Kami suggested that he could probably raise about fifty thousand dollars from his savings. He added that he thought he could take a second mortgage on his house but was more interested in *why* the question.

"Have you ever been in their house...the people who were just here? What do you think it's worth?" Robby asked.

Kami replied that he knew the couple for many years and had often visited the house. He estimated it to be worth about a hundred and fifty thousand dollars. He thought that the couple had been having marital problems for the past month or so.

"Let me make some phone calls. I'll bet we can get it for one twenty five. That could solve the space and security problems. It's going to get much worse, not better," Robby said, and then found a quiet corner and dialed on his cellular phone.

Kami answered the door and signed for a messenger-delivered envelope from American News. He and Larry did not know what the contents were. When asked, Nancy explained to them that they were Purchase Orders for the equipment that was due to arrive. She added that she was sure the deliverymen would accept them, as this was the way most companies who had accounting departments conducted their business.

Robby finished his calls and told Kami to go to the bank and get all the cash he could lay his hands on. He said he was going to go talk to the people across the street and then go to the bank that had the mortgage on the house and meet with his nephew who was a loan officer there.

* * * * *

Ralph Jackson, one of his assistants and the Physician-In-Charge sat at the head of the table in the conference room. His department heads had been briefed earlier to bring him all of the

66

details and records concerning Kathy. A hospital courier was waiting to bring her old records from the archives that were located in a big, tilt-up building in the Industrial Park. Old records for the corporation's many facilities were consolidated in the lower-rent structure.

The records, which were extensive, could not be located and a tracer in the computer led back to General Hospital. The Medical Records Supervisor conducted a frantic search, returned with one of his clerks, and had an explanation for the apparent loss of the records. The clerk had taken a call from the Police Dept. on the previous day. He showed his log indicating Badge Number Forty-Three and the Police Department phone-number, which he checked out and verified. He personally spoke to the officer and when he located her current files, he called back with the information. There wasn't much in the file as she hadn't been treated at the hospital for seven months and that was for a bad case of the flu. The officer wanted the auto-accident report, which was ten-year-old information. The clerk submitted a request for the records that were in the archives when the computer verified their existence. Ralph thanked them and told them to keep looking and to return as soon as the records were found.

Doctors, nurses, orderlies, and staff members who recalled Kathy filed in and out of the conference room and in short time Ralph had a pretty good accounting of her condition and treatment. On a much lower key, his assistant was accumulating a very thick file of information concerning Emily Mullin, physical therapist. Someone, a secretary no doubt, entered and said the records were found. They were on the delivery truck that made daily rounds. They were now trying to find out where it was and divert it or make other arrangements for speedier delivery. Ralph displayed his pleasure at the way the staff was reacting efficiently, as he thought of the best way to handle this crisis.

His PIC, an elderly, but respected pediatrician had been skeptical of the story from the outset. He was a major stockholder and was more concerned about publicity regarding the shooting of Emily. His initial instructions to Ralph were to avoid any publicity at all. If that could not be done, then they would emphasize how

67

professional and thorough the medical treatment of Kathy had been. As far as the physical therapist was concerned, the hospital regretted the loss of a capable employee; however, it occurred long after work hours, in a location far from the hospital. Period. If pressed further the position would be that there was an investigation in progress and refer any further queries to the DA's office.

Two heavy boxes of records were rushed into the meeting room. The PIC asked one of his assistants to find the Emergency Room x-rays and bring him a portable back light to read them. They were found along with a folder of Polaroid pictures. The PIC studied the pictures and x-rays for several minutes and looked seriously at Ralph. "This girl can *walk*?"

"That's what the editor of the American News told me. He personally witnessed it and took her interview. Otherwise, I'd share your view completely that this was a temporary recovery or a fraud. There's been so many. Do you have anything on the spleen removal? That, and a chipped tooth. He told me that there is no closure scar and no crown on her front tooth. Twelve years old, that's not a baby tooth, right?" the Administrator asked.

The pediatrician in him responded. "All I want for Christmas is my two front teeth. At twelve, definitely permanent front teeth. Maybe we better prepare for a press conference. I'll go to my office and call the Board of Directors and let you know. We have some Public Relations specialists in the central office. I'll see what they say."

Ralph reread the handwritten agreement that would allow the hospital to disclose records and make use of Kathy's recovery in return for discounted medical bills of local leukemia patients. Professor Makino also agreed to bring Kathy to the hospital, walking, when he had a signed agreement to that effect. The letter was delivered earlier in the morning by a young bicycle courier with a Jewish accent.

* * * * *

Bad news travels fast. A local talk-show host was handed the fax by one of his staff. "Verify it!" he said off-mike, as he let the caller rattle on. CONFIRMED appeared on his monitor. He took a deep breath and cut off his caller. "OK, all you born-again-freaks out there. I've been listening to your calls about this *Kathy* for the past two hours and I would rather talk about the more important things, like the coming elections and the *issues*. Listen to this. Just in from a reporter who was there. (He didn't say that the reporter worked for a newspaper that was also owned by the radio-station transmitting his voice.)

"The disks, claimed to be delivered by god, are in fact, CDs that can be bought in any music store and they were painted. Infrared photos, taken by my photographer identified the black disk as The Best of Eric Carmen, made in New York City. The other, apparently covered with ordinary whiteout, looks like it may be a pirated version of Air Supply as the writing is in Spanish and the retail code number cannot be found in any catalog. One title, positively identified as 'Perdido En El Amor', has been translated to Lost In Love, one of Air Supply's top hits."

"I'm not making this up folks. I'm reading it straight from the words of a reporter who was there. He goes on to say...."

"The backrest on the wheelchair was new. There was no indication that the chair had ever been used as the seat was covered with a fluffy pillow...hardly the type that a person would sit on."

"There's a lot more detail in here. I suggest you religious-right-freaks read about it in the paper and then call me back and apologize."

"So...it looks like I was right one more time," and then in a warm, concerned-for-humanity voice, added, "I can't figure out the scam. Why would anyone want to make up a story like that?" Then, back to his familiar radio voice. "OK, I'm ready for the next caller who wants to talk about the *issues*..."

* * * * *

The dominoes had not begun to fall inside the Makino residence. Outside, reporters began to depart after answering their mobile phones and receiving new assignments. The word traveled quickly through the line of people. Fraud. The TV van, parked across the street, packed it in. This one was over.

The first indication of anything wrong was a flurry of telephone activity, which quickly tapered off to a stream of angry callers. The new equipment, which was supposed to be hooked-up by now, wasn't, and the new staff did not notice the change of attitude. Kathy, watching the news on TV while waiting for Larry and the workers to solve their computer problems and clean the place up, saw and heard the quick news item. There was a picture of the two disks on her chair, followed by close-ups, which revealed their identity. The announcer made matter-of-fact remarks about the method of detection, showed a picture of the new backrest and then changed to another topic. About the same time, Nancy recognized that the callers were angry and expressing their resentment, not calling for information or encouragement. Negative comments passed quickly and activity all but ceased. An air of disenchantment overtook them.

Kathy called them all to the kitchen table. They pieced together all the information they had received so far. It seemed to her that the world outside was ready to accept that the *miracle* never happened and ready to sweep it under the carpet and go on about its business. Kathy was not satisfied with any of the suggestions being made for a course of action and wished that Rabinowitz or Kami were there to furnish some leadership. Then, she got an idea and asked Nancy and Larry if either computer could be made to run. The electricians replied that they were done with the electrical work; just some minor items left...covers and some markings. The phone men were carrying all of the empty boxes for their equipment outside. Larry said he thought the machines could be turned on.

Kathy said she knew where to get answers and went to her computer. She confirmed that one of the disks was in the CD drawer and turned it on. When the monitor came to life, she typed: I TRUST IN YOU, and pressed ENTER. She asked the others to leave her alone a moment.

"What seems to be the problem, Kathy?" came from the speakers.

"I don't really know. Everyone seems to think we are liars here.

We don't even know what we are being accused of. The disclosure is supposed to be out in the afternoon paper, two more hours yet. Without the support of the newspapers, how can I get You the press conference that You want?

"Oh, thank you for Victor! Do you think he likes me? Where is he?"

"OK. First things, first. Victor. Needs work. Very rough on the inside. He needs to look at that. He's never spoken to Me. Attractive people seem to have this problem. Do you think you can help him with that?" God advised.

"You know. Emily told me that same thing once. She said young, attractive people don't need to think or work hard to be successful, but then, when things go wrong they don't have the experience or training to handle problems. Emily and I were discussing the possible reasons for the large percentage of entertainers, athletes, politicians, and celebrities with AIDS, alcohol, drug, and other problems."

The voice responded, "They come up with some lulu's, don't they? I have to laugh at times. They usually do end up talking to Me, and, of course, I have to be serious and help them out.

"While we're on the subject, remember what I told you about egos...see a connection? Now...about Victor. Are you going to help him? Remember, he has a free will like you and neither of you know what a holy relationship is."

"Yes, I'll talk to him. Where is he?" Kathy continued the conversation as though she were talking to a close friend.

"Ask Rabinowitz. As a matter-of-fact, Robby is coming in the front door now and I want him to answer the rest of your questions. You won't forget Victor?"

"No, I won't forget," Kathy promised and ended the conversation.

She left the computer-room to greet Robby and looked outside hoping to catch a glimpse of Victor, working with the police, but he wasn't there. There was only a hand-full of people waiting. The religious group was gone. "Thank god, you're here. We have a lot of problems. Where's Victor?" Kathy greeted Robby.

"You think we got problems! I don't think so. Look at this!

71

These guys are calling us frauds," he said, holding up a copy of the Evening Star.

"I don't see any frauds here. Anyone see any frauds here? I think we have a great lawsuit here. That's what I think we have. Now...what do you think your problems are?"

Everyone gathered around to read the story in the paper.

"How did you get this? It won't be out for a couple of hours yet," Kathy asked.

"The printing press is in the back of the lot where my offices are. One of my in-laws works there and walked a copy over to me when I was in checking on my employees. Downtown, near the bank. The bus comes right out this way. Faster than driving and no problem parking."

Robby saw Kami returning and stopped him in the entryway. "Kami. I've got great news! We own a house. I closed it. Ironclad...for one-eighteen, five. My nephew is the loan officer for the mortgage company and we assume the balance of the loan...a good rate of interest...we gotta' pay some equity. I need twenty-three grand from you by quitting time...six-o'clock. I already paid my half. Any problems with that? They'll be out by five this afternoon. My cousin, Lenny, is going to move them free. He owes me and had no work for his crew today."

He continued on, not waiting for answers to his questions. "Larry, you ought to go over there and start planning on how to use the place for your work. Kathy needs to stay here...in her own house. We're getting too many people in here. Before you go, look at this." He reached into the group reading the paper, re-folded it for them, and kept the sport pages. "You'll get a kick out of this," he said as he shuffled through to find a particular article. He pointed to it and continued talking, "Look here...the track writer reports that some jockeys were complaining of unusual conditions on the track yesterday. Three jockeys turned in the lowest times, ever, for their mounts. The groundskeeper swears that there has been no new turf added and no changes to the watering procedures. The racing commission wants an investigation. It looked like a fix to them, but there were no big money winners.

He turned his attention back to the group. "OK. You all

72

finished reading the lead story? They're calling us frauds. What have they got? Two things. One. The backrest on the wheelchair. Two. The disks. The bastard! Infrared film, he uses.

"Let's start with the backrest. This is news to me. Kathy, what's the story here?"

"The picture here only shows the backrest and not the whole chair. I bought a new backrest a couple of weeks ago. But I didn't get around to changing it right away. As you can see, it does look like it's never been used. If they had taken a picture of the whole chair, anyone can see that it is well used," Kathy answered.

"You have a receipt for it...with the date of purchase?" Robby asked as though he were conducting a cross-examination of a witness at a trial.

Kami responded, seemingly peeved at the tone of the question. "Yes. I bought that for her. The medical supply store is on Oxford Street. Six or seven blocks from here. We have known the manager for years. Ever since we needed equipment like this for Kathy. I also have the old backrest around here somewhere. You try it. Go ahead, sit down in the chair, and try to change the backrest. That's why she didn't change it right away. I changed it for her, as she was unable to do it herself."

"All right!" Robby exclaimed. "We'll blow their asses right out of the water! Put the old backrest on when you find that. Larry...Nancy, make me a lot of copies of the receipt.

"Next. The disks. I'll take the blame for that one. Infrared. I'll be damned...didn't think of that. We'll use the real ones. Can we do that, Kathy? Will the computers run without the disks?" Robby asked.

"I don't know but I know how to find out. I'll ask the computer when Larry gets back from across the street. I *think* the hard drives have all the files they need to operate now that things have slowed down," Kathy responded.

"That's going to be a security problem with the disks in view. Where the hell is Victor? He should be back by now. Kami, when you go to the bank for the money, stop by National Security Service and see Irving, my brother-in-law. We have to do a better job on securing the disks. My idea is for Victor to have them chained to his wrist. Irving knows where to get this kind of stuff. You see them used in the movies all the time.

"Also. Ask him for a price for two guards around the clock. No kids. Big blacks, with no bellies hanging out. Mean looking, but no guns. No...clean cut... We need a good image here. When he gives you a price, offer him two bucks an hour more for dependable guys. Wait a minute...female guards. No...make it one male and one female...on each shift. That'll keep everyone awake. Got it? It's getting late, you better get going."

"General Hospital canceled a press conference that I thought you set up. I just received this from a courier. They could not get through by phone," Kami said handing Robby an envelope.

"Don't know a thing about it. You sent them the agreement that I wrote up for you? Fill me in before you go." Robby asked.

"I rewrote the agreement, in my handwriting, without the legalese. I sent it with your uncle's courier service as you suggested. Everything else is in this folder. I got myself organized as you recommended." Kami handed him all the material and headed out the door, smiling.

Larry returned, and went straight to the computers with Nancy and her crew. He inspected the connections and turned everything on. All of the printers began to operate and the girls opened-up paper packs and loaded them fully. Larry and Nancy began reading the information that was being printed and collated them into piles in the confined space.

Robby read Kami's file of notes. He didn't know about Briggs's tip-off to the hospital or what Kami had left out of the agreement he sent them. He did not like the message from the hospital administrator saying that the agreement was being forwarded to the DA's office. Kathy was watching TV news and switching channels, looking for more information about her. She glanced outside occasionally to see if she could find Victor. There were a few more people, but no sign of him.

Robby called everyone back into the kitchen. There was another problem that he needed answers for. Larry stayed behind to monitor the equipment.

Robby opened his meeting with a question. "Who knows

anything about *superconductors*? What is this thing? To me, a superconductor is the guy who lets the old lady ride free. Anybody got a clue?"

Nancy raised her hand and Robby pointed to her.

"We now have three computers working and Kathy's is free. It didn't have enough memory to suit Larry. I noticed that Kathy has an encyclopedia in her software. I'm sure that would have the basic information to explain superconductivity."

"Great! Let's do it," Robby replied.

"A few more things?" Nancy asked of Robby, who nodded his approval. "The computers have printed manuals for each of us. The manual has your job-description and answers to most of your questions. It contains a summary of the events that have taken place since Kathy's experience yesterday. We'll pass them out when we have them in folders."

"There are statistics and spreadsheets that we are just now receiving. We don't know how the computers are doing all these things. For example, we have names, addresses, and phone-numbers for all who have called in. We have what we believe are summaries, printed in many different languages.

"Right now, we are just sorting and collating the information.

"It's kind of spooky. For example, there is a manual for each security guard and Professor Makino has only just left to arrange for them."

"Has anyone got more questions?" Robby continued. "If not, I suggest that we read our manuals when they become available and get some more reporters in here to refute this evidence, *and* report the whole story. I think we are going to be visited by the DA and we have to look good.

"Dammit. Kami left without getting me the old backrest or the receipt. Kathy, can you...." Robby stopped short when she held out both items.

"OK. Show time! Those guys have been out in the street all night and all morning. They're the hard-core. Let's give them a good show. Fifteen minutes. We start with Number One and real disks this time.

"When Larry's free I want to talk to him.

"Kathy. What were the problems you mentioned when I arrived? Victor is getting a new suit and a haircut. You won't like either one." Robby followed Kathy to the living room and sat beside her.

She smiled and said that she didn't think she had them any more. He had solved most of them since his arrival. "How can you be so sure of yourself?" she asked him.

"Sure of myself? It's show business. All on the outside. For years, I was scared to death most of the time. I grew up scared. Probably because I'm a Jew. I was always trying to prove that I was just as good as everyone else. It took me a long time and your computer to get over it. I know, finally, who I am, and for the first time in my life, I am at peace," Robby replied.

"And who are you? I know I like you and right now, I need you."

"I am just another person, like everyone else. The only thing 'special' about me is my purpose here. I am going to help you in any way that I can. That's who I am, now. I even like myself now and I need me, now, *sober*, to make my wife and son proud of me. God...how I used to miss them!"

"And you don't now?" Kathy asked, puzzled.

"Nope. No more. I know where they are, and they're watching me, cheering me on. I have God's word on that," Robby replied.

"I have another question. What's a *holy relationship*?" Kathy asked.

For once, Robby didn't have a quick answer and he thought a bit. "A holy relationship? I suppose the opposite of an unholy one. How the hell do I know? That's a new one on me. Maybe two gay priests? Was it used in a phrase? At the moment, it's like superconductivity. I don't get the concept. Nothing registers."

"I just heard it used for the first time this morning. I thought you might know. How you feel about your wife was what made me ask," Kathy said.

Robby looked at his watch, nearly two-o'clock, and shouted out, "Show time! Let's do this right, everyone."

He looked around one last time to see what had been done and if anything had been over-looked. The house had been cleaned up, the furniture arranged neatly, the telephone workers and electricians had gone. Both original disks were placed on the wheelchair seat and a smaller pillow selected so that the worn seat showed up clearly, in front. Someone thought of draping the old backrest over the new one and affixed a copy of the receipt to it. It made a rather solid statement. Larry set up his table in the hallway, furnished him with his manual and a neat stack of brochures to be handed to the reporters.

Pleased with everything, he motioned to Kathy to have a seat and to receive the first reporter. He called out to the street. "Please send in number one."

Kathy took one more glance out the window, but she didn't see Victor.

Chapter 7

There was little activity at the SuperCee office complex when Lewis arrived. He was ushered to the reception desk and introduced to Chad by the security guard who met him in the vestibule. Lewis made mental note that SuperCee must not have many visitors and those who did come, were probably accompanied by an employee. There seemed to be little need for a security guard as the reception desk dominated the entry and a stranger would not know where to go from that point.

Chad put down the celebrity magazine that he had been reading and invited Lewis to join him in a cup of coffee, at a chair behind the reception desk. While waiting for Chad to return with coffee, he looked about and confirmed that the information he received from Victor was accurate. He had to devise a way to first get past Chad. He had nothing except instinct to go on and searched his brain for an idea, when he noticed the magazines that were lying about. Tabloids, entertainment, and fashion. One caught his attention...a crime magazine...for armchair detectives. Someone in this place was paranoid about security. Perhaps he could use that to his advantage.

After exchanging a few more pleasantries with Chad, Lewis explained the purpose of his visit. He told of his role as the initial reporter on the Kathy case after playing a hunch when he read a police report. He downplayed the actual event, expecting it to turn out to be a fraud, but he wrote the column because that was his job. He put two-and-two together after discovering that Larry, Victor and *superconductors,* spelled SuperCee and that there might be some theft of company property or proprietary rights involved. He went on to say that as a responsible reporter it was his duty to notify the victim of misconduct and secondly, to provide a story for the newspaper. He was also concerned that since his paper had the lead story, he didn't want them to be embarrassed by giving news space to some scam. He said that he knew Victor personally, and he wasn't your average security guard. He held a degree in computer science and was working on highly advanced projects. He saw

Chad's expression change when Victor's name was mentioned...so he added that he knew him socially as well. He felt a pang of guilt flash through him when he added further that he met him in a "bathe house" and they both seemed to like the same kind of wine, if he knew what that meant. He asked Chad what he liked, and he said Pinot Noir. Lewis raised his eyebrows and remarked, "What a coincidence."

He asked Chad if there was a copy of the American News about and he would show him what he meant about reporting only the minimum. Chad went to several offices and returned with a copy of Lewis' article. Lewis read the front page to him and explained how he could have easily brought SuperCee into the story, which may yet turn out to be a criminal offense.

Chad took the bait and called Mr. Hudson, giving him a more paranoid scenario than Lewis had hoped for. Chad returned the phone to its cradle and told him that Mr. Hudson, the Operations Director, would be right out. Seconds later, a short, pudgy man, came from an office nearby.

He took quick, short steps and extended his hand in greeting and introduction. He did his best to hide his emotions, but Lewis could see a rage going on inside the man. Lewis and Chad were invited to his office. There was a rage going on in the office as well. Although very large, the room was filled with boxes of records, stacks of papers on the floor, chairs and tables; two computers, an answering machine with a white telephone on a separate line, a multiplex telephone on his desk, a red phone on the wall, a cellular phone, a beeper, and a portable two-way radio on the console behind his chair. He invited Lewis to sit on the one empty chair, directly in front of him between the two computers. Chad was left standing.

"OK, give it to me again. Do you mind if we record this conversation ... company policy?" Hudson asked, reaching into a desk drawer to bring forth a recorder, fumbled with the controls a few times before he had it working, and then he placed it on the desk between the two computers.

Lewis surmised that it was not company policy or a procedure used frequently, as the recorder would have been on the desk and not in a drawer. "No, not at all. I was going to recommend that we make a record. By the way, I'm not wired. I'm here to offer information, not to gather it. Here are my press credentials and the number for American News if you'd like to check me out. My editor's name is Gordon Briggs. My name is Lewis Anderson...my by-line...here on the front page."

Hudson inspected the credentials very quickly and nodded in approval. "From the beginning."

Lewis related what he had told Chad earlier, frequently turning to Chad to have him fill in, speculate, editorialize and, in general, to sell the story. When he finished, Hudson sent Chad back to watch the front desk, leaving the two men to discuss the issue further in private.

"What you're telling me is that we may have a conspiracy here? Some collusion with Larry and Victor? Why is it always the *security* people that you can't trust? I knew he was too good-looking to be just a security guard. I'm not surprised that he has a solid degree. He can start anywhere at sixty grand. And he's working for a buck over minimum wage? I should have checked him out myself," Hudson said.

"I'm not saying this is a conspiracy at this point. I'm just as new to this story as you are. But when two guys work for the same superconductor company, both computer experts with access to company records, and some lady claims she was miraculously cured by a computer with disks that have superconductors in them, I think it's time to look for the real story. What I think, is that if *we*...American News and SuperCee, put our collective brains and information together, we can find out what's behind it, expose these guys and cut our losses," Lewis responded.

"I need to speak to the company president. He's in Baltimore at this time. Do you have a number where I can get in touch with you after clearing this with him?" Hudson replied nervously.

"Here's my card. If I get anything more, I'll call you...or Chad out front?" Lewis asked. He was given Hudson's business card with the number to call. Just what he wanted...he got past Chad. He thought he'd push his luck a little farther. "We have other reporters working on the story, in other directions. I'll keep this from them, as my editor does not want SuperCee mentioned. If you discover what the two of them were up to, or find material missing, please make sure you get me, and not one of the other two. I promise you we'll publish nothing that you give us without your consent.

"You could do *me* one big favor," Lewis said as though he had actually helped Hudson. "Is there someone around here who can tell me what a superconductor is? I haven't a clue."

"I'll make sure you're told first. I can agree to that. Wait a minute and I'll see if Dr. Jordan is in," Hudson said while dialing on the phone complex and made an immediate appointment for Lewis. "Jordan will tell you more about superconductors than you really want to know. His office is on the second floor, next to the Lab. You can't miss it." Hudson showed Lewis to the door and pointed to the elevator. Lewis was smiling to himself as he walked across the large lobby. Two hours later, knowing *much* more than he really wanted to know about superconductors, he was leaving SuperCee. He intended to give his respects to Chad, but thought the better of it. However, Chad spotted him, called for him to stop and he saw the security guard get up and block his exit. "Oh, oh," he thought.

"Mr. Lewis!" Chad exclaimed when Lewis turned and approached his desk. "I just heard it on the radio. The *miraculous recovery* is a fake. Some reporter broke the case. Do you know who Eric Carmen is...some old singer...I think? He's on one of the CDs. You were right."

Lewis was momentarily stunned by this information. Then he recalled his moment in front of the computer and his faith was restored. The information was playing right into his hands. "May I speak with Mr. Hudson again? This is exactly what I was afraid would happen," he asked.

"Hudson left for Baltimore right after he spoke to you earlier," Lewis was informed.

"Hungry Eyes. Eric Carmen," Lewis said to Chad as he hurried out the door, just recalling the hit recording.

* * * * *

The first reporters to be greeted by Rabinowitz were journeymen for a prominent national weekly. They stayed on the story because they thought there was money in it either way. Big bucks if there was something new from the medical side, such as the by-products of superconductivity or the materials used to manufacture them in the present state-of-the-art. If it proved to be some sort of con game or swindle, they could sell it to the tabloids. They did not have the problem of a daily deadline to meet. After reading the handout and the initial conversation with Rabinowitz, they were surprised to find that American News, a local newspaper, had control of the story. They were hoping to get an in-depth interview to get the complete story in an analytical manner. Rabinowitz emphasized that the story was completely true, had no idea where the other reporters came up with their information...which was obviously false, as he pointed to the wheelchair.

"Does that look like a new wheelchair to you guys? The *backrest* is new. There's the receipt for it. Look at the old one. Does this chair look like it needed a new backrest? That other stuff about the disks...I have no idea where they got that," Rabinowitz said, and then pointed to the remaining reporters outside. "We have to let everyone in. Kathy wants to get the word out as quickly as possible."

He got an idea and told the reporters to go in and start their interview with Kathy, who was ready. He called American News and found Briggs, who agreed to talk to him. Rabinowitz began by asking for advice. He advised the editor of the situation with a weekly and asked if some arrangement could be made with them without hurting American News's interests. Briggs told him how it could be advantageous to the newspaper since the weeklies had very sophisticated writers and researchers that would relieve the paper of staff and equipment and told him how to draw up the contract.

Briggs had been informed of the fraud issue, had only the sketchy information from his reporter at the house, and wanted to know the full story. Robby informed him, in detail, what had occurred, and the remedies that he had made. Briggs was much relieved at the up-date. Robby asked if the paper still had the same law firm representing them and Briggs acknowledged that they did. Robby asked the editor to call them and arrange for the firm to represent Professor Makino in a libel suit against the Evening Star. Briggs howled at the suggestion and asked Robby why he wanted his competition to handle the case instead of himself. Robby said he really believed Kathy and the whole story, was dedicated to helping her and he just wouldn't have the time.

Briggs asked if there had been any news from the hospital. Robby mentioned that they canceled a press conference, and that *he* hadn't set it up in the first place. Briggs mentioned how he thought that had come about and explained his role in it. He said he would call the Administrator and personally give him an up-date and, perhaps, re-schedule after thinking it over. He emphasized that Kathy *was* walking, a fact that could not be ignored. The conversation ended satisfactorily in an exchange of pleasantries, surprising to both of them. Both men smiled to themselves and felt better about things in general.

Larry left for more supplies, a visit to the bookie with the money that Kami left for him, and wanted to find some college students to move the larger pieces of furniture from Kathy's bedroom, which was now being used for more office space. Apparently, everything was going well in the computer department. Robby called for Nancy and asked if she could take dictation. She replied that all of the new staff *could*, but it was rather old-fashioned. If he wished to dictate a letter all he had to do was dial a number and the computer would do it for him. He managed a nod of the head and asked her to set it up for him. She brought him a phone on a long cord, dialed a number, and offered it to him. "Showtime!" she said with a smile. "Do you want me to edit it before it's ready for your signature, or is it just a memo?"

"Use your judgment," Robby replied, adding, "Nancy, you're cute, but too damned smart for me," and began dictating a contract into the phone. By the time the reporters had used their time allotment with Kathy, Robby had a four-page agreement waiting for their signature. Essentially, they were given complete access to all the information that was available. They would provide TV photography and voice recording throughout all interviews. They would keep one journeyman reporter on site for copy to be furnished to the American News for a percentage of the profits...left blank, to be filled in by the official agent, Professor Makino.

Kathy was into her third interview and Rabinowitz had finished reading his manual of instructions when the Assistant District Attorney arrived, surprised to be met by a man he had faced several times in the courtroom. After some informal discussion the Assistant presented Robby with the handwritten contract and wanted to discuss the matter with Professor Makino. The letter, in a plastic evidence bag, was opened and read by Robby while he explained that the professor, legally Kathy's agent, was not available and that he was filling in temporarily. After reading the letter, he asked if he could make a copy. He called Nancy to take care of the request and returned his attention to the real reason why the Assistant District Attorney was there, since the document that was presented to him was unsigned by the hospital, it was not worth the paper it was printed on as far as being a legal contract. The worst case that could be made of it was an unsolicited sales presentation. But since the hospital signed for the document, even that was questionable.

The Assistant nodded his legally trained head and said there were questions of fraud, reported in the media, concerning the case. Robby looked surprised and called in to interrupt Kathy's interview and asked her if she would mind standing up and walking a bit for the benefit of the Assistant District Attorney. Kathy did so, going directly to the window to see if Victor was there, aiding the police. She noticed there were more people than before. But she didn't see Victor. She asked Robby if the DA's Office had any news about Emily yet and he shook his head from side-to-side. "Anything else you want to see?" Robby asked.

The Assistant said there were some disks that were supposed to contain superconductors and that the wheelchair was new. Robby took the man by the arm, and showed him the wheelchair that was on display just inside the living room. "Does that chair look new to you? The *backrest* is new. Here's the receipt with the date of purchase. There is the old backrest. Would a reasonable person buy a new backrest if they didn't intend to use the chair? Look at the entire chair! Look at the wear-rings on the leg adjustments. Would you buy this chair and call it *new*?

"I call this chair *old* and *well used*. Kathy's father has not yet located the receipt for the chair, which was bought over ten years ago, but it was purchased from, and maintained by the same man; a reliable witness. Did you interview him? Here's his business-address and phone-number on the decal. It matches the receipt for the new backrest.

"While you're here, look at the disks. You tell me...have you ever seen anything like them before? I heard it reported that you could buy these in any record store. You think you can buy these *anywhere*?" Robby went to his table and returned with a magnifying glass. "Here, use this. I want you to look them over real good and then tell me that you can buy these at the mall for fourteen bucks. I've seen what these things did in the computer. You ever see what a music CD does in a computer? It plays music. People with broken backs do not get up and walk. That girl in there is walking. I've heard she can even dance."

The Assistant completed his investigation and returned the glass. He asked Robby what incident Kathy referred to earlier. "Emily?" Robby asked.

"Yes, I think that is who she mentioned. Who is that?" the man asked.

"Emily. Emily Mullin. Kathy's physical therapist at General Hospital," Robby answered. He saw that the man did not make a connection and continued.

"Let me get this straight, what you're telling me. The DA's Office receives a complaint from General Hospital that one of their patients is *cured* and you come right over here to investigate, but that you are completely unaware that one of their employees is gunned-down in broad daylight, in the center of the city, by drug dealers, and *you don't even know about it?* That's what I'm understanding here." Hearing no response, Robby continued, "Emily Mullin. Write it down. About a week ago. Shot and killed with a bullet to the head. Where are you in the investigation? You'll call me when you get back to the office, right.

"I'd like your opinion, since you're here, on what this paper, the Evening Star, told their readers. Forgetting all the legal jargon for a minute, the average reader is left with the impression that *fraud* has been committed here. After what you've seen here today, do you think this is responsible reporting?" Robby asked.

Halfway through the article, the Assistant replied, "I think a libel case would hold up, from what I've seen here. I mean, if you presented the medical evidence, which I haven't seen, and then she *walks* into the courtroom. Is this what this is all about? You're setting up a libel suit?"

"If you think about that a little bit, you'll find it similar to hitting a hammer with a nail," Robby replied, showing the man the door. He was glad to see Larry returning with two husky young men carrying boxes of supplies.

Without Kami to make decisions, Robby suggested, for now, to put the bedroom furniture in the garage. Larry instructed the helpers on what to do. After checking with Nancy that all was going well, he began to read his manual and was interrupted by Robby who wanted to know if there was any news of Kami's where-abouts. Having none, he told Robby what had been accomplished so far. He placed the bets. The guy was glad to see him, but what was going to happen with a big pay-off? Will there be trouble? Robby didn't think so. Larry explained about the layout of the neighbor's house and thought it less expensive to move Kathy over there, as there was a huge, sunken living room for the reporters and cameramen. Moving computers, communications and putting in the extra electrical service was much more complicated. Robby thought about that and said it was more important to have Kathy in *her* house.

Kami entered the house whistling and smiling. He ignored Robby for the moment and embraced Kathy when she got up to greet him. He was glad to see her walking and asked if there was any pain or any remission of any kind. She said no, and danced around for him, smiling. Then she returned to her task. Kami met with Rabinowitz.

He said he had taken the money to the bank, signed the papers and presented Robby with his copy of the deed for their new house.

He told of his successful meeting with Irving and remarked at how little the guards were paid. The first shift would be on duty at six-o'clock. Irving located a supplier for the courier cases with an attached wrist chain and the first shift of guards would bring that along with them. When asked what took him so long, Kami responded that he and Irving had become engrossed in conversation after the completion of business. Kami presented him with a monthly track sheet, provided by Irving, which had reams of comparative data on racehorses and scheduled events. Kami went on to show how he had picked the winners for today's races. Robby said he was lucky because Larry had already placed the bets, but if he wanted to, he could throw the money in the toilet instead of going back to the bookie.

Robby showed him a copy of the hospital agreement and said he was lucky he changed it because the DA had given them a visit and told him the results. He told Kami that he better talk to Larry about the moves that were going on and since they had the other house, why not move stuff over there. And that he had wanted Kathy to remain in her own house. Kami preferred that also.

When Robby admitted Number Six, he thought he had seen the reporter and his photographer the night before and casually asked what paper they represented. The reporter showed him his credentials for "American News". Robby asked for the name of their editor and he hesitated and finally said "Lewis Anderson". Gears clicked and Robby asked them to wait just a moment and went to get one of the police officers. The photographer was shooting pictures when he returned with a police sergeant. Robby explained to the officer that he thought the two men were not legitimate reporters for American News since they didn't know the editor's name and there was no reason for American News to send more reporters. He asked the officer to please check them out further and they were asked for some other means of identification. With that, they bolted through the door and ran down the street. The photographer left behind a very expensive Nikon camera. The officer picked it up and read the engraved name and phone-number of the owner aloud. "Can't run fast enough," he said as he copied the information to his notepad.

The incident alerted Robby to the fact that there needed to be better security for the disks and he thought of Victor. He asked if anyone had seen him without receiving a reply. He found Victor's home phone number in his manual and placed a call. Victor answered.

"What the hell are you doing home? Did you get everything done that I told you to do?" Robby asked.

Victor explained that he did, that the suit wouldn't be ready until quitting time. He said Sammy was not happy because it is right in the middle of his big season with spring fashions, Passover and Easter. He thought he better get some sleep, as he would be up all night again.

"How about the haircut?" Robby asked.

Victor replied that he got the haircut first and that it was "violent". He went on to say that he was called again by SuperCee and had to go and turn in his uniforms. He explained that he had heard the bad news and was wondering if he even had a job. He asked if he could keep the suit, since it was "custom fit" and no one else would want to buy it.

Robby asked him what he was doing now and what he was wearing. Victor said he was in bed and only wearing a "violent" haircut. Robby hesitated a bit and thought of his own son and then asked Victor, "What do you think of Kathy? Do you think she is a phony?"

Victor replied that he really liked Kathy, but he had only met her and had spent most of the night outside or alone in the early hours and really had no idea of what was going on. Realizing the slim information that Victor had, he told him that he still had a job, that a professional security company was furnishing guards and for him to come in now as he was needed.

Victor asked about the uniforms again. Robby told him to wear one now because a security presence was needed and that SuperCee could pick up the uniforms when they deliver his severance pay. Victor wanted to know how he was going to get his suit from Sammy. Thinking of his son again, Robby asked Victor if he had dress-shirts, neckties, shoes, and other accessories to go along with it. Victor replied that he did not. Robby asked him for his shoe size and he would have Sammy deliver everything to the Makino residence. Victor replied that Sammy was a "megabyte" tailor and had all of his sizes, including his hat size and could he get a hat to cover his "violent" haircut.

Robby concluded by telling him he was, "...glad it wasn't a *violet* haircut. The hat's out. No hat. Get your ass over here as fast as you can."

Lewis came by to pay his respects to Kathy. He, too, had heard the bad news, didn't understand it, and said that he had been temporarily removed from the story, being replaced by an "old pro".

Kami gained everyone's attention and announced that a banquet had been arranged for five o'clock, in the house across the street, and that everyone was invited to attend.

* * * * *

Ralph Jackson was in a quandary at General Hospital. The phones were ringing off the wall and disrupting patient care. He had accumulated sufficient medical information, first-hand, from records and staff to know that Kathy could not walk, had irrecoverable scarring, loss of spleen, and a crown on a permanent front tooth. All prognoses were that she would never walk with the current technology. All of his staff had positive information regarding Kathy, her father, and more troublesome, Emily Mullin. He had spoken personally to the editor of the Evening Star who reassured him that his reporters had reported their findings accurately, albeit not completely; omitting pictures of Kathy standing, observations of her walking, and only a close-up of the wheelchair backrest. They did have pictures of the entire chair and it was old and used. They felt that the results of their investigation by infrared film could not be overlooked, and the paper was within their rights to publish it.

Ralph looked at the smiling faces of his staff waiting in line outside his office, some with documents in their hands, waiting to provide him more positive information. He was wishing he had ignored the PIC's instructions to forward the professor's letter to the DA's Office. His secretary signaled him that she had finally gotten

90

through and had Professor Makino and a "Mr. Rabinowitz" on the phone.

Ralph introduced himself and was amiably received by Kami. He inquired of Kathy's condition and was assured that she was fully recovered and that Kathy had asked the hospital to notify several of the doctors that she recalled who first attended to her, but none had called back. She was having a photo session at the present time but would be available shortly, if the doctors were on the line. Kami knew the administrator of ten years past and inquired of his health and where-abouts. Following Robby's signals, he said he could see no value in Kathy speaking to the present administration in light of their turning his contract over to the DA. That canceled what he thought was a scheduled meeting with the hospital staff, and that there had been no pressure from the hospital to investigate the death of Emily Mullin.

The Administrator apologized, explaining that he was new to this hospital, and that some decisions were being made at a higher level and wondered if there could be a compromise position. Rabinowitz, waiting in the wings, had the terms written out, introduced himself as Kami's assistant, and read the following into the phone, "General Hospital to name the next wing in it's construction plans in honor of Emily Mullin. General Hospital to provide *free* treatment for ten leukemia patients from this state per year. General Hospital to duplicate in a medically and legally acceptable manner, all records they currently maintain on their patient, Kathryn Makino, and be delivered to her in person by the Administrator. No. Make that the Administrator *and* the person who made the decisions you referred to earlier. None of these records will be released to anyone including the FBI, the State Department of Health, the Pope, or any media service. No one; without the express, written consent of the patient.

"When the records are received and the agreement, written by the hospital, is acceptable and filed with the District Attorney's Office, Kathryn Makino will *walk, unaided,* from her residence, to General Hospital to be examined and answer any questions your staff may have. She will not accept questions from the press at that time, but they may be present to cover the story as a news event.

"American News, represented by a Mr. Gordon Briggs, will be given priority arrangements over all other media within your facilities." Robby stopped and Kami came back on the phone.

"Is there anything you'd like to change, or find unreasonable?"

Ralph Jackson said he lacked the authority to agree to several items, such as the naming of a new wing, and the potential future costs for free treatment, but otherwise thought it reasonable. Personally, he didn't like the idea of putting heat on his PIC and asked if that could be changed. Kami thought about it a moment and said, "No. I want to see what that guy looks like."

Ralph promised to get back within the hour and asked for a number to call. Kami said that would not be necessary. If they did not receive the information by eight in the morning, the protest march would probably start anyway and there would be complete chaos at the hospital.

"What protest march? This hospital?" Ralph asked.

"You haven't heard? The Black community is very upset over Emily's lack of support from your hospital. They want the violence stopped. Kathy's walk would have a calming effect. We'll be up late, so come by anytime."

Ralph thought the better of saying "Blackmail" and said he would get to work on it right away instead. Kami hung up smiling and said he enjoyed being an agent.

Chapter 8

Alot of controversy was taking place on the local radio talk show. The afternoon host was a man with an amiable voice and a great sense-of-humor. He had a slightly conservative viewpoint that matched the backwoods bent to his comments. He had an established audience; commuters...hard working people on their way home to eat dinner and watch TV. Today's show was particularly easy for him.

A radical-liberal followed the noon news and had the Evening Star's story to work with. In his two and a half hour show he and his callers had pretty much covered all of the negative implications that could be made from the disclosure of the unused chair and the phony disks. Kathy had been tried, found guilty and hung. Towards the end of the broadcast the callers began changing the subject, and drifted to the upcoming campaigns, the candidates, and their favorite issues.

Immediately preceding the current program was a segment hosted by a physician whose bleeding heart and lack of medical practitioner experience, a good speaking voice, and robust good looks made him the dandy of the housewives. Because of the large amount of time he devoted to herpes, AIDS and the other problems, both physical and emotional, associated with same-sex relationships, he was the dandy of the homosexual community as well. He spent the first twelve minutes of his show expounding in medical terms why the miraculous recovery and the apparent fraudulent claims came as no surprise to him. With the commercials, and a few new drugs that he was pushing, there was only time for one or two callers and then the present program.

Friends, acquaintances, and people with first-hand knowledge of Kathy and Professor Makino, who had been listening to the mud slinging at anything of a positive nature, began phoning in and were allowed to complete their calls. One caller, a friend of Emily Mullin, made a connection with Emily, Kathy, and General Hospital, which up until now, was not publicized. (The host sent his assistant scrambling for information on the shooting of Emily and within minutes had her press history on the computer in front of him). With that information, he had his audience trying to make second-guesses and maybe this story was not dead after-all.

Another caller, who had spent the night outside the house, reported seeing a man in a SuperCee uniform and knew that the company was involved in research of superconductors which were reported to be in the disk. Positive information was still coming in towards the end of his show and he had managed to entertain and inform the tens-of-thousands of drivers out in the commuter traffic who were staring into the brake lights of the car ahead.

The six-o'clock news would be coming along soon. That, followed by two liberal hosts for the evening audience. He enjoyed leaving them with a hot potato whenever he could. It came in the form of a fax, leaked from the District Attorney's Office. It was an internal memo stating that the residence of Kathryn and Professor Makino was investigated. It stated that the disks were not of the musical variety, that the wheelchair backrest had been replaced and a receipt for it was shown. The chair had been well used and that Kathryn Makino was observed walking, unassisted. There was no evidence of criminal activity found at the scene.

The memo went on to say that the disks needed to be investigated further to determine their actual content, function, and capabilities. If they were musical disks that had somehow been reprogrammed or altered, a case would have to be initiated by the company whose rights had been violated, if indeed, they were, and a civil case for damages. If a new technology resulted from the alteration, the company could achieve a monetary benefit. This was speculation only. A researcher was assigned the duty of finding case history on altered products. For information only.

The memo made the next point clear. The Assistant District Attorney wanted a thorough briefing on the shooting of Emily Mullin by the detective in charge of the case first thing tomorrow morning.

The memo ended with a request for information on superconductors. If anyone in the office knew what they were, would they please inform the Assistant DA.

The talk-show host read the memo in the closing minutes of his

94

show and invited his listeners to return tomorrow to see how Kathy was doing.

* * * * *

Robby asked Kami where he had heard about the protest march, as it was news to him. Kami said he just made it up...it was part of the agent's job. Robby thought it was a great idea, but Kathy would *lead* the march, if she were up to it. Both men grinned and asked Kathy to join them for a discussion. She was happy to get up and stretch, as she had been sitting for interviews for the past two hours. She was hungry also. They decided to close down for an hour and informed the people outside. They noticed that the TV van was back and many more people were waiting.

Victor showed up in his SuperCee uniform. Robby told him to sit and watch the disks while they went across the street to eat. Kathy asked him if he had eaten and he replied that he hadn't. She told him to put the disks in a shipping envelope and join them.

They walked to the house across the street. A moving van was picking up the last of their packing material and tying down the load inside. They found a beautifully decorated buffet with an abundance of delicious food. Larry, Nancy, and Shirley were already eating. Kami asked Larry if he had invited his family to join him for dinner as he intended to work late. Larry said that he was expecting them any moment, but the food was so good he couldn't wait.

Robby said he thought it was a lot of food, but Kami noted that they would have three shifts of guards plus the police to feed. He said it was part of the agent's job to keep the employees happy; smiling at Robby as he showed him the bill. "For tax purposes."

Their new house had a big U-shaped kitchen with a long counter along one side. They joined there, standing up, since there were no chairs and Robby brought up the subject of a "march" to Kathy. She liked the idea and asked where to and how far. "Let's go to the University! We have so many friends there," Kami requested. He could arrange for one of the larger classrooms to meet their friends. He estimated the distance to be about two miles and asked Kathy if she thought she could walk that far. She didn't hesitate in answering and said she felt like she could walk forever. It really felt good to her.

Robby asked if she could walk from there to the General Hospital. He was sure the hospital was going to come through with an acceptable agreement. Kathy said she could, but Kami wanted to know how far it was. All three estimated that it was almost three miles, depending how they went. Victor joined them with a huge plate of food. Kathy told Robby he was wrong and he started drawing a map on a napkin with estimated distances for Kami's review. "No. Not about the distance to the hospital. You were wrong about Victor's haircut. I like it! I can't wait to see him in a suit!"

Being reminded of Victor's duties and seeing him eating with both hands, Robby asked him suspiciously where the disks were. Victor put down his plate and tapped on his chest. He had them under his shirt. Robby apologized and told him that his new clothes would be delivered soon and that he would have a courier case to keep the disks in. He explained to Victor and Kathy what his duties would be. For now, until things got hectic, he was to get her anything she wanted and run her errands. Secondly, he was to have the disks with him at all times. Kathy explained that that was impractical, since Larry had to have immediate access to them. They called Larry to join them for a moment and Nancy took the opportunity to excuse herself and relieve Marcy for some of the great food.

They asked Larry's advice on the disk problem and he recalled seeing a safe in one of the office-supply stores that would fit in the computer room. The disks could be kept there and Victor used only when they were transported. Robby didn't like that arrangement, because two people were then responsible. He asked Larry to find a safe small enough that required two keys to open or close it and then Victor and he would not be able to forget. Larry said he'd do it in the morning. Larry continued to explain about the disks. He needed them whenever he went interactive in present time, like when Kathy speaks to the computer. He needed them whenever he put a new hard disk on line; such as a new computer. They were impossible to copy as they contained too much information and there were so many files, the hard disks ran out of memory, but he knew how to prevent that now.

The other times that he needed them...at least one disk...was when the computer finished a task and had files that could be deleted, he was instructed by the computer to delete the files and then install the disk to fill it back up with new information. Operationally, it was all very simple. What was mind-boggling was the power they had at their disposal. Robby asked if it could explain in layman terms what a superconductor was because he was still confused after reading the summary that Nancy prepared for him.

Larry said that Shirley had prepared the summary from the information on Kathy's Encyclopedia CD and it should be in easily understood terms. Shirley had gone further, to God's disks and asked the computer to give her the formula for superconductivity and the computer said it was currently restricted information that was not able to be accessed until after His press conference. Shirley was one smart computer operator...to which Victor said, "Amen, brother." Kathy gave him a frown and a soft nudge with her elbow.

Marcie arrived with a message and a package for Victor. The message was that Sammy The Tailor had delivered his new clothes, and the package contained his case for the disks, complete with cipher lock and book of instructions. He made a conscious effort to remove his gaze from Marcie's derriere as she went to the buffet for food. He was too slow. Kathy was glaring at him when he looked over at her.

As long as they were all there, Kami announced that they were making plans to walk to the University at nine in the morning and perhaps to General Hospital afterwards. Larry could use the day to prepare moving his operation over here and as far as he knew, he and the girls were through for today. Larry confirmed that nothing new had come in during Marcie's watch.

Kami said Kathy would speak to the press for two more hours only, as everyone needed to get some rest for the day ahead. He told everyone about the new security guards that were watching the premises and reminded all to read their manuals and come to him if

97

there were questions or new information. There would be coffee, blintzes, fresh-fruit salads, and juice at eight in the morning.

Kami and Robby returned to the Makino residence together. They were greeted by Kami's and Kathy's friends who had been waiting to see them and unable to get through the police cordon. Robby excused himself, went in, and turned on the TV to watch the six-o'clock news.

Kami shook as many hands as he could and was soon joined by Kathy as she and Victor walked back to the other house. They were quickly surrounded by the crowd of well wishers, and Victor had to motion them back to maintain order. He realized he had a real job. His first one. He decided, right then, to take it seriously.

Robby watched the Kathy story unfold before his eyes. Commentators were showing side-by-side photos of the Evening Star's "evidence" and photographs taken by other services. Whoever said that a picture was worth a thousand words made a very valid statement. Interview clips with people who knew Kathy's medical history conflicted severely with the Star's version. Pictures of her standing and video clips of her walking around in her living room were shown at least three times during the commentary. Several "talking heads" in medical uniforms with stethoscopes around their necks held x-ray film in their hands while explaining the paralysis that would occur from such an injury, and, "…in my medical opinion...this patient would never regain the use of her legs."

Robby called them in to watch, but they were surrounded by their friends and unable to leave. Nancy was watching over his shoulder and said she was very pleased to be on this assignment and part of the "team". Robby asked her what perfume she was wearing and she told him and then asked why. Robby said he thought it smelled familiar...that was all. Then he asked her if the computer could make him a map of the city, as he had to plan a route to walk tomorrow. Nancy was back in less than a minute with a city map and the route outlined, all in color. She said, "Thank God. It was already made," a statement, not an exclamation.

Robby asked, "This was available before we decided on the march?"

Nancy looked at it and replied that she thought it had been printed about four that afternoon...before they went to eat, she was certain of that. She asked if that was significant.

"Damn right it's significant. That line goes all the way to General Hospital! I'm coming to work in my walking shoes tomorrow."

* * * * *

It was after nine-o'clock when Ralph Jackson introduced himself and Doctor Edwards, the Physician-In-Charge of General Hospital, to Rabinowitz. They wished to speak to Professor and Kathy Makino who had abandoned any idea of returning to interviews and were in the street surrounded by friends, inside the circle held by Victor and three police officers. Robby knew why the two men were there and asked if they had complied with all of Kami's requests. Ralph tried to explain the logistic problem they had with the duplication of records and the legal problems that were facing him. Robby inquired into the legal problems, as he could see none. It was with the lawyers at corporate level. Robby explained that the administrators and the doctors ran the hospitals, and if they just used common sense, they didn't need the lawyers.

Doctor Edwards spoke up and apologized for the way things had gone. He said he was responsible for the earlier decision but had been convinced to accept a second opinion. He said he been assured the support of the majority of the directors who were presently meeting to iron out the details and that's where the lawyers came in. "Such as?" Robby asked.

"A new wing is on the drawing boards. It was to be dedicated to a certain individual. A physician of long standing. Currently a director. You see the complications," Dr. Edwards explained.

"None at all. He's out and Emily Mullin, the best healer in the history of General Hospital, is in," Robby replied. "Let's cut through the political and legal bull. We'll bend on the duplication problem. Spell out what the records are, and the duplication problem, and put it as an addendum with a guaranteed completion date, one that you can make.

"If you do that, and complete all the other items, bring the entire package here at eight-thirty in the morning. Kathy will begin the parade at nine-o'clock. She would be pleased to have General Hospital at her side. I suggest you wear comfortable shoes."

"Christ! We're going to be up all night," the Administrator complained.

Robby turned to the PIC and replied, "I think your patient could use a little exercise, what's your opinion?" referring to Ralph's portly physique.

"It will be my honor to walk beside Kathy. I don't think the hospital can run without Ralph, especially with the preparations that need to be made for her arrival. I suggest we get to work and I can assure you that the hospital will meet your conditions.

"By the way, I worked for Mt. Sinai for a time and went through some of my old records. I'm sorry about your wife and son. I performed some evaluations on your boy. We haven't come much further in treating leukemia, I'm afraid."

Both men shook hands with Robby and left together in one car that had been allowed through the police roadblock.

* * * * *

Lewis Anderson looked at the front-page layout of the American News that had been written by his editor, Gordon Briggs. He read the lead-in and speed-read the remainder of the article. "Textbook journalism," he commented. Briggs showed him the stacks of information and the choice of pictures that were available to him and he reiterated that he could write for a week without leaving his desk.

Then he noticed the by-line. "Lewis Anderson". He asked if it was going to press with credit given to him and Briggs said that he deserved it. If it had not been for him, their reporters would be standing outside the Makino house waiting their turn in line. He told him he had spoken to the owner of the paper and that he might be the new nighttime editor. Lewis said that wouldn't work for his present assignment. He thought that, for now, he wanted to be the reporter that was cheated out of credit for the story. Then he thought again and said aloud, "Fired. Yeah. Put the word out that I blew the story. I failed to make the connection with Emily or SuperCee. I was there, remember? I can work a lot better if I've been fired. SuperCee just might be looking for someone to handle the press and who better than me?"

"Clever, very clever. Do you think you can pull it off?"

"Don't know. How long to get to Baltimore, dump a bucket of garbage on your boss and get back with instructions on how to clean it up?" Lewis asked.

"Depends. Especially on what part of Baltimore," Briggs answered, puzzled.

Lewis wrote down some names and phone-numbers and gave them to Briggs. "I always wanted to do this. I'm going to slam your door shut on the way out. You open the door and yell out that I've been fired. Then, I'll be on the phone in the car. Hook me up with Kanisha and let me know where I can pick her up. She's working for our paper now. Give her the by-line. If I'm not in the car, I'll be at the Brass Rail drowning my sorrow.

"I need to know where Mr. Hudson is. Chad knows. Both numbers are there. Use your imagination. Say you're a friend of Victor's."

"That'll fit perfectly. I told the editor of the Chron that I needed Kanisha for a special project and he decided to grant her a leave-of-absence. The Kathy story with her by-line will not hurt her career at all.

"Before I *fire* you, you might want to read some notes that I have." Briggs unlocked an office cabinet drawer and pulled out a folder. "My notes on Fenhauser, SuperCee, hookers who never do time, and the attorneys who keep them in business. Some rumors I checked on.

"Well! Don't look at me so startled. I *do* have some reporter's instincts left in this old brain of mine.

"I just remembered...there's a big political meeting going on in Baltimore right now," Briggs informed Lewis.

Lewis looked at his watch after taking the packet of information. "I'll read this at the Brass Rail." He walked to the door, took hold of the handle, turned to his boss, and smiled. He turned, slammed the door, and hurried across the newsroom floor towards the exit. Hearing the invective that followed him, he thought that Briggs might have been a great actor as well as a great journalist.

* * * * *

Badge Number Forty-Three finally completed his paperwork. It had been another strange day for him. Doing traffic control, he heard the call from the officer in front of the Makino residence to be on the lookout for two suspects fleeing the residence, with a description, etc. He noticed a small, compact car speeding and changing lanes behind him. He slowed, turned onto a wide street, watched the car pass in his rear view mirror, did a U-turn, and pursued. He clocked him and had him on three counts; speeding, reckless driving, and not coming to a complete halt at a stop sign. Forty-Three was good at this job. He found just the right spot to accelerate, hit the lights and siren, and was in the guy's rear-view mirror right now... the driver never saw him coming.

He thought the two young men looked nervous as he went through the pre-citation formalities. He looked them and the car contents over thoroughly. Camera stuff in the back. The passenger was in a sweat. The registration and license information checked. He asked where they were coming from and they said they were late for work. Home. They were coming from home. He checked the passenger's ID and looked for the residence. The two did not live in the same part of town. The passenger's family name, "Fenstermaker", rang a bell. He got on the radio and checked back with the officer at the Makino residence who had the name from the camera. He had the two get out of the car and called for his "back-up" as he informed the station that he had the two suspects.

A second patrol car arrived, cuffed, and drove away with the two men. He called for a tow truck to pick up their vehicle and then drove to the station himself, missing several opportunities for citations along the way. At the station, there was some confusion and the problem of what to charge the men with. After the police made a few phone-calls to check out the two sets of press credentials, the reporter explained that he was the one who "broke" the miraculous recovery case. They were going back in with some newer equipment to see if they could discover anything else wrong. When they were recognized, they panicked and ran.

Forty-Three asked if Kathy was walking and the two reported that she was. They said they also would like to get some fingerprints to check her out further, because this is how a lot of these frauds are pulled off...using a double. Forty-Three was the first person to see her walking, after her father. He smiled at the two young men, made no comment about their occupation, and wrote out the citations.

It wasn't very long after he was back patrolling the streets that he was summoned to the District Attorney's office. He was asked to brief the Assistant DA on the arrest he made earlier. While explaining his role in the arrest of the two pressmen, he made mention of the fact that he was the first officer on the case after "escorting" Professor Makino the previous day. The Assistant DA sent him back to the station to make a complete, detailed report of both incidents.

By the time he finished his paperwork, he was on overtime, in the middle of the commute traffic, listening to the talk show.

* * * * *

Kanisha Porter entered the Brass Rail, looking for Lewis Anderson. She was a very attractive, black woman, in her mid-twenties. She wore her hair in the style of Tina Turner, her favorite singer. Men usually turned to admire her. Today she was wearing a business suit, as she had just left work. There were enough of her voluptuous body parts moving under it to make the alcoholics at the bar stare and fantasize a moment before returning to their drug of choice.

She located Lewis at a table in a corner, and joined him. They spoke for almost a half-hour before Lewis was able to present her with all the facts he had at his disposal. Briggs phoned him and said that Hudson was still in Baltimore and was going to catch a commuter flight back in the morning. Lewis invited Kanisha to

103

dinner and maybe they could come up with some sort of plan. He realized he was not a detective, nor was Kanisha, and he doubted if the life of a detective was anything like most detective and mystery writers describe. Mike Hammer, he was not.

It was nearly eleven PM before the couple had digested the sketchy notes of Briggs and speculated on what could be beneath it all...if anything. Lewis decided he would go to SuperCee in the morning and try his luck with Chad again. He drove Kanisha home, and as she departed, she told him she had another approach and some contacts to make and would call him in the morning.

She changed into a mini-skirt and a flimsy, leopard-skin patterned blouse that she sometimes wore on a disco-dancing date. She found some red shoes, designer pantyhose, and pulled her hair into a tight ponytail and jelled it down. She looked in the mirror and thought she could pass for a hooker. As an after-thought she sprinkled herself liberally with perfume, had her press recorder in her purse and walked a short distance on the streets to a location that she recalled crawled with prostitutes in the evening.

She began making friends with them. By four in the morning she had a wealth of information and met several women that she could really call friends. She was going shopping with one of them in the afternoon and going to dinner with the other one before starting another night's work. She hoped that no one had noticed that she earned no money on her first night on the street.

Chapter 9

Kathy got up when she heard her father moving around downstairs. It was only a bit past six and the sun had not yet cleared the horizon. She found him having tea and made herself a cup. They discussed the events of yesterday and their plans for the coming day. Kathy had no doubt in her mind that she could walk the distance. She and Kami were both wondering what would happen at the hospital when they arrived. Kami told her that, if the hospital came through on their promises, he would insist that any questions be limited to medical matters. She wondered what to say if questioned about the disks that were not the real ones. Neither had an answer.

Kathy switched the subject to Victor and asked her father what she thought of him. Kami replied that he certainly was attractive in his new suit. When he finally got to try it on, it was very late; after they said goodnight to the crowd. He said that Victor had a positive manner about him that he liked. He referred to his taking charge the previous night when they were suddenly surrounded by the crowd of people. Kathy thought about that and the fact that Victor had the disks under his shirt and thought that he could be put in jeopardy, or else the disks stolen or damaged. She asked where the disks were and Kami said that they were with Victor. He was sleeping in one of the bedrooms in the house across the street. She said she would like to get one disk to see if there were any new instructions. She was hoping to go and get them herself and to see Victor, but Kami opened the door and spoke to the new security woman and asked her to take care of the chore.

When Kathy received the disk, she went to the computer room and installed it. After typing in her message, she was greeted by God who asked her how she was feeling...more of a formality, since He already knew. She asked if there was anything new that she needed to do. She was told that Larry needed to solve the riddle of the Air Supply disk. He purchased it in Mexico when he was on vacation, visiting his relatives. That is why the retail number does not show up in the music store catalogs in the United States. It was legally made and sold in Mexico. He gave the CD to her for Christmas a few years ago, when he found that she enjoyed listening to Air Supply.

She was told that she needed to spend two to three hours each morning alone in front of the computer to prepare for the upcoming events. For example, today she should change the route of the parade slightly and walk the street where Emily lived, meet her niece and give the software to a person in the neighborhood who could use it. Otherwise, she was going to forget. God told her to make sure that if she promised to do something, she had to follow through and do it. Good *intentions* were not sufficient. God signed off, looking forward to His meeting with her tomorrow.

Kathy told her father about the discussion. Kami wrote down the instructions and agreed that he would take care of the business with Larry. They found the software that Kathy bought for Emily's birthday and gift-wrapped it, with a short letter explaining the gift. It was to be given to the most promising student in the neighborhood high school. They looked at the city map and saw that on the route from the University to the Hospital they were within two blocks of Emily's street. Kami said that he would call Briggs with the new information and have him locate Emily's niece, and to arrange with the high school principal to receive the gift when the parade passed by.

A large crowd was gathering outside. Kathy dressed and found that she had several good pairs of walking shoes to wear, the soles having never been used. She was well groomed when she was offered some food by Victor. Robby arrived and he and Kami left for some coffee and blintzes with Dr. Edwards, who did more than was specified. Two of the physicians who provided emergency care to Kathy were present with him. They, too, were going to march. The orderly, who worked on the Emergency ward at the time, volunteered to follow behind, pushing her wheelchair. The hospital provided an ambulance to follow the parade and administer cold water and any medical attention that might be needed along the way.

Nine-o'clock was fast approaching. Nancy presented Kathy with a bouquet of flowers from the staff. Victor was standing by in a very smart suit, white shirt, and nice tie. He had shined shoes, and a courier case chained to his wrist. With his new haircut, he could pass for a young FBI agent. Kami completed his last phone call and announced that the parade was ready to begin.

He took Kathy by the arm and started walking towards the University, a route familiar to him. Robby, Dr. Edwards and the two physicians fell in behind them. The orderly, pushing her wheelchair, and two General Hospital nurses that he located in the crowd, made a nice entry behind the four men. Kathy called for Victor to walk at her other side. The waiting media personnel, friends and well wishers, joined in behind. At the corner, where a roadblock had been set up, another large group of people were waiting. Two more short blocks and they would join the main thoroughfare. The TV crew was filming the event from their van.

Forty-Three had just issued a citation and was sitting in his cruiser completing the form when he heard the noise. He glanced in the direction of the sound and saw that the parade was advancing toward him! He called in to find out what was going on and was informed that there were no parades scheduled for this day. He called his fellow-troopers at the Makino residence and "No," they were not instructed to clear a path for a parade. Their instructions were to provide crowd control at the residence, which they were doing, however, the crowd had vanished.

A senior officer at the station told Forty-Three to halt the parade as they did not file a permit. The parade was already upon him and he was still talking on the radio. He turned on the flashing lights and swerved his car around to block oncoming traffic when he saw the direction in which they were heading. He asked for any patrols nearby to start blocking side streets in front. He recognized Kathy walking in front and relayed the information to the station. Another patrol arrived with lights flashing and Forty-Three instructed him to stay here until they passed and then guard the rear. He flew past the marchers and pulled back into the lane in front of Kathy. He smiled at her, said she was costing the taxpayers an awful lot of money, and called in to report that, "In the interest of public safety, I'm leading the parade...and did anyone know where they were headed?"

The Sergeant at the Makino residence said they were going to the University. It sounded like he had a mouth full of food when he talked on the radio. The station came on the radio shortly after and directed the patrol at the Makino residence to pack it in and start clearing streets ahead. After walking the first mile, the number of marchers had nearly doubled in size, and more and more people were lining the street to wave and add their good wishes to Kathy. Television was providing good coverage and accounted for the majority of the new marchers. Many, listening to the radio, also decided to join in.

Kathy was in good spirits and the walk hardly affected her. She waved and smiled, often recognizing someone as she passed by. They passed in front of the medical supply store and the owner came out and gave Kathy a big hug. He said that he had tried to call and couldn't get through the answering devices on the phone and that when he tried to visit, the police at the roadblock stopped him. She invited him to join the march. He would get a lot of publicity for his business. He thought a second and said, "Why not? Elmer can run the store." He waved to his clerk and fell in step as the parade continued. Before dropping back to walk beside the orderly and nurses, he told Kathy that he never felt so good about losing a customer.

* * * * *

Lewis Anderson had no trouble getting to see Chad at the SuperCee offices. He went to the Makino residence early to see if he could get more inside information from Victor or Larry. While speaking to Victor about SuperCee the subject of his uniforms came up and Lewis asked if he could turn them in for him. Lewis took the one Victor had at the Makino residence and arranged for the landlady to let him get the other ones at his boarding house.

Lewis called Briggs on his private line and asked him to get some American News reporters at SuperCee's front door and to ask some of his friends at other papers to do the same. And, it wouldn't hurt if they started getting flooded with calls and, if the talk-show people would cooperate, they would announce the inside-numbers on the air. All you got on the listed number was a machine and a promise to call back if you left your name and number and the nature of your business. Briggs didn't question his reporter further and complied with the request.

Several reporters were already at SuperCee when Lewis arrived. He waltzed around them, said, "Good morning," to the Security Guard while waving a SuperCee uniform, and went directly to Chad's desk. He was watching TV and met him coolly until he saw the uniforms. Lewis asked if Mr. Hudson was in because he would probably want his advice. Chad replied that he had not returned and then Lewis turned to a more personal topic...Victor. He said that the uniforms were Victors and then asked if he had seen him on TV. Chad said he hadn't and Lewis asked if he could get the local news that was showing clips of the unscheduled parade. Chad said he had been watching, but hadn't seen Victor. Lewis asked if he could come behind the desk and point out Victor the next time an update came on. Chad said it was OK and Lewis joined him on the other side.

The guard came by to advise Chad that a TV van was filming the outside of the building and that more reporters were wanting to come in and talk to someone about the Kathy story. Chad told him to keep them out of the building. They were wasting film on pictures of the outside of the building and there was no law against it. Lewis offered a sympathetic smile to the guard as though he was another concerned SuperCee employee.

An update of the parade came on and Lewis pointed out Victor to Chad. With a haircut and suit he hadn't recognized him before and took a closer look and agreed that it was, indeed, Victor walking beside Kathy on the screen. "Damn switch hitters," Lewis said like a dejected lover. "You think you have something going and the first skirt with money comes along, and pfffttt," Lewis added, making a fleeing gesture with his hand. He let that sink in.

"Nothing, not a word. Just turn in the uniforms for him. Then I see him with the Kathy bitch...all smiling, lovey-dovey." Lewis thought he had pushed it far enough. Chad was buying it.

He tried to get more information about Hudson's schedule but he believed that Chad just did not know. He thought he might as well practice his story on Chad to see if there were any major flaws.

"You know, I've been fired because I kept SuperCee out of my column. The owner said that a first year reporter would see two SuperCee employees, a SuperCee uniform running around, and disks with superconductors in them, and be intelligent enough to report what he saw. And then, the other paper scooping us with the phony disks," Lewis tried to continue, but the switchboard was lighting up and Chad was trying to put the lights out and failing. The return of the guard to report that more people were showing up out front was met with an order to call his supervisor and get more security staff on the job.

Employees were leaving their offices to take in the scene in front of their place of work. Chad could not answer their questions and asked if one of the secretaries could assist with the phone. There was only one instrument on the multiplex phone and that didn't help matters as the secretary only got in the way. Lewis suggested to Chad that there was another multiplex on Hudson's desk and if the numbers were on the same exchange and could be switched, she could help from there. He turned the phone over to her and went looking for a key to Hudson's office, which he knew was locked. He tried it anyway and Lewis accompanied him, noticing that it was the same type of lock as on all the other doors. "Do you own the building or are you renting it?" Lewis asked.

Chad replied that it was a rented building and Lewis asked if the property management offices were very far away. The manager would probably have a master key. Chad agreed and dispatched a low ranking employee to inform the property manager and return with a key; also to inquire if they could think of something to remove the people from in front of their door, as they could not conduct business.

A couple of men, obviously senior department heads, were standing in the lobby watching the commotion outside and offering Chad some really off-the-wall advice. Nothing practical.

Hudson arrived by cab. He looked at the mob and entered the building like a bulldog, not actually running, but going as fast as his stubby legs could manage. "Jesus Christ! What the hell is going on around here? Who *are* all these god-damned people?" were the first words from his mouth. The department heads disappeared when they saw him coming. Chad was left standing with Lewis to explain the situation, and it was obvious he was not informed and completely unprepared. Lewis spoke calmly, "Mr. Hudson, you have a major problem here that is going to get much worse if you try to stonewall these folks. I know where they're coming from and what they want. That *was* my business, remember?

"I've been fired. Because I tried to help you out and blew the story. I need a job. Unless you have some really good PR people on staff, I can take care of this in four hours and get back to normal around here."

"Four hours? You think this will be over in four hours?" Hudson asked.

"Or less, if you follow my advice," Lewis replied confidently.

"Which is?" Hudson asked.

"First, am I your new public relations officer or not? I need a job. When you don't have your ex-employees marching at the head of the parade on TV, and there are no media people knocking at your door, I can write articles for your company. No one knows much about superconductivity and your company is a leader in the field. You need a *positive* public image. Right now, you have none, and if you don't handle *this* situation right your company is going to have a negative image." Lewis paused long enough for Hudson to ask Chad what the TV comment was all about. Chad explained that Victor was leading the march to the University with Kathy. Hudson's jowls tightened and his eyes bulged further at this information.

Lewis saw the hopeless situation that confronted Hudson and said, "I can start right now. Four hours or less. Guaranteed. Just give me the go ahead. Am I hired or not?"

"What kind of salary are we talking about here? And I'll need to get the president's approval," Hudson replied.

"For starters, the same as the two overpaid jerks who ran back to their offices when they saw you coming. I'll have this solved by the time you get approval. If I can't earn my keep, I'd rather leave on my own. You won't have to fire me," Lewis stated his terms.

Hudson looked at Chad and asked who the *jerks* were. Chad mentioned two last names and Hudson smiled. "All right, Mr.

Anderson. You're hired. Now, how do we get back to business around here?"

"One. Tell Doctor Jordan that he has a captive audience starting in one hour.

"Two. I want the largest room with the worst acoustics that you have, made available in ten minutes.

"Three. Send someone to the nearest coffee shop or store and bring coffee and donuts. Cheap shit, no expresso. Paper cups, cream in a carton and sugar in a bag. No spoons. Reporters know how to stir coffee with their pencils.

"Four. I will write your opening speech and you will read it exactly as written. It will say that Victor *was* an employee. He was fired when he failed to provide security at a critical time. He was not authorized to wear a SuperCee uniform away from the workplace.

"Lawrence submitted his resignation with no reasons given. That *is* correct?

"There is no known connection between SuperCee and Kathy Makino, except that the company extends their best wishes regarding her recovery and hopes that it is permanent.

"I'll fill in more details. You read that and then introduce Doctor Jordan to explain superconductivity to them.

"I will handle the questions and answers after you introduce me as the public relations officer and then you can all go back to work.

"One last thing. Chad. Just leave the phone off the hook. One small slip of the tongue is all these guys need to write a new story. Everyone's looking for a spin that is going to hit the jackpot. Don't provide it. That's what you're paying me for."

Hudson looked at his watch and then at Lewis. "It might just damn work," he said with a glimmer of hope in his otherwise "man-on-the-verge-of-a-heart-attack" disposition.

* * * * *

Larry returned from his office-supply errands and met with the phone company technicians and electricians. An engineer was with them and they devised a workable plan for converting the newly acquired house into a communication and computer center. They promised full service for 100 lines within 24 hours if the electrical contractor provided the required routing for their cables. The contractor was standing by with men and equipment and guaranteed he could finish the job by quitting time, today. That met nicely with the phone company's work plan as they could work on the other two ends of the job and no one would be in the other's way. Nancy called him from the meeting. A computer problem.

He went to the Makino house and she explained that the computer was asking for a disk and Victor had both of them chained to his wrist. Larry called the safe company and asked why the safe he ordered had not been delivered. He was told that one of the other sets of keys had been misplaced and because of the security problem he described, they decided to change the combination of the lock and make new keys. It took some more time to do that, but the safe would be there shortly. Nancy was assigned the task of locating Victor and having him return to the house with the disks.

She could see Victor and Kathy on TV every thirty minutes. How was she going to get a message to him? She saw the police car in front. Of course! Call the policeman and have him tell Victor to return. She called the police station and after working through several layers of supervision finally got the approval of the shift chief to have a police car bring Victor back to the house. He called Forty-Three and told him to bring Victor back to the Makino residence as soon as he could get another car to lead the parade. The Chief of Police was approaching the head of the parade in his marked vehicle and told Forty-Three to hold his position and he would take them to the University himself. Nancy watched on TV as the action took place and Victor was on the way back. The commentators had no clue about what was happening, but reported it anyway, as though it was a significant event.

* * * * *

The Racing Commissioner's meeting was concluding. In front of him were the results of drug testing on all of the horses that raced the previous evening. All normal. Every inch of the track was

113

inspected and soil sampling indicated a uniform, acceptable turf for racing. Animal feed was analyzed and the weather bureau provided atmospheric conditions at the time of the races.

The TV film was examined and every rider and every horse was observed making a positive attempt to reach the finish line first. Every jockey had been interviewed and asked for an explanation for the poor performance of horses that finished much worse than their track record would indicate. Not much was revealed. The speaker for the jockeys was not satisfied, and wanted the commissioner to do *something* because the jockeys were the ones getting the heat from horse owners.

The Commissioner could find no evidence of foul-play and promised to check with Vegas and see if something was going on there...any big winners, etc. He closed the meeting philosophically, saying that there were only three or four aberrations per night and that was what made horse races. He recalled to the group that Babe Ruth struck out more times than he hit home runs.

* * * * *

Victor enjoyed the ride in the patrol car with the lights flashing and the siren howling. He was in front of Kathy's house in minutes. Larry greeted him, asked for the disks, and relieved him of the responsibility of carrying them. Victor wanted to go back to his bodyguard job and the officer said he could take him back. Forty-Three sure asked him a lot of questions. He laughed at the one when he was asked if he had a permit to carry the gun. Victor took out the bible and said he didn't know he needed a permit to carry it. The parade was approaching the University grounds when Victor rejoined them. One astute commentator told his audience that the courier case was no longer in view on Victor's wrist.

Larry inserted one of the disks after telling his staff to leave him alone until he was done. He typed in the message and God welcomed him on the speakers. Larry was told to write down eight numbers. These were the winners for tomorrow afternoon's races. When he asked if there was going to be trouble collecting after the race he was told, "Only if you take Victor with you...he looks like

114

a young FBI agent now. Take Rabinowitz with you when arrangements are made to pay you. Give twenty thousand to the courier, twenty thousand to the bookie and twenty thousand to Lewis. Put the rest in the safe and an accounting to Professor Makino."

"Anything else?" Larry asked.

"Yes. Go to the flower shop in the mall. It's called Abie's Irish Rose. Buy flowers to be sent by courier to Nancy. Do this every day. No name, just the florist's business card. When the lady at the florist asks your name, tell her it's Rabinowitz. She won't believe you, but don't worry."

"Got it. Anything else?" Larry asked as he wrote down the florist's name.

"Yes. You say prayers a lot. I don't know what you want. You are going through a ritual and not communicating with Me. I am not confused with Spanish or Engish words or thoughts."

"This was how I was taught. What am I doing wrong?" Larry asked.

"Try this. *Invite* the Holy Spirit into your life. I communicate through this means. Then be specific about what you want. Rattling off twenty Our Fathers and fifty Hail Marys doesn't do a thing except to show that you are a good, deserving person, which I already know. I need to know what is going to make you happy. Because you have free will, the only thing that will make you happy is what *you* think will make you happy," God instructed.

"I'll give it a try," Larry responded as the screen returned to the heart prompt and the speakers went silent.

* * * * *

Editor Gordon Briggs had two reporters assembling the data that was flowing into his office. The lead story was already written and the Sunday supplement was sold nationwide. It was just a matter of making updates as the information continued coming in. Circulation was way up, and the public was waiting for his paper to come out. TV and radio were beating him to the punch, but they were paying a premium for access, and there were still a lot of people out there who didn't believe anything unless it was in the paper.

He was puzzled a bit when Lewis called him and requested that the calls to SuperCee be halted and to recall the American News's reporters and use them on the march coverage and to "leak" to the other papers that the SuperCee story was over. He complied with his requests, but was puzzled when Lewis closed the conversation as the "SuperCee Public Relations Officer."

Chapter 10

Students lined both sides of the wide University pavements, forming a path to lead Kathy into an unoccupied study lounge. When his students recognized him they began cheering, "Ma-kee-no!... Ma-kee-no!... Ma-kee-no!..." He smiled and waved to them and tried to quiet them using a referee's time-out signal, but it helped little. Faculty, staff, and students were milling around inside waiting to meet Kathy and her father. Victor quickly formed them into a reception line with the Dean, Kathy, Kami, Robby, and the doctors, in that order, standing at one end of the room. He led those waiting, one at a time, and managed an orderly process. American News photographers were allowed to take pictures along with the University newspaper staff.

Kathy was feeling great and not the least bit tired. They still had a long way to go and the Dean announced that the march was going to continue shortly and that the students who wanted to participate in the parade would be excused from classes. He reminded them to maintain proper decorum, as they were representatives of the University. After a refreshment, provided by the Student Union, Kathy led the way to General Hospital.

When they left the other side of the University grounds, they were joined by about a thousand friends of Emily who said they wished to make the walk with Kathy. Victor asked who their leader was and they seemed to have none. He asked if there were kin and a black man introduced himself as Emily's brother. He and his wife were invited to march with them, one on each side of Kathy. By the time they got back to the main thoroughfare, there were about ten thousand people out for a walk.

They expected some trouble at the downtown junction where two major roads crossed and there was usually very much traffic. There was a major bus stop and a shopping center and the intersection would be full of people in the older, small, family-owned businesses that still existed after two generations of malls. As they approached they saw that the police had re-routed traffic and had barriers up for their safe passage. Emily's brother showed

117

Kathy where Emily had been gunned down when they passed the spot. They were surprised at the confetti, which showered them when they passed a tall office building. Looking up at the source, they saw hands waving and people watching from every window.

Several blocks further they left the main street and turned into Emily's neighborhood. Forty years earlier, this was a model community. The single-story family residences were built after W.W.II and were the first homes for many of the city residents who now lived up in the mansions near the University or in newer suburbs. The area consisted of a very high percentage of blacks, or those who lacked the money to move. It was not a nice place to live. Kathy knew Emily's street well. She accompanied her father here many times when he drove Emily home after a visit. She had never been in Emily's house, because the steep steps in front made it inaccessible from her wheelchair, and she hated to be carried in public.

She saw a very pretty, black girl of about ten waiting in front of Emily's house. She had a bouquet of flowers in her hand. A large black man at her side introduced himself as the principal of the school and Emily's brother introduced Kathy to his daughter, who had to be reminded to present the flowers. Kathy saw the girl's liking of them and presented her with the flowers that she had been carrying. Robby came forward with the computer software and Kathy presented it to the principal. Kathy asked if she could see inside the house where Emily lived. Her brother escorted her and Kathy looked at the pictures she had on the wall. She recognized herself in several of them. Her Physical Therapist diploma was proudly displayed above the sofa in the living room. She looked in the bedroom and saw a large collection of books and remembered how Emily said she preferred to read instead of watching TV. Kathy saw a set of books that caught her eye. Three books in blue jackets with gold titles. She read the titles. A Course In Miracles. She opened one to glance at the contents and found that it was full of Emily's notes. Emily's brother noticed her interest in them. She put them back with the others and went outside to the waiting marchers.

Emily's niece was offered a ride in the wheelchair and the parade resumed.

One commentator estimated the marchers to number well over fifteen thousand when they rejoined the main road leading to the hospital. Television cameras from the helicopters overhead were sending their data to be transmitted to the viewing audience. Other vans with their camera data being relayed via satellite were filming along the way. Ralph Jackson watched the procession heading his way and hoped he was prepared. Nancy had forwarded to him a set of instructions that she received from the computer.

A decision was made by Kami to halt the parade in a large public park near the hospital. He had conferred with Robby and Dr. Edwards and, because of the size of the group, there would be a problem providing medical service at General Hospital. Patients would be unable to get to the parking lots, the Emergency Entrance would be blocked. Deliveries of supplies, etc. would be interrupted. The park was a convenient place and had some public lavatories, water, and places to sit down. The change of plan met with the Police Chief's approval and he turned the parade in that direction. He led them into a big, open, pasture that was sometimes used for outdoor concerts.

Using the Chief's loudspeaker, Kami directed his followers onto the field and after they were all off of the street, he thanked them for their support. He advised them to go home and watch the meeting as it was going to be televised live by the local TV company. A limousine, sent by the Administrator, took Kathy, Victor, Kami, and the PIC to the hospital, instructed to return for Robby, the doctors, and the others who would attend the meeting.

The hospital had an auditorium where they conducted meetings, held seminars for their staff, and had audio-visual equipment on hand. Kathy and the group were led through the room to a small guest lounge where they were offered snacks and refreshments and introduced to the Administrator. Ralph Jackson showed Kathy the messages he had received from her computer and they went over the list; item-by-item. Everything was satisfactory to her. She felt relieved that there was an agenda and that the Administrator would

119

be the Master of Ceremonies, able to assist her, if she was presented with something new.

When Robby arrived, he was shown the list, and asked that he be allowed to make an opening remark following the MC's instructions to the audience. Professor Makino would make a few comments and then introduce Kathy. She would say a few words and then the PIC would use pictures, x-rays and medical facts contained in her records to explain the scope and nature of her injuries and the treatment received. Several doctors who attended her were available to testify to the facts of the injuries. Then Kathy would take questions from the audience.

The auditorium filled quickly. There were about twenty chairs in front of the raised portion that was used as a stage. The Mayor, a few council-members, directors of the hospital, the Chief of Police, the District Attorney and senior hospital staff filled the chairs. Gordon Briggs was also offered a seat for the event. The remaining people stood behind. Directly in the center of the room, there was another raised platform for cameramen and projectors. Other TV cameras were on the sides of the room.

Ralph checked the room to see that all was ready. The orderly and the wheelchair were on stage, Emily's brother and spouse were seated with the attending physicians and the room was filled to capacity. He announced that all was prepared and asked the dignitaries to follow him to the stage and to be seated. When Kathy made her appearance, there was sustained applause.

Ralph Jackson checked the mike and called for silence. He began by welcoming everyone to the meeting and especially pleased to see Kathy Makino, a former patient, *walking* so confidently to be here today. He said that there was an ongoing investigation by the District Attorney's Office into the shooting of Emily Mullin, a hospital employee, and close friend of Kathy's. Because of the investigation, questions and comments regarding her should be limited to her role in the treatment of Kathy. He then asked Emily's brother and her niece to stand and take a bow on her behalf. They were applauded, and quickly sat down. Ralph requested that questions be limited to medical treatment that she received at the hospital. He then introduced Mr. Abraham Rabinowitz who had asked to make some comments.

Robby accepted the mike and looked around at his audience. He knew he was speaking to tens of millions of people who would see him now, or later this evening on TV. He thought of his wife and son.

"My name is Abraham Rabinowitz. I am an alcoholic. I am an attorney with offices in this city. My friends call me Robby.

"I was requested by Kathy and Professor Makino to assist them when Kathy discovered that she could walk. I let them down. I am the person who substituted music CDs for the two disks that Kathy received. They were hurriedly painted at my direction and, of course, later found to be of no use in a computer except for music.

"The CD with the music of Air Supply was manufactured in Mexico under license to the copyright holder. It was a gift from a friend-of-the-family who purchased it during a visit to Mexico, which explains why it was in the Makino residence.

"By now you have all seen pictures of Kathy's well used wheelchair," he said while pointing to it on stage, "and you can see why a new backrest was purchased.

"I wish to offer my apologies for the lapse in judgment that I made which cast a cloud of suspicion and disbelief upon my friends. At that time, I was not convinced of the nature of her recovery myself, and due to my drinking problem, was looking for the possibility of work for my firm.

"I can attest to the validity of the power contained in the authentic disks. At three-o'clock in the morning on the day that the phony disks were disclosed to the public, I was summoned to the computer operating with a good disk and I believe that I conversed with God. That discussion has made a profound change in my life.

"I have found a new purpose in life and the forgiveness of the Makinos for the problem I caused them. I hope that I receive the same from this audience and the public, especially from the DA who is sitting there in the front row. Thank you." Robby returned to his seat while receiving a loud, sincere applause.

Ralph introduced Professor Makino after telling Robby that he certainly had received *his* forgiveness and thanked him for setting the record straight.

"I am Tamo Makino. I teach advanced physics at the University. I am the third generation of Makinos to be born on American soil. My father served in the US Army during World War II and did not survive. I was the first Makino to abandon the samurai traditions, becoming instead, a liberal college student and marrying an Irish Catholic.

"We had one daughter, Kathy. My wife was taking her to school in the car one morning and driving at normal speed along the frontage road when a truck hauling rolls of sheet metal was involved in an accident on the freeway above and alongside. The cargo broke loose. Ten tons of metal rolled down the embankment and struck the car on the left side. My wife died instantly and Kathy received major injuries. She was transported and treated here at General Hospital. She was a patient for six months before being allowed to come home. She continued her treatment here for another three years and it was fairly well decided that she would never regain the use of her legs.

"Emily Mullin, who was Kathy's physical therapist, became a friend of the family and introduced Kathy to computers during one of their frequent trips to town together. For three years, Kathy could not manage the chair by herself and was confined to the house most of the time.

"Several days ago, I was summoned home from classes to find Kathy *walking!* I'll leave it to her to tell you how that came about."

He then introduced Kathy.

She walked to the center of the stage and bounced around a little in time with the audience's clapping. She took the mike from her father and asked for quiet, but it was a few minutes before she could speak above the applause.

"Thank you. Thank you all for coming. As you can see, I'm *walking!* And it feels great!

"Before I tell you about how I got out of that chair, I think you are entitled to know the extent of the damage that I received, and to meet some of the people who saved my life some ten years ago. At

122

this time, I want to introduce you to the Physician-In-Charge of General Hospital, Doctor Charles Edwards." As Kathy went back to her chair, it was difficult to tell if the applause was for her or for the PIC, who was very popular with the medical staff.

Dr. Edwards asked for the first slide and pictures of a crashed car were shown on the screen. Apparently, Mr.Briggs's staff found some news coverage and photos in the newspaper's archives. The doctor was motioning the projector operator to change scenes more rapidly as the graphic newspaper photos were not pleasant to look at. Next, there were a series of photos taken in the Emergency Room showing Kathy's external injuries. There were close-ups of a broken front tooth, a deep gash on the left side of her face, just in front of the ear, multiple cuts and bruises on the front of her face and forehead.

Then he switched projections and asked that the x-rays be shown to explain the extent of her internal injuries. A broken collarbone was very easy to see on the screen. The broken bones in her vertebrae required some assistance in finding and they were pointed out by the physician. He asked that the lights to be turned back on and then read from the medical records that her vital signs were observed changing, indicating a ruptured spleen and that intervention was needed immediately. He read from another report the medical terms and then told the audience what the doctor said...he removed her spleen...and there were no apparent complications as a result. Doctor Fischer? Was he here? If so, please say hello to Kathy.

A distinguished looking man with graying hair, wearing a physician's uniform, took the stage and embraced Kathy, to the applause of the audience. He indicated that he didn't wish to make a comment and left the stage.

Dr. Edwards continued with more detailed x-rays of her spine. Even laymen could see on the screen that something was broken. A hand was raised from the front row and the PIC broke with the format and recognized a young physician from the State Department of Health. The question was raised about whether a certain medication had been administered after the spleen removal. The PIC searched for Dr Fischer to answer the question. He was found and replied loudly, "If my memory serves me correctly, I don't believe that product was available ten years ago." There was a polite muffling of laughter and the PIC continued with his presentation.

The orthopedic surgeon who was summoned to make the evaluation and immobilize Kathy's spine was introduced. He explained how he worked with the neurologist and the operating room technicians to determine the best possible method and procedure to heal the injury after determining that surgery was not appropriate. He indicated what might happen if surgery was attempted and the risk factors were definitely against it. When he ended his presentation he was applauded and the PIC introduced the doctor who was her primary physician through recovery, her extended stay in the hospital, and her physical-therapy program, Doctor Clancy.

"How do you tell a twelve-year-old girl that she is never going to walk again? For me, that was the most difficult part of Kathy's recovery.

"My job was to review all of the treatment that she had received, monitor her progress, and examine the state-of-the-art for any new developments that could be used beneficially in her case. I arranged for her scan as soon as she was able to be safely moved. Now we have the equipment on site. I met with dozens of the best surgeons and neurologists to examine her case, hoping that I was not going to have to tell her the bad news. Unfortunately, that search was unsuccessful and I was left with the task of notifying the patient and her father, Professor Makino.

"I was fortunate to have Emily Mullin assigned to my department and I thought she was the best medicine that I could offer Kathy. I think that I made the right decision from what has been reported to me.

"I am delighted to see Kathy using her legs. I hope that she will give me the opportunity to be my patient once more so that I can enlighten myself and pass on to others, the details of her recovery. Is that a deal, Kathy?" The doctor finished his presentation with the question when Kathy nodded her approval.

The PIC asked, wisely, if there were any medical questions

before introducing Kathy and, of course, there were none. He motioned Kathy to take the mike and she was met with applause when she stood and walked center-stage.

"Thank you all for your part in my life. Without the excellent treatment that I received here, I probably would not be speaking to you today.

"My real recovery began a short time ago when I was very depressed. I was confined to this chair, I failed my driving test, my friends were all out working at jobs or married and raising their families. I had not seen Emily, my best friend, and she didn't answer her phone. I remembered an idea that Emily taught me. When things are not going right, *invite* God into your life. I did that. I felt immediate relief and thought that was the end of it.

"Then I received the disk in the mail and after a few mistakes, put it into my computer. A voice asserting that it was God spoke to me after I followed the instructions. We had a discussion and I spoke with Emily, who told me the reason why she had broken her appointments with me.

"After that I made a promise to assist God with a project of His and then He cured me.

"Only my closest friends know of this project, as I was instructed later, by God, not to reveal it until the conclusion of today's examination by the media.

"I do not know what superconductors are, but I was told, again, by God, that they were in the disks.

"One of the most frequently asked questions is, 'Do I think superconductivity had anything to do with my recovery?'

"The answer. 'No.' The disks are merely a means of storing and transmitting data. Of themselves, they have no curative powers. Robby joked one time when he heard an interviewer ask that question, that if a person got a headache from using DOS, the disks would certainly relieve that problem.

"Because of the frequency of the question, I have developed a new response. Why do you search for a remedy in a product that you cannot even comprehend when I have already given you a simple, complete, answer? *Invite God into your life.* I did that and *that* is why I am walking today.

125

"Why is this so difficult to comprehend? Everyone can do it. It costs no money. It takes very little time. You can do it anywhere. Nothing that you already have is at risk...well, maybe some goofy ideas...like evolution, martyrdom, reincarnation, or predicting the end of the world each year. Or that God is vengeful and to be feared. Or perhaps, you just don't believe there is a divine order to this life of yours. If that is the case, then I challenge you...make a sincere invitation. Then you will know for sure.

"I'm ready for questions."

The Administrator resumed his task as Master of Ceremonies and stood beside Kathy where they could pass the mike between them. He reminded the audience to keep the questions confined to her treatment at the hospital, but he knew from her presentation that it was going to be a difficult task. He pointed to a reporter to his left who was frantically waving his hand.

"I believe this is a fair question, within the ground-rules. I have done a lot of coverage on so-called miraculous recoveries in the past. One of the most common frauds is the use of a double. Another person, same age, close resemblance. My question is: How do we know that you are who you say you are? The accident was ten years ago and the best witness, Emily Mullin, is dead."

Ralph said she did not need to answer the question. Kathy calmly took the mike from his hand and looked at the reporter. "Thomas, would you hand me that glass after you wipe it clean with one of those napkins," she said as she pointed to the items on a folding table in front of the celebrities that had water available for them. There was silence as the reporter cleaned a glass and Kathy asked, "You will accept fingerprints as positive evidence, won't you?"

"Yes," the man said, handing her both items. "My name is Rick, not Thomas," he added.

Kathy continued cleaning the glass, then held it by the napkin on the bottom and put her right hand around the top of the glass. She looked at the reporter again and said, "I'm sorry Rick, I must have had you confused with Doubting Thomas." She continued amidst the laughter, "I believe that is a Police Officer beside you. There, in the front row. Sir, would you take custody of the evidence

126

and have your people check out my fingerprints. Make sure that Thomas, I mean *Rick*, gets a full report."

The Chief of Police took the evidence, reached in his pocket for a pen, and carefully placed the glass on it.

Ralph took a question from another waving hand to his right. "Robby, Mr. Rabinowitz, said that he, too, spoke to God. This is the first that we have heard of it. Could you fill us in on the details?"

Kathy took the mike and replied, "Robby is shy. It's the first that I've heard about it too. Maybe if you give his law firm a little publicity, he'll tell you about it." She glanced at Robby and he was smiling. Kathy breathed a sigh of relief after fielding her first unexpected question.

Ralph took a question from the center of the room. "You indicated to Doctor Clancy that you were agreeable to a new medical examination. Will the information be restricted or will all staff members be allowed to review it. I have several ideas about the spleen removal and its side-effects that I would like to examine," apparently a question from a doctor.

"Just a minute. I'll let my father answer that." Kathy turned and offered the mike to her father.

"The answer to your specific question is perhaps better dealt with by Doctor Edwards. Kathy's agreement with General Hospital is that she will make herself available for a complete examination by qualified medical staff. I think the idea is that she would make a one-time visit. X-rays, Lab, etc. I certainly don't want her to be treated as though she were a medical experiment or suffering from some type of abnormality.

"We have her scheduled for a visit tomorrow, at another facility where there will be no distractions, such as a parade. It should not take a lot of time.

"If you discover something of medical value, Kathy and I have no objections to sharing it for the public welfare. However, I don't think you will find the answer in her body. The answer we all search for is in her mind."

Ralph took another question from the rear of the room. A woman's voice asked, "You said you made a promise to God to help

Him with a project. Can you tell us what that project was? I assume you did it since you are walking." There was a murmur of approval of the question.

Kathy took the mike again and said, "I thought you'd never ask!"

She let the laughter fade. "If I answer this question, the meeting is over. Do we all agree to that?"

The approval was overwhelming. She asked for all those in favor and there was more applause. She asked for those opposed and the room was silent.

"OK. Here goes. First. I saw Mr. Briggs when the lights were up. Please stand up. Mr. Briggs is the editor of American News. He knows.

"My father, of course. Please stand.

"Robby. When he isn't speaking to my computer and keeping secrets from me...he, too, knows. Please stand up, Robby.

"Victor. My personal bodyguard and keeper of the disks. Please stand."

She turned to the audience and asked, "Do you like that haircut? I do." There was overwhelming feminine voice approval.

"Larry, Nancy, Marcie and Shirley. The computer-room staff, who are busily answering your calls and filing the information being provided by the disks...they all know.

"One nice patrolman is running around with the information, but he doesn't believe me.

"These are all my friends and they have kept this secret for me.

"I did not know that I would be healed when I made the promise to assist. I just said I would do it, on faith. That promise....

"To put together a press conference for God so that He can determine if He wants to change anything, on what He calls...this project.

"When I receive further instructions, I will let you know.

"The meeting is over."

Chapter 11

It was very quiet at SuperCee. By the time Doctor Jordan was really getting into the subject of superconductors, half of his audience had departed. Mr. Hudson had no idea that they had been withdrawn to cover the Kathy parade or that Briggs had terminated the calls to the offices. Lewis Anderson used the time allotted to Dr. Jordan to form an outline of his feature story on superconductors. Using that and some pictures that he saw on the wall of the lobby was all he needed to earn his first week's salary. He handled the remaining reporter's questions in quick fashion and the meeting was over. Mr. Hudson was delighted and went to his office to call Baltimore.

Chad was reading his magazines and watching the parade. The switchboard was dead...a few outgoing calls were in progress. Chad told him that was a good idea about seeing the property manager because they delivered a key. While managing some small talk, and glancing through a magazine, Lewis pocketed the key and put the magazine where it had been. He asked where the mens-room was and excused himself. Inside he found what he had hoped for...a bar of soap. He pressed the key into the bar, turned it over to get an accurate impression of the splines and pressed again. He wrapped the soap in a paper towel and stuck it in his pocket. He washed the key and returned to Chad. He slipped the key back into position while picking up the magazine once more.

He glanced at his watch and said he had to go and cancel a job interview that he set up. He said he'd return in a couple of hours, asked if he had an office yet, and told Chad to be more careful with master keys and not leave them lying about. He saw a key-box attached to the wall and put the key on top. He got Chad's attention turned from the TV long enough to indicate to him where the key was. He also got a good look at the numbers and codes stamped on the key. He called Kanisha as soon as he was out of sight of SuperCee. They decided to meet at the Brass Rail again. He visited a locksmith shop in the downtown area and a new key was made for him in a few minutes.

He arrived at the lounge ahead of her and located a table away from the bar again. He ordered a Virgin Mary, explaining to the bosomy waitress that he had a heart condition and couldn't drink alcohol. He made detailed notes of what he had accomplished so far. It wasn't much and there were no leads in other directions. He looked at the key he had made and wondered why. Was the paranoia rubbing off on him?

He noticed the movement at the bar as all heads turned and some groans filled the air. Then he saw Kanisha looking for him in the dim light and waved. Then he saw what caused the commotion. She was wearing almost nothing. A leotard and some flimsy underthings, and the red, high-heel shoes that attracted attention to her legs.

She joined him and began talking excitedly about all the information she had accumulated. He had no idea of what she had been up to and more curious about the clothing she was wearing. He almost said she looked like a hooker and he was embarrassed, but she could already see that. She asked him if he was married and he replied that he wasn't. She said she wasn't either. She suggested that they go by car to the park along the river as she had a lot to tell him and he would probably feel more comfortable there. She asked him if he wanted to leave alone or exit with her. He decided on the latter and endured the snickers and comments as they walked past the bar arm-in-arm. Outside, Kanisha laughed, and commented on what a bunch of jerks they were. Lewis admitted that he enjoyed it and it hadn't hurt his reputation at all as she was a very attractive lady under all that hair.

On the drive to the park, Kanisha explained why she was dressed the way she was and what she had done the night before after Lewis dropped her at home. Today, she had lunch with one of her new friends and went shopping for the clothes that she was presently wearing, with another. Lewis asked the purpose for her actions, as he hadn't been out at night in years and no idea of what was going on after dark.

She said she thought she found some connections with SuperCee and prostitution. By then they arrived at the park and could talk more comfortably. She said that the first girl used to be in trouble with the police all the time. Then she met a high-class hooker at a party who told her how to stay out of jail and gave her a number to call the next time she was hassled. The attorney who got her released had a long talk with her and arranged for her to be an "escort" for a visiting politician instead of payment for legal services.

This is what she had been doing for the past two years. She was back on the streets now because things were slow before the election. She was supposed to go to *Baltimore*, all expenses paid, but her mother was ill and needed her here. "First clue. You said Mr. Hudson went to see his boss in *Baltimore.*"

Kanisha told about her conversations with the other hooker. She was older and not as attractive and back on the street on her own because of it. She had been around and knew how the system worked. *They* were always looking for young, beautiful, intelligent, women. If you had the qualifications and the connections, there was a good life. You answered the phone, dressed well, arrived on time, took care of business, stayed healthy, and banked your money. No taxes, but no retirement plan.

Lewis asked who *they* were. Kanisha asked if Lewis thought she had the qualifications for finding out. He couldn't help but laugh out his approval. He asked if she was seriously going to take care of business and she told him not to worry, she was going to get arrested before it came to that.

Lewis filled her in on his progress. She did not approve of him writing the feature on superconductivity. She said he was a *news* reporter. She mentioned a travel writer who worked for the Chron who could, "turn on the "sunshine-pump" and make you want to run right out and buy a ticket for a leisurely paradise vacation on the beach in Altus, Oklahoma."

Lewis agreed with her criticism but insisted that he had to be given credit for the article. Kanisha said she thought that would be a problem, but what if Lewis invited the writer to SuperCee? He agreed with that approach. She said she would make the arrangements.

Lewis thought he had better return to his new job and Kanisha said she had to get some sleep. Lewis expressed his concerns for her safety. It was agreed that he would solicit her favors at exactly midnight at an intersection that they were both familiar with. That way it would appear that she was "working" and they could exchange more ideas. Lewis told her about the key he made with absolutely no idea of what he was going to do with it. They laughed.

* * * * *

Television and radio were beating the press with "breaking news". Unfortunately, the manner of presentation left little for the viewer or listener to analyze or to consider other options to what was selected to be aired. There was no balance as to what was important and what wasn't. You either got it the first time around and accepted it, or it was gone into outer space. With the paper, it was a little different. The important things to most people were on page one. If you disagreed with that, you could spend some time reading the *funnies*. If buying a new car was important to you, you could spend your time reading the new car ads. If you disagreed with the paper or the editorials, you could write to the editor and explain your dissatisfaction.

The American News was getting very few complaints on their coverage of Kathryn Makino. After today's press conference at the hospital, tomorrow's edition would be a masterpiece of information. Gordon Briggs went home early to watch the evening news on *network* TV. For once, he was ahead of them. Now he was going to see how the big boys play.

* * * * *

The computer room crew stayed on the job until the hospital limousine arrived with Kathy, Kami, Robby and Victor. Larry explained what had been accomplished during the day and that the entire operation would move to the other house in the morning. One computer was already installed and was handling the telephones. Nancy had updates for everyone and passed them out. There was only one sheet for Kathy and Nancy looked inquisitively at her

132

when presenting it. It said: When Are You Going To Speak To Victor? Kathy read it and folded it, before putting it in her instruction manual.

Victor was given his key, which was necessary to open or close the safe. The two disks were presently locked inside. Victor and Larry left together to try out the keys and for Victor to verify their presence. Nancy had a stack of bills, which she presented to Kami. He just smiled as he leafed through them until he got to the last page. A knot appeared in his stomach when he saw that the total amount due was over a hundred thousand dollars! He had always managed his personal finances conservatively, having the money in the bank before purchasing anything. He was broke. The money he put out for Larry's bets, and the purchase of the house left him with very little cash on hand. He shoved the pile of bills in front of Robby and pointed to the bottom line on the last page. Robby said, "The race is tomorrow."

Kami looked around for today's paper and opened it up to the racing sheet. Apparently, Larry had already been there, as there were circles penciled in around last nights *losers*. He was engrossed in reading the report of the Racing Commissioner's meeting when Larry and Victor returned. Larry dismissed the girls and said he wanted to go home and spend some time with his family.

Kami announced that dinner was coming soon and after that, suggested everyone could relax and see themselves on TV. Nancy was carrying a bouquet of flowers and asked Robby what his plans were. He said he had none and she invited him to her house to watch TV. Victor asked if there was another TV around that he could watch, as he had to guard the disks in the other house. Kathy remembered that she had a small TV that she used when she was confined to bed a lot. Kami remembered it and located it in a closet. He offered it to Victor. Kathy re-read her note and smiled.

* * * * *

The local talk-show hosts were not enjoying crow for dinner. They wanted to talk about *elections* but very few of their listeners did. They were left with their dependable cronies who called in to hear themselves on the radio. It was apparent that they were not going to let anyone talk about Kathy when they went into long commentaries on other subjects.

National talk shows were spreading the story. Throughout the Biblebelt, this was the only story going.

The night before, newsstands ran out of copies of the Evening Star. The paper's namesake is really the planet Venus and not a star at all. Tonight it was high in the sky, seeming to follow the moon as the earth continued its daily-rotation and not at all concerned that today's edition was being ignored and would be recycled. All of the alibis and the cleverly worded lead story would go unread. The editor wasn't concerned about his job. On his desk, in a plastic envelope, were six fillings and a crown. His reporters had gone through the Makino trash and found them. He didn't know where or when they were going to come into play, only that he had a story yet to tell.

* * * * *

Professor Makino fell asleep in front of the TV. Today, he was presented with another household problem that he never thought was coming and he was unprepared for it. After dinner, Kathy wanted to stay behind and join Victor to watch TV. He decided to stay up and wait for her. He joined the millions of other parents who were doing likewise...sleeping in front of the TV set, waiting for their children to come home.

* * * * *

The Professor need not have worried and developed a crick in his neck from sleeping so uncomfortably. Kathy and Victor were dancing. "One, two, three, four, turn, that's right, smile, head up, one, two, three, four," Victor was teaching her to dance to the music that was on the radio late in the evening. It was mostly romantic music for young people in love, and the announcer was taking calls and answering their requests which were almost entirely from the current top twenty.

134

They had been at it for over two hours without a break. The walk in the morning didn't seem to have any effect on their energy level, but Kathy said she was ready to sit one out. It was a nice evening and they sat on the front stairs, as there was no suitable furniture in the house yet.

Kathy asked Victor how he liked his job so far and he responded that he was really pleased, but, it was a little scary for him, like when the crowd gathered around quickly the night before. She said that he knew almost everything about her, but that she didn't know much about him, and asked him to tell her about himself.

Victor spoke about his parents, born and raised in New York City when it was a good place to live. His father owned a retail store for men's clothing, but the business held no future for the next generation. He had two older brothers, then a sister, then him, and then three younger sisters. His older sister was his favorite and the one that taught him to dance so well. He did well in school, having a lot of help from his older brothers. After high school the family all went together and got him through college. It was a struggle and he worked part-time, but he made it. He could see no future for himself in the retail business and his best subjects were in math and physics. He said he wasn't very good in them, but his grades were better than the females in those subjects. He thought of engineering as a profession, but looked at the courses and didn't think he could make it before he was too old to get a job. His next-to-oldest brother went to a Technical School and learned computers. He already was making more money than his father and oldest brother combined. So, he made an abrupt change and took some Computer Science courses. He was good at it. His brother is sending him some money and with the part-time security job, he will be able to complete his education and maybe open a company with his older brother.

Then, he met Larry at SuperCee and they became good friends. Larry is an expert, in his opinion, and he learned so much from him that he couldn't turn him down when he was asked to provide Kathy some security. He really needed the job to make ends meet. He laughed when he told her that his father owned a clothing store, but this was the first suit he ever wore.

Kathy asked him about sports. He said that he tried and liked everything. The problem was that football practice took too many hours. The blacks in his neighborhood were too good at basketball for him to make the team. He threw his arm out playing baseball and the doctors made him quit. The Puerto Ricans and the Cubans dominated the court games. He could swim well, but his school didn't have a team. In college, he just wasn't good enough at any one sport to try out for a team and he worked after school most of the time anyway.

She asked him about entertainment. What did he do when he found some time? Dancing was his number one activity. He didn't have money to go out to the discos, but there were a lot of free socials at the University. He rattled off a list of places where there was good music and space to dance and no one ever asked if you had a ticket if you just danced well and minded your manners.

That gave Kathy an opening to find out what was really on her mind. "Don't you need a date to go to some of those places?" she asked.

Victor said he hardly ever took a date. There are usually more females than males at the Sorority dances and the Church socials and once you become known, you are welcome. He volunteered that he liked being with the females, probably because of his sister, and he usually got along with them very well. He hadn't met anyone special and wanted to play the field until he had a job and could settle down. Finding a female to keep him company just came naturally to him and until now, he hadn't given it much thought. "Yeah, some guys have a lot of trouble finding a girl. But, they are egotistical jerks." He told her the story of one guy he knows, on the football team, that thinks if he drinks two six-packs of beer before a party he is irresistible to the girls. "He's just a loud, foul-mouthed, drunk. No girl in her right mind is going to enjoy his company. He always ends up getting more drunk and wanting to fight."

Kathy related how she had no first-hand knowledge of that type of social life. All of her socializing has been on TV, and there seemed to be an awful lot of violence. She asked Victor if life was like that.

He said it was if you were looking for trouble. He had never had any. If he sees something brewing, he just gets out of the way. He had never seen any robbers, or car-chases, or met any violent characters as they are portrayed on TV and in the movies. He described his life as pretty calm and peaceful. Just a lot of work and a lot of study.

Kathy thought of her promise and wondered how to approach the subject. She asked him if he went to church. "No." He told about going to church when he was a child. His parents were Catholic and it was church every Sunday, rain or shine. His father still goes, but his mother got out of the practice about the time she started taking birth control pills. He barely recalls the discussions his parents had over that, but she ended up not going to church anymore. He went to Catechism and made his First Holy Communion and Confirmation, but then he just dropped off when he started working. A couple of times he went to Mass on Christmas and on Easter. He recalled going to one of his younger sister's First Holy Communion; the whole family went together.

He told her that the best dances were with the Baptists. The church where he goes to dance has many black girls, "...and *they* can dance!" He said he went to a Lutheran church one time and they wanted him to enroll in classes to convert to their religion before he was allowed to dance with the girls. That wasn't his kind of church. He asked Kathy, "Why do all these people want you to change and be like them? I don't even know who Luther was or what he believed in. Same way with the Mormons. Every girl I met who was a Mormon wanted me to become one too. None of them seemed very happy to me. Sneaking around back to have a cigarette or hiding a can of beer in a bag. Maybe misery loves company?"

"I don't have any religion. My mother was a Catholic and I was baptized a Catholic. I remember going to church with my mother but I never went to any to any of the other stuff you mentioned. I don't know what my father is. He goes to some church with some of his Japanese friends. But, not regularly. Sundays, he usually spends with me. We always go out to dinner and he likes to take me

137

to different places, like the concerts, or ball games. Sunday is our special day together.

"My Dad's a character. Like, one time *he* wanted to go to Classic Village to hear Zamfir. Have you ever been there? It's up on the side of this huge hill and only a dirt path and log stairs, lots of them, and about a mile from the parking. Emily and I already made plans to see the Pointer Sisters, but, no, my father already had the tickets for the three of us. He really embarrassed Emily into going. When we got there, we found out why the *three* of us had to go. There was no way he could have gotten me, and the chair, up that incline. It was bad enough with the two of them carrying me. Luckily, about half way up the hill, a group of young men, I think they were college students, saw them struggling and took me the rest of the way.

"Actually, it was a very memorable occasion. Zamfir was terrific! We laid out on the lawn...I forgot to tell you about that part. We also had this big basket of food along for a picnic. That had to go up the hill also. My father buys Southern fried chicken and watermelon...to bribe Emily...can you believe that! Anyway, we spread out on the lawn, have a picnic and listen to good music."

"How did you get back down?" Victor asked.

"The same guys. They looked for me after the concert and we went in style, everyone whistling Zamfir's music and spitting out watermelon seeds along the way," Kathy replied.

"We were talking about religion before. Do you believe in God? I mean, right now it must be difficult for you. Thrust into this position of guarding a freak who talks to God," Kathy asked.

"I don't think you're a freak. Actually, I believe everything is on the level here. I was surprised at Rabinowitz's comments at the hospital today. I had him figured for a 'wise-ass' before. I didn't like him. Now, I've changed my mind. Something happened last night when the crowd came at you. I could feel it inside me.

"You could say that I believe there is some order, something that makes us humans different from all other living things...the ability to think and make decisions that affect our lives. For example, my career. I had choices. I *decided* that I wanted to study

Computer Science and then I did the things necessary; to enroll myself, pay the tuition, buy the books and go to class.

"I believe in something, I just don't know what it is. Maybe I should have stayed with the Catholics. My father sure seems to know. Yet, he could never explain it to me when I spoke to him about it. He repeated what was in the Catechism and that was what I was asking him about. He never really answered the question."

"Do you remember what you asked?" Kathy inquired.

"I think it was about the Holy Ghost. Catholics always say this at the beginning and the end of everything. "In the name of the Father, the Son, and the Holy Ghost." The Father, I guess, is God. The Son is Jesus. Then, who is the Holy Ghost?" Victor explained his confusion.

"Would you like the answer? From someone who speaks to the Father," Kathy asked.

"Let's hear it," Victor replied.

"I hope I get this right. First-of-all, we have a name change. It's now politically correct to refer to the Holy *Spirit*, not the Holy Ghost. Oh, I wish Larry were here! I'd like to know if that was changed in Spanish as well. I'll ask him tomorrow. Maybe a Cardinal saw the movie, 'Ghost Busters', and put in for a name change.

"The Holy Spirit is how God communicates with our mind. I think it is this spirit you referred to when you said something happened inside your mind when the crowd rushed in.

"There is a way to find out. You are all alone here in the house. The guards are watching outside. When I leave to get some sleep you will have nothing to disturb you. Make yourself relax and look within yourself. Don't think of anything else, just you and the empty feeling within. Then *invite* the Holy Spirit into that space and see what happens," Kathy instructed him.

"OK. I'll do it. Like you said this afternoon, it doesn't cost anything."

"Now. You can do a favor for me. If you get a response and you make communication, find out what a Holy Relationship is. I think I'll go now and try to find that answer myself," Kathy concluded as she stood up, stretched, said goodnight and walked to her house.

Chapter 12

Lewis was not accustomed to being up this late. He had never been up this late in this part of town. He checked that the door locks were down on his car. He stayed on the Boulevard, which was well lit. There was a shorter way to get to the intersection where Kanisha was waiting, but he didn't want to chance it. There was a lot of action on the street if you knew what to look for. A parked car, with the exhaust visible and the driver slunk low in the seat. Solitary females, walking slowly along the wide pavement. Some others, resting with their backs against the wall in a doorway or a building entrance. A few solitary men, smoking cigarettes, were walking clumsily with their drink in their hand. A lot of cars, newer than those parked or abandoned along the Boulevard, were driving slowly with only the driver's seat occupied by a male.

Run-down stores, many boarded up, some gutted by fire in the past, comprised the majority of structures on this stretch of the Boulevard. Every block or so there were bright lights inviting a person in to see the girls and have another drink. An occasional Adult Book Store. One all-night restaurant. A Mini-Market was open, well lighted with strong bars on the windows. Several hotels were still open offering inexpensive rates on neon signs. They were very old, maybe two or three stories at the most. The windows were small and hardly any lights were on upstairs.

Lewis recognized the street where he was to turn and made a left onto it. Two blocks and then look for Kanisha. He was going to have trouble. The street was lined with hookers and about three cars parked with lights still on. High heels, long legs, short skirts, bodies bent over, talking to the drivers. He passed slowly across the intersection. He didn't recognize her. He made a U-turn and passed on the other side. No sign of her that he could recognize in the poor street lighting. He thought he might try it from a different angle and made three right hand turns. He parked in a well-lit space just short of the intersection. He turned off the lights and waited, motor running.

A hooker was coming over to talk to him. He lowered the window about two inches, no more. Then he saw the big hair. Kanisha. Thank God. She was wearing a long black leather coat and he had been looking for the clothes he had seen her in earlier. She went immediately to the passenger side and wanted in. He reached over and unlocked it. "Man, it's freezing out here! Turn on the heater!" Lewis could feel the cold from her jacket after she closed the door. "Roll up that window!" she demanded through her shivering lips. She snuggled close to him and then found the heater controls and put everything to full hot.

Lewis asked her, jokingly, "Don't you think it would be more natural if you stood out there with your fanny in the middle of the street talking to me through the window? That's what the other girls are doing."

Kanisha replied, "No. We're cool. I told everyone I had a 'date' with you and to be looking for your car, as you were new in town and not familiar with the area. It worked out just right when you drove on through. What name do you like? My street name is Kenya. Do you like it?"

"Why not call me Lewis. I like that name. Why do I need another name? I'm not one foot out of this car around here," Lewis replied.

"I want to introduce you to my friends as we leave together. Also, I have to return this coat to one of the girls. She let me borrow it when she saw I wasn't used to cold nights like this. I said that I hadn't been on the streets for a long time and had been working only pre-arranged 'dates'. Not bad, eh? I'll tell you, some of the stories you hear out here are truly unbelievable. I might do some features on this when I get back to my regular job." She managed to get the coat off now that she was warmed up. She turned on the radio and found some music that had a nice beat to it. She pointed out a tall, slender, blonde wearing a yellow top and black, stretch pants. "I gotta' return it to him. He's probably freezing by now."

"Him?" Lewis asked. "Not *her?*"

"Oh, she's a *he*. I told you some funny things were going on

142

out here," Kanisha said as Lewis pulled away from the curb and slowly approached the group of five or six that were standing on the corner. She rolled down her window and handed the rolled-up coat to the blonde. She asked if any of them wanted to party later on. She said she was going with *Lewis* to the Sheraton and if his friends wanted to party, they'd come back and pick them up. Obviously, they all said yes.

Kanisha's new friend pushed the others away and stuck her head in the window and said hello to Lewis with an expression of approval. Then she told Kanisha she really needed to work and if anything came up to call her first. *Kenya* said she would. Lewis made a two hundred and seventy-degree turn, drove two blocks, and was back on the well-lit Boulevard. "Where to?" he asked.

"You want to go to my place? I gotta' get out of these clothes and into something warm. We can talk there. I have a lot of good information," Kanisha said and then moved closer to him.

"Yeah. I know the way from here. Do you think you can find some *music* on the radio? I hate that shit that's on there," Lewis remarked.

Kanisha began pushing buttons and turning knobs and complained, "You got no soul, brother."

Lewis retorted, "Maybe I've got no soul, but I've got *ears* and that shit stinks. What do you think they made for cutting that, fifty cents?" Then he sang, "....critics raving about our rap, and the record's making fifty cents."

"Where did I hear that? Isn't that a new song?" Kanisha asked.

"New? I don't think so. That's Eric Carmen. A singer with *soul*. It's been on all the stations ever since the Star discovered Robby switched disks. That, and Air Supply."

"I like Air Supply. I don't remember Eric Carmen though," Kanisha said.

"When you hear the music, you'll remember. Hungry Eyes. All By Myself. It Hurts Too Much.

"Did you get to see Robby's speech today? TV's showing him every half-hour or so. It was very moving. Kathy was great."

"Yeah. I almost cried. Especially after I read what I got credit for writing. You guys did a beautiful story," Kanisha replied.

143

"I had nothing to do with it. Remember? I got fired. That was all Briggs at his finest. I never knew he was that good of a writer himself. He's been at the same desk ever since I went to work there and this is the first time I ever heard of him doing anything but criticizing," Lewis said.

It was approaching one in the morning when Lewis arrived at Kanisha's apartment. She invited him in and put on some coffee. She excused herself to change clothes and he surveyed her living quarters. She had done very well for herself. The apartment was small, but it was complete, well designed, and tastefully furnished. She had a computer and a row of software manuals. Not many books, but he figured she had them available on the computer.

The kitchen looked like she used it a lot. He opened the refrigerator and saw that it was well stocked. The coffee was done and he poured a cup for himself. Nice china. Nice silverware...not stainless. The girl had some class. He admired the art as he waited for her to change. He didn't like her music when he looked at what she listened to. Some of it was good. She had a Neil Diamond and a Barbara Striesand with her Whitney Houston. He could live with that.

When she arrived, she looked gorgeous. Her street make-up was gone and she was wearing a comfortable sweat suit. He whistled his approval and got up to bring her a cup of coffee when she sat beside him on the sofa. He returned with the coffee and resumed the same seat.

She took a sip of coffee and remarked how good it was after being out in the cold for so long. She suggested they finish business and Lewis nodded. He said nothing new happened when he got back. Hudson seemed pleased and he had the blessing of his boss. They gave him a nice office and an open hand to run the PR. They just wanted to see what was going out before he sent it. It was going to take some time to work through the system to find out what was going on there.

Kanisha said she was able to verify almost everything she had been told. Briggs has an employee who is working with her and supplies her with all of the information she needs. Court records have the names of counsel and clients. The researcher checked

144

backwards on counsel and found that the majority of them were connected with Fenhauser's firm at one time or the other. Now she is trying to make a comparison with the judges and the sentences given. That's a little harder to do, but she said a pattern had already developed between counsel and judge match-ups.

She said she would be arrested tomorrow to see what else she could find out. Lewis raised his eyebrows at that bit of information and asked her for clarification.

She said it was all arranged and would be done in broad-daylight, so there was not much danger. One of the girls has a pimp who was on Vice. He was under suspicion and transferred to Theft, daytime work. He'll make the bust. It'll look good on his record. The only thing she was worried about was if the counsel who gets her released wants some free sex in exchange for introducing her into the club.

Lewis said he had no ideas. He was already in way over his skill level. He had a key though. He was prepared. They laughed.

Kanisha told him not to worry. She asked him if he had ever been married as he seemed to be Puritanical about the subject of sex.

"Divorced. Five years," Lewis stated flatly. He went on to explain that he had no children because his wife didn't want the responsibility. She was a socialite and liked parties and spending money. She had her own money to spend and she met some guy who helped her spend it. He caught them and it was over. He just couldn't accept her back even though she wanted to give it another try. He liked her and she was fun and interesting, but there was just no way he could forget what happened.

"Anyone special since then?" Kanisha asked.

Lewis said he dated a lot and had some steady relationships, but no one that he wanted to spend the rest of his life with. He always compared them to his ex and they fell short of his expectations. Once he thought of trying to get back together with her, but she had remarried.

Kanisha stood up and posed for him. "Do I meet with your expectations?" she asked pertly. Lewis was temporarily at a loss for words. He started to say something, but she cut him off. "Prejudiced? Because I'm black."

Lewis had his thoughts in order and told her, "Yeah, I'm prejudiced. But not because you're black. Don't you think you're a little too young for me? We're almost a generation apart. As a woman, you're beautiful. You are also intelligent and we are both in the same line of work. Frankly, I never considered I'd have a chance with someone like you. So, yes, I guess you could say I was prejudiced against you."

"What's age? I've always liked older men. They are less egotistical. They are more caring and thoughtful. And afterwards...there is something to talk about. Do you know what I mean?" Kanisha asked.

"I know *exactly* what you mean. All of the younger women I ever dated were looking for Prince Charming to come riding in on a white charger and carry them off to 'never-never land'. I remember one lady, about your age, wanted to get married right away. I found out she had already had four other marriages. She lived like a queen. She got half of everything four times," Lewis said.

"And you think I might be the same way?" Kanisha asked.

"No. Of course, not. You're crazy. I never met anyone like you. I like everything about you. But, you were right. I was prejudiced about your age. Hell, you didn't even know who Eric Carmen was." Lewis knew he shouldn't have said the last part, but was surprised at her answer.

"I'd like to hear some of your music. Maybe I've been prejudiced by my peers. Did you know that Mr. Briggs told me I was prejudiced? I was. I used to be prejudiced against white people. He told me that I needed to look at each story and each person individually and not generalize. It really helped.

"I like you because of who you are. You took a stand on issues of honesty and fair reporting. You are the most respected reporter on the News's staff. Even at the Chron, your reputation is known.

"So how about it? After I get out of jail tomorrow, we'll listen to some of your music."

Lewis inhaled the last of his coffee, which was now cold. "I've got a better idea. Maybe *I'm* the one who is prejudiced about music. Let's listen to some of your's and you can drop me off at SuperCee in the morning *before* you get arrested."

Kanisha held out her hand.

Chapter 13

Saturday morning was quiet on Elm Street, where the Makinos lived. Except for the roadblocks, everything was back to normal in the neighborhood. The early morning sun was making its way through the dew and the trees, plants and lawns had a glow to them. It seemed as though everyone were sleeping in today.

Larry made his way through the checkpoint, driving Kami's van. The security guard on the new house helped him unload some cartons. The furniture company's enclosed truck lumbered down the street and parked behind the van. Two young men got out holding plastic cups of coffee. They all went into the house. Victor emerged from the doorway, glanced over at the Makino residence, stretched, and went back inside.

Robby, Nancy, and Marcie arrived together in Nancy's car. Robby had an armful of newspapers. They went into the new house. The catering van arrived and a man and a woman dressed in whites took their wares inside. A security company four-door sedan arrived to make the shift change. Irving drove the car and was in uniform. He walked around both premises with all four of his employees. Three went into the new house and the replacements stayed outside. Robby and Irving emerged with coffee and had a discussion in the middle of the street. Nancy emerged with coffee and a pastry and went to the front door of the Makino residence. She was met by the security guard, who took out a key and opened the door for her. The caterers departed.

Larry and Victor departed in the van. Victor was in casual clothes and had a courier-case in his hand. Irving and the two guards left. The furniture movers went to work, unloading their goods and carrying them into the house. It was ten-o-clock before anything else was visible from outside. A black limousine pulled up in front of the house and a driver in a gray suit got out and stretched. He spoke to the female security guard and went across the street to wait for his passengers. Larry and Victor returned. Victor had a garment bag over his shoulder when he re-entered the house. Larry diverted the movers long enough to move a large carton into the house on one of their dollies.

At ten fifteen, Kami and Nancy walked from his house to the other. He was dressed in a suit and rubbed his neck and shoulder with his hand as he walked. A young man arrived by bicycle with a bouquet of flowers, spoke to the uniformed lady, and went to the other house. His protective helmet bobbed up and down as he sped down the street while leaving. Shirley arrived in a red sport car and parked behind the van. She brushed something off the front of her skirt while standing beside her car. The moving men continued holding a heavy piece of furniture in the air as they admired her actions and moved only their glances until she passed from their view on the other side of their truck. Kami returned to his house with some food on one of the caterer's serving trays. The guard opened the door for him.

There was a sudden flurry of activity around ten thirty, initiated by Kami speaking to the guard who then relayed information to the other house. Larry responded first and then returned, Nancy changed addresses, then Marcie. Larry and Victor hustled across the street, Victor hugging the case to his chest. Nancy and Marcie returned, each with a stack of paper. Then everyone went to the other house...leaving Kathy alone with one of the disks and the computer.

The moving men closed up the doors on their truck and returned inside. At eleven, Kathy announced that she was ready to go to the hospital for her examination. Kami went to the house and led her to the waiting limo. Robby joined them, briefcase in hand. The driver made several nice maneuvers and was heading back in the direction from which he arrived. Nancy got his attention and handed a bouquet of flowers through an open rear window. The large vehicle moved elegantly down the street and turned out of view.

A heavy-set man allowed the high-power binoculars to rest on top of the large fat-storage unit that he had for a belly. He stopped dictating to a frail little man who sat cross-legged, taking down notes on a yellow pad with a white ball-point pen that had advertising for a law firm on it. They were in the attic of a house

150

several blocks away on a perpendicular street. Beside the man with the binoculars was a huge TV camera aimed out the window. The first man signaled to the cameraman to take a break. "Where do you think they are?" he asked.

The cameraman responded without taking his eye from the viewer. "I think *one* is still at Makinos. It depends. Did he have one or two to start with?"

The big man asked the little man, "You're the computer expert. What do you think?"

The little man replied, "Not enough information. Even if we knew how many disks went into the house. And maybe there was one already there. You aren't even sure of that, right? You don't even know how many computers are still in the house. Maybe there was just a Danish in the case. Like I said before, we have to find out more information."

The cameraman said he was going to re-run the part when they all left the house at one time. He was sure Victor had the case with him, but maybe something might be a tip-off on slow motion.

The big man turned to leave, "Keep watching. I'm gonna' call in and see if Hudson has any other instructions. Yell down if something comes up."

The limo was met by a police patrol and guided to a side road. The driver raised his hand, reassuring his passengers. "They'll make sure we aren't tailed. We're going to Mount Sinai if you haven't been told." Another officer, on foot with a portable radio in his hand, signaled them ahead. They wound their way through a residential area and the driver turned onto the freeway that led to the hospital. They parked outside the maternity ward without drawing attention and Kathy was ushered inside where she was met by the PIC of General Hospital. He explained to her the security measures they had taken to insure her comfort and asked if she had objections to being taken by gurney to the room where she would be x-rayed and examined. She saw her orderly standing by with a gurney and a big smile.

"Starlight Express, my favorite pusher. I'd trust him to take me anywhere," Kathy said as she sat up onto the gurney. A surgical cap was put over her hair; a mask covered her nose and mouth. The orderly lifted her legs up and turned her, motioning her to lay her head back on the pillow. He covered her up to the neck with a sheet. Then he saw her flowers. He crossed her hands on her chest, plucked a rose from the bouquet, and stuck it between her fingers. He laid the bouquet at her feet.

"Don't play dead...its bad publicity," he said as he wheeled her off to a long corridor.

"How did you ever get the name, Starlight Express?" Kathy asked as she watched the ceiling go by.

"Don't know. Emily nicknamed me. It just stuck. I kind of like it. She had nicknames for everybody. Remember Nurse Cutter? We used to call her Nurse Clutter...because her desk was always such a mess. Emily named her. We had the German boy who broke both legs. No one could pronounce his name correctly and he used to get angry until Emily named him Rainbow, which sounded pretty close. He liked that. He colored the picture of the rainbow himself and we hung it behind his bed. Sure do miss that gal." They stopped to let a group of patients get by.

"Starlight Express! I know that name from somewhere," Kathy said. "It's a good name. If I find out, I'll let you know."

They passed through two large doors and the orderly closed them behind him. She glanced up and saw that they were in a long corridor. Starlight Express told her she could get up now and walk the rest of the way. The applause began when her feet touched the floor and she walked quickly to the large assembly of medical personnel who were gowned and waiting. She appeared to be in a surgical teaching room. Robby and Kami were the first to greet her. Her father said that everyone there had a medical purpose, had seen lots of naked bodies and to not be embarrassed about anything. She said she didn't think that she would be. Kami said he and Robby would be waiting in the lounge for her.

"What's going on with you and Nancy?" Kathy said while winking at Robby. She turned and met her examiners.

* * * * *

Another masterful edition of the American News was quickly

bought out and the presses were still making copies to re-fill the empty racks and newsstands. The paper owners left their semi-retired life to deal with the profitable business opportunities that this story presented. The *big boys* from the networks and TV, in general, were annoyed with the agreements that they were being forced to sign to obtain information. It was nothing more than an agreement to present facts accurately and balanced, a claim that they usually make when accused of bias anyway. The American News didn't see it as a problem. What the media did with the information after it was presented as *news* was unrestricted. Editors could print anything they wanted to, and talking heads could say whatever was on their mind. However, they would do it on the editorial page or on TV programs that were not presented as *news*.

Kathy's computer had provided a list of radio programs and segments that provided *news*. The same applied to television. The list was quite comprehensive as it contained information on all frequencies in the broadcast bands, worldwide. Most complained, but signed.

Printed information was more easily handled. News was on the front page and editorials on the editorial page. American News did not restrict the weeklies as the events were happening too rapidly for them to form and alter opinions. The tabloids decided to work outside of the system, using their own resources. American News was delighted with their decision as they felt they would not keep their agreements in any event.

* * * * *

Lewis Anderson made sure that Kanisha had his mobile phone number memorized. He had a list of all the phone-numbers and contacts that she would be relying on during her arrest and jail visit. He didn't like the fact that it was Saturday. Things could go wrong on the weekend. She assured him that she could take care of herself.

He didn't like the idea of her using his car, but agreed that she needed it to go to the place where she was to be arrested. He checked that he had the spare set of keys and where to pick the car up...if there was anything left of it. He leaned over and gave her a kiss when she dropped him in front of SuperCee.

His first problem was getting in the building. There was a cipher lock to electrically open the door. He didn't have the combination. There was an unfamiliar security guard. No one else was entering or leaving. He explained his situation to the guard. The guard checked his book and didn't find his name on the list. The guard made a phone-call and waited for a call back. He waited five minutes and was getting antsy. Five minutes more of waiting and he was thinking about getting a taxi and going back to Kanisha's apartment and call the whole thing off. Mr. Hudson opened the door from the inside and let him in.

He said he was surprised to see him on a Saturday morning since the company worked a five-day week. Lewis wanted to show him the outline he had been working on, but Hudson said he was busy now. Lewis suggested meeting for lunch and Hudson said he never ate lunch. He said he'd see him on Monday, maybe, if he had time and went to his office and closed the door.

Lewis went to his new office to work on his project. The door was locked and he recalled leaving it unlocked when he left. The key Chad gave him opened it. He tried the other key he had copied. It also worked. He checked his phone and it worked. Briggs answered. Lewis said he was sorry; he must have dialed the wrong number. He remembered what Larry told him about the phone monitoring that went on here. He called Briggs back on his portable. He said he was at work and worried about Kanisha. Briggs told him not to worry; he was also aware of her plans. He told Lewis to meet him at his house for dinner on Sunday for some very interesting information.

* * * * *

There was a full day's work for the computer crew. Larry had to get a mainframe on line with the help of a team of technicians from the company that leased it. The master bedroom upstairs was a nice quiet place to organize all of the output from the printers. The living room was made into a meeting room with two long tables and a dozen chairs. Victor took the small guest room downstairs with attached bath, was out of the way, and had some privacy. He arranged all of the new clothes that he had picked up from Sammy The Tailor in the morning.

He helped where he could, but was better at watching TV and informing the team of how things were going. Some of the kid's programs were pre-empted for news of God's press conference. Politicians, clergy, celebrities, authorities of one sort or another were making their evaluations. On one channel Victor heard a spokesman for one of the religious groups calling Kathy's comments "blasphemous" and told the audience where they could find the event prophesied; chapter and verse, in the Bible. Send in your money to support the new religious information highway that his church was sponsoring. Victor kind of liked the guy's style. As he was shown on some other station's film clips, Victor began imitating him. The others heard him a few more times, and by noon everyone was repeating the phrase, "Just a few more dollars, folks, and we'll have this information highway on line."

Nancy was getting some seriously heavy phone-calls. There were a number of calls that she screened out for Kami and Kathy. The DA's office...urgent. Both State Senators phoned in wanting their calls returned. Many, many clergymen wanted a call back. The State Department of Health...sounded very serious and official. The FBI, sending an agent...request utmost cooperation. Actually, the agents, two of them, had already arrived and were permitted through the roadblock.

They waited outside in their car, although they had been invited to come inside and wait for Kathy's return. Nancy told Larry that the FBI must not let their people watch TV since they were probably the only two people in town that didn't know she was being examined today.

* * * * *

Kathy recognized Dr. Clancy even with his mask on. His voice was still familiar to her as he explained what was going to happen here today. He was the director, would get her through this ordeal

155

as quickly and painlessly as possible, and assured her that only the routine Lab work, for blood samples would cause any pain at all. Moveable x-ray machines were standing by to take their pictures as soon as she was gowned properly by the surgical staff. He said everyone would leave the room for that, then she would have the Lab specimens, and then a thorough visual and audio exam. She nodded that she understood.

A female attendant ushered her to a small room just outside a pair of doors, and she changed into a surgical gown. She was handed a plastic container with a lid, a roll of paper towels, and instructed to, "Leave it on the shelf." The attendant said her things were safe there and left the room. When Kathy was ready, they returned to the main room to begin the x-rays. She recognized Dr. Edwards also, and he came to her and asked if she could help with a problem that they were having. It seems that the hospital released all of her original dental records to her family dentist. He has been located and will be here with all of his records for the last couple of years. The service that stores and maintains his files has been unable to locate the originals. Kathy said she thought she had them at home. Dr. Edwards spoke to another gowned and masked physician and said very sternly that they would finish the dental exam, " Here, today, quickly." He and Dr. Clancy guided her to the table in the center of the room and introduced her to the x-ray technicians. Everyone filed out, leaving the three of them alone. The pair worked efficiently and professionally and was finished in less than five minutes.

Someone was summoned in and left quickly with a box on wheels. The last machine was rolled back and Kathy was told she could sit up.

More technicians came in and attached all kinds of stuff to her, her blood pressure was measured, her temperature taken, her oxygen level measured; gadgets and probes of all kinds were placed on her body. She barely felt the pinprick at her elbow and saw her blood running into the sampling tube when she had the nerve to look. It seemed that they were taking a lot. The needle was withdrawn after the cotton swab was pressed on it and her arm raised to hold it in position.

All of the stuff was taken from her and she was asked to breathe into a machine and she did that. Next came some equipment for an eye exam, which she liked doing. No problem with that. Everyone was quiet as the doctor performed the exam. When he finished the check for glaucoma, he looked at her and smiled. "Twenty-twenty," he announced, turned off his machine, and left the room. The Lab personnel had all departed and Dr. Clancy returned with perhaps thirty gowned and gloved physicians.

As she was led again to the table in the center of the room, Kathy saw x-rays being clipped to the viewing boxes and some of the members moved closer to see them. "Unbelievable! This is not the same person," she heard a female voice say loudly. A few more members turned to look at the x-rays.

"Please keep the noise down and your attention focused on the patient," Dr. Clancy said professionally.

Dr. Edwards added, "Please keep your opinions to yourself until the examination is completed." A hush fell over the group and all eyes were directed to the patient in the center of the room.

Kathy was assisted onto the table by Dr. Clancy and told to lie back. He removed the top portion of her gown and folded it across her abdomen. There was an inrush of air amongst the viewing members who expected to see *some* scarring, not a perfectly formed, unblemished solarplexus.

Dr. Clancy opened his clipboard and began speaking into a microphone to record the proceeding. "Patient: Kathryn Makino. Female. Age, twenty-three. Height, sixty-five inches. Weight: One hundred and twelve pounds. Hair: black. Eyes: blue. Father: Japanese descent, living. Mother: Irish descent, deceased.

"Patient treated at General Hospital following automobile accident...."

Dr. Clancy continued in clinical detail, describing each injury that she received, what treatment was provided and the name of the physician who provided it. It was quite a lengthy report by the time he got to the point where she was released to him for recovery and maintenance. Dr. Edwards interrupted and said that in view of the nature of the injuries it was only common sense to halt at that point in her recovery. He suggested that since all of the current x-rays were posted and some of the Lab work completed, that they be examined and then to continue with Kathy. While they were doing that, the dental exam would be accomplished. No one commented.

Dr. Clancy replaced her gown and said she could sit up. She did and then she was helped off the table and there was a mix-up. The dentist wanted her back on the table, as his new equipment needed her in a prone position, if possible. Kathy recognized her dentist and said hello to him. She asked him why he wasn't wearing his Groucho Marx glasses and fake nose. He asked her why she wasn't wearing her fillings and the crown...as he heard on TV. They both laughed. He told her to open up and she could not talk more. His equipment clicked a few times and he asked her to open again. He did it again and then asked her what happened to her fillings. She said she threw them in the wastebasket.

He asked her to open wide. He directed one of the surgery lights into her open mouth and he checked around with a mirror and dental pick. He really worked on the front tooth, tapping and picking away. He selected another tool from his kit and probed under her gum. He checked a chart he had with him and did some more picking and tapping. He was finished and put his things away. He said she had perfect choppers and hoped his other patients didn't do the same thing or he'd be out of a job. He filled out a form, signed it, and passed it to Dr. Edwards. He said he had a patient in a great deal of pain and had to leave but wanted to talk more to Kathy. She said she would call him.

Most of the doctors had finished looking at the x-rays. A few were back on the other side of the room re-examining her original x-rays. Dr. Clancy helped Kathy to sit on the table and called for resumption of the examination. He asked a colleague to perform a reflex test on her legs and when that was completed, he asked her to perform a series of twisting and bending movements of all her limbs and body. He asked Kathy if she had any pain anywhere in her body or any discomfort when she made any of the required movements. She replied that she was quite free of pain and what a relief it was. She volunteered that she was taking no medication of any kind. She said the stretching actually felt good.

Dr. Clancy asked if there were any more tests that needed to be done. If not, he would accept questions for the patient to answer...confined to *medical* questions.

A doctor identified himself as Chief of the Psychiatric Department. He wanted to know, for the record, what her family history was concerning mental health. Kathy laughed and said, "My father's crazy," and was joined by the crowd.

The doctor said aloud, "For the record, no problems noted."

A doctor identifying himself as a Pediatrician asked if she had ever used drugs other than those prescribed by a qualified doctor, including alcohol, marijuana, or tobacco. Again, for the record.

Kathy thought a bit and admitted that she tried smoking cigarettes a couple of times. Then she added, "For the record, put down that I didn't inhale!"

A doctor identified himself as Internal Medicine, said he was having trouble phrasing his question but thought it legitimate. Dr. Clancy told him to give it a try.

"Well, OK. Here goes. You said you *invited* God into your life some time before the recovery. Do I have that right? And the way I heard it, you were depressed at the time...at the time you made the *invitation*. OK. Here's my question. I think it has medical significance. Do you think there is a connection between being depressed and a decision to make the *invitation* you spoke of?"

Dr. Clancy said she need not answer if she didn't want to.

Kathy wanted to reply. "This is the type of question I love. *Think* about what you've just said. When you are depressed, you've already exhausted every solution to the problem you think faces you. If you had the right answer, you wouldn't be depressed any longer, would you? You are depressed because the answers that your ego are presenting are everything other than the one I suggested, and none of them work. Have you tried my solution to the problem yet? No. So you are still depressed because your ego is strong and holding out hope that maybe it can think up some other things that won't work either. The stronger your ego is, the longer it is going to take, the deeper the depression; and more chaos, injury and destruction.

"Finally, a little bell comes on inside, when you are *really* depressed, and you say, 'this is it, I can't go on like this any longer,' and you *decide* to give it a try.

"Hello! I'm not depressed anymore.

"I think if you try my idea *first*, like so many millions of people out there have already figured out, you won't have reason to be depressed in the first place.

"How that fits into the medical equation, I don't know. How many healthy, happy, productive, people are you treating? Perhaps it could be a part of your preventive medicine practice. Instead of 'take two aspirins and call me in the morning,' you might suggest that they spend a moment or two with their Creator and call you when they break a leg skiing, or to replace some skin they lost while sliding into third base.

"I think that was a good question because it led to my present condition."

Kathy received a warm applause. Dr. Clancy suggested that they had run out of time and that he felt the medical information was more than adequate. One more waving hand was allowed a question. "Was she going to get a scan?"

Dr. Edwards said it was a waste of energy and resources to give a perfectly healthy young lady a scan when others who needed it were waiting. He adjourned the examination. Kathy dressed and walked with Drs. Clancy and Edwards to join Robby and her father.

160

Chapter 14

It was common knowledge on the streets that you did not conduct business in front of a certain fast-food chain store. The manager/owner was influential in local politics and he wanted a wholesome, family image for his business. The food was good, plenty of it, inexpensive and a favorite eating place for policemen. For a hundred dollars, Kanisha had arranged for a new friend of hers to meet a certain police officer for lunch there.

Kanisha waited in Lewis' car on the street where he could find it later. She waited about twenty minutes after she saw the patrol car park in the lot, and went to work. The restaurant was on a corner and the occupants inside had a nice, open view while eating. There was some activity on a Saturday afternoon. A lot of guys were leaving the office after catching up on the previous week's work. The ball games hadn't started yet. Most of the lounges were closed in preparation for the big night ahead. Kanisha learned quickly from the other girls how to keep from having a "date". She priced herself out of the market. From all appearances, she was actively soliciting.

The manager noticed her first. He was about to call into the station when he saw that he had a patrolman right there in his restaurant. He walked to the booth and pointed to the offender outside and asked if he would mind telling her to take her business somewhere else. The officer said he would take care of it, and was just about finished eating. The manager took the lunch bill and said it was, "on the house." His *date* complained that the girl on the street was new in town and making it tough on everyone. She told him she was very aggressive, but heard that she needed money badly. She made a date to meet him when he got off work and left by a side exit. The officer went outside, observed Kanisha waving down a car with a solitary male driver, and arrested her. Halfway to the station, after he reported in with the arrest information, he pulled into an unused parking lot. He told her that if she cooperated with him, he could make her life a lot easier. She listened to what he had to say, which verified what she had already been told. He took out

161

a business card and offered it to her. In return, she was to be available for free sex. She took the card. He asked her if they had a thorough understanding and she said they did. He advised her to be straight with the guy whose card she had and listen to what he had to say. He asked her where she could be reached in the future and she reached in her purse and found Lewis' new phone-number at SuperCee. She said that it was OK to talk to him and he would know how to find her.

He left the lot and continued in to the station. On the way, he told her that she had a lot of class and, if she worked with him, she could do all right for herself. He asked if she was interested in working some parties for him. He said it was big bucks and not the penny-ante streets. He told her about some of the girls that he had helped to move up the ladder of success. Some even got lucky and married the Johns. As he took her from the car at the station, she took hold of his hand and gave it a squeeze. She said she liked him and would keep her end of the bargain.

She was allowed to make her phone-call and then booked. The process was unpleasant, but she remembered all of the phony numbers and addresses and got through the ordeal. She was seated beside a clerk who was taking down information from her when a man in a smart, brown suit asked for Kenya. She raised her hand and saw the smile when he looked her over. He introduced himself to the clerk as "counsel" and handed her a set of forms to type. The clerk pulled out the paper she had been typing on and inserted his and began typing. He motioned Kenya to stand. He took her aside where they could talk privately in the busy office, only half-staffed today. He looked her over thoroughly and the first thing he said to her was that he was impressed and asked why she was on the street. She related her well-rehearsed story about her mother's illness and the need for money. He asked her if she had any money and she replied no. He gave her five twenties and directions to his offices. He said everything had been arranged for her release and to be at the address in two hours. He had another appointment. If he wasn't there when she arrived, to wait. If she skipped, he promised her she would do hard time. She promised to be there.

She was back on the street before Lewis had finished his chores

162

and come to pick up the car, so she sat in it and waited. She went to a liquor store and picked up a couple of newspapers to read. She hadn't completed reading the American News' lead story with Kanisha Porter's by-line, when Lewis arrived by taxi to pick up his car. "Chickened out...eh?" was what he said when he saw her in the car.

"No. Mission complete. Crime committed, arrested, charged, booked, hearing date set, bail set, bail met, released. On the street in less than two hours. We have a very efficient system...all computerized except for some legal forms, but I'll bet they change that soon." Kanisha rattled off the experience, which was still fresh in her mind.

She had Lewis write down the arresting officer's name to refer to later if he called for her. She explained about that. She told of the upcoming meeting with the attorney who arranged her release. They decided to go and have some lunch while Lewis filled her in on what he had been doing. He gave her a ten-page outline on superconductivity, and some pictures he clipped from science magazines lying about in SuperCee. Kanisha looked at it and after the first page told him that it would never do. She told him again that he should stick to news and that she would take it to the Chron and have it pumped up.

They were early for Kanisha's appointment when Lewis drove by the downtown office. She said she wanted to get it over with. Lewis parked a block away and she walked to the Law Offices, which opened into a small lobby. No one was at the reception desk. She located the name and office of the attorney on the directory and took the elevator to the third floor. It opened onto a very attractive office complex and she was greeted by a bespectacled, well-dressed, jewelry-covered woman, who looked as though she had just come from the beauty parlor. Kanisha handed her the card and said her name was Kenya. She was asked to take a seat and Mr. Scalia would see her shortly. A very attractive blonde was already seated and waiting. She could not have been more than twenty, but she looked about thirty. Very high mileage.

The blonde stared straight ahead, moving her position frequently and seemed to have a lot of anxiety. Her hands were locked tightly in her lap. Her nose seemed to be bothering her as she rubbed it every thirty seconds or so with her index finger. Her clothes seemed new, but apparently they hadn't been laundered lately. Kenya's name was called and the receptionist pointed her toward a corridor. "Second office," she said and handed her a bright yellow folder to take with her. She found the office and the door open. The attorney signed some papers, and motioned her to close the door. He took the folder from her and opened it, telling her to sit down.

"Your story checks, but we can't seem to locate a history on you. No priors, the court record is clean. Can you explain that...it's unusual?"

"I'm not stupid...until today, at least. I'm not used to the streets. Oh, I can handle myself. Most of the Vice guys will let you go for a little action. Especially if you have some class. I got away from that for the last couple of years. I got in with the right circle of friends. Nice people, good parties, travel, a week out on a yacht...huge, man," Kanisha sounded very convincing as she stretched her arms way out, displaying a very nice pair under her tight stretch jersey.

"Then my mother had a gall bladder go bad and I tapped out for the operation. She had complications and no one else to care for her so I came back home. I guess you could say I *over-extended* myself. That's what my business friends are talking about these days. Don't *over-extend*.

"So, I'm over-extended and hit the streets. I made a mistake. It won't happen again. I can pay you off in three to four days, including the hundred you loaned me. Don't worry; I pay my bills. Is that what you wanted to see me about?"

"No. I think I have a better solution. How much care does your mother require? What I'm asking is can you leave town...maybe for a week?"

"Yeah, if I had the money to hire a sitter. Someone who can get her meals. She can't get out of bed and walk around. Another couple of weeks and she should be fine. A grand would cover her for a month. I can make that in one good weekend."

The attorney looked her over and agreed with her.

'So, when you worked at a higher level before. Tell me how it worked. Did you have a pimp? Who made the dates? Who did you work for?"

"Another girl got me started. I did a few parties with her and her friends liked me. I sort of became a regular. But it was too infrequent, and didn't always pay well. I was always having to borrow money from the other girl. She just told me one day that I was "in". She gave me a beeper and I had a phone-number to call when I wanted work. I heard it was a small-time operation run by some night club owner," Kanisha bluffed her way through the interview.

Mr. Scalia asked her if she wanted to work for him. He said it was her chance for the "golden ring" if she would join his organization. He said she would have complete protection. She could not work the street or run something on the side. She would answer the phone, do as she was told, and work for tips only until she finished her apprenticeship. All her living expenses would be paid, including travel.

He said he understood about her mother, but these things happen. He would advance her the money if she could leave for Baltimore this evening. There was a shortage reported.

She asked him about the apprenticeship. How long did that take? He said it varied. If she were as good as she looked, it wouldn't take long. He said that they just wanted to be sure they had class people working for them. He said *reputation* was extremely important. Next to *performance*. He re-phrased his presentation, "We guarantee satisfaction."

She said she did also and accepted the job. She had to wait nearly another half-hour until she was given a packet of instructions and a thousand dollars...cash. Her airline ticket would be waiting at the airport. The well-dressed receptionist said all the information was inside.

The blonde was on the verge of tears when Kanisha left the office.

* * * * *

There was a meeting in the new house late Saturday afternoon. Kathy, Kami, and Robby had returned. Larry and his crew had everything under control and were wondering if they had to work on Sunday. Kathy said, "If the Bible is correct, God will rest tomorrow. So should we."

Robby offered that no medical information could be released until the Makino's read it and that was going to be Monday morning. He said that the FBI agents were here to verify that a match-up had been made with Kathy's application for a driving license and the fingerprints on the glass that was turned over to the DA. However, there had been no crime committed that was under their jurisdiction to investigate, and they did not release the information. Professor Makino authorized them to release the information to Gordon Briggs at American News and they were headed his way now, so that it might be reported tonight on the news.

Kathy thanked them for their support and for everyone to get some rest for the coming week. She wanted to spend some time with her father who needed a massage for his stiff neck and was interested in the race results, if anyone knew where to find out. Nancy recalled that she could obtain racing information on the computer and went looking through the paper to see how to do it. She found the number to call and went over to Kathy's computer to set it up for her.

Victor got permission to move the rest of his belongings in Kami's van. Kathy said she had better show him how to operate it because it had been modified for her. She and Victor walked to the van. He said her idea didn't work. He tried to relax and did everything she told him to do, but he fell asleep and woke up this morning. Kathy told him to try it again. She said she had no luck with her problem either, probably because her mind was spinning with new, exciting information.

* * * * *

"The van is leaving with only Victor in it. It stopped in the middle of the street. The van is jerking. It stopped again. He's

166

making a U-turn. Stopped again. It's backing up. Whoa! Did you see that? He almost hit the girl! Kathy is talking to Victor again. She's going back to the house. The van is jerking again. OK, it's coming this way. Kathy is back in the house." The fat man was talking into a recorder.

The cameraman asked if anyone got the license number of the van. "Yeah, I got it. What for?" the small man asked.

"If I see that sucker coming towards me, I'm getting the hell out of the way!"

The big man again, "Where are they? I say both disks are in the other house."

Cameraman, "I agree."

Little man, "Too early to tell. Nancy went to the other house. You said she had a paper. The disk could be in the paper. She returned without the paper. You screw up a heist now, you'll never get a second chance."

Big man, "Hudson's nuts. Wants to know the odds for hitting the safe, like, four in the morning. The guards are unarmed. Maybe six guys barge in, grab the safe, put it in a fast truck and hike out the back streets."

Little man, "I agree."

Cameraman, "Not a chance. The guards have radios. How do you get the truck in? What if the safe is alarmed? What if it's *bolted* down. You lost track of all the different workers that went in there. The lock company took a toolbox in. You don't need a toolbox to deliver a safe. What if the disks are in the *computers* and not in the safe...?"

Big man to little man, "That's what we got you for. You check to see if they are in the computers."

"No. No. No. I don't go in on the heist. My job is to tell you anything you want to know about computers. *Information*, not part of a half-assed team of SWAT rejects," the little man said.

Big man, "I thought you said you agreed."

Little man, "I said I agreed with you; Hudson's nuts."

Big man, "Robby and Nancy leaving together in her car. Anybody remember how he arrived in the morning? Larry, leaving on foot. He doesn't live too far away, right? Remind me to call and see if he wants a tail on Larry. Now the two temps are leaving. Marcie and Shirley...getting in Shirley's car."

Cameraman, "I'd like to put a tail on that Shirley one time."

Big man, "Kathy and the professor returning to their residence. Anyone left in the house?"

Cameraman, "Now is the time to hit it. Silencers. Two guards down. Walk in, check the joint out, take what you came for, and walk out whistling."

Little man, "You've been watching too many movies."

Big man, "Shift change. Here comes the sheriff with the posse."

* * * * *

Larry had wanted to stay for the race results, but Kami told him to go home to his family and he would keep him posted on the results. Kami and Kathy were sitting at her computer and Nancy had the race information on the screen. This wasn't a spectator-sport. This was numbers, percentages, odds, and results. Maybe a spectator-sport for accountants. Kami explained what the numbers represented, but all Kathy perceived was that there was a lot of money moving around.

At the track, the Commissioner was concerned. He personally inspected the track. His aides had all checked in with their findings. Everything he could think of had been examined and there was no sign of wrongdoing. Vegas was as surprised as he was, but not concerned, volume was up. There had been a couple of bigger than normal winners because some favorites were not performing, but no repeaters. He was pleased with the meeting that the jockeys had. They were concerned about their jobs and their leader promised the commissioner that they were not involved and would do everything possible to run clean races.

Kami had analyzed God's picks pretty well. Most were favored to win. All had been turning in good times. He didn't agree with the fifth race. The favored horse had very good times and should finish well in the lead, by his reckoning. The eighth race looked like it was going to be a race. Three horses had very similar records.

The numbers scrambled on the screen as the computer updated the results of the first race. Kami quickly analyzed the numbers and told Kathy, "One for God." Kathy said she was bored. An advertisement ran across the screen with the frequency for the radio station that was broadcasting the races live. She got her little portable and tuned it in. Much better. She called Larry to let him know he had won the first race and gave him the radio station frequency that he could listen to. When she returned from the kitchen with a snack Kami told her, "Two for God."

Kathy stayed interested through the third and fourth races. She found the liniment that her father used to massage her feet and legs and gave him a neck and shoulders massage. The radio announcer agreed with her father when he was giving his commentary on the odds and the favorites for this race. Kami showed her on the screen where all the money was being placed. The large majority on one horse to win and the rest scattered throughout the field. He looked at God's choice and checked the numbers. A good, solid performer, but outclassed in this race. He crossed his fingers as the announcer described what was happening and his opinions of the probable winner. "And they're off. A good, clean start…."

Kami had his ear close to the speaker and pointing to God's horse on the monitor. The announcer informed the listeners in a fast, but clear voice, "…into the first turn, Jim Dandy by a length, running strong as expected. Neck and neck behind, looks like…Oooh, dear god! Jim Dandy! This is terrible, folks. Oh god, Jim Dandy's thrown his jockey. Oh no! Jim Dandy is down! No. He's clear. He's up! Vern. Vern Hopkins…the jockey, is clear of the track. He's down now. Definitely hurt. Jim Dandy's pulled up.

"It looks like Melody in the lead coming out of the turn on the back rail. Melody by a half. Satan's Pleasure pushing on the outside. Jim Dandy under control. His trainers have him. Vern is down, but clear of the track. Midway through the turn, its Melody, loosing some to Satan's Pleasure, the pack too close to call. It's still anybody's race. Melody falling off the pace, Irish Summer breaking from the pack, coming on strong. Satan's Pleasure in the lead. Irish Summer challenging. It's Satan's Pleasure holding the lead. A race to the wire. Satan's Pleasure, Irish Summer, Melody. Satan's

Pleasure giving ground. Irish Summer coming. Irish Summer! Wait until its official before throwing those Jim Dandy tickets away, folks. Very close at the wire, but this announcer is calling it Irish Summer. Let's take a short commercial break and I'll come right back and fill you in on the terrible spill we just witnessed here."

"Five for God," Kami said. "Call Larry again."

"What for? He's listening too. This is boring...I'm going upstairs to my room. A lot of new information came in on the computer for me to read."

"Boring? This is exciting! Who would have ever expected that to happen? The favorite, pulling up lame and dumping the jockey like that." Kami tried to talk her into staying up and keeping him company.

"Daddy, that's dumb. You *know* who is going to win. I think you have an ego problem. Did they tell you at the hospital that I said you were crazy?" Kathy asked.

"No. No one mentioned it to me. You told them I was crazy? Like mentally unbalanced? Wait a minute...the next race is about to start."

Kathy rubbed his neck, gave him a kiss, and said goodnight. "Crazy. I told them you were crazy. I was right," she smiled as she departed. Kami never heard her as he concentrated on the race.

She had just gotten in bed and adjusted the light to read her manual when she heard him screaming and running up the stairs. "He did it! Eight for eight! Kathy! Can I come in? Eight for eight!" He opened the door to tell her the results. "Do you know what the pay-off is? I figured it roughly over eight hundred thousand. We can pay all our bills! Aren't you happy?"

"Yes, Daddy. I'm happy that I have a crazy father. Why don't *you* call Larry now. Now that you have something to say. I want to get some required reading done; I think this is a little more important, OK?"

After Kami went downstairs, she read for about an hour. She turned off the light and walked to the window. She looked across the street and saw the glare of the TV. She thought about the feelings she got when she danced with Victor. She went back to

170

bed, turned on the light, and read some more. There was nothing about holy relationships in her new instructions.

* * * * *

Kanisha Porter's flight was nearly empty and she chose a seat over the wing. She read the articles she "wrote" several times. She wondered how she ever got herself involved in a situation like this. Was she being immature and wanting some excitement? Was she overgenerous in repaying Briggs for the favors she owed him? Maybe she was overly ambitious? No. She didn't know she'd be given credit when she accepted the job. She took it because, one, she owed Briggs, and two, because she liked and respected Lewis. She should have asked more questions. Yes, that was her problem; she never asked enough questions.

Here she was, halfway to Baltimore, a place she had never been before, in the middle of the night, a hastily-thrown-together bag of the most whorish looking clothes she could find in her wardrobe. She should have listened to Lewis's objections and told Briggs that the job was just too dangerous. She could be in a nice warm bed with Lewis right now instead of on the way to meet some creep who was going to try to make some money with her body. And Scalia...*slime-ball* is a compliment. And the ex-vice cop. And the police station booking. Slime. What was she thinking of?

She took out a pencil and underlined the direct quotes in the American News article. It was a habit of hers. She liked to try to figure out what else was in the same paragraph that had been omitted. Oh, oh. Briggs tricked her. Yes. There were some quotes on the front-page that seemed to make the major points. For the speed-readers. But on page four there was a word-for-word record of the hospital press conference. She read it. She was impressed. Lewis was right. Kathy was for real. Quite an idea, *inviting* God into your life.

She decided to give it a try. She made herself comfortable, put her head back on the airline seat, closed her eyes, and relaxed. She envisioned the plane breaking through the cloud of problems that surrounded her and asked God to tell her what to do. She listened

171

and she *knew* why she was doing this. It had nothing to do with Briggs or Lewis. She was doing this for her sisters. For the black and white females who had to work in the world's oldest profession. Women who never had the opportunity or the ability to go to college, or even finish high school. That was what this was all about. Only she could do it. That's why she was chosen. She had the looks, she had the street smarts ever since she was a teen-ager.

She opened her eyes and was alert. She was going to expose the bastards who were oppressing her sisters. Will this plane go any faster?

Chapter 15

Out West, a man wearing a suit similar to Victor's was reading the Los Angeles Times, which was readily available in Las Vegas. The pilot informed him that they were at a cruising altitude of thirty five thousand feet and that the stewards would be serving drinks in just a few minutes. He mentioned that the weather was forecast to be beautiful in Kathy's hometown and for everyone who loved Kathy to raise their hand and the airline would provide a complimentary drink. The man raised his hand, although he was carrying half a million dollars in his carry-on bag.

The Kathy story intrigued him and he read it entirely. He thought Kathy reminded him of his daughter. He hoped she would turn out the same way. It was tough raising kids in Las Vegas these days. Too many undesirables were drawn by the gambling action and, now, with the druggies, it wasn't a nice place to live anymore. Moving large amounts of gambling money around was a respectable job. It was hard work, long hours, unscheduled and carried a lot of responsibility. The airport security employees certainly respected him. When he turned his gun in for transportation in the hold, he wasn't even asked to show his permit. They even sent someone along to protect him until he got to his boarding gate.

He checked the name and address of the big winner. Lorenzo Garcia. Damned Mexicans. They jump the line, work for peanuts and hit the big jackpots. But, then, they spend a lot on gambling. Only people worse were the Orientals. Been paying a lot of them off lately. He was refreshing himself on the new information that the attorney for the casinos had presented at the seminar for a pay-off like the present case. He thought he had it down pat. The Internal Revenue Service rules were certainly unfair to the mind of a risk-taker. No matter who won, they won. They took no risk at all. The casinos took some risk, as in the present case, but the odds were in their favor...it was not a sure thing.

The name Lorenzo Garcia came to mind again and he was sure that the guy was not going to want to withhold a portion for taxes.

He was taking the money and heading back to Mexico. If he were a working taxpayer, he'd have played the money above board at the track or with a licensed house. The computer checked him out. A new player. Just got lucky. He'd be back home in time to see his daughter's tennis match. She'd really come a long way since he hired the new instructor.

* * * * *

Gordon Briggs' wife was upset when he canceled their night out at the Elks. She accepted his explanation that he had received new, significant information and had to rewrite the all-important Sunday edition. This had not happened many times before and he did have a good story going. Also, he'd been very thoughtful of her lately. She decided to watch TV and wait up for him. Maybe have some of his favorite homemade brownies when he got home.

After talking to the FBI and signing for the fingerprint report, he was in a quandary as to what to do with the information. It was a technical problem due to the time frame. The large Sunday paper was waiting to be printed by the press foreman. He called the owner for suggestions. Together, they decided to roll the presses and insert an update by hand. Old fashioned, but no other way to do it. So, Gordon Briggs was finally one step ahead of TV!

He called in the night shift supervisor and told him the story. He told him to assign as many people as he could find to put together a one-page supplement. It had to be absolutely accurate, clear, and concise. Load it with appropriate pictures, and it had to be ready in an hour and a half or they would miss the trucks taking out the first loads. He told him to start immediately. Then he called the rest of his team to let them know the change in routine. He could hear the presses rolling in the background when he called the shop foreman. It sounded good.

By the time the big boys had their big guns blasting away for their canned weekly show, the American News had verification from the FBI that Kathy's fingerprints *were* Kathy's. There were some religious programs already filmed and ready to be broadcast that were still not convinced of Kathy's recovery. Some TV ministers had worked all week on their Sunday speeches. One preacher had spent two whole days researching the Bible for anything that was *blasphemous*. He really liked that word and wanted to work it into his presentation as many times as he could. They should hear the first TV reports just before they go on the air. The week ahead would be very interesting to watch.

Briggs thought as he waited for the supplement to be written and laid out. It suddenly dawned on him. "God is going to have a press conference!" he exclaimed. He called in one of the night clerks.

"Telephone all department heads. There will be a very important meeting here, in this office, at ten-o'clock in the morning. No one is excused. Call my secretary and have her here, also."

* * * * *

Kanisha was inspired and excited when she met her contact in Baltimore. The well-dressed man came to the room that she was provided in one of the major, downtown hotels. He leered at her while explaining the ground rules. He said she got in too late, but tomorrow would be a good day. He asked if she had any preferences, but explained that they were really short on girls and she would have to take whatever came up. Kanisha said she wanted "top dollar" and no "coke parties". She needed money badly. She was reminded that she was working for tips.

"No drugs. I just say no to drugs," Kanisha said firmly.

"Whatever comes up," the man said, leaving.

Kanisha waited until she thought he would be gone, went downstairs and got a taxi. She was glad that Lewis put the money into her account. She could use the automatic teller and not have to walk around with a lot of cash. A few minutes later, the taxi dropped her off on a wide street that had very little traffic. She took the driver's card, said, "Seven. Sharp", closed the door, and didn't pay him anything. She walked over to join her sisters. She was glad she brought her flesh colored pantyhose and a short, sexy jacket. It was cold.

The taxi driver admired her long legs and thought she was a

pretty friendly hooker as she walked through the lights of his vehicle. He was sure going to enjoy some of that at seven in the morning, after a long night's work. "Been a long time since I changed my luck," he said to himself.

Kanisha introduced herself to the others, explaining that she was new in town. They gave her a thorough briefing on how to stay out of trouble, and advised her to move on, as there was nothing happening this evening. All of the big-spenders were at the political meeting. They weren't there because they were not pretty enough, classy enough, or educated enough. Kanisha moved on to speak with others on corners, sometimes in groups, sometimes to a single girl. They were all tough on the outside, but she could see the fear, tension and lack of self-respect inside. This was a dangerous, short-lived, and degrading occupation.

By four in the morning she decided she was not going to find what she had hoped for...a stand in. None of the girls she met could possibly double for her. The others were right. The ones out here tonight were not in demand. Many were going hungry tomorrow. Some others were going to struggle through until tomorrow night without their fixes.

She went back to the hotel and took a shower. The phone rang. She answered it and the caller was angry, wanting to know where she had been. She said she got something to eat, and took a shower. He told her he had bad news. She had a date for brunch at eleven. She wasn't going to like it. She asked why not and the caller laughed and hung up after telling her to be in her room at ten thirty.

* * * * *

Big man, "Nancy's car returning. Rabinowitz getting out. Nancy. Going inside the residence. The professor greeting them. Light still on upstairs."

Cameraman, "How much longer are we gonna' stay here? Man, my eyes hurt."

Big man, "Until it's quiet. I was ready to call-it-a-day before this came up. If they leave and Victor is still in the other house,

176

we'll go. We were supposed to get some relief, but he can't find anybody he trusts. Nice to know we're wanted."

Cameraman, "Got someone coming on the sidewalk. Off to the right. Let me adjust the light level...yeah, Larry. Got Larry returning on foot. Something up?"

Little man, "I'm checking out. I'll be in at six in the morning. I can cover with the binoculars. You can tell Hudson, for me, a heist isn't going to work. I think we need to get someone inside. These disks are light, they're small, and I think, loosely guarded. The smartest way is to pull a switch. If I follow this story right, they'll never know the difference. One day they work and the next they don't and Hudson has his superconductors. This Dick Tracy shit is a waste of time."

Big man, "I'm beginning to agree with you. The new roadblocks over on Cherry and Walnut to keep people out...no way to get *our* people out."

Cameraman, "Lots of ways. Stash the stuff here, for example. Cut the chain link fence and go out through the woods. Easy for a 4 X 4. A helicopter!"

Little man, "You been watching too many movies again. See you in the morning."

Big man, "Larry and Robby going to Nancy's car. Larry driving. Making a U-turn. Heading out this way. Didn't see Nancy. Must be still inside the residence..."

* * * * *

Larry drove anxiously to the bookie's place of business. The front was a used-book store, it didn't make much money these days. The primary business was done in the rear offices that were accessible from a small parking lot that had a lot of foot traffic. The lot and surrounding streets were jammed with cars due to the nearby movie theater and the hamburger joints that were popular with University students. He finally found a parking space and the two of them walked a block to the meeting. Robby said to just play it cool and let him do the talking. It was nearly midnight.

They found the bookie waiting and a bit perplexed, but he told them not to worry, the money was coming. He showed them the canvas sack containing three hundred-and eighty-five thousand dollars and asked if they wanted to count it.

Robby asked for the total amount and how it was determined. The bookie had the numbers already prepared in a loose-leaf binder. He said that the odds were eight-to-one per race, adjusted for the pari-mutual. He went down the list of races with the payoff for each one. Beside that, to the right, was another column with the odds factor and the third column for the product of the numbers.

The numbers jumped at the fifth race. The bookie said that he was damned lucky...the jockey. A broken arm was the worst of it. He asked if they watched it on TV and both replied that they hadn't as the races weren't televised. The bookie said it was on all the stations at the end of the news, usually with the sports coverage. The jockey said he was trying for a record and pushed Jim Dandy too hard, too soon. He said it was, "Pretty obvious. Two lengths ahead at the first turn. They been under a lot of pressure by the 'Commish'. Vern turned in a couple of bad times earlier. I think *you* lost on him one day."

He continued going down through the list and the results. He kept his finger on the grand total of eight hundred and eighty-five thousand dollars!

The bookie told them they should count it. The rest was coming in by courier and he thought the guy would be here by now. He excused himself to make a phone-call as they counted the money. He waited until they finished and then told him he had the wrong information. He gave them the expected arrival time at the airport. He figured it would take another half hour or so for the rest of the money to get there.

There wasn't much in common to talk about with your local bookie at midnight so he was asked to turn the volume up on the radio so they could listen. The talk-show host had a forensic expert in the studio explaining that Kathy's true identity was not yet known and that the teeth x-rays were a better and more accurate identification than the fingerprints. The bookie asked Larry and Robby why they were smiling at that information. It was no surprise to him. They use dental records to positively identify corpses. The bookie agreed with the expert. He added that the whole thing was some kind of publicity stunt. "A press conference for God...for Christ's sake."

The host took two callers who agreed with his studio expert. A third caller started out talking about Kathy and then switched somehow to denigration of the religious right and time for a commercial break. There was a knock on the door.

The bookie unlocked the door and let the courier in. Really nasty looking, Larry thought.

The bookie made the introductions. The man wasted no time in pleasantries.

"Show me some ID." He looked at Larry's drivers license. "Lawrence? I have Lorenzo."

Larry explained that he used his original name. The bookie said that he was the person who placed the wager and paid the money. That resulted in a change of subject, one hurdle over. "US citizen?" Larry nodded yes.

"Paying taxes? We got no Lorenzo Garcia on our computer."

"Yes, but it would be under Lawrence," Larry replied.

Robby spoke up and asked why the questions. The bet was placed with the bookie and Larry won. The courier asked who he was and Robby said a friend of the family who came along because of the late hour.

The courier said it was necessary to find out if money was going to be withheld for taxes. This bet was not placed through the regular channels and he was protecting the source. He wanted to know if they were legitimate bettors and not revenue agents...which was his next question. "Were they now, or in the past, any agents of any branch of government, or under hire by anyone known to be an agent of the government?" They said they were not.

Next, he said he was going to read them their rights. They looked puzzled.

"We operate a dependable service for our clients. We make our money on volume. We pay our debts to maintain our reputation. We aren't stupid. We know the odds. You beat them. We pay you.

The odds of a repeat performance are not within your lifetime. We won't pay you again. Do you understand that?"

Robby and Larry said they did. Robby thought Sammy could do a better job with the bulge in the courier's suit coat. Maybe a little padding on the right side for balance.

The man went on, "If you have filed a tax return in the past, and plan to remain in the USA, our recommendation is that we re-invest the money for you. It will cost you about twenty-five percent. Maybe only twenty percent for a purse this size. If you decline the offer, you run a risky business. If you evade and try to finger the bookie here, we can make you look real bad.

"My *personal* advice, since it looks like you're staying here...pay unto Caesar."

Larry looked at Robby. Robby didn't hesitate. "We paid unto Caesar. This is God's money. We'll take it for Him."

"Better count it," the man said, looking at his watch after putting the briefcase on the desk.

Robby asked if it was all there. The man said it was. Robby reached in the other bag, took out about twenty thousand dollars, and offered it to him for the advice. The man declined the money. "Unprofessional. Like I said, we have a reputation to maintain."

Robby picked up the sack and handed it to Larry. He picked up the briefcase and motioned Larry to leave. On the way out he asked the bookie if he wanted a tip and the man put out his hand. "Satan's Pleasure...never drop a dime on him."

Outside, Larry said that wasn't nice and he should have given the bookie a tip. Robby said he left the bundle on the other desk when they were watching them pick up the bag and briefcase. Inside, the courier and the bookie were completing their paperwork. The courier said he thought he had seen Robby somewhere before. "Maybe on TV." As the courier was about to leave, the bookie found the bundle of money. He remembered where he, too, had seen the man.

"That's the guy who made the opening speech about the switching of the disks on Kathy's press conference. I'm sure of it now."

The courier looked at his watch. "I'll be damned. You're right. Wait 'til I tell my daughter."

Chapter 16

Kanisha was waiting in her room at ten-thirty when the phone rang. Her New Age pimp said he was glad she was there. Did she have a cocktail dress with her? Yes, she did. She would be picked up at eleven. Be in the lobby. She was going to escort a Representative from North Carolina. There was a brunch and a meeting scheduled for noon. She asked what was the bad news. "He's gay!" he laughed and hung up.

She checked herself in the mirror and thought she was a pretty good-looking lady. Her short, black cocktail dress showed off her legs, which, she thought were her best asset. She changed bracelets to something a little smaller. Satisfied, she went to the lobby just before eleven. She found a discarded copy of the Baltimore paper and read the latest information on Kathy. There was a feature supplement on Kathy and she was surprised at the credit for the article. Kanisha Porter.

"Kenya?" a uniformed chauffeur asked her.

She got up and accompanied the man to a waiting limousine. He was black and she found it easy to talk to him. He drove for thirty minutes and they approached a very nice residential area. By then, she found out that her date was black also and they would meet at a local politician's house and then go to the Country Club for brunch. He didn't have a schedule for what happened after that.

He drove into a gated entry and up to a beautiful ivy-covered mansion. The driver escorted her inside and she met three other sisters waiting in a small room just off the entry. She was dressed appropriately. She was presented with a floral decoration for her dress and one of the girls helped her put it on her dress. She was from Chicago, a very attractive brunette with green eyes.

She met a bottled blonde from New York City who had a very nice tan and a bad attitude. The other girl was black, real class. From Kansas City. Beautiful smile. She befriended her and found out she was working on her law degree, had a daughter, and was divorced. She laughed when she mentioned that. The *bitch* he left her for put on about twenty pounds and then he lost his job, which

183

wasn't all that good to start with. She was doing much better without him. "...should'a dumped yo' ass a long time ago, oh oh oh," she sang. Good voice.

Their dates arrived from another part of the large house and the introductions were made from a list that the host, and seemingly the homeowner, had on a piece of paper. Her date, Representative James, "Jimmy", Franklin, was a handsome black man in his late thirties. He looked her over casually and made a few complementary remarks and returned to his conversation with the host. His parting comment was that he would listen with an "open mind". The group headed to the waiting limousines and she was led to the one that she arrived in. She got stuck with the New Yorker to talk to as Jimmy and her date, a small, elderly, white man with a pallid complexion and a strong southern accent talked all the way to the Country Club.

They were waved in by a uniformed attendant and pulled up to a side entrance that was red-carpeted. Jimmy finally acknowledged her presence when they got out of the car. He took her by the hand, placed it on his arm, and then smiled to the well-dressed people who were there to greet them. There was some polite applause and some photos were taken. They were ushered inside to a large party room that had a magnificent banquet displayed. They were seated at the head table and served coffee immediately. Her date finally stopped talking politics and really introduced himself. This time he made some sincere compliments. He asked about her background and she said she was going to college and was studying to be a journalist. He remarked that he approved, and did she know that the reporter who broke the Kathy story was black? She said she hadn't been following the story as her mother was very sick, etc., etc. Champagne was served and then breakfast. It was delicious Southern cooking, no doubt in honor of the guests. Jimmy made small talk and told her that the presentation was probably going to be boring and if she wanted to excuse herself when it started it would be quite all right. She asked what it was going to be about and he said, "Superconductors. A sales pitch."

She asked if it was all right to stay, as she wanted to know more about them. He said it was all right and would enjoy the company, frankly surprised that she was interested. He joked that it wouldn't help much with her journalistic career, as it was all rather theoretical at this point. The last guest had departed the buffet table with a plate of food. A podium was moved from the wall into a waiting spot light and a distinguished looking man with a graying, blow-dried hair style introduced himself as Doctor Jeffries, the Director of SuperCee, Incorporated. Without the use of props of any kind, he was able to leave his listeners with a clear picture of what superconductors were and the marvelous things that could be done with them. The presentation left the listener with no doubt that the breakthrough would come at any moment, and come from the work being done at his company. He related how he had just come from briefing the President and many of his staff who showed a very recent interest in superconductors. This part of the presentation took only twenty-five minutes.

Doctor Jeffries read the text of a bill that would be coming up for a vote the following week. He referred to one section and said that the funding for Research and Development was in there and how a yes vote would get his company over the last hurdle and launch the Era of the Superconductor, a roadbed for the Information Highway.

He received an enthusiastic round of applause.

Kanisha was intrigued with the conversation that followed in the limousine on the return trip. She and the New Yorker sat quietly while the older man did most of the talking. He told the younger man that North Carolina would not benefit. He said that it was another Fenhauser project and more than likely had the necessary votes. He reminded him that Jeffries made no mention of other companies that were working without public support and were probably just as far along. Dr. Jeffries made no mention of the possibility that the superconductors had already been invented, as reported in the Kathy headlines. He recommended a no vote. He looked at the New Yorker and said that if the bill got to him he would have to recommend it's approval. He hoped that it was killed before it got to him.

The driver took a different route on the return trip and stopped at a larger estate. A solitary man met them and opened the door.

The older man and the New Yorker got out of the car. Jimmy remained seated and made no attempt to get up. The two men shook hands and Jimmy assured him of his vote. The driver returned to the previous estate, and Kanisha got her first case of jitters. Jimmy invited her into the house, which seemed to be unoccupied. The limo driver parked beside a large structure with doors for at least four cars. The upstairs might have been servant quarters.

Jimmy announced his arrival and a female servant informed him that the others had already departed and would return at six. Three hours, Kanisha calculated quickly. Jimmy took note and asked Kanisha if she would like to stay and keep him company. The way he put the question was what made her accept the offer. Ever since she met him, she considered the possibilities. She decided after the coincidence of the superconductor presentation, and the mention of Fenhauser, that she was on to something. If she had to, she would.

Jimmy went to the kitchen and opened the refrigerator. "Damn. No Dr.Pepper." He yelled back at the female employee and asked her if they had any more Dr. Pepper around the house. She said she would look. He asked Kanisha if she wanted anything and she said she was very thirsty and plain water would do. "Too much salt in the gravy," he remarked.

He told the servant that he would be in the den, and to bring them water and a julep, if she couldn't find a Dr. Pepper. He led Kanisha to another part of the house into a guest suite consisting of a bedroom, a den, a bath, and a patio overlooking a beautiful garden and swimming pool. Kanisha accepted a seat beside him after he clicked on the TV. He asked her the channel for sports and she said she didn't know, and then he recalled that she wasn't from Baltimore. The servant arrived with a tray carrying a pitcher of ice, a pitcher of water, two glasses, and a Dr. Pepper. The tray and tongs were silver. He obtained the sports channel from her and clicked it on.

She asked him who the other man was...he seemed important. Jimmy said he was the party leader. Not in office but was the real power in his section of the country. "Very influential," he remarked, without stating a name. She got up the courage during a commercial, and asked who Fenhauser was. She said she had had a date once with a "Fenhauser" and described him exactly as she had seen in the photo in Briggs' file.

"Michael Jordan played on this team," Jimmy said as the ball game resumed.

It was a good game and she watched it with him. "End of the first quarter," the announcer said and a commercial was already on the screen.

"Sounds like the same guy. What did you think of him? As ruthless as they say?" Jimmy responding to her last statement.

"Oh, Fenhauser. A jerk. A first-class jerk." Kanisha was faking it very well. For effect, she said, "Couldn't get it up."

A tracer message appeared across the screen: Important update on the Kathy Makino recovery. Official FBI report verified that fingerprints match. Detailed report on News Channel. The message repeated and a new ad was shown.

"What do you make of that?" Jimmy asked her.

Kanisha said she wasn't following the story, her mother was sick and she needed money.

The game resumed and both watched in silence until half time, as Jimmy was very interested. There was a back-court foul and the director took the opportunity to show the film clip of Vern Hopkins, a veteran jockey, being thrown from his mount, Jim Dandy. Rider reported in good condition after barely escaping the hooves of the pack two lengths behind. Jim Dandy retired from racing as a result of injuries. They showed him taking a header again as though no one got the message the first time.

North Carolina was leading at half time. Jimmy pushed a button and the servant returned. He asked for another Dr. Pepper and pointed to Kanisha. She felt like a Dr. Pepper too, and asked for it. "Ham. Too salty for my likes. My daddy, now there's a man knows how to smoke a ham!" Jimmy said.

Kanisha felt more comfortable when Jimmy turned the volume down. She asked him what the other man meant when he said a "Fenhauser project".

Jimmy said Fenhauser was a household word in political circles. He had a huge conglomeration of interests, but what it boiled down to was that he represented special interest groups and could come up with about ten percent of the vote on any given issue. He told Kanisha that she was probably working for him and didn't even know it.

She asked him to explain because her arrangements were with an attorney in her hometown. Jimmy told her that Fenhauser had access to a huge database and could use the information beneficially, but he liked power and used the information as blackmail to swing votes; depending on who was going to pay the most to him. Because he represented so many different interests, some of them opposing, only his computers knew for sure who was being blackmailed.

The game resumed. The servant waited until an appropriate time out to inform Jimmy that his hosts were not returning until much later, and that he was free to use the limo to the airport to catch his flight. "Bastards," he said when she was out of earshot. "They have me figured for a no vote. So kind and charming. Until you vote against their interests. I wonder what Fenhauser has on them. Probably pictures of you and Charlie making it, right?"

"Charlie is the man who owns this house? I've never met him until today. Give me a break, he's over seventy," Kanisha said.

"And gay," Billy said as he turned back to the ball game.

They watched TV until the game was over. Billy was pleased with the results.

"Well, that makes my day," he said, turning off the TV.

"Would you like to make my day?" Kanisha asked.

"I would if I could, but I can't. I'm gay too," Billy said rather jokingly.

Kanisha said that she had already figured that out. She wanted to know if and at what time he was going to the airport, as she understood his intentions. He told her his plans, which gave them about two hours more time. She asked if they had time to go to her hotel on the way to get the rest of her belongings. He said it was on the way to the airport. She asked him how he liked press interviews and he said they were OK as long as the reporters, etc. were friendly.

She picked up the Baltimore paper, which was in the room and asked him if he read the entire lead story. He replied that he was interested in the story and hoped that it was not some kind of publicity stunt. She asked if he thought the reporter had done a thorough and honest job of reporting. He said that he didn't know, only that she was reported to be black.

Kanisha lifted her skirt and reached into her pantyhose, bringing forth a plastic pouch. She opened it and presented her drivers license and press credentials for the Chronicle. "I'm Kanisha Porter. Look at the by-line on the story. One-and-the-same. I'm friendly, and I'm trying to put Fenhauser away. I *guarantee* your confidentiality, one brother to another. I need information so anything you can tell me is off the record." She saw his approval and said, "Let's get started. See if the slave can find me something to write with," motioning to the button.

* * * * *

"I hate to drag you away from your families on a Sunday morning," Gordon Briggs stated at the beginning of his meeting.

"I missed the whole point. Everyone did. Kathy is not the story. **God** is going to have a press conference and we are sitting here debating whether her *fingerprints* take priority over her *dental work* as a means of identification. Ladies and gentlemen...**God** is going to have a press conference! Exactly as Kathy said in her closing remarks at the hospital press conference. Not only is He going to have a press conference, **we** are in the middle of it. No. As of this morning, we are leading. We have not had one call from anyone, questioning the validity of our FBI report. It is here, in my hand, and I have not received one call. Not one question. We hit the street with the supplement this morning. Our paper is the *Bible.*

"So, what does that mean? We have some responsibilities. We better put on our thinking caps and see how we are going to pull this off. What I want to do right now is some target practice.

"Let's assume that the press conference is a global project. Maybe like the Olympics. Who is going to attend? Who is going to be the MC? Let's assume Kathy at this point. Who is going to ask the questions? How is the problem of language to be handled?

189

What old stuff do we have on the UN communication system? The technology is here. Who is going to broadcast it?

"I think you all get the picture. I want you to go home and spend the rest of the day writing up a scenario of how you think it will go. Write down everything that might be an issue. We need answers but first we need the questions. We might have to work late tomorrow night, so be prepared.

"I know I'm asking you to do in one day what the Olympic Committee has four years to work out."

* * * * *

Lewis was caught off guard when he answered his phone and Mr. Hudson was on the line. He was informed that something important had come up and would he mind coming into the SuperCee Headquarters. Hudson sounded like the police officer who had the duty of informing a parent that their child had been killed in an auto accident. He immediately thought of Kanisha having been detected and her body found floating in a river in Baltimore.

He worried about his own safety. No one would be near the SuperCee building on a Sunday morning. He decided to go, even after he called Briggs' office and got no answer. He tried him at home and was informed that he was on the way home from an office meeting and reminded Lewis not to be late for dinner as she was going to prepare Gordon's special roast. He said he would be there with bells on and to inform Mr. Briggs that he had been called to work for something important. It couldn't possibly be regarding the fingerprint report, which was the only new thing that he was aware of.

Hudson was waiting for him when he drove up to the front door of SuperCee. There was a limousine parked in front with a driver waiting. He caught sight of the license plate, D FENSTER. He put it together quickly. A defense attorney and Fenhauser. *He* wouldn't be there if they were going to kill him right away. And there was a chance Kanisha was still alive. There were five cars in the company parking lot. The guard said good-morning. He followed Hudson who moved along pretty fast for such short legs. Hudson took the stairs and not the elevator, which was standing on the ground floor waiting for passengers. At the top of the stairs he made a right turn and invited Lewis into a small office with sparse, hard furniture.

Hudson started right in asking questions before Lewis had a chance to be seated. Where had he been last night? He said he was with his girlfriend...and wanted to ask if that was against company rules, but didn't. He was asked a lot of information that was already on the employment form that he filled out. He was asked to repeat his role in writing the original Kathy story. Lewis related his story again and how he was fired. That wasn't what Hudson wanted. He wanted a detailed; step-by-step description of what happened at the interview. How many rooms in the house, how were they laid out? Where was the computer? In other words, draw a blueprint of the house. He found a piece of blank paper and drew it out from memory, wasn't sure of the kitchen details, and of course, hadn't been upstairs. Hudson liked the drawing.

He was then asked if had seen the real disks and he said he had. He was asked to describe them and he did. He said the color photos that showed up the following day in other publications were accurate, to the best of his recollection.

He was asked about his relationship with Kathy. Did he think he could get another interview with her? He said he thought so; his problem was with his paper. As it turned out, it appears he was right, but for the wrong reasons. Lewis asked what all the questions were for and maybe he could save some time.

Hudson was not a clever liar. He said he was just doing some background work, but Lewis saw through that. He asked, "Mr. Hudson, what do you really want to know?" A door inside the room opened and Mr. Fenhauser walked through it. Lewis could see that he had been watching the proceedings through a one-way mirror. The man looked exactly like the photo that Briggs showed him.

Without introducing himself, he told Lewis that he could answer that question. He said he knew that Lewis and Kanisha Porter had spent the preceding night together and they had been seen together around town. He wanted to know how Kanisha Porter was obtaining the information for her paper when she had not been

191

seen entering or leaving the Makino residence and her name was not on the police officer's authorized list. Lewis laughed, now that he had an idea of what they were looking for. "Why didn't you break her door down and read her E-mail? She works out of her apartment most of the time. I'm sure she has a private number into the house. They were talking about that when I was there. I think American News gave her the story for two reasons. She's black and she works cheap. Also, if you know anything about the business, you can see that she is a damned good writer. She learned a lot from me while she was at American News. Before they learned that it is bad business to fire black reporters."

The man motioned Hudson from his chair and sat down in it himself. He leaned forward and looked Lewis directly in the eye. "Mr. Anderson, what turns you on?"

Lewis thought a minute and said, "Money. I've never had enough money. I've worked all my life and I've got nothing. Why do you ask?"

The seated man leaned back in his chair and said, "Mr. Anderson, you seem to be in the right places at the right time. Mr. Hudson tells me you did a good job here with the press yesterday. For a man to be rich he has to take a few chances in life. How do you feel about taking a few risks?"

Lewis replied that he agreed with that assessment. He was willing to take some risks as long as no one got hurt in the process. He didn't yet know where this conversation was headed. They either had Kanisha in Baltimore or they wanted something else.

Hudson's phone came on and he answered it. Before he found the switch to turn off the speaker, Lewis heard the caller say that they haven't picked up Porter's trail. Hudson listened to the rest of the call and mentioned a few more places that they could look. After some expletives, he told them to call back as soon as they found anything. Switching the phone off, he made an apologetic look towards the other man, saying he had to do all the thinking himself.

So, they hadn't found Kanisha yet, Lewis thought. He changed tactics. "Look, I work *for* you people. If you let me know what it is you want maybe I can help you get it. If those guys were looking

192

for Kanisha, I know where she is. My god. I spend the night with her and you don't ask me if I know where she is?"

"OK." The seated man asked him, "Where is she?"

"Out of town on another assignment," Lewis replied. "Now, are you going to tell me what this is about?"

"Can you get into the house? Or can you get Kanisha into the house?"

"Yeah, I think so. It would fit in with the story I'm writing about SuperCee." Lewis figured it out. "You want the disks! Right? The superconductors are in them. Not a bad idea."

"That's right, Mr. Anderson. And I'm willing to make it worth your while. Normally I don't conduct business in this manner. I prefer to talk things out on my yacht or in the Caymans, but there isn't time in this case. The President has taken an interest in superconductors and there are other government agencies with a deep interest. My friends in Japan, well, they don't like to be caught by surprise. Europe is begging for a project of this type. The former Soviet Union is an untapped market. There are millions of computer-oriented Russians.

"You can see the potential that exists if we can get out hands on them and get a jump on the other people that are working as we are. You get one of those disks in my hands and you'll never have to worry about money again."

"I don't work well under pressure. Give me a day and I'll give you a plan on how to get a disk. In the meantime, can your Lab people make me a, no, make that *two* disks. One black and one white. I think the way to do it is with a switch. Meanwhile I'll figure out a way to get inside. Either myself or Kanisha. She is interested in making some money also. A very ambitious young, lady. It just so happens that I'm having dinner with the man who fired me. I think, from the phone conversation, that he's seen the error of his ways and they would like to re-hire me. For the record, I'm on SuperCee's payroll. I like your retirement plan much better.

"Give me until tomorrow evening. I think I can come up with a plan."

"You have it. Thank you for your time, Mr. Anderson."

"And you, sir? I didn't get your name," Lewis asked politely.

"Let's just leave it that way for now. You can work through Mr. Hudson with assurance that he speaks for me."

Chapter 17

Kathy got up early on Sunday morning. She read everything in her work manual before going to sleep when her eyes got tired. They were fine this morning and she had no trouble focusing on the house across the street. There was no sign of anyone stirring. Her father was up half the night celebrating and disappointed when Larry informed him that just he and Robby were going for the money. He stayed up to keep Nancy company until they returned with the money. It was after two in the morning before he turned in. She put on some tea for him and made a pot of coffee. She went to the computer, forgetting that she needed a disk for her "live" morning update. She called Victor on his new, private line. She told him coffee was on and to bring a disk over for her. He asked what time it was as his sleep was interrupted when they came over and put the money in the safe, and he said he couldn't open the safe without Larry. She said it was a little after nine. She said she'd call Larry about ten. In the meantime, she'd come over and visit with him if that was OK.

She asked if there was any food over there and Victor replied that there was none. She said she would call the catering service and was there anything he wanted especially for breakfast, now that they had money to meet expenses. He said he liked ham and eggs if it could be done. She said she'd see. Kathy found her father's manual and the caterer's number. They were open and took the call. The owner hinted a bit about when they would be paid and Kathy sounded surprised. She told them that if they delivered after about ten thirty, the safe would be open and they would be paid. The lady asked why they kept the coffee-fund in the safe; she heard it was a nice neighborhood. Kathy didn't have a ready answer and the woman asked if she was the *Kathy* that was on TV as the voice seemed the same. Kathy said she was and the lady said, "I'll believe you when you order ten loaves and two fishes."

Kathy said, with a smile, "Please add ten loaves and two fishes to the order. I wasn't expecting company, but now that the FBI says I'm really me, a crowd may show up."

She found the American News and two other papers on her front porch. She took them with her and kept a tight hold on the coffeepot as she crossed the street. She announced her arrival to Victor who said he was shaving and would be right out. This afternoon she was going shopping for a big-screen TV, now that they had some money. She poured the coffee and had it waiting for Victor.

He arrived in suit pants and a clean, white shirt that had only the top button buttoned. He took a sip of the coffee and said, "Perfect." He sat beside her, reached for a paper, opened it, and read. She was going through the American News, reading some of the related articles. She tore one page out and Victor asked her what that was about.

"Look at this! The directors of General Hospital announced their plans for construction of the largest and best equipped Sports Medicine Center in the state.

"The facility will be named in honor of Emily Mullin, a member of the staff with extraordinary healing powers." Kathy read the highlights of the article aloud.

They went back to their individual reading. Victor found something of interest. "Here's another one on Emily. The District Attorney's Office has ordered a reopening of the Emily Mullin case after a meeting with the Mayor and local leaders. Through efforts of the community and the police, one suspect has been apprehended and charged. One vehicle, identified as being at the scene of the shooting, has been sighted in Los Angeles County. Local police there have been alerted and are on the lookout." They returned to their reading. Kathy called Larry just before ten and he was awake. He said he'd be over in about ten minutes to open the safe.

Kathy asked Victor if he had made the *invitation* yet. His reply disappointed her. He was watching the Late Show and fell asleep. When he woke up he went to bed and fell asleep immediately. She said she had no luck with her project either. Victor changed subjects and asked her about the money. When the three of them were over last night, he heard them talking about all the bills they had to pay and what should they do with the rest. Victor said he had

196

never seen that much money in his entire lifetime, let alone at one time.

Kathy asked him what was worth more, the money or the disks? He didn't have a good answer. He said if push came to a shove, he'd take the money. Kathy said he had no vision and he didn't understand that. He said she was the hardest girl to understand that he ever met. She said that was because he was used to getting his way with the other girls. Victor got up and turned off the small TV that was showing news. Kathy thought he was mad at her. He turned on the radio, found some music, and asked her if he could have this dance, since none of the other girls were available.

Larry came in and found them dancing, poured himself a cup of coffee and read the paper until they were done. He said he would like to get back home as the family was waiting to go to church. They opened the safe and removed a disk.

The safe was stacked full of money. Larry said one of the computers in the next room was available, but Kathy said she wanted to use her own, in private. She took the disk and walked back to her house. She paused and curtsied at the door on the way out and thanked Victor for the dance.

She went to her computer, inserted the disk, and typed in her message.

"Good morning, Kathy," God said to her on the speakers.

"Good morning. Question. Do you have a morning? What I mean is, the earth turns and there are more people in the sun and it gets darker on the other side. It seems like you never get a rest. Is this a dumb question?"

"No. I don't have a body like yours to rest. Also, I am everywhere at the same time. On to more important things. I see that you spoke to Victor. He tried, but he is not focusing. He's like a loose cannon. Try improving his aim. A lot of people are like that; it is part of the free will package. Alone and isolated, people figure it out quickly. In a modern society with so many diversions, it sometimes takes longer. Have you noticed how much time he spends in front of the TV? His mind is being filled with nonsense and he is not thinking of anything."

"Do you have any instructions about what to do with the money?" Kathy asked.

"Leave that to Robby and your father. You will be given instructions tomorrow. For today, I want you to call Mr. Briggs and let him know that you wish to speak to Kanisha Porter. Then, why don't you teach Victor how to drive and go to a rock-concert?

"I've done enough work today, I think I'll take a rest," God said and the speakers remained silent to Kathy's questions.

Gordon Briggs was surprised to hear from Kathy. After some exchange of pleasantries, he told her of the plans that he had been making, commenting that his staff had a meeting earlier and were all at home now thinking of how to proceed. She was pleased to hear that. He said he would like to meet with her on Monday to brief her on the outcome of the meeting and they scheduled a time. Kathy told him that she wanted to meet with Kanisha Porter, but had no details. Briggs remarked that he was having Lewis over for dinner this evening and it was a coincidence since he would be able to locate Kanisha. Kathy remarked that she didn't think it was a coincidence.

* * * * *

Conservative talk-show hosts were having a field day. The FBI report was in their hands, having been copied and faxed in it's entirety from the American News supplement. NBA stars were being interviewed before the games and asked to comment on the news and didn't add much to what had already been analyzed for the public by talking-heads. "Kathy" had become a household word across the nation and was spreading rapidly to other parts of the world. Soon the Pacific Rim nations would know of the FBI report and Europe would have it on the evening news.

Kanisha Porter was creating news. Her interview of James Franklin continued in the limousine through the short visit to the hotel to pick up her belongings. She almost panicked when she met her pimp walking in as she was walking out, but her street smarts saved her. She pointed to the waiting limo and said, "*Used* to be gay. I'm going to North Carolina."

"Hey, I never said you weren't a looker. When you coming back? he asked.

"*Jimmy* wants to take me to visit his mother! I'll call," Kanisha said.

"Hey! Good luck, hear," the man said, resuming his way into the building.

She studied investigative reporting. This was her first real attempt at it and it felt good to her. Jimmy was giving her some pretty good leads. It appeared that the limo driver was unable to hear their conversation and they were able to converse openly on the way to the airport. Kanisha thanked him sincerely and confirmed her promises to him when the driver dropped her at the main entrance. The limo continued on to the VIP entrance. Jimmy Franklin felt good about his Baltimore visit.

Kanisha Porter looked like a successful business woman used to traveling as she went to the commuter airline and purchased a ticket with her Versatel card and then went to the phone to make a long distance call.

* * * * *

Lewis was en-route to Briggs' house for dinner and didn't hear her call at his home number, however the answering machine picked it up. Mrs. Briggs met him at the door and welcomed him inside. Gordon was trying to figure out what the point was that the popular liberal was trying to make on one of the Sunday evening news up-dates. Anyone in their right mind would see that the next step, if you followed this person's reasoning, would lead to another government program, disclaimers to the contrary. He greeted Lewis and motioned him to sit down and watch the rest of the show with him while Mrs. Briggs went for some drinks. The subject was campaign reform and seemed to come up every four years with little ever being accomplished. Briggs commented that if the Founding Fathers were listening to the show they would have no idea of what it was about.

Before dinner was served, Lewis informed Briggs of everything that had occurred to date, including Kanisha's venture to Baltimore and the meeting he had with Fenhauser. Briggs told him to write everything down. Lewis said he already had and gave him an envelope with the reports. Briggs said that he wanted to continue making contact at his house as he had had reports from his staff that some of the competition was not adverse to tapping the paper's phone and data lines. He had even heard rumors that one publication had screened the garbage and had Kathy's old fillings. Lewis asked about that. Why hadn't there been a disclosure of her dental x-rays? The public was clamoring for it. Briggs laughed.

He said he really admired Kathy's dentist. The dentist said that the person he examined at the hospital, during the medical session, was Kathryn Makino, the same patient that he had been treating for a number of years. He was not going to release any patient information without a court order. Since the patient was not dead, decomposed, or mutilated in any way, the fingerprints would have to suffice for identification. Professor Makino gave him permission to release the information, but since the dentist was taking a stand, based on ethics and his professional standards, he would not interfere. The Court didn't know what to do. So far, no judge has issued an order to release the records.

Lewis had not eaten this well for a long time. Mrs. Briggs was, perhaps, not an excellent bridge player, but her art in the kitchen was flawless. He noted Gordon's paunch and remarked that it might be due to the food he was getting at home. Gordon said his wife was "...killing him with kindness." But, that was how he preferred to go and he could take it to the grave with him.

After dinner, they chatted in the living room. Lewis remarked that things have certainly changed. He was very upset when he didn't get the job of campaign reporting and that was what led him to make his invitation.

Briggs looked at his wife and asked her if she recalled the bridge game with the Catholic priest who had recently retired from the Navy as a Chaplain. She said that she did and added that he held services on an aircraft carrier during Desert Storm, and had many interesting stories to tell. The priest held Mass at a church that was different from theirs but they decided to go hear him. His sermon that day said exactly the same thing that Kathy said. God was waiting for the invitation and that the Holy Spirit was how it all worked.

Gordon said he had been upset also as he was overworked and was not editing the paper. No one was. He was *managing* it since the owners retired. That was what triggered his invitation and now he is out *writing* for a change and much happier.

Briggs released the latest bit of information that he received. "Kathy wishes to speak to Kanisha Porter. She called me this morning, around lunch-time. She figured I would know how to find her."

They talked until almost ten-o'clock, exhausting the information they possessed. Briggs asked Lewis, on parting, if he had any ideas about God's press conference, he would welcome them.

Lewis thought about that on the drive home. *God* is going to have a press conference. He recalled what had happened in the last week and was jarred. *God really is going to have a press conference!*

When he arrived home he checked his messages and was overjoyed to hear that Kanisha was on the way home and to meet her at the airport if he got the message in time. Otherwise she would take a taxi home and he could call her there. She gave him the flight number and arrival time.

Lewis looked at his watch, ran back to his car, and headed to the airport, driving with fervor. There wasn't much traffic on a Sunday night and he picked up the tail that was following him. There was a lot of traffic and many people at the airport. He found a parking spot and ran to the arrival gates. He found the flight number on the TV monitor. It was reported on the ground and he ran to the gate. Her big hair was easy to spot and he breathed a sigh of relief when he saw her. He picked her up and planted a big kiss on her. "Can't it wait until we get home?" she asked.

He told her that they needed to talk and she agreed. She had tons of information. They went to an almost deserted bar at the airport and got two really high-priced drinks. Kanisha began right in with a summary of her trip to Baltimore and how the system worked. She showed him about twenty pages of handwritten notes with names, dates, bills, and how the officials voted. With more detail and her computer, she could put together a list of people that were owned by Fenhauser. She said she met Doctor Jeffries from SuperCee and he was a very good salesman.

Lewis asked her to guess who he had met. "My god, no. Not God again!" Lewis said no, just the opposite. He had met Fenhauser. He told her about the meeting he had earlier.

"So, they want one of us to steal the disks. Is that it? Can we pull a double switch?" Kanisha asked.

"What I think is that we should let Kathy know what's going on. By the way, she called Briggs and wants to meet with you. Neither one of us knows what it is about. I think we should go to my house and not yours. I think I screwed up when I mentioned that you worked out of your home. It wouldn't surprise me if your apartment has been broken into. I am sure you will be tailed, once they find you.

They went to a public phone and called Briggs. He was glad to hear that Kanisha was all right and said he had a private number to get through to Kathy. Briggs looked at the time and said he was sure that Kanisha's name was on the entry list, but he would double check and add both names. He suggested that due to the late hour they talk to Kathy tomorrow.

The arrival gate was deserted except for airline employees. Whoever was following him was watching his car. Lewis told Kanisha to wait at the departure entrance and to jump in his car when he pulled in. He went to his car in the parking structure and headed for the exit. After paying his fee he drove quickly back to the departure level and saw no car following them. He pulled in and picked up Kanisha and told her to stay low until he was home. He drove to his house and opened the garage door with the automatic door opener. He made sure all the lights were out then he turned on the bedroom light and returned for Kanisha. They watched from the living room window, in the dark, and waited until the car pulled up with the lights out and parked nearby.

Lewis commented that they could get a good night's sleep, now that they had a bodyguard watching the house.

Chapter 18

Big man, "Nancy and Rabinowitz arriving."

Cameraman, "He's driving her car now. Looks like Larry walking in. He looks happy in the telescopic."

Big man, "Shirley and Marcie arriving together."

Cameraman, "Take a look at this, I got 'em zoomed in." The cameraman moved so the other man could look through his camera.

Big man, "Man, what a pair!"

Cameraman, "In your dreams."

Big man, "Catering truck. Hey, that's a good cover for a get-away."

Little man, "Right! *Everybody's* here when the caterer's here. I say we need someone inside."

Big man, "Hudson's working on it. He agrees with you, but you gotta' look at all the options."

Little man, "You guys been following this story? What happens if God is really on the disks and you get away with a heist?"

Big man, "I'll say the devil made me do it."

Cameraman, "*God* on the disks. Now, who's been seeing too many movies?"

Big man, "Zoom! Zoom. Get me some plate numbers. Two people in the car...that's a Chevy...what?..two, three years old. Man driving, business suit, looks like a minister. Passenger...female...Look at that hair!...black...looks black...yeah, a nigger. Going to the residence. Door's opening. Looks like the professor is up early. Going inside. You getting this all down?"

Cameraman, "Got it all. I'm locked on the plates. Here, you read 'em. My eyes hurt after looking at that Shirley."

Little man, "What does a minister look like?"

Big man, "You look at him when he comes out. I'm gonna' run a check on the plates."

* * * * *

203

Kathy was pleased to see Lewis again and especially pleased
meet Kanisha...they seemed to have formed a fondness for ea
other from the outset. Kanisha accepted a cup of tea from t
professor while Lewis had coffee. Kathy brought up the subje
first. She said she had no idea of why Kanisha was summoned, b
the timing was great as she was going to have her morning meeti
with God and would find out. Victor was dressed, shaved, a
smelled of cologne as he brought one disk over and presented it
Kathy. She said she might be awhile and suggested they wait at t
other house with the others who were expecting a meeting short
Kathy excused herself and went to her computer with the disk.

Everyone had finished breakfast and was waiting for Kathy
arrive so that the meeting could begin. Kami and Larry had count
out all of the money that would be used to pay bills. The caterer h
been paid in full, given a big tip, and left smiling. Larry had t
money and the bills in individual envelopes and inside the briefca
that the courier donated.

Kathy arrived, smiling, and instructed Kanisha to return to t
house and Victor would show her to the computer. She sa
everything was ready to go; all she had to do to speak to God w
to press ENTER. She said Victor would wait and return with h
and the disk.

Kathy took a seat in the center of the table and said she had l
of news.

"First, congratulations to Robby and Nancy! They are going
New York to speak to Robby's more successful relatives. Fro
there, they will be going to Switzerland, probably to open
account. His relatives will know how to do it. On the return tr
they will visit the Caymans. Probably something to do with taxe
I talked to a very special lady who explained to me what a ho
relationship is. So, when they are finished with business, they ha
my permission, also, to spend some time in Niagara Falls.

"We have money for postage, so the staff will be busy maili
out all of the press conference preparations to all of the countries
the world. That has to take priority over everything else because
the delay in getting the mail to some countries. Fortunately, m

have embassies here in the USA and it can be officially received and forwarded.

"My father is to have an office at American News so that he can work closely with Mr. Briggs. American News is conducting a meeting right now to see how they are going to proceed. I'll meet with him later and we should...better, I'll ask him come to our meeting tomorrow. I think we have to keep each other informed and that is the best way to do it.

"Daddy, after yesterday's FBI report, many TV hosts are going to want me on their show. My instructions are that you will turn them all down, no matter how tempting the offers.

"It gets a little tricky here. Do we have a list of all the reporters who were here at the beginning? Following Mr. Anderson?"

Shirley said she had the list filed and could find it.

"Good," Kathy continued, "Please call them and schedule a half-hour private interview for each. We'll do three hours a day."

Robby raised his hand and Kathy recognized him. "Does that include the two Evening Star creeps?"

"Yes. The purpose is to get me familiar with the different questions that I will be asked in the future. It is training for me and this is a fair way to do it since those people were first. Remember, we did not disclose the 'press conference for God' information at that time. Only my recovery and the information about the disks. Lewis was the only reporter that was aware of the real reason and he did not report it.

"The rest of you may not be aware of this, but Mr. Anderson and Kanisha have been working for God in a completely different manner. It has something to do with dispelling the myth of the 'devil'. Their progress has been splendid and he will be back on our 'team' very soon, reporting with fervor. Correct, Lewis?"

"I've never been so scared in my life. But, yes, I do enjoy it, and this is the first that I have known that my other assignment was part of any plan.

"Where does Kanisha fit in? Has she heard from the computer before?" Lewis asked.

"No, she hasn't. I think she already had a line of communication established," Kathy replied.

Kanisha returned with Victor. He went to the safe and replaced the disk. Everyone looked at Kanisha and Kathy asked her if she had anything to report.

"Amazing machine you have over there!" Kanisha exclaimed. She looked around to see if anyone else could hear and asked Kathy if she could speak openly in the present company. Kathy assured her she was with friends.

"I am supposed to take one of the disks. Larry will be given a list of directories and files to copy to the mainframe. That will take some time. The black one is the one to be taken. I asked why, but no reason was given. We will all know the reason in due course. Victor was summoned to witness this part of the conversation.

"You will hear shortly on TV that Representative "Jimmie" Franklin was found murdered in his mother's home in North Carolina. The police will be looking for a prostitute by the name of Kenya in connection with the murder. She is black, five feet six, one hundred twenty-five pounds, hair blown-dried, wearing a black cocktail dress and red high-heeled shoes. Last seen near the Baltimore airport.

Some other people will be looking for her also. Lesson: My interview with "Jimmie" Franklin was recorded while driving to the airport in a limousine.

"Lewis. A hundred and twenty-five pounds? I don't think so," she concluded.

"Is that what you heard via the computer?" Lewis asked.

"Yes. I wasn't making it up," Kanisha said defensively.

"God only knows how much you really weigh," Lewis said, smiling. Everyone else in the room was smiling also.

* * * * *

Everyone was on time and the meeting began in the conference room at American News. One of the owners was present and introduced to the staff and then Gordon Briggs opened the meeting.

"*GOD is going to have a press conference.* We are going to produce and direct it. I'd like to go around the table and listen to how we should go about it. Anyone want to start?"

206

Several hands went up and Briggs gave preference to Roy Atkins, the night editor. The nephew of the owner who was present at the meeting stood up and cleared his throat before speaking. "I was not at the meeting yesterday, but I was informed of it. Like so many other things around here, I am informed and I do nothing about it. I've been the night editor here for four years and I haven't done anything yet except to be informed.

"I am not a journalist. I don't have ink running in my veins. English was my worst subject in college. I did not study journalism. I have this position because the night shift here are professionals and require little supervision. I went to school to study *management*. I graduated with honors and I understand management. I like management and I am a good manager. Mr. Briggs can verify that I am a good manager, because any time a technical problem came up at night, I *managed* to find him and solve the problem correctly. I managed the night shift. I did not edit it.

"So, to the subject at hand. I am convinced that there will be a worldwide press conference. It will need a manager. I will not be missed on the night shift and that job should be given to a senior journalist. I would like to volunteer for this job.

"I have already made a list of the major subjects. We need to identify each item, assign responsibility and authority, make a timetable, and then follow-up to see that it is done on time. It will require monitoring and someone's time to do it.

"I think I am the best-qualified person to take on the job."

There was a long applause. The owner sat in awe and finally joined in the applause. Briggs looked at the owner and said, "We're off to a good start here. My number one problem is solved, unless you have another idea." There were tears in the man's eyes, so Briggs asked the "new manager" to take over the meeting and start with the first item on his list.

In an hour, they had a complete, detailed package with answers for most questions. There was a list of assumptions that would have to be checked out.

The new manager of Project Invitation was assigned two assistants and a larger office. It was decided by Briggs that Roy should be the one to meet with Kathy and interface with her team and get some answers to the hundreds of unanswered questions that came from the meeting. It was, indeed, going to require a full-time manager to make this operation successful.

* * * * *

Lewis and Kanisha returned to her apartment. Earlier in the morning they had discovered the break-in, which was partially disguised. The lock must have been picked to get in, but the deadlock couldn't be engaged when the burglars left, and Kanisha knew that she turned the dead bolt when she locked up. Kanisha purchased discounted floppies. Someone had painstakingly removed the labels from her floppies and placed them on new, name-brand disks. Whoever had done it was not computer-oriented. It would have been much faster to make copies and leave no evidence behind. She put a disk in her computer and tried it. Empty! All of her files had been stolen.

"Thug," came to Lewis's mind and he called Chad to see if Hudson was in yet. Hudson came on the line and Lewis told him that it was stupid to burglar Kanisha's apartment. Hudson denied it, but Lewis saw through it and said that he would be in the office soon and had a plan to get one of the disks. Hudson said he would be waiting.

Lewis felt that Kanisha was in jeopardy. It wouldn't be long before someone put together the pictures of Jimmy Franklin and his "escort" in Baltimore and discovered the amazing resemblance. Especially the big hair. He decided to keep her out of the way at Briggs' house and knew how to get rid of the tail that was following him. She packed a small bag and they headed for the car. He drove to American News and she got out of the car. He pulled into the employee parking lot and walked in the front door of the paper's business office with her.

Kanisha exited a side door, got in the back of Lewis's car and stayed low. Lewis came out of the office after saying a few kind words to some startled staff. He left the lot and observed his tail in the rear-view mirror. He could see the signal to the other car that

208

came in to stay on Kanisha's trail. He drove to the Makino residence and was permitted through the roadblock. He drove straight through and exited at another roadblock on the other side of the residential area. He drove quickly to Briggs' house and ushered Kanisha to the front door. Mrs. Briggs understood the reason that Lewis offered for hiding her in a safe place. He said he would call after his meeting with Hudson. He headed for SuperCee.

Chad directed him immediately to Hudson's office. Hudson was staring into one of his computers and had a phone cradled on his shoulder. Two serious-looking men in cheap suits were standing behind the only available chair. Their boss was seated. Hudson hung up the phone after grunting that he'd call back. He motioned the boss to get up and for Lewis to sit down. Hudson said he could talk in front of the others.

Lewis asked if these were the "amateurs" who burgled Kanisha's apartment. Hudson asked him what his plan was for getting the disks. Lewis pointed to the stack of imported floppies with gummy material on some of them and no labels and asked Hudson how he kept track of them. They seemed to be at a liar's convention with questions being answered by other questions. Lewis broke the ice. "I don't work with amateurs. All you get are files of personal letters to mom and big-time if you get caught." He got up to leave and said he'd return the disks to Kanisha. Hudson stopped him and pointed the three others to the door.

"OK, Hotshot, let's hear your plan."

"There are two ways to go, actually three, counting your way. Your way isn't going to work. If the police don't catch you, Kathy's supporters will. And they'll lynch you. Have you tried to get through that neighborhood? There are people lined up on the entire perimeter. Four entries. Twenty-four hour guards. I know. I checked it out in person," Lewis began the conversation.

"So? How do we do it?" Hudson interrupted.

"It depends. Do you trust Kanisha Porter or not? If you don't trust her then I can get one out. I'll need the support of your Lab people and maybe three or four days. I was in there today and they are an unsophisticated bunch. I talked to the professor, the guy who is supposed to know about physics. He was interested in my

209

proposal. I told him that we have a superconductor detector and would like to check it out. He puts in the disk, our detector whirls and blinks, a few lights flash. The meter pegs out and verifies that it is a superconductor. I push the button and the disk comes out...only it isn't the same one. I leave with the original inside and promise to send him a free detector.

"Your Lab boys need to make the detector. They can use the guts of a CD-changer so nothing has to be invented. I wasn't able to actually see the disk or measure it, but there is enough data available that your boys in the Lab can duplicate it. It has to pass muster. If the color is slightly off, or the density, etc., I can get nabbed when I pass the disk back to them. It can't be too hard to do. If it works in her computer, it has to have certain dimensions. Can you get the model of her computer? If so, we can buy one and test it before we try the switch."

Hudson was excited and said that he thought it would work. "And, plan B, assuming we trust Porter?"

"I like Kanisha. She is a lot of fun, if you know what I mean. But, she is very, very ambitious. I understand that, she came from a really poor family. But, she will stop at nothing once she gets an idea in her head. She can get in and she can switch disks. It depends on *if* she wants to. It just so happens that she brought this subject up two or three days ago. I haven't approached her on it. drove her to work this morning; she and Kathy seem to have made a strong relationship. She had to pick up some information for her column. On the way out, she commented on the lack of security.

"So. You might want to consider this; I already have. Kanisha may beat us to the punch. Remember, she is an intelligent, liberated woman," Lewis concluded.

'You haven't broached the subject with her; is that what I'm hearing?" Hudson asked.

"That's right. I just know she'll do it. Especially if I have fence for her and the price is right," Lewis replied confidently.

"So, if we trust Kanisha, what do we need you for? We can deal directly with her," Hudson asked.

"I thought of that possibility. That's why I have all of the tapes of her interview with James Franklin stashed away in a safe place

You guys are all over the place, aren't you? I think Mr. Fenhauser would be very unhappy with you if something unfortunate happened to me.

"So, what's it going to be? I prefer to do it myself and cut her out. I only hope she doesn't beat me to it. And you can tell your boss I want *two million*. I don't think Kanisha will work that cheap, but then, she's young, and not thinking of retirement."

"For now, until I get further instructions, we work on both plans. I'll have the Lab start on the device now," Hudson said.

"I have a date to take Kanisha back for a meeting this afternoon. I'd like to have a fake disk in my hand. In case there is an opportunity. Agreed?" Lewis asked.

"I'll do the best I can," Hudson said as Lewis departed. He was talking to himself as he dialed a number on his secure phone...*two million, if he only knew what they were worth!*

"Hello...Hudson here. Tell the man I have a sure thing. Ten million. Proceeding."

On the way out, Lewis stopped by to see Chad. He said he'd be back at five to pick up a package and since he was really short on time, would Chad do him a big favor and provide him with a text processing program that was compatible with SuperCee's. He wanted to do some work at home and his software was too hard to use for the format that Mr. Hudson wanted. He thought it was on CD-ROM and his home computer had the drive for it. He wanted to pick up both disks at the same time, if he could.

* * * * *

Big man, "Another pair arriving. What's that now, the third or fourth? You guys got any clues as to what is going on...Hudson's been bugging me."

Cameraman, "Too many people in and out all day. We need to get some sound. I still think the disks went out with Rabinowitz. He has a briefcase and is picked up by the head of a private security company. Like those people have a lot of jewelry and furs down there."

Little man, "That is the fifth unidentified visitor or pair. They come and spend almost forty minutes exactly and then leave. OK? You know two of them were journalists if your spy at the checkpoint is reliable. I'll just make a wild-ass guess and say they were reporters doing interviews. You guys do this shit all the time? Jeez."

Cameraman, "Hey, it's a living. What's your excuse?"

Little man, "Divorced in California. Got this problem about wanting to eat every day. I'm augmenting my income."

Big man, "Action, action. New van arriving. American News. Four...no, five people. The big guy. What's his name? Camera...got a name?"

Cameraman, "Forgot it. Marcie leaving...c'mon Shirl! I wan'na see you bounce those beauties. Focused on the doorway."

Big man, "Marcie walked past the car. Walking out. Maybe going home on the bus. Everybody in the house. No Shirley."

Little man, "And maybe she's going to meet her boyfriend at Denny's. He can bench-press both of you. And the camera."

Big man, "Lookee here, would you. I'd say that was Lewis Anderson's car. Don't change film now. Hudson wants details. Yes! The nigger is with him. Concentrate on her. Positive ID if you can get that close."

Cameraman, "I can spot a pimple on her ass with this baby."

Little man, "But neither of you have a clue as to the location of the two disks. Remember? They are about six inches 'round. A hole in the middle. If you see one of those, wake me up. This is really dumb shit we're doing here."

Big man, "Reporters leaving, Kathy going to other house. The professor going too. No one in the house."

Little man, "And now the private security guard is standing in the doorway. Go ahead and say it. I already wrote it down."

Big man, "Private security guard. In the doorway. Feel better now? I can see why your old lady divorced you. You're a smart-ass, did you know that?"

* * * * *

Gordon Briggs introduced Roy Atkins, the manager of

PROJECT INVITATION. Roy explained to the team that his group would be the focal point between Kathy and her team and the news media. He laid out a scenario of what had to be done and the answers that they had come up with so far.

Kathy was pleased and said that she would probably be able to get answers to all of the questions in the morning. She said not to worry about money as that was going to be provided. She said that there would be no sponsors, and that this would be a news event and reported freely as such. The owners of satellites, cable, etc. could provide their services free or not. However, if they did not provide free public service, they would not have access to the events. If they wanted to have sponsors for follow-ups with human beings talking, there was no problem with that. She made it very clear that no one was going to have to pay to hear God.

Shirley was filling in for Nancy who had left for New York with Robby. She said that there was a small manual for Roy. There was a database several inches thick and a folder full of spreadsheets. The computer printed it at ten-oh-eight this morning and she had no idea of who Roy Atkins was until the meeting.

A decision was made that the American News group could use the rest of the house. A bell rang in Larry's head and he commented, "That's what all this other stuff is for. I was wondering who was going to be using it. All we have to do is run the phone lines to wherever you want your desks."

After the meeting concluded, Lewis and Kanisha asked Kathy if they could *steal* the black disk now. Kathy said it was very convenient as both Larry and Victor were there. They would take the disk to the other house, make an exchange, and return. No one else would know except Larry.

She asked Victor for the black disk and he provided it. The three walked to her residence. Lewis said he had a problem since he had two disks with him. One was made by the Lab at SuperCee and the other was an idea of his. He showed her the disk that contained text-processing software that he had spray-painted. The software probably had a trace back to SuperCee, either in the .EXE file or back to the firm that sold the software. Kathy said she would use the one that looked the best to her. Kanisha carefully placed the real disk in her purse and Kathy couldn't make up her mind. She finally chose the painted one.

It was almost eight when the meeting was over and there was going to be a big day tomorrow.

* * * * *

Lewis was nervous as they sat and waited for the taxi. Kanisha said she would be all right and was worried about him. Lewis was concerned about her. But, he couldn't come up with a better idea than hers. The taxi arrived at the downtown corner. Kanisha kissed him good-bye, got a firm grip on the carry-on bag she had and went to the taxi. She gave the driver instructions to the airport. Lewis got out of the car and went in to get some junk food. He kept his eye on the car following him and it did not go after Kanisha. So far, so good.

She used Mrs. Briggs' credit card to purchase her commuter flight to New York City. She hoped there was a machine to purchase her ticket to North Carolina after she got to Kennedy Airport. She went to the ladies restroom and checked her hair again. She hated it plastered down like that and it itched. She reached into her panty hose and removed the disk in the bubble wrap. She scratched her belly and put it back. She arrived at the boarding gate, which was now accepting the last of its passengers.

She wondered about the airport security. Her jewelry usually had to be removed when she went through the metal detector. The inspector noticed the jewelry too, but his wand didn't detect anything.

Lewis finished eating, got in his car, and listened to a talk show on the way home. The liberal host wanted to talk about some hot campaign issues, but his callers started talking in that direction and then switched to Kathy. Lewis smiled, thinking that he had a good job, reporting impartially and not having to justify an agenda.

Chapter 19

The caterer was smiling as he left the new offices of PROJECT INVITATION. Not because of the tip he had received, but because of the good humor of the group inside. Kathy was finishing her morning session using the white disk. Victor was waiting to escort her to the meeting and watching news on the new, big-screen TV. He saw a picture of Kanisha Porter, identified as Kenya Roberts being presented, with a number to call if anyone saw her. She was wanted in connection with the murder of a North Carolina elected official. Victor told Kathy about it when they were returning to the new offices. She said not to worry and asked him how he was doing with his project. He replied that he was trying and really concentrating but, so far, nothing was happening. She told him to keep trying. He said it felt like he was sitting outside of church on a Sunday morning.

Kathy referred to her note-pad after opening the meeting with the announcement that she had lots of answers.

"The press conference will take place at Ground Zero for the first man-made atomic reaction.

"It will take place on Easter Sunday, coming up quickly.

"My father will be the Master of Ceremonies.

"Larry will operate the computer.

"I will answer the questions.

"The United Nations will decide who will ask the questions and the order in which they will be asked. The questions must be limited to the use of man's free will. No new technology will be revealed.

"Ten million dollars will be added to our operating budget.

"Larry is to update the spare computer now, with the black disk. We are all invited to watch him do it. Larry, it's your show." Kathy concluded her part of the meeting.

"Like, right now? Before the meeting is over?" Larry asked.

"I believe so." Kathy replied.

"Victor, lets get the disk and do it," Larry said. He and Victor re-opened the safe and took out the black disk. All got up and circled around as he went to the spare computer and put in the disk. He put in a few commands and nothing happened. After a few more attempts with deeper programming commands, he received a message that informed him the disk in D drive was unreadable.

"So, it appears that one of our disks has been disabled," Kathy said rather calmly. "Worse yet, it could have been stolen and switched. Larry, why don't you take a good look at the disk and see of you can determine if it is genuine or not?"

Larry removed the disk and inspected it in the light. He used his fingernail and chipped some black paint from the plastic. "This disk is a phony!" he said.

Kathy told her father that he might want to call the Police and let them know that it looks like someone switched disks on them.

* * * * *

Hudson called Lewis in response to the latter's request.

"I have the disk. There is a problem." Lewis began the conversation.

"You have one of the disks in your possession? Is that what I'm hearing?" Hudson asked excitedly.

"You could say that. I told you Kanisha was good. She took it out last night. It's a good thing I had the replacement or she couldn't have pulled it off," Lewis said.

"Where is it now and when can I pick it up?" Hudson asked.

"Whoa, whoa. I said there was a problem. Perhaps if I came in and spoke to you in person we could find a solution together. As a-matter-of-fact, I know we can find a solution. So, for starters, I don't have the disk here. Call off your goons. As soon as I see them leave, I'll come in to your office," Lewis said confidently.

"And how do I know you won't just take off with the disk?" Hudson asked.

"If I was going to split, I'd do it the way I did yesterday. I wouldn't bother to phone you," Lewis said, exasperated with the paranoid thinking of Hudson.

"OK. Come right over," Hudson said.

Lewis waited and made a bowl of cereal and checked to see

how long it would take the message to get through. "Four minutes," he noted, glancing at his watch when the car outside departed. He concluded that there was a central control somewhere. It would have taken only a minute or less, if Hudson was controlling the action.

He drove to SuperCee very relaxed. He felt Kanisha was safe since her picture was still being shown on TV. He couldn't figure out why God wanted the disk to end up in the hands of SuperCee. Hudson was waiting for him in front of the building, motioned him to park in the reserved space and come right in. They went to the office of Doctor Jeffries, the president of the company. He was introduced, and offered a cup of coffee.

"I understand that you have some good news for our company. I hear that you have one of the disks that have superconductors in them?" Dr. Jeffries began.

"Yes. I don't know if it has superconductors in it, but it is the black disk that was reported to have super storage capacity," Lewis answered.

"Tell me, how did you come about this? There has been a lot in the papers about phony disks concerning this Kathy person," Dr. Jeffries asked.

"Kanisha Porter has become a friend of Kathy. She is the American News reporter that took over my assignment. We've been friends for many years. We visited Kathy last night and Kanisha asked Kathy if she could see a demonstration of the disk in action. Kathy obliged and Kanisha made the switch with the disk that Hudson provided. It looked pretty good to me. I couldn't tell any difference." Lewis stopped talking.

"When can I have this disk in my hands? I understand that you want five million dollars for your service," Dr. Jeffries asked.

"That's where the problem comes up. I told Hudson this might happen but *he* authorized me to go," Lewis said, looking at Hudson, after taking note of the price difference. "You told me to execute both plans. I wanted to wait until I could make the switch myself. She couldn't have pulled this off without the disk that was made here."

217

"I don't understand. What's the problem? You and Porter have the disk," the president asked for an explanation.

"Kanisha wants...get this...*ten million dollars*. I told her she was crazy, but she stood firm. That's her price." Lewis looked at the floor, sheepishly.

"That's a lot of money. How did she arrive at that figure?"

"It seems that your company is not the only one that wants the disk. She mentioned to me that a foreign country offered her seven-and-a-half for the same service," Lewis lied.

"Japanese or Middle-East?" Dr. Jeffries asked.

"She didn't say. Oh, she did say she would like to see it stay here in the US."

"Very patriotic. Let's say that the price is not too far out of reach and we decide to purchase it. How long will that take? How will the purchase be made? I would be seriously unhappy if I purchased a disk that was made right here in this building for ten million dollars. Some other people would be unhappy also and it is not nice when they are unhappy," Dr. Jeffries said seriously.

"She is putting it in a 'safe haven', as she called it. The money is to be deposited in a Swiss account. I am to be your hostage until you receive the disk. She will get it to me or perhaps let you know where to find it. She wasn't clear on this point. I trust her, or I wouldn't be here," Lewis thought he made a clear summary.

"And, if we decide not to meet the price? You are in a very precarious position here," Dr. Jeffries asked.

Lewis looked at Hudson and asked, "You haven't told him about the Jimmy Franklin interview?"

It was Hudson's turn to take some of the heat. "I haven't finished checking it out. He claims he has the interview that Jimmy Franklin gave on the limo ride. The hooker we think is Kanisha Porter. He's blackmailing us."

"That *was* Kanisha Porter and I have the interview. It's not blackmail, it's insurance," Lewis replied.

"So? What happens now?" Dr. Jeffries asked.

"If we have a deal, I go home and wait for Kanisha to contact me. You can decide now or wait and watch TV. Kathy should be finding out just about now that a disk has been stolen, or not working anymore...depending on how good of a job your Lab boys did," Lewis concluded.

"We have a deal. Keep in touch," Dr. Jeffries pointed Lewis to the door.

When Lewis was gone and the door closed, Dr. Jeffries said, "I hate being blackmailed like this. That jerk...doesn't he know that as soon as Porter has the money, he's history. Pathetic."

Hudson didn't respond as Chad called him on intercom and told him there were two important calls waiting. Jeffries indicated he could take them there, in his office. After identifying himself he listened to the caller on one line and then the other.

"My surveillance people just reported that a Police car came screaming in to the Makino residence. My snitch at the station said one of the disks has been stolen and replaced with a phony. I wish to hell Kanisha Porter was working for me.

"I didn't tell you about the interview holdout because Baltimore tells me there is nothing incriminating in it. Do you know something different?" Hudson asked.

"Baltimore doesn't know what was said in the house before they got in the limo. I heard the whole tape from the limo and it seemed to only fill in the holes. The real damage could have been done earlier. If Lewis has *that* tape, he may have us by the balls."

"That's the one he said he had. If he's a no-show, the tape goes public."

"I hope the disk is worth the price. *If* the superconductors are in there, we could turn this into a legitimate business." Dr. Jeffries ended the conversation.

* * * * *

Badge Number Forty-Three was the first police vehicle to arrive at the Makino residence. He came in with sirens screaming and was now familiar with the route so he was driving at a relatively high speed. He hit the brakes hard, blocked the street with his vehicle, silenced the sirens, and doused all but the blue lights. He was really good at this. He approached Kathy's house with caution before

219

noticing the people who were trying to get his attention from the other house across the street.

Kathy greeted him and explained to him that the disk didn't work and found that it was a phony. Forty-Three asked how she was doing and said he was following her story closely. He said he better get a detective and a fingerprint team. Kathy said that it was probably useless for fingerprints, as Larry had just about removed all of the paint from the phony disk. He asked if he could use a phone and thought that the District Attorney should be informed, as he was really interested in this case. He saw Professor Makino waving at him and went across the room to talk to him.

He reminded Professor Makino that Kathy had told him the very first time he met her that God was going to have a press conference. He said he thought she was an emotionally upset person and never mentioned that fact to anyone. He remarked that it was only a week and look at all that happened. Now, a disk stolen. He asked the professor if there was a list of everyone who had been in the premises since the last time the disk was known to be the right one. Kami asked Marcie to see if she could come up with the list.

Shirley was seated at the spare computer with the C:\ prompt blinking, waiting for Larry to remove the last specks of paint from the bottom of the disk. He cleaned it with a damp kitchen towel and said it looked like spray latex paint and it did not adhere to the plastic very well. He put it in the D drive and she stayed in DOS and found that it was a text-processing program. Larry told her to install it and she typed in the commands. She followed instructions from the monitor and completed the installation. Larry told her to open the .EXE file and she complied. He gave her a few more instructions and the screen reported the information that he requested. "Print it!" he said and she hit the Print Screen button.

"Kathy! Kathy! Come quick! The President of the United States is on the phone!" Marcie came into the meeting room with a long extension and a telephone and handed it to her. Kathy took the instrument and sat down.

"Hello, Mr. President. This is Kathryn Makino...Yes, still walking...Yes, he's fine, thank you...That's right, a press conference...Yes, I believe so at this point. I'm sorry, you don't understand. We have just had one disk replaced with a phony. We need one of the disks to go interactive. If we have one disk, I believe you will hear God speak. That's why I said I believe so...The police are here now...Yes, I believe the Secret Service would help...Yes, if you want to send them, but I think we have an excellent police force here. If you want to help out, can you do something about all of these helicopters flying around here? ...Yes, very noisy. This is a residential area and the school is just a few blocks away. I'm more concerned for the safety of the children...Thank you very much. No one here seems to know how to control them...Yes, the information I have is Easter Sunday...No, I wasn't aware of that, but I did not make the schedule and I believe that God would take preference over the play-offs...I need to discuss that with someone in government. I believe it is to be on government land...Yes... may I bring my father with me? ...I think Mr. Roy Atkins also...The manager of PROJECT INVITATION...No, he hasn't been in office. He volunteered, from American News...Yes, they were mailed from my home...Don't your Cabinet members read the paper and listen to TV? ...Just a moment, sir, I think I can answer that. Shirley, do you recall if the Secretary of State was sent a list of instructions and an information packet? It seems like we sent them to everyone else...Sir, the Secretary of State was notified. That went out as registered mail and we have a signature for it. Would you like the name of the individual? ...Uhh, just three, sir, and one of them is on vacation...Yes, to Switzerland...Yes, I believe He did have twelve, but that was before computers...Yes, you have a sense-of-humor too, I saw your latest explanation on TV...This afternoon is fine...We'll look forward to it. Thank you very much for calling." Kathy put the phone down.

"Well, that was the President. He says that he's been following my progress very closely. I think he really called because the Secretary of State threw our information in the trashcan and now the foreign embassies are calling him for more details after receiving the information we sent *them*. Shirley, if you will make me another copy, I'll hand-carry it to the White House and the President can give it to him.

"Daddy. You and Roy will visit the President with me. We should be there in time for dinner. He's sending a plane to pick us up.

"Larry, I guess you'll be in charge until Daddy gets back. Lock up that disk and don't open the safe until I return. Victor, no one goes in that safe. There *may* be some Secret Service people here. I prefer to work with our own people until we can check the Secret Service out and see how they perform. But, with this president, maybe we'll see them and maybe we won't. I know the plane will be here because this will be a great opportunity for pictures.

"Shirley, continue looking up all of the information you can find on the test site. I want to become a walking encyclopedia on radioactivity when I get back. What am I thinking! Cancel that. I have the walking encyclopedia in my house. I'll walk to the test site on my Daddy's arm and he can answer all of the questions."

"It's on TV already!" Victor announced excitedly. The group looked at the message as it ran across the bottom of the screen without interrupting the soap opera in progress. UNCONFIRMED REPORT: ONE OF KATHY MAKINO'S DISKS HAS BEEN STOLEN FROM RESIDENCE. REPEAT: UNCONFIRMED....

Larry showed the printout from the computer to Kathy. She folded it and asked Larry to walk across the street with her.

"There is a reason for a SuperCee disk to show up here. Do you remember the conversation you had with God concerning the ego and SuperCee?" Kathy asked Larry. He said he recalled it.

"And you know all of their codes and how to break them...correct?" Kathy asked. He said that he did.

"While I'm in Washington, I want you to take that disk apart and find out everything that it contains. In the meantime, we want no mention of the fact that it came from SuperCee. We'll let the police find that out during their investigation.

"Who would pay ten million dollars for a disk that is reported to have superconductors in them?" Kathy concluded.

"Besides SuperCee, only about a hundred others. In this country alone. New technology is like finding oil."

"I hope that I'll be back by morning. I look forward to my daily meeting," Kathy said as she looked at her idle computer in the other room. She looked at her wheelchair. "Give that to someone who can't afford to buy one. It needs a complete overhaul first."

When they returned to the INVITATION office, Nancy was waiting to speak to Kathy on the phone. They spoke for about ten minutes and Kathy put the phone down and said she had some announcements to make. She waited until everyone was seated.

"First, Robby has five hundred thousand in the bank. Larry, Daddy and Robby have signature cards, but it's better if we open a business account locally for our daily needs and move funds electronically. Robby will FAX us with the account numbers and details.

"Robbie's mother is preparing the wedding and reception for them when they return to New York. We are all invited. Daddy, if our budget allows, can we all go to the wedding? Robby would like Victor to be the Best Man. Sammy makes great looking tuxedoes and he can bring one along for Robby to wear at the wedding.

"That's about it. We better get packed to go to Washington."

She called Victor aside. "Would you ask Sammy if he does ladies dresses? If not, ask him who he recommends. I haven't a thing to wear."

* * * * *

Kanisha called Lewis on his cellular phone. She was safe and ready to make a deal. Lewis was to find out the Swiss bank number from Kathy and when the money was in the account, she would tell him where the disk was. She asked how he was doing. He was scared a little, but had faith that all was going to work out. She said she missed him and that it would all be over soon. Lewis asked her if she was making notes and maybe when it was all over the two of them could collaborate on a book. Kanisha thought that was a great idea.

* * * * *

Kathy wore a plain black dress and her first pair of high-heeled shoes that Sammy selected for her. He didn't like the way the shoes

223

fit her and promised they would be replaced before the limo showed up. He was a magician with a sewing machine and her dress was quickly altered. She selected the jewelry from his case after listening to his advice. As she looked herself over in the mirror, Sammy suggested some changes in her cosmetics. Kathy agreed. Sammy said maybe his sister could ride to the airport with them and make the changes on the way. She agreed to that. Sammy took one more look at Victor, tugged his lapels and patted his bible bulge and seemed satisfied with his appearance.

Kathy was glad that Victor could come along now that there were two Secret Service men with nothing to do except watch the safe. Victor had his key with him, so no one could open it anyway. Professor Makino looked very distinguished in a dark suit and University necktie. Kathy said he should blow-dry his hair to be in keeping with the President. Kami said he would look like a Japanese Einstein. Roy had gone home to change and they were waiting for him to return. A pair of shoes was delivered and Sammy was right, they were more comfortable. Kathy was pacing the floor, breaking them in while waiting for Roy. It was getting late.

They heard the sirens in the distance and they were getting closer. Forty- Three came charging down the street and made one of his procedure stops. Roy stepped out, wiped his brow, and seemed pleased to be on foot. He was nicely dressed and wore a tie that matched Kami's. Kami spotted it immediately and they established another link in their friendship. Sammy's sister showed up and she examined her model. She asked who picked out the jewelry and Kathy said she had. Ethel suggested some changes and took the jewelry case from Sammy. It was time to go.

Kathy wanted to see the crowd, but Ethel kept moving her face and applying various potions from her kit. She completed the work and handed Kathy a mirror. Kathy was amazed when she looked at herself. She felt she really could be a model. She asked Kami what he thought of it. He stopped his conversation with Roy, gave a quick glance, and said she was beautiful. She was about to ask Victor, but he let out a long whistle and smiled. He gave her a thumbs-up. The limo was approaching the airport.

The driver turned short of the main entrance, onto a gated street and along a frontage road. They came to a small, elegant building and saw the jet with official markings parked on the apron in front. A crowd was waiting to greet them and take pictures. A path was roped off for them to walk from the limo to the entrance. Kami took his daughter by the arm and Victor handed her the bouquet of flowers that he remembered to buy for her. They walked inside amidst the applause and the questions and comments that were being shouted to Kathy.

She recognized the Governor immediately. He introduced himself and said that he would be accompanying her to Washington and then he introduced his wife. After a few words, they were led to the waiting aircraft. Victor, Roy, and Kami were ushered aboard with the Governor's wife. The Governor and Kathy were stopped at the top of the boarding ramp, turned to wave good-bye to the crowd and have their pictures taken. The stewards, in Air Force uniform, seated Kathy at a lounge beside the Governor's wife. Her father and the Governor sat across. The plane began to move as soon as the Governor was seated.

Kathy noticed that there were about twenty seats behind that were occupied. She said she was glad that others were going and that the President hadn't sent a plane just for her. The Governor laughed and said that the others were members of his staff and some Washington press. And they were all there, just for her. She asked him what she could expect on her arrival in Washington. The Governor laid out the scenario, with a transfer to limousine service at Andrews AFB, and then to the White House. There would be some people to greet her at Andrews and arrange for her return flight.

The Governor and Kami spoke much of the time during the flight and Kathy and the Governor's wife became friends. Kathy asked her what she thought about the upcoming press conference with God and the woman's body language revealed that she was a complete skeptic and accustomed to keeping her thoughts to herself. Kathy said to go ahead and tell her what was on her mind, as she wasn't going to tell anyone what was said.

"Most of them think it's a big joke. There isn't much happening in the world right now to occupy their attention. The primaries are coming up and every bit of publicity helps. Right now, you're the biggest controversy going. The only show in town. They'll humor you for now," the older woman said.

"That's what's on *their* minds. What's on *your* mind? Do you think I'm a joke?" Kathy asked, remembering her lesson.

"Perhaps you are. I'm the wife of a very important man. It's best that I keep my opinions to myself."

"And perhaps I'm not. So there is a glimmer of hope that there is a separate, thinking, intelligent, and free spirit in your body. I wonder what she thinks of me. Am I a joke to her? Is God a joke to her?" Kathy asked.

"I haven't been in touch with her lately," the official's wife answered softly.

"I'm sorry. It's just that I thought I saw a sign of sadness in your face. Have you ever thought how great life would be if you invited God to one of your parties. I hear that you throw great parties at the mansion," Kathy continued.

"Would you come to one of my parties? I'm having one this weekend," the woman asked.

"You don't get it. I'm not God. I was suggesting that you invite God into your life. The real you. The one you haven't talked to lately," Kathy explained.

The woman was locked in thought and finally replied, "You're right. I saw that on TV and thought you were onto something. Then I forgot about it. I think I'll do that. We're staying in Washington and I'll be alone in the guest house for a day or two."

"You can't lose," Kathy informed her. She felt the landing gear being extended and the Governor and Kami joined in the conversation.

226

Chapter 20

"Mr. Hudson, this is Lewis Anderson. Kanisha has advised me that she is ready to deal. I am on the way to get the account number for the bank. When the money is deposited, you will have your disk. She wants to know how long it is going to take to get the money together. She has other buyers interested and they are at ten-and-a-half, but they are foreigners."

"Give me a number to call you back. Moving ten million dollars out of the country quickly may require some special expertise that I'm not familiar with. By the way, Lewis, what's in this for you?" Hudson asked.

"I'm just trying to stay alive at this point. I'm caught in the middle. Kanisha is going to run as soon as she gets the money. I know that. I hope that I can continue working for SuperCee doing your PR. I know how to keep my mouth shut. I only stole the tape from Kanisha to keep my mouth from being shut permanently. You guys put Jimmy Franklin away, didn't you?" Lewis asked.

"What was on the tape, Lewis?" Hudson fished with no skill what so ever.

"Bad. Bad business. How you guys tried to blackmail him because he was gay and how he beat you by going public. Many, many, names of politicos who you set up, who chose not to go public for one reason or the other. But, hey, it's all yours man. Just let me work for you, see what a good job I can do and the tape is yours," Lewis pleaded his case.

"I'll see what they say. From me, personally, I got no hard feelings. I think if the disk is genuine and you pull this off without any more problems it may work out for you. We always need some men around that we can count on. We could even go legit if the superconductors are for real," Hudson responded.

* * * * *

"It's going to be two in the morning before we get back home,"

227

Kathy said to her father. They were arranging for the return flight. The Governor said that he could arrange for them to stay over in Washington, but Kathy said she needed to be home for her morning session. More drinks were offered and declined and the limo departed for the White House.

There was little activity outside of the White House this evening and they were through the security procedures rapidly. Victor was relieved of his Bible and then it was replaced. He was able to find someone to take the documents for the Secretary of State.

The Governor introduced them to the other guests who were invited to dinner. The minister who was going to say grace asked Kathy if there any thoughts that she would like included. She thought about that and said, "It all starts with the *invitation*. Maybe you can expound on that."

"Ladies and gentleman, the President of the United States." All eyes turned to the staircase as the President made his entry. He located Kathy immediately and walked to her after announcing his regrets for his wife who was at a seminar.

Kathy was a bit flustered at first, as she was not used to all of the handshaking and endless congratulatory dialog that took place before any serious thought occurred. Her father said she would get used to it, as it was very much the same with his students when he met them socially. After shaking hands and listening to how nice it was for her to come, etc., she introduced the President to her father, Victor, and Roy. The President excused himself to shake more hands. The Governor took her around and introduced her to the ones she had missed earlier. The Guest of Honor was a finance minister from a Mid-East nation wearing his country's traditional headdress. Kathy was startled at his perfect English pronunciation. His wife was about twenty years younger, dressed elegantly. Today was her birthday and she wanted to spend it having dinner with the President. The Governor, seemingly bored with his duties, excused himself to glad hand some friends, and said he would seat her for dinner. She found her father surrounded by a group listening to him expound on the virtues of Kosher food. Victor and Roy were having a cocktail and entertaining the Governor's wife and two other women. They seemed interested in what the men had to say.

228

The President made a boyish gesture of running off to the dining room with the Mid-East wife and dinner was announced. The Governor found Kathy and escorted her to her seat, three down on the right side between the Governor and an empty seat. The President pointed and Rev. Jacobs said grace. His theme was that when Christ knocks, for God's sake, open the door. *Invite* Him in. He then came and took the empty chair. Kathy thanked him for his effort on such short notice.

She and the Reverend established some common ground quickly and they conversed amongst themselves throughout dinner, while the Governor seemed to have someone to talk to on his right and across the table. Victor and Roy were far down. Her father was in the middle on the other side and everyone around was listening to him.

Towards the end of the meal, the President announced the birthday of his guest. Her husband motioned to a servant who entered with a diamond bracelet on a black velvet pillow and he rose and presented it to her. It must have cost a million dollars. There was applause and then a cake with candles and all sang, "Happy Birthday To You." The cake departed to be cut and served. The President said he had *invited* a special guest tonight who had been receiving a lot of publicity lately. He said he wished some of the people he was sponsoring in the campaign would do as well. He waited for the polite laughter to subside and then he asked the guests if they would like to see Kathy Makino walk. They all applauded and Kathy got an idea. She rose and the applause resumed. She walked to the head of the table and whispered to the President. He nodded his head and called one of his staff. By the time she circled the table and got to Victor the music began...a Strauss waltz.

"May I have this dance, sir?" she asked.

Victor got up, tugged at his suit coat, and took her hand.

He started her slowly and gracefully. As she fell into the rhythm, he lengthened the steps. By the time one circle of the table was complete the guests were clapping in time with the music. Victor spun her to the concluding bars and she arched back over his strong supporting arm to a sincere applause.

As they resumed their seats, the President said that was truly remarkable. He asked her how long she had been confined to a wheelchair and Kathy said that it was over ten years. The President indicated that he would speak to her later and announced the entertainment for the evening. A relatively unknown but very funny comedian kept them entertained for an hour. There were a few Kathy jokes mixed in with his routine.

After dinner the President summoned Kathy and said that he was not informed about her scheduled departure and thought he might be able to speak to her in a few days. Kathy replied that she had agreed to come to Washington to conduct business and not as entertainment. She told him that her organization was announcing to the press in the morning that the press conference would be held at Alamogordo, New Mexico, on Easter Sunday, not very far off. She expected the Pope, all Heads of State, and the President, naturally, to attend. He told her she could not do that, it was government land. She told him it was public land and the government only represented the public. He said they had better have a meeting now and they left for the oval office.

Inside, Kathy said that the President should inform himself better. She said that the foreign gentleman and his wife knew more about what was going on than he did. Or, perhaps the President had been informed and thought it was a joke. The President assured her that was not the case, but it was not convincing. Kathy asked him if he had read the packet of material that was addressed to him. He said he couldn't read everything that was sent to him. Kathy said that someone on his staff had decided for him that an opportunity for the people of the world to communicate with the Creator of Mankind was not a suitable subject for the President whose nation was going to sponsor the event.

"Sponsor? I have not agreed to sponsor your event," the President said angrily.

"You would be foolish not to, when eighty-five percent of the population is in favor. We sent you the statistics. Our poll covered a significantly larger number of people than any of the services you presently subscribe to and I can assure you that *my computer projections are flawless.*

230

"And, of that eighty-five percent, ninety-two percent said they were willing to spend public funds to put it on. At this time, we do not anticipate the expenditure of *any* public funds to organize and broadcast the event. We only want permission to use the site and the services that are presently idle. The people have already paid for them."

"You mentioned Alamogordo. That rings a bell. What is the significance of that? Why not in New York or Los Angeles?" the President asked.

"Not exactly Alamogordo. Ground Zero for the first man-made nuclear fission device. Alamogordo is the closest place. There is an Air Force Base nearby that is serviceable. As I told you this morning, I did not choose the location, and do not yet know it's significance. I just know that's where it's going to be," Kathy said rather firmly.

"Superconductors. This isn't a scheme for public funding? Where do they come in?" the President asked.

"They are the 'holy spirit' of PROJECT INVITATION. The means of communication with the staff. The real Holy Spirit is much less sophisticated and every single person in the world has access. It is not necessary to wait for the knock on the door. God is there, waiting now. Waiting for *the invitation*," Kathy informed the President.

"I'm going to do my homework. I see you have to leave soon to get home at a reasonable time. Can you arrange your schedule to meet with my cabinet?"

"I can come to Washington at your convenience. If you have a personal computer around here, I could even stay for a few days. I promised to be on the computer each morning.

"If I plan to stay overnight, I would have to bring the one remaining disk with me. I'm sure there is a personal computer around here that I could use."

The President told her he would like to see the disk, maybe even have a demonstration. Kathy said she would work on it.

* * * * *

231

After explaining who she was and what she had been doing with her son, Kanisha Porter was gracefully accepted into the household of Mrs. Franklin. Kanisha kept the disk on her person but let no one be informed that she had it. She was introduced to everyone as a close friend of the family. She kept her hair tied back and jelled down to maintain a low profile. The interment ceremonies were scheduled for the following afternoon and she planned to attend.

Lewis obtained the Swiss account number and gave it to Hudson.

All was quiet at PROJECT INVITATION. The phone-calls were being answered by the computer and statistics compiled.

American News had its headlines and lead-story completed and were adding the latest bits of news that had come in from around the world. The press foreman was waiting for the word to start. The circulation had increased so rapidly that he had to put another shift on as the machinery could only print so many copies per hour.

Moving the PROJECT INVITATION staff to the Makino office allowed some space for the conducting of business with the various media agencies.

* * * * *

One or two reporters stayed on the flight, hoping that Kathy would break the press protocol controlled by American News. Except for Kathy, Kami, Victor, and Roy, the plane cabin was empty. Kathy sat next to Victor and looked at the lights on the ground from thirty-five thousand feet. This had been his first jet ride. Kathy had been on several before. One time to a special clinic for evaluation. The other time she went on vacation to her grandmother's home in California.

She wondered if people who flew airplanes had any special insight, as she never heard of too many problems associated with pilots and they certainly would be a group with a strong ego. She asked an attendant if she could speak to one of the pilots. He left and returned with a handsome man in his early thirties. He introduced himself as a Major and said that he was a flight-examiner and would not be missed up front.

Kathy explained her idea to him and he thought a bit. He said that his present job presented no real moral challenge, but before this assignment, he was a pilot on a B-52, carrying nuclear weapons. He said he thought people in that line of work were very dependable, hard-working, dedicated, and knew that if they all worked together and did their job, they would never have to drop a bomb.

In response to her specific idea of a strong ego, he said he thought that if the ego was trained to go in the right direction it need not cause chaos. He mentioned that some of the pilots he knew, who let themselves stray, were soon discovered, and were out looking for other work. He said that was what he was presently doing as a check pilot; observing how the pilots perform, and making recommendations to make them better pilots. He said that he had been keeping up with the news coverage and saw her making the statement about the *invitation*. He said he hadn't tried it yet, but was going to.

He said that what troubled him most about the nuclear bomber was the way his job was depicted in the media; some sort of madman who wanted to kill millions of people, when just the opposite was true. And, after all the hard work and the victory, the very same people were unprepared to offer any leadership to resolve the economic hardships that followed. So, they didn't want to kill them with a bomb, they wanted them to slowly starve to death.

"Identify those people and you will find your ego problem."

Kathy asked him if it were possible that he had already made the *invitation*.

The pilot said that was a very good question and that maybe he had. He recalled several training missions that were very arduous, with in-flight refueling and he had actually prayed for a safe return. He also said that crossing large bodies of water is often very boring and you have a lot of time to just think and watch the wondrous world go by underneath the plane. He said he knew that there was a God. He didn't know how to really get in touch with Him. Kathy thought that he already had, but added that another *invitation* couldn't hurt.

Victor listened to the conversation intently without saying anything. When the pilot left to resume his duties Victor said he was going to make the *invitation* this evening when they got back home. Kathy said that was a good idea and asked if he knew how to do it. Victor asked for more information. Kathy told him to wait until everything was peaceful and then to lie as quietly and comfortably as he could and look inside his mind. She said there were two opposing forces at work, one to distract and one to come through. Of the two, the spirit was stronger and would emerge. The opposing force was the ego; the spirit was the real Victor. She wished him luck, and assured him that the real Victor would only bring joy. God set it up that way so that the power cannot be used for the wrong purposes.

She said that she thought she had discovered what a holy relationship was and Victor asked her about that. She said it was one in which the two partners had turned the relationship to the hands of the Holy Spirit to work for God's purposes. Kathy said she thought that Robby and his deceased wife had one and that she hoped that Nancy and Robby would share one too. Victor said he had never seen two people so attracted to each other in such a short time. Kathy said that they had help, without mentioning the flowers.

* * * * *

Another day had already begun on the other side of the world. The President of the Philippines was informed of the packet of instructions, indicated that he was interested and scheduled a meeting with the Catholic Archbishop to discuss it later in the afternoon.

Japan's Prime Minister considered it something for his Secretary of State to handle. In China, there was some interest. The Australians had their fax copies and were waiting for the courier to arrive with the original documents. They informed the heads of clergy for the most prominent religions. There was a serious meeting of the closest friends of the Indian Prime Minister. They assigned the task to a scholar of renown. The Israeli Prime Minister wondered why Alamogordo, New Mexico and why not a site with religious significance. He assigned one of his ministers to investigate and see if the site could be changed. Saddam Huessien was informed of it by one of his confidants. He asked him what the texture of the paper was. Perhaps it could be useful...they laughed.

The Vatican had followed the story from the beginning. A group of Cardinals were studying details of the information packet that they were furnished. They were vitally interested in the project, but unfortunately, the Pope had already made plans for the Easter services. They had already sent a return message to PROJECT INVITATION requesting that the event be postponed for a month due to the conflict with the Easter ceremonies.

The Russians knew about Alamogordo. Their first concern was the threat of nuclear radioactivity. But, they wanted to send someone. They needed help and maybe they could find *something* there. Their presence would certainly be beneficial to them. Maybe if they could send representatives from each of their divided parts, and they acted in union, it would aid their cause.

The German Chancellor was quite interested in the information. Yes, they were interested and would send a government official and many clergy. The Italians had lost the packet of information and asked their Embassy to obtain another. The employee who stole it and turned it over to his Catholic priest thought he was doing the right thing. No one knew what to do with the information in Greece, it was finally sent to the Head of the Orthodox Church.

Spain was definitely interested in the outcome and would wait and see what came of it. South Africa would send clergy. Kenya and Ethiopia would send clergy. Some African nations would send relatives on vacation if some agency would sponsor them. The Archbishop of Canterbury met with the Prime Minister and they called a meeting of Parliament. The Queen's Office requested postponement due to Easter plans.

Chapter 21

The FBI Director knew how to play hardball. So did Kanisha Porter. Moreover, she had the support of Mrs. Franklin. Summoned to North Carolina by his Regional Chief, the Director listened to Kanisha's plan after he was sworn to secrecy. If he did not approve, he could withdraw his men and expertise, but would tell no one of his knowledge of the plan.

The ceremony would be over by four in the afternoon. The casket would be switched by the funeral director after leaving the church. Kanisha would ride in the hearse, place the disk in the casket, and remain with it so there would be no possibility of a mix-up. The remains would be given proper care and placed in a mausoleum. The casket containing the disk and some weights would be interred. The cemetery staff would leave their work vehicles, a portable tent and on old step-van close to the gravesite. The FBI agents had access to night vision equipment and cameras and could work out of the van or the tent. Kanisha would inform the people who wanted the disk and let the FBI photograph them in the act of digging up the gravesite. The evidence would be used later.

The Director said he couldn't comply because the disk was stolen and he would be breaking the law himself. Kanisha corrected him. The disk was not stolen; it was given to her. She asked him to investigate and see if a report had been made by Kathryn Makino. He said that he would check it out and if she were telling the truth, he would cooperate. He would give her forty-eight hours and then he would have to notify the President. She and Mrs. Franklin agreed to that. Mrs. Franklin said she thought her son would want it this way.

* * * * *

Lewis Anderson was on the phone with Mr. Hudson wanting to know how the money transfer was going. Hudson said that half was already in the account. It took some time to move this much money without attracting attention. He told Lewis to call back later.

* * * * *

The President was pleased with the information he got at his morning briefing. Alamogordo was OFF LIMITS due to residual radioactivity. That was the end of that. A nicely worded message was sent to OPERATION INVITATION.

* * * * *

Larry had no trouble deciphering the codes on the CD that Lewis got from SuperCee. Apparently, they had not found a replacement for him. The CD was a text-processing software program that the company purchased at a discount and coded so that it could not be used in any computer other than SuperCee's. The manufacturer and license number codes were printed out for reference. But, Kathy told him to take it apart, so he started looking at everything. He ran it through an anti-virus check. It passed. He knew something else was in there. It took him about an hour and he finally found it. The disk was coded to work in conjunction with another computer system. He always suspected that SuperCee had another mainframe somewhere; he never bothered to look for the access code before. He now had the code to get in, if he ever wanted to. He committed it to memory.

In spite of the late arrival home, Kami was up when the President's message arrived. He called one of his colleagues at the University who was an atom-bomb trivia collector. The scholar had intimate details of the materials used in the first chain reaction. The professor did some quick calculations in his head and asked how the site could still be radioactive. His colleague said it wasn't...to any extent that anyone was in danger...unless, of course, you ate ten tons of sand a day for six years. Then you would definitely die of radioactivity. His friend recalled that the second bomb dropped on Nagasaki was identical to the original test device. He had visited Ground Zero at both Nagasaki and Hiroshima and there were no ill

238

effects. He stated that the memorial in Hiroshima was visited by tens of thousands of people every year. Professor Makino asked his friend to fax the information that he had in his library with details of the materials used in the test bomb.

* * * * *

Arnulfo Sanchez was not a happy man. He was a mason and many houses and stores in his pueblo were constructed by him. He was proud of his skills and respected by his neighbors. He had managed to send his oldest daughter, Rosa, to college in Cuidad Juarez because he was then in his forties and could work longer hours. His remaining two sons and three daughters wanted to go, but his body was incapable of doing more work. He tried using his head and became a strong voice in his union. It took so much of his time that he ended up making less money, and greatly disillusioned with the politics. His wife tried to help with a small store, but the government taxes and credit and thievery resulted in very little profit. The biggest problem was the rate of inflation. Unless she sold her goods immediately, there was no profit unless she raised prices, and then her customers went to another store. Arnulfo experienced the same problem. The price of cement would rise monthly, but his wages remained the same. He was always behind. He wanted a better way.

His daughter was becoming a problem for him. She was not content to accept the situation and kept telling him to open his eyes, to look across the border and to observe what works. She made him sit with her one afternoon and observe the cars going by on the highway near their house. The Mexicans were going to work and the Americans and Canadians were going on vacation. She pointed out the differences in the age and condition of the cars and compared the price of the identical car purchased in Mexico with the price one paid on the other side.

She showed him her passport and visa that was forged, but it wouldn't work anymore since the Americans installed the computers. She reminded him that there was no waiting list for Americans who wanted a visa to visit Mexico.

He told her that he already knew it was better on the other side, and that was because the Americans stole the Mexican land. She laughed at that and told him that the land was worthless when the Americans accepted the treaty that had already been negotiated before the war began. If the government of Mexico had not already sold the valuable parts of the land to individuals, there would have been no war to start with. He asked her where she had learned that and she said she was told about it from other students at college, and then looked up the facts in history books.

What concerned him most about her was that she had abandoned the Church. She told him that hardly any of the students in college took Church seriously anymore. He was really upset with her when she said she had placed an ad in a publication to find an American husband. She explained that she would never be able to get across the line legally any other way.

She told her father that many of the students had heard about a meeting in Alamogordo and there were plans to cross the line with tens of thousands of Mexicans who were looking for a better way to live. She wanted his permission to join them. He looked in her eyes and saw himself as a younger man, full of hope and willing to take chances. He told her he had less than one thousand pesos, but she could go with his blessing.

* * * * *

Kathy was radiant after her morning session with the computer. When she went to the office for the morning meeting there was a bouquet of flowers and a note saying, "It worked! I love you." She looked at Victor, who was also smiling and blew him a kiss. While waiting for her father to join them, she read a copy of the morning American News that was open and her picture, dancing with Victor, was on the front page. The lead story contained information on the upcoming event. She was shown other national newspapers with her and the President smiling for the photographers. Her father arrived and continued doing some radioactivity calculations on his scientific calculator while enjoying a cup of tea. Larry informed her that the disk contained only a text-processing program that was able

240

to work in two computer systems and access to one of them was very sophisticated, more so than the SuperCee office system. Kathy began the meeting by describing her visit to Washington and her meeting with the President. Kami interrupted and said that the President had sent a message declaring the site off-limits due to radioactivity. He said that he had just completed his calculations and that there could be no harmful products left from the explosion. Kathy said that was her number one project, to return to Washington and have a meeting with scientific, rather than political advisors, and that her father was all the material that would be necessary. His brain and his calculator would suffice.

She said that Roy and Larry needed to have a meeting and figure out how everyone could go to New York City for the big wedding of Robby and Nancy.

She assigned Roy the task of making a budget for the cost of equipment and technicians to broadcast the conference to the world. He should investigate renting rather than purchasing equipment and, if they had to, they would buy time from owners of satellites.

Marcie raised her hand and informed the group that someone was putting money *into* their account, large amounts of money. She had received confirmation slips for balances of over ten million dollars!

Roy said he wanted to hire a company in New York City that specialized in this type of event. Kathy said he should approach them for a budget price and also to contact the Fundamentalist organizations, which had equipment and stations already in place.

Shirley said that they had already been sent information packets, as had all the religious organizations. She read that a request for their support was included, naming their stations, frequencies, and hours of operation. Two had already replied with tentative approval, asking for more details. Of course, the details went out with the second mailing.

The meeting concluded after asking Roy to made arrangements for her and her father and Victor to return to Washington. She asked the Secret Servicemen if they could arrange for safe transport of the disk and that Victor would be in charge of it.

Shirley said she had a private call for either Kathy or Professor

241

Makino...the Director of the FBI. Kathy took the call and told him to cooperate with Kanisha as far as he could, and that she did, in fact, give the disk to Kanisha. They did not file a stolen report and had no intention of doing so. The purpose was not yet known to her and they had broken no laws. They reported to the police only that the disk had been replaced. Kathy understood the ethical questions that the Director had and said she admired his detail but explained that she was following instructions.

After the call ended Kathy invited Victor to go for a walk to the park. She hadn't been on a swing for years and wanted to try it again.

* * * * *

Big man, "Kathy and Victor leaving the office, going back to the residence. No, they're turning! Heading this way. No vehicles parked on this part of the street. Where are they going? Got any ideas?"

Cameraman, "Close-up, holding hands. Looks like they're going for a walk!"

Big man, "That's a change in routine. Nobody's done that before."

Cameraman, "Sure, lots of people have. You never done that with a broad?"

Big man, "Nobody *here* is what I meant. Sure I done that. Me and my ex, used to walk to the park like that all the time."

Cameraman, "I didn't know you were married before. Wait...I just spotted something. He packing, man! Here, you take a look. Is that heat or what?"

Big man, looking through the zoom camera lens, "Yeah, I'd say he's packing."

Cameraman, "He's got the Secret Service in there with the disks, what the hell does he need a gun for?"

Big man, "Yeah, I was a lot lighter then. A good-looking chick, my ex."

Cameraman, "So why'd ya dump her?"

Big man, "She dumped me. I was screwing around on her and

242

she caught us. That's how I put on weight. The other chick could put together some good chow. For ten years, I ate real good, but look at this gut."

Cameraman, "Too bad, you ought'a walk more."

Big man, "You think Shirley's going out for lunch today?"

Cameraman, "I hope so. This is getting really boring. Hey, what'd ya think of the DA busting the editor of the Evening Star? Somebody snitched, I'll bet."

Big man, "I never seen anybody as lucky as Kathy. It seems like everyone's on her side. I even heard a rumor going around that she picked the horses for her old man and he par-layed it into eight mil."

Cameraman, "I ain't heard that. So, it looks like we don't get to see Kathy's old fillings. Did you know there was a law against that...going through the garbage? I hope they don't have a law against surveillance like we're doing."

Big man, "Nah, we're in the clear. We're only looking. No law against that."

Little man, finished reading the paper, "Maybe there ought to be."

Big man, "And maybe there ought'a be a law to *invite* yourself to shut up. You get on my nerves, do you know that?"

Little man, getting up and leaving, "That's the first intelligent remark I've heard all week. I think I'll do just that."

Big man, "Where the hell's he going? What'd I say that was so bad?"

Cameraman, "I think he is going to make an *invitation.*"

* * * * *

"So, tell me about your experience. You said you made the *invitation*?" Kathy asked Victor.

"Remember when we took off from Andrews? It was real dark and the plane ran into the clouds and we could see nothing. Then we broke out and the moon was lighting the tops of the clouds. And the stars were shining. We made a turn and then we could see the ground and the lights beneath us. It was nighttime, but we were

243

able to see where we were going. I don't know how the pilots did it in the clouds, but we could see the coastline and the highways and I knew which direction we were going.

"Anyway, I was thinking about that when I went to bed and I wasn't tired this time. I did as you said and looked far into my mind, I saw myself leaving the dark and coming up into the light, and, I actually said this, 'Please come into my life.' Nothing happened. I had this picture of God in my mind. Michaelangelo's painting. Then I remembered that I was supposed to speak through the Holy Spirit and asked Him to enter my mind. Whoosh...just like that. Something happened inside me. I felt good. I almost came over to tell you about it, but I wanted to do it again, so I did. This time I was asked what I wanted. I didn't know. I got up and wrote some things down, but I have to figure out what I really want before I do it again."

"So. What do you want out of life?" Kathy asked.

Victor said he didn't know but that he really felt happy and that's why he bought her the flowers.

"And the note, who wrote that?" Kathy asked.

Victor took her by the hands and lifted her from the swing. He looked into her eyes and said that he did. Their heads moved closer and they were joined in a kiss.

* * * * *

Jimmy Franklin's mother was flanked by the Governor and the Director of the FBI as they stood in the center of hundreds of mourners at the cemetery. The Governor and his wife had been friends of hers for many years and were great comfort to her at this time. It was quite natural for the Director of the FBI to be in attendance, as this was a case that came under his jurisdiction.

Mrs. Franklin was a fighter. She marched with the Kings in Montgomery. Her husband was a prominent black politician until he passed away from a heart attack. She thought she was the one who pushed him too hard. She thought her domineering demeanor was responsible for her son's sexual preference. She couldn't help it, she was born to fight for equality. But, it had taken the lives of

244

her two most loved ones. She was going to see if she needed to change, but first she was going to help Kanisha put away her son's murderers. Tears finally came to her eyes when the casket was covered.

Kanisha called Lewis and told him where the disk was and as soon as all the money was transferred, he could tell Hudson. She was planning to leave North Carolina in another day as she felt safe with Mrs. Franklin and enjoyed her company. Lewis asked if she had read the morning papers and she said that she had. He asked her if she would like to do some reporting from Albuquerque, as that was where he might be heading. She said she'd get back to him after she thought it over.

Lewis was granted access to the OPERATION INVITATION office to meet with Kathy. He was surprised to see Roy heading up the staff, and actually busy. He had neat piles of documents that he was reviewing and signing. There was a flowchart with a schedule of events on the wall. Marcie and Shirley were in and out of his office, moving paper and updating his chart. He was asking them questions and actually directing them to act. Lewis was impressed; more so when Shirley told him he had a call from Lucas Productions, and Roy waved him out of the office to conduct a private conversation.

Kathy was glad to see Lewis again and he explained his plight to her. She told him not to worry; he could stay at the residence. She had Larry check on the balance of money and it appeared that ten million dollars had been deposited. Kathy told him to call in from there and tell them where the disk was. Then he needed to get some clothes to travel in as they were all going to New York City and then to Washington.

Lewis phoned Hudson and told him where the disk was. When the invective and expletives diminished enough that he could get in another word, he said he was sorry, it was not of his doing and wanted Hudson to be sure that he understood the location and repeated it. He told Hudson that if the disk was not there he would walk into SuperCee...but he knew it was there.

* * * * *

Roy was still working after everyone else was finished for the day. He wanted to be organized in the morning when the two new temps came in to replace Shirley and Marcie. He decided that someone had to stay behind to tend the store and since he had never met the bride and groom, he volunteered for the job. There was an increase in the volume of printing and he decided to look at what was happening. The bulk of it was requests for more specific details on the location of the conference and assistance with travel plans. El Paso, Santa Fe, and Albuquerque hotels were booked solid and airline flights were impossible to obtain.

A new instruction manual for Lewis started printing. He summoned one of the security guards to get Lewis who was staying in Victor's old room. He began reading the instructions and burst out laughing. He found the folder that contained the names of entertainers and celebrities who had volunteered their services for the upcoming event, returned to his office and waited for Lewis.

He was really pleased with the responses that he received for a company to produce the equipment and technicians. His New York City lead fizzled out on him as they were booked for the Easter weekend, but they recommended a friend of theirs who was somewhere down in Texas. Roy located the man, a former partner who left the New York firm to get out of the hard winters and the hustle-and-bustle of the East Coast. He had only a part of his crew working on Easter. When he discovered it was for Kathy he promised he could get anything that was needed and would do the job for cost! The man had access to mobile generators, portable stage, sound and lighting equipment and an experienced crew. He was flying in to meet with Roy in the morning and go over the details of what would be required.

Lewis arrived and went to Roy's office and was offered a chair. "Wait 'til you get a load of this!" Roy said, handing him his manual and the folder of entertainers. Lewis began reading.

"Oh, no. No, no, no. Impossible. Out of the question. No, no, no. You've got the wrong man," he said to Roy. Lewis looked in the front of his manual again and handed it back to Roy. "This is a joke, right?"

Roy shook his head.

"I heard Kami was going to be the MC. No way," Lewis continued.

"It's no joke. Let me see if anything new came in for my manual. I've been holding the other folder open as I didn't know what to do with it." Roy got up and checked through the new data that was being printed. He found an update for his manual and read it to Lewis.

"Saturday is going to be a slow day. The sound systems and translators will need to be checked out. Kathy's computer is available. Lewis has nothing to do. He can rehearse his act and select the entertainers that he wants in time for the show. Provide transportation and travel expenses for all those participating."

Roy handed the manual and folder back to Lewis. "I'll cancel your trip to the wedding and see if Rabinowitz has any more relatives that want to go.

"Don't look at me. I had nothing to do with it. You better get to work. If anything else comes in for you, I'll have it sent over." Roy concluded the meeting by pointing to the Makino residence.

Lewis opened the manual and began reading aloud as he walked across the street, "...Type: DESKTOP...Enter... From the Desktop Display, Click on the ENTERTAINMENT icon...Enter the last four digits of your Social Security Number...Follow the instructions...To Exit, type QUIT and enter...Return to the Desktop Display."

* * * * *

Bruce Fischer shut and locked the door on his big Apollo RV. He had her loaded with food, propane and gasoline. He was surprised how easily the big engine started after a winter of sitting out in the cold New Hampshire weather.

The generator was a little cranky and wasn't keeping frequency exactly, but then, it did that last year when he started it for the first time. His brother-in-law was just going to have to get used to working a little harder until he got back. The doctors didn't give his wife much hope of making it through another winter, but Bruce wasn't going to let her go without trying everything he could. He had never been west of the Mississippi and it was about time he went. He knew the RV could make it, he just hoped he could. He went inside and added up the mileage again. Then he sat beside her and watched the rest of the program on TV. The comedians had some new material to work with now that Kathy could walk.

* * * * *

SuperCee had to bring some operatives up from Miami. They were enroute to North Carolina. They were people who could be trusted. They wanted more money, but they were worth it. Their leader and first man on the scene drove down from Arlington in a rented van and he had a good layout of the cemetery when he met his team at the airport. He had located a 24-hour hardware store and purchased all of the tools they would need. Shovels, wrecking bars, and bolt cutters to get through the chain link fence. They went to a fast food restaurant and went over the plan.

They would case the cemetery one more time to make sure nothing had changed. The burial plot was in an expensive wing and more secure. They would have no trouble locating the right plot, as it was decorated with many fresh flowers and the ground crew left all their equipment nearby. The area had strong gates at both entrances, so the plan would be to cut through the chain-link fence in an area that was covered with tall brush. The van would continue to circulate on the outside perimeter road and keep in contact by radio. If there were any visitors, they would call it off, but there was big bonus money if they could get the job done tonight.

The leader was so thorough that he bought a CD to show them what they were looking for. He answered a few "what if's", and the group headed to the cemetery. Grave robbing is not considered high-tech. It was three in the morning when the van made it's first round. By three-thirty, he placed a call on his cellular, "Mission Complete. Have disk, will travel."

He dropped his men off at the airport entrance and drove to the helicopter pad. He made a complete report to the well-dressed man who was waiting.

Chapter 22

B riggs got wind of the plan from Roy. He made a special trip to her house to convince her to change her mind. He told her about all of the problems her group was going to have traveling tourist class. The Secret Service Agents and Victor. How was the airline staff going to ensure them seats together? And what would happen if someone recognized her at the airport. Her father wasn't going to like the food that they served. And the idea of taking the Airporter bus to the airport was out of the question. What if it was already loaded with other people and there was no room. And traveling with all of Rabinowitz's relatives, that was no way for her to fly. If it were a question of money, American News would gladly charter a plane for her to take all of them to New York and then to Washington and return.

Kathy stuck to her plan. The trip to New York was a personal matter and had nothing to do with OPERATION INVITATION or with government business. She wanted to go with Robby's relatives and get to know them. She had never had any Jewish friends before and she thought flying together was a nice way to meet people. Besides, Robby's aunt had a travel business and she needed to get fifteen more seats sold so that Robby's nephew and his wife could' go on the trip. They were young and starting out in business and didn't have the money to make the trip otherwise. Robby would like them to attend, she was sure of that. If Mr. Briggs wanted to help out, he could help advertise to fill the seats. The price was very low for such a short-notice flight.

Then she remembered a promise she had forgotten. She never called back to the owner of the Medical Supply Store. Shirley got the owner on the line and Kathy talked to him for nearly half an hour. His business had doubled and he had just gotten approval for a portable traction device that he and his friend, Elmer, had been working on for some time. It had state-of-the-art sensors, and used elastic tension instead of water for weight and took up less space than a pair of socks. It was great for people with back problems going on a trip. Kathy said she wouldn't be needing one, and that she was going on a trip to New York for Robby's and Nancy's wedding. The owner said he wanted to go to New York to find a company that could manufacture the device. When Kathy told him the low price for the package, he got the number to call to reserve a seat on the flight. She said she hoped to see him on board and he could tell her more about it. She told him to make sure he talked to Sammy The Tailor because he would know who did that kind of work. Maybe Sammy might be interested, but right now, he had more work than he could handle due to the publicity.

* * * * *

The UN secretary-general happened to be watching the TV program when Kathy made her statement at the hospital regarding the press conference. "What a marvelous idea!" he thought. The ramifications of such an event would certainly make his job easier...if only it were going to happen. He really liked the idea and wondered if the United Nations were finally going to unite. Several times he thought of a question that he'd like to ask while enjoying a cigar. He was informed of the receipt of the instructions from PROJECT INVITATION and asked to see them personally. He read them in detail and decided that, due to the time frame, his office would receive any and all questions. He found money in his staff budget to sort and analyze the input. He informed all member nations of what he was doing and those that did not wish to participate were free to decline. Some nations offered clerical assistance. Many scholars, informed through other means, requested to have access to the questions for review and possible inclusion of their own.

* * * * *

The "Snow Birds" were glad they came down to the desert this year after such a bad winter up north. Many had made plans to drive their rigs back home as soon as the weather changed. The news of Kathy and OPERATION INVITATION was the main topic in this mobile, retired or semi-retired community. When the announcement was made that the event would be in New Mexico these free thinking people pulled out maps and started making plans. Some had already set up their RVs outside the fence of the test site. They ignored the warnings to move on as they were breaking no laws and there were more of them than there were Military or State Police. The word traveled quickly to the Pentagon and thence to the President.

Many students decided to go to the Kathy event rather than Fort Lauderdale on Spring Break this year. For two days there was not a bottle or can of beer to be found in Alamogordo. Finally, the delivery trucks got through.

Bernie Rich flew his Cessna Skywagon down from Boise and was talking with Bill Perkins from Oklahoma City about Bill's Cessna 195. They were in El Paso, wondering how to get to the test site. Bill called a retired military friend of his to see if he could make some calls and grant permission for them to land in the desert. They had heard that one crop-duster from Georgia had declared engine trouble and put down on the road and some people helped him push his plane onto the shoulder.

* * * * *

The President took note that when the Chief of Staff of the Armed Forces said that he could not "…in good faith, order his men to fire on unarmed citizens," that a change in strategy was needed. He ordered his staff to send a message to Kathy that she had a sponsor for the event.

The Chief of Staff signed the order to dispatch a Mobile Communication Group to Holloman Air Force Base and set up their equipment. He had a meeting with his Generals and Admirals and instructed them to assist in any way possible. He directed that there would be no guns within a one hundred-mile radius of the site and the men would wear their service uniforms and not field equipment. The Navy was given permission for the Blue Angels to perform as they wanted to participate in some manner and the desert was out of their environment. They would have to coordinate with PROJECT INVITATION. All branches of service were to direct their field

251

kitchens and medical teams to assist. Any personnel that were qualified and volunteered should report to the Base Commanders at Biggs AFB, Holloman AFB and Kirtland AFB to assist with the increased workload.

The only thing he didn't understand was why the President wouldn't allow helicopters to be used within twenty miles of the site.

* * * * *

A helicopter was passing Arlington National Cemetery and the noise hardly bothered the occupants. The pilot eased off on the throttle and lowered the collective slightly to begin his descent into the pad at the large estate along the river. Inside the mansion, Fenhauser and six of his cronies were waiting to see what they had paid ten million dollars for. They watched as the well-dressed man embarked from the helicopter with a briefcase. He hurried toward the house, ducking down for no apparent reason; the swirling blades were several yards above his head. The man was ushered to a pool table that was well lit in the nearest room to the garden entrance. He put the briefcase on the table and opened it. The disk was in the same condition as it was when delivered to him; wrapped in bubble-wrap, inside pantyhose.

Fenhauser picked it up with a handkerchief and examined it in the pool-table light. Satisfied, he handed it to his computer expert who had a ten thousand-dollar laptop open and ready to go. He put it in the computer and the C:\ prompt changed to a pulsing red heart. "Looks like we got the genuine article," he informed the group. He tried some commands and nothing worked, but the man said not to worry about that, they would take it to the SuperCee command center and dissect the information on it there. But, before that they were going to do a lot of non-destructive testing on the disk itself.

Three of the men went to the helicopter with the disk and they took off, heading for Dulles International Airport.

* * * * *

Nancy was glad that they had stayed overnight in Miami and Robby had a chance to meet with some of her family who would not be able to make the wedding. Her family was scattered about the USA and some had already departed by car and others by plane to be there. They stayed with Nancy's aunt who was widowed, and had a comfortable house in what used to be a nice part of the city. Nephews, nieces, aunts and uncles, cousins and one sister came by to wish them well. The conversation centered almost entirely on Robby and Kathy. Everyone thought he would be taller after seeing him on TV.

They took an early flight to Newark and were over Dulles about the time that Fenhauser's private jet was taking off with the disk aboard. Robby was explaining to Nancy how much Miami had changed. He used to go there almost every winter when he a kid. The best kosher food in the world used to be served there. No one had steel bars on their windows in those days. He remembered discussing with his father one time how the windows on the houses in Miami differed from those in New York and the reason was for wanting the tropical air to circulate and not to keep out the cold. Now there are bars over the windows to keep out robbers. He wondered if there was really an increase in the number of house burglaries or just the perception. Her relatives certainly believed that there was an increase and the cause was Cubans. They also all admitted that the Cubans they met and knew were honest, hard-working people.

Nancy said that the reason her sister could not go to the wedding was because she had to go to court with her son. He was charged with substance abuse and had probably burgled some houses along the way to support his habit. Robby said he was lucky so far. Only one brother of his had a drug problem and he let his business go down the drain before the family found out about it. Robby said he handled the case and got his brother into rehab, but the money was gone, stuffed up his nose.

They changed the subject back to the wedding when they felt the power reduction and the long descent into the New York area.

253

Nancy was excited about seeing her gown that Robby's mother was making by hand for her. She said her mother must be worth over twenty million dollars, and making a dress by hand? Robby said that was how the family made the twenty million, one stitch at a time and *invested* part of it. 'This dress is an investment and she is going to make you promise to keep it in the family to be worn by other relatives. Not only that, she likes to sew." They still hadn't decided where to go on their honeymoon.

* * * * *

The SuperCee jet made a beautiful landing in spite of the crosswind. It was a little chilly when the door opened and the three men hurried down the boarding steps and into the waiting car. They drove directly to SuperCee's front door, passed Chad without saying anything, and walked upstairs to the locked Lab. Hudson was chasing behind on his stubby legs. He looked like he had been up all night. They went through the Lab and met some men in sport shirts who were holding doors open that were marked "Keep Out! High-Voltage". They took the short cut instead of going in by the rear entrance that was almost hidden from view. It looked like an office for a shipping and receiving department. Inside was an area that looked like it was a warehouse and inside that was the Control Room. It was a concrete structure with no windows and only one heavy door. It was marked with large "Radio-active" decals. The control room contained a plush meeting room with a wet-bar that was sectioned off from the other half that consisted of a row of computer stations and a mainframe. One wall of that room had a row of computers and workstations. It really wasn't what one might expect to find in a business that was controlling about fifteen percent of the government's political activities.

The first thing they needed to do was have a meeting to decide what to do. Hudson did not want the responsibility, as this was a technical problem. They decided long ago to keep Professor Jordan in the dark. The computer expert who programmed the mainframe stated flatly that he was not qualified to do anything with the disk until it was installed in a computer. He did have enough technical knowledge to explain that they could not expose it to heat, intense light, intense cold or magnetic fields. He certainly wouldn't expose it to x-rays, ultra-sound, ultra-violet or infrared. No one knew how a metal-detector worked so someone was dispatched to find out and to buy one.

They weighed it. Previously they tested the weight of a thousand other disks, both for computer and music types. This disk's weight fell right in the middle of both kinds. They decided a metal detector would serve no purpose. The programmer wanted to get on with it and Hudson decided that he could examine the data while waiting for other ideas to develop.

The programmer put it one of the company's standard computers that he had completely downloaded. It had only the basic operating system. DOS had not been installed. He held down Ctrl and Alt with his left hand and pressed Del. There were some clicking sounds and some flashes and then the pulsing red heart appeared and two messages. Message one read that the hard drive was full. The second said: "You should have used Windows. I didn't pay Mr. Gates his royalty so I didn't put it on this disk. Please install *your* Windows program. *My* operating system can handle it."

The programmer typed some commands and nothing happened. He stopped to think, and then he figured it out. His computer just became useless. The hard disk was completely full of information and he had no way to get to it.

After some more thought he went to the next computer and downloaded everything except DOS and Windows. He checked that there was nothing else on the hard drive. "OK, let's try it again. Give me the disk." Hudson removed the disk, looked at it again, and gave it to his chief programmer. He put it in the drive and clicked on File in the Program Manager window to install the disk. However, the computer flashed back out of Windows into the DOS prompt. The operator typed in the DOS commands to install the disk. The installation suggested they were about out of room on the hard drive and wanted to know if it should continue to fill it up with files or halt here. A caricature of a face with a winking eye was above the "halt here" option and the operator clicked on it. The pulsing red heart command prompt appeared in the upper left corner of the screen. The chief programmer sat back, rubbing his hands with the success.

"Now for the hard part," he said. "I have a good idea about how this works after reading the accounts in the paper. Kathy said she typed IN GOD WE TRUST and got the computer to respond. That's right, Hudson?"

Hudson acknowledged with a nod of the head and the man typed in the command and entered it.

"OH, NO YOU DON'T!," appeared in big bold letters on the monitor.

* * * * *

The FBI Director spoke to Mrs. Franklin for about an hour before returning to his office in Washington. The leader and two of the grave robbers had been identified. The van had been returned and impounded for evidence. The helicopter flight path was recorded and they were presently trying to pinpoint the exact coordinates of the destination. They had the subsequent flight information to Dulles and the name of the pilot. It was but a matter of routine detective work to put all the pieces together. The Director said they had already investigated and found that a private jet, registered to a foreign holding, but believed controlled by SuperCee, had been parked adjacent to the helicopter landing area and had departed a short time after the helicopter landed. They have the flight plan information on the jet and the name of the pilot. There appears to have been a violation of FAA crew-rest procedures as the plane and pilot had previously been to North Carolina and believed to be carrying Dr. Jeffries of SuperCee. They would use that violation to interview the pilot and obtain an itinerary and passenger list. It was all coming together to make an airtight case, but the Director was convinced that the disk was in the hands of SuperCee.

Mrs. Franklin expressed concern for Kanisha's safety and Kanisha was concerned for the safety of Lewis Anderson. The Director said he could provide witness protection for both. Kanisha said she would stay with Mrs. Franklin until things settled down a bit. They thought they might go on a trip to the desert for the Easter weekend.

Chapter 23

Everyone connected with OPERATION INVITATION had had a good night's sleep. Hudson had been up for over thirty-six hours, having overseen the operation of retrieval of the disk and now that he had it, to make it do something. Dr. Jeffries came in to see what he could do to contribute to the effort of breaking the codes. The computer chief knew there was something of value in there. He just could not get access to it. He gave up with programming commands. All he saw on the monitor were strings of letters and numbers and the computer's response: Bad command or file name. He gave up. The monitor suddenly came to life with a caricature sobbing tears and a high, squeaky voice on the speakers said, "Boo hoo, I want Lawrence."

Dr. Jeffries looked at Hudson and asked if that could be Larry Garcia, the programmer who resigned to work for PROJECT INVITATION. "Could be. Ask it if wants Lawrence Garcia," Hudson told the programmer.

"How?" the programmer wanted to know.

"Type in the question and see what happens," Hudson replied.

He typed in the question and the caricature smiled and the voice said, "Yes, he's such a nice man."

They tried typing other questions but nothing happened and the voice repeated, "Yes, he's such a nice man," every ten seconds.

After fifteen minutes of that, Dr. Jeffries told Hudson to find Larry and bring him in.

* * * * *

Big man, "Two Airporters coming in. Right on schedule. Make that three."

Cameraman, "Look at what Shirley's wearing! She sure knows how to show those babies off."

Big man, "She's gonna freeze 'em off in New York. I hear they had a cold spell, this late in the year too."

Cameraman, "Whoa, whoa, looka this. I'd say a cross between

Arnold Swartzenegger and Sylvester Stallone. I told you she had a stud somewhere."

Big man, "I still think Marcie's better. I'm a leg-man. My ex, she had some real nice legs. Used to walk a lot."

Cameraman, "Larry won't be walking for awhile. What do you think Hudson wants *him* for?"

Big man, "I don't know, but I'm getting' a little nervous about this shit. That's kidnapping and I set it up for Hudson. Get him at his house when everyone is sleeping. That's what I told him."

Cameraman, "Hey, it must have worked, he hasn't shown up yet. You got a plan for Anderson and the black bitch with the hair?"

Big man, "No. This ain't my regular style. I much prefer watching them screwing and getting the pictures. Hey, nobody gets hurt. This is kidnapping. I didn't bargain for that."

Cameraman, "Looks like they're heading out. Roy and the professor having a discussion. Pointing in the direction of Larry's house. Your plan must have worked. Oh, oh. Here, take a look!"

Big man, "Dammit! The whole damned family. Maybe Hudson didn't want him after all. Next stop, New York City."

Cameraman, "I'm all for that. I can use a break. Hudson got us lined up for the next job? I got just about enough money to open that camera store I was telling you about."

* * * * *

The Head of the Immigration Service met with the Texas and New Mexico State Police and their top aides in El Paso. The Mayors of both El Paso and Ciudad Juarez agreed that it was a mistake to close the border station to vehicle traffic. Americans could not get through as the Mexicans abandoned the vehicles and joined the pilgrimage on foot. Their estimate was fifty thousand cars and trucks backed up on the highways in Mexico. The barricades on both sides of the city had been breached. An estimated ten thousand people had broken through to the west and were walking to Deming.

The INS Chief didn't want another Waco, Texas on his hands

260

and instructed his men not to shoot unarmed people who only wanted a chance to hear God's voice. He reminded the mayors that they should concern themselves with looting and vandalism, but none had been reported so far. Some juveniles, mostly American, were letting off some steam but nothing else was reported. Those with enough water were heading up the highway directly to Alamogordo, but the majority was walking highway 25 to Las Cruces.

The Chief suggested that they talk to the Governors and see about getting the National Guard Units to provide transportation and water at Las Cruces while the roads were still open.

* * * * *

The President found himself powerless. Events were out of his control. He too, was reminded of Waco and was not going to order the shooting of unarmed people. Of immediate concern were the dignitaries that were visiting from around the world requesting security and accommodations. Terrorist threats were received in large volume earlier in the week, but had completely fallen off as the days wore on.

* * * * *

"What do you mean; he wasn't there? My surveillance people staked him leaving Makino's house early. Then, this morning, they tell me he and the whole damned family walk four blocks, with no one around, and leisurely get on the bus for the airport!" Hudson was yelling at his top goon.

"Right. We went to the house. The address Chad gave me. Hell, it's like an apartment house. It didn't look like a place for a family with kids. His car wasn't anywhere around either. The only person around that time of night was an old lady and she didn't know anyone by the name of Larry living there. They didn't allow kids, besides. We called Chad back, but he only had his answering machine on," the goon explained.

"So, why didn't you call me? I told you this was top priority," Hudson demanded.

"We did, been trying to get you all night. No answer on your phone. I called your house, from the phone book. I even *went* to your house. We went to Chad's house first. He never came home. The first we got through to you was like eight this morning..."

"Here's Chad now. Come with me, I want to get to the bottom of this," Hudson was in a bit of a rage.

"What's the screw-up here? What address did you give these guys? And where the hell have you been all night? I told you to wear your beeper at all times."

"I *had* my beeper on when you called. I left the theater and called them like you told me to do. I gave them Victor's address like you told me, and went back to watch the movie. Maybe I left the beeper off, because the people were pissed when it went off during the movie," Chad explained.

"You gave them *Victor's* address? I told you to give them *Larry's* address!" Hudson screamed and grabbed Chad by the throat. The goon pulled the hands free so Chad could talk.

"You told me to give them *Victor's* address!" Chad began to sob. "You can take this job and shove it. I quit." He ran out through the door, turned, and gave SuperCee a one-fingered salute.

Hudson calmed a bit. "You said you tried to call me all night. What number? The one on my cellular here?"

The goon pulled out his notebook and checked the number. "That's it. Must have called ten or twelve times. No answer. No busy signal or I'd have kept trying."

"Try it now."

The goon said, "It's working now. I already called you an hour ago." He dialed in the number of Hudson's phone. The phone rang. He shrugged his shoulders and hung up.

"Call me in three minutes," Hudson said and left in the direction of the control room.

He returned in about five minutes. "That's it. I was in the control room and it has a copper shield to keep radio signals out. I tried dialing out and couldn't get through. OK. You're through for now, unless you want to go to New York and try to get him there."

"I'm free, how about you guys?" the top goon asked.

"Fine with me. My old lady's heading out to see her aunt in Phoenix."

"Nah, I got plans for Easter and we were leaving this afternoon," the third goon said.

"OK. You're finished for now. It's better if we have our man in New York take over. I've been up for two days straight now."

* * * * *

Roy was wishing he had kept more people behind. He called over to Briggs and got some office help. His call from the Commander of the entire US military left him shaking. He didn't know much about the military but he remembered seeing them in action on TV during Desert Storm. The pictures of the Chief of Staff stating that they were going to blind the enemy and then kill them contrasted sharply with the new Commander's offer to render assistance and the request for his strategy. He didn't know anything about strategy.

The police returned the disk to him after they finished their investigation and wanted to know if charges were going to be filed. They had positive information that the disk had been sold to SuperCee. Roy wished that Kathy, or her father was available to make a decision. He really had no legal counsel.

His contractor called several times wanting to know how to proceed. He hadn't expected all these people to be in the way. His trucks with extra speakers were still out on the highway. All he had was directional speakers and the people there were a mixture of English and Spanish speaking. How was that going to work? Roy didn't quite understand, and the contractor explained it again to him, "The speakers can transmit one language only. No problem with the amplifiers, I got lots of power. The problem is the people are all mixed up. If I had the other speakers, I could space them out and the people could form groups, depending on the language they understood. The ones I got blast out in one direction only. I thought I was going to set up in the center. Now I have two languages to worry about. I need to have some kind of a decision

263

if I'm going to make this by Sunday. Also, we can't move out here. The people are camped and I can't get my men and equipment through."

Roy said he'd call back with an answer.

He closed his eyes and sat back, searching for answers and wished to God that he could think of something. He received a message, "Play with the disk."

He opened his eyes and picked up the disk that was on his desk. He looked at it and felt it. Held it on his finger. And then he noticed that there was a pattern reflected on the clear side. Rays, in different colors, moved about as he tilted the disk. They started narrow in the center and got wider toward the edge. He played some more and got the rays to form a perfect X. "That's it!"

He called the Pentagon and got the Chief of Staff. "Have you got any tanks out there? Anything that can clear a path through the crowd?" Roy asked.

The Chief said that he had a whole battalion on standby.

Roy told him to start clearing the center. He'd call back as soon as he found out from his contractor how far his cables would reach from center stage. The General's troops were to create four sectors, with corridors, so the people had some way to move about.

The Chief said his tank commanders could do that without anyone getting hurt and would issue the orders. He thought that was a very good strategy and wondered why none of his field commanders had recommended it.

Next, Roy called his contractor back and told him what was going to happen. His man was delighted. He had everything and the manpower to get it done already in place. Roy asked how were they going to get the two language groups to move.

"Hey, no problema. As soon as I get the first speakers up I'll play *banda* and the Mexicans will start to move in. In four hours, the Americans will gladly give up their seats."

"What's banda?" Roy asked.

"High School music. Tuba for bass, squeaky clarinets for counterpoint. Every verse ends in O, A, or corazon. The Mexicans love it. It wears a little thin on American ears after a few hours though," the contractor replied.

264

"I'll have to take your word on it. I'll keep you posted on a time frame, but you should see some tanks moving in soon."

"You made a mistake, boss. You should have painted those tanks green and white like the Border Patrol vehicles and you'd have seen some Mexicans moving."

"Spanish-speaking. This is a language problem," Roy emphasized.

The contractor asked if he could have more money to set up the other equipment out on the highways when they were able to move. Roy asked if the people had access to car radios and the man said he thought so. Roy reminded him that this was a low-cost operation and the program would be broadcast in English and Spanish, as well as other languages and the people would just have to figure out for themselves which station to listen to on the car radios.

Roy called the Chief back and asked for a time frame and if there was time to paint the tanks green and white, explaining why. The Chief didn't think there was time or that it would be effective. He also said he was glad that he didn't have the President's job of smoothing out all of the egos of those who wanted to be in the center. He had heard that some heads of state were "absolutely furious" over the restrictions on helicopter traffic. The President had a good answer though. He had Kathy's promise that she would walk to the stage with him, after they got to the edge of the crowd by limousine. "Now that they had a path to get through."

The Chief asked Roy who had started all of this mass migration. Had his group been setting this up for some time?

"No," Roy replied, "They're just people looking for answers."

* * * * *

The three Airporters arrived in front of the terminal and found an area roped off and a red carpet waiting for them. The group looked like an average bunch of tourists on a package deal. There was curbside check-in and the reporters and well wishers were held back by a heavy showing of security. An airline employee checked each ticket and issued a boarding pass. All of the carry-on luggage was put on a cart and Larry's wife tried to get hers back and

265

couldn't find it. Two airline employees came to her assistance and took charge of the children.

Inside the terminal, their path to the departure gate was provided by more red carpet. They walked to the Security check-in and were quickly ushered through, as they had no baggage to put through the screening devices. They went to the boarding gate and were met by the Governor once more for photos. Several other dignitaries and some high-powered TV personalities were there to greet them. Kathy was a bit shocked and just a little upset and told her father that she felt like she was being used. The Governor was a nice man, but she certainly didn't share his philosophy on governing. And why the TV personalities? Why were they there?

"Egos. Remember? You were told about this at the beginning," her father reminded her.

"And that guy, I suppose he was a reporter, yelling at me about what am I going to do if God doesn't show up on Sunday. I didn't know what to say and he stuck a microphone in my face," Kathy complained.

"He was only doing his job," Kami replied.

"Oh! My god! That's our airplane? I thought we were going on a smaller one. This is a 747. And who is paying for all of this? I'll bet the airline sold so many tickets when they found out I was going on this flight that they had to get a bigger plane," Kathy said sarcastically.

"Honey, did you have your meeting this morning on the computer?" Kami asked her.

"No. I was up late. Then I hurried around to pack and then the disk got locked up and Larry was late so we couldn't open the safe. Why do you ask?" Kathy explained.

"Why don't you sit with me on the flight and we'll chat, OK? I have a lot of things to tell you before we get to New York. For right now, think of everyone who is here to see you off as being a friend of Emily," her father told her.

"I feel better already. How is it you are always so calm and peaceful?"

"It's a long story, I'll tell you on the plane," her father replied.

266

* * * * *

The President was happy to hear that things were going peacefully at Ground Zero. He had been briefed earlier by top scientists from the Department of Energy and was satisfied that there was no problem with radiation. The Transportation Chief had air and ground traffic under control. The only problem was transporting dignitaries from the surrounding airfields, military and civilian, and parking for the aircraft. The personality conflicts that were expected did not occur, as the pilots seemed to be making the decisions, based on the facilities that were available and the type of aircraft that they were flying. The expected problems with small, general aviation aircraft did not come about. Many returned home to watch on TV. He was especially pleased when his military commander informed him that the center area had been "depopulated" and that there were now four, wide corridors for movement and access.

"So, how far do you think I have to walk?" the President asked.

"Why don't you get Starlight Express to push you in a wheelchair? I saw on TV this morning that he has already put out tee shirts with his logo on it. A lot of the wheelchair attendants are wearing them at the airports...or selling them...I forget which," the Chief of Staff said.

"Well, I heard one last night that made my hair stand on end," the President said. "Someone has some statistics that show a complete change in how nations are solving their differences ever since some New Age...you know, people like Kathy, were made advisors to the National Security Council. Anybody want to look into that?"

There were no volunteers. "OK. I'll hold it for the new Secretary of State. He's got his hands full right now."

Chapter 24

"Are you feeling better now that we've leveled-off?" Kami asked Kathy.

"Yes. Are you going to tell me that long story now?" Kathy asked.

"Now's a good time. You will be busy after we land and I have some other things to do in New York," her father replied.

"I think there are two lessons here for you today. The first deals with the people at the airport, the reporter who shouted at you and the Governor. This is the problem of specialness. The people who upset you consider themselves "special". Rules were not made for them. If you want to see how the strong ego works, look at the laws that our Congress passes. Who is exempt from them? The very people who write and pass the laws. For themselves, they have "special" provisions. You were told that you were going to have to deal with these people. Remember?

"And now for the important lesson. You didn't make an invitation today for the perfectly good reasons that you told me. So, little things are upsetting you. You promised that you would get new instructions every morning."

"You're right. On both counts. I wish there was a computer here and I could listen now," Kathy replied.

"Everything is happening so fast! Where are all those people coming from? I had no idea that it was going to be live, in front of *millions* of people. When I agreed to this I had a picture in my mind of a TV studio and a panel of experts asking questions and I would get the answers from the computer. Now, Roy tells me he is all set up with enormous sound systems and he has equipment to translate in almost every language and transmitters to broadcast to the world and practically all of the radio and TV networks are prepared to cover the event live."

"And that he has used about all of the money. I still don't understand where the ten million came from. I know we are receiving a lot of contributions that we did not ask for. I hope Roy has checked with someone who knows the tax codes and is accounting for all the money," Kami offered.

"No problem. Marcie received the tax information and updated Roy's manual with the latest financial report with income and expenses. Roy sure came along at the right time, didn't he?" Kathy remarked.

Kami said, "I certainly couldn't have run this operation. Spending that much money scares me.

"Did you hear Roy tell about his conversation with the head of the military? He was scared to death at first and now he has the guy eating out of the palm of his hand. If he wants tanks, he gets a battalion of tanks. He needs to locate some sound equipment that is stalled in traffic out on the highway and he gets helicopters to fly them in. A four-star general has to check with Roy to see if it is OK to bring the helicopters past the 20-mile restricted zone."

"Yes, I heard. It's a riot the way Roy tells it. And it's always 'Yes, sir, no, sir, or I don't know, sir.' The man is not wishy-washy. Actually, Roy said he has a lot of respect for him and his concern for safety so that there are no *casualties*, as he calls them. The general even suggested setting up nurseries for the infants, but there was no time to implement such a proposal," Kathy said.

"Three more days to go. Roy says he's ready and has just a few sound tests to make and maybe some relocation of speakers or people," Kami replied.

Kathy glanced out the window and looked at the white clouds below before returning to the conversation. "So, why aren't you going to be with me in New York?"

Kami glanced at his watch and told her they had time to discuss it.

"Many things happened to me after the accident. I was angry. I was angry with the owners of the dog that got onto the highway. I was angry with the driver of the car that slammed on his brakes and swerved in front of the truck. I was angry with the driver of the truck. If he had just kept going straight, he wouldn't have lost control of his trailer. I was mad at the people that loaded the trailer. I thought they should have used more chain to keep the roll of metal tied down.

270

"I was angry with my union because of the insurance policy that they had. The cost of your treatment was far more than the policy covered. I was even mad at you. If you had your seat-belt fastened and hadn't been reaching into the rear seat for your comb, maybe your mother would not have been distracted and could have avoided the collision...the metal was not rolling that fast."

"Daddy, it was an *accident*," Kathy consoled.

"Maybe not. Let me finish my story," Kami replied.

"The first year was horrible. I had a good job, but it took all of that and the insurance to keep my head above water. And the loss of your mother weighed heavily on me. I couldn't get her out of my mind. I was all alone here in the house. The only diversion I had was bridge and it was at one of the games that I met a woman, a professor from Columbia University who was visiting for a research seminar. She talked to me about my problems and I started finding solutions. She sent me a set of books to read when she returned to New York. More solutions appeared. I took a second mortgage on the house, went and bought a car, and started fixing up the house for you. Remember that old station wagon? I thought it was a good idea, but we couldn't get the chair in and out and the only way you were comfortable was lying down and then you couldn't see anything. And then, the big day when you came home!

"I had some company and a purpose in life.

"Anyway, I kept in touch with my friend over the years. I really studied bridge, got very good at it, and had a satisfactory social life. She visited me, and I visited her, and we corresponded a lot."

"Daddy! Are you telling me you have a girl-friend and I don't even know about it?" Kathy interjected.

"Wait just a minute. I'm trying to answer your question about this being just an accident.

"So, my friend and I are getting along very well. I can see that she likes to work and to travel and I know it isn't going to work with me taking care of you. I reached a point where I was happy. I stopped reading the books she sent me and just enjoyed life. Then your miracle happened. Everything has changed."

"So, now that you don't have me to worry about are you going to get married?" Kathy asked.

271

"I'm still trying to answer your question about it being an accident.

"I began reading the books she gave me after your recovery was called a *miracle*. The name of the books is A Course In Miracles. They were on the shelf where I have piles of old papers and records. When I moved them, an old folder dumped its contents onto the bed and floor. It was the folder with the papers for the negligence claim that my attorney wanted to pursue. I was gathering them up and placing them in order when I caught sight of the name of the law-firm that represented the freight company and the driver. Guess who was the attorney that made an offer to settle out-of-court?"

"Not Robby!" Kathy exclaimed.

"The very same. He must have worked this out in his office. I never saw him before he agreed to help us out with all of this publicity. The law was definitely on his side. My attorney had no grounds to prove negligence against the truck driver or the freight company. The load was secured better than the law required. The cause of the accident was a dog in the road...an act of god. He must have figured out the excess medical costs, my assets, the insurance company's liability, the cost of legal action and arrived at a settlement figure that was just."

"Daddy, it was an *accident*," Kathy said firmly.

"How can you be so sure?" her father asked.

"God would not have put us through such pain in order to have a press conference. He chose us afterwards.

"So. Are you going to get married?" Kathy asked again.

"I want to talk about it. I don't want problems with my family like I had with your mother. Your mother was very unhappy with my family because they would not accept her," Kami replied.

"Another long story?"

"Let's talk about it on the return. Right now, I think you had better inform yourself about how to handle the meeting with the rabbi after the wedding. This will be your first real encounter with religious people since this all began," Kami remarked.

"I wish I hadn't promised Robby that I would meet with them. There are going to be representatives from several other faiths.

They are friends of the rabbi. I haven't thought about the impact of all this on organized religions at all."

"At least you won't have the Catholics to worry about. Their position is that if and when God shows up they will listen and then take appropriate action," Kami said.

"I know how to solve this. I am going to have a talk with my computer before the meeting with them," Kathy said.

* * * * *

Dr. Jeffries returned to the control room and listened to Hudson's explanation of the latest bungle. He received the information calmly. He took down the numbers that Hudson had for his people in New York, what instructions they had been given and relieved Hudson of the project. He sent Hudson to get some sleep in his office in case he needed him.

The computer kept repeating, "He's such a nice man." Over-and-over. It continued to annoy Dr. Jeffries and he told the computer chief to get rid of it. The man said he couldn't. Dr. Jeffries pointed to the sound switch and turned it off. There was a slight bit of static, then the voice continued, "He's such a nice man."

The computer chief said the disk had found the internal sound system and the only way to turn it off or lower the volume was to change the settings. He couldn't do that without loosing the present screen and he was told not to change anything until they brought Larry in.

"Who told you that?" Dr. Jeffries asked.

"You did, before you left last night," the chief replied.

He called the operatives in New York and they informed Dr. Jeffries of their plan: Kathy's group was booked in an older, but nice, medium-priced hotel. Her request for privacy, due to the wedding being a private celebration, was being honored by everyone. But that could change. They had three Spanish-speaking men and a woman who would pretend to be friends of the family to gain access to Larry's room. After explaining the rules to them all, two men would leave with Larry and the other two stay with the family until they were sure he was gone. Then they would leave. They would drive Larry to the company plane and bring him in to SuperCee.

Dr. Jeffries was a salesman, not a kidnapper. He couldn't think of a better idea. He told them to go ahead and they would get a bonus if it was done quickly and cleanly with no problems.

* * * * *

Good Friday was a day of peace and tranquillity in the Sonoran Desert. Those who had made the journey thus far were satisfied with their effort. Many could not continue further. The only movements were the trucks and the volunteers offering food and water. Roy's contractor surveyed his system and decided to wait until Saturday to test the sound. His people were tired and needed a rest. Tarps thrown over the cactus and tumbleweed to provide some relief from the sun turned the desert into a sea of blue. Under them the people waited with hope. Many, with faith. Those with charity shared their provisions with those less fortunate. No one suffered. The guilt had long ago been removed. Now, but to wait for the challenge that lies ahead.

* * * * *

It was not peaceful and tranquil at the airport in New York and many other major terminals. People were hurrying to and from their flights. This was vacation time. Students were everywhere, the highways jammed with happy parents listening to their kids telling about their adventures at school.

In Mexico, the beaches and the mountain resorts were jammed to capacity and food supplies were low in the *tiendas*. No milk or bread in many of them, but plenty of beer and sodas...new cases were ready to be loaded and cooled. The finishing touches on the floats for the parade were being made. The churches were decorated with everything the priest could ever hope for. Flowers everywhere! The little girls looked beautiful in their new dresses.

"Fiesta!" the men were shouting. It's time to get drunk and be somebody.

Kathy was in a hurry also. It was only two hours before the wedding and she wanted to get in front of the computer now. As much as she wanted to meet Robby and Nancy her anxiety stemmed from the meeting afterwards for which she was not prepared. It seemed like an eternity getting from the airport to the hotel, changing clothes, and then waiting for someone to find a personal computer. The hotel just happened to have one with a CD in their accounting office. It was private and she was welcome to use it at her convenience since the office was closed today. Then, Larry going to get a haircut with his relatives but fortunately his wife found the key to the safe on the floor. It seemed that Victor was the only one she could really depend on. She couldn't wait to see him in his tuxedo.

She finally got to spend some time with the computer. As she left the accounting office, she walked directly to the lobby where the police and hotel staff were trying to console Mrs. Garcia and find information. She urged them aside and took Mrs. Garcia's hand.

"Your husband is safe. He is doing God's work at the moment, but he will be returned to you in a couple of days. If I had kept my promise, you would have known about it before it happened and not had to go through this terrible experience. I apologize. Are the children OK?"

"Yes. The woman who was with the kidnappers diverted their attention and they have no idea of what happened, except that I may have upset them with my crying. When Larry left with the two men, he told them he was going to get a haircut and then he handed me the key and said it was for the luggage. The man who stayed behind tried to open the luggage with it and when it didn't work, he threw it on the floor. Later, the man and woman left and told me to sit quietly for ten minutes or Larry was dead. That's what I did."

"You have God's promise that Larry is going to be fine. You and Larry may even get a few laughs out of this. Since my father has also disappeared, why don't you and the children sit with me at the wedding? Victor is going to be the Best Man and I'll be all alone," Kathy motioned someone to find the children and helped

Mrs. Garcia to her feet. "We better get going. It's bad manners to be late for the bride and groom."

* * * * *

Dr. Jeffries' phone rang in SuperCee's control room. He removed his feet from the conference table, adjusted his chair upright, and answered it. "Great news! When will he be available here?...My time...Right. Got it... No. Don't bother him now. I know it's only forty minutes away...Another crew rest problem? We have another pilot in New York...the one that used to be a hooker. Then a flight attendant. Or was it the other way around?...The one that Fenhauser fell in love with and sent to flying school. The other pilot will know how to find her...Yeah...Call me when you're about an hour out. I'll meet you in person. I'm supposed to be in Chicago right now. There's been so many mistakes I'm running this end myself. You wouldn't believe the people Hudson's been working with.

"Yeah...I told him he'd get a bonus. I'll leave it up to you, but if it looks like a good clean job... No. We don't have a thing without Larry.

"I don't think this is something we should discuss over the phone. You can see for yourself when you get here."

When he hung up Dr. Jeffries sent someone to get Hudson. He arrived in wrinkled clothes, yawning.

"Larry's on the way in. D'ya see what you can do with a little bit of supervision and common sense? If you keep things simple and use good people, you get results.

"Do you think you can figure out a way to shut off this, 'He's such a nice man'? It's beginning to get on my nerves," the Director asked.

The computer expert answered, "It's getting on all of our nerves. The only way is to shut off the computer. The last command I put in was the question that you posed about wanting Larry Garcia. If I had a prompt or something, maybe I could make it do something."

"Go ahead. Give it a try," Dr. Jeffries ordered.

The expert held down Ctrl, Alt and Del and the computer turned itself off and back on. Before he realized what he had done, the computer notified him that the hard drive was full. "Damn it, another hard-drive down the drain! I give up. This disk is driving me crazy."

One of his assistants suggested that he should have removed the disk before he booted. The expert suggested that they wait until Larry comes in and they all agreed. The computer speakers began once more, "Yes, he's such a nice man."

* * * * *

The wedding of Nancy and Robby was beautiful. The only disturbing thing was the attention that Kathy was receiving from the media. She didn't let it bother her and it did not detract from the main event. It was also providing the couple with photos, film, and TV coverage that would have cost a fortune to obtain otherwise. Kathy sat on the bride's side with Mrs. Garcia and the two children to her left. It made a beautiful picture to complement the wedding couple. It was also shown on national television many times with the daily news coverage.

The wedding party and guests left the synagogue and went to the reception at a beautiful and expensive restaurant that was owned by a member of Robby's family. Kathy tried to stay out of the limelight as much as possible after offering her best wishes to the newly-weds and thanking them for the work they did for OPERATION INVITATION.

She saw Shirley sitting alone and went to talk to her. She was on the verge of tears and asked her what the problem was. Shirley explained that she had broken up with her boyfriend. He didn't want to come to New York in the first place and he didn't want to go to a party with a "bunch of Jewish people that he didn't know." He wanted to stay in the hotel and watch the ball games on TV and lay around in bed. That was all he ever thought about. That and the gym crowd that he worked out with every day. All he did was body-build and sponge off his parents. He never had a real job. He was always asking her for money and thought he would get by forever on his looks. She bought him a plane ticket and he went back home.

Kathy started to console her when she spotted her father, alone, talking to Robby. She excused herself to greet him. She could see that he was very upset and found some empty chairs where they could sit and talk. She asked him what had happened.

"She turned me down! Can you believe that? After all that time we spent talking and her interest in me. I thought surely..." Kami said dejectedly.

"Well, what did you two do before, when you were together?" Kathy asked.

"We talked mostly. Went out to dinner and normal things like that. Played bridge when she was visiting. But, we talked mostly about my problems. You know, she isn't near as pretty as your mother.

"She said I completely misunderstood our relationship and that she was interested in me as a person, and how to help solve my problems. She said she certainly wasn't interested in me for a husband. She said I didn't understand people and saw no purpose in our getting married.

"She said she had been dating a tall psychologist and they had much more in common. Then she said that she loved to dance and couldn't do that with short men. That was the final straw," Kami revealed.

"Oh dear. This has been a bad day. Would you mind if I leave you with Shirley for a bit? I have to find Victor and see that Mrs. Garcia has someone to talk with. Then I have to go meet with the rabbi. *That*, I am prepared for.

"Shirley's over there. Come on, I'll walk over with you," Kathy said while leading the way.

"Wow! You sure are dressed nicely for the wedding. Where's your date?" Kami asked Shirley.

"Do you like this dress? I got it from Sammy. Such a deal he made me."

"I sure like Victor's tux. Now that Kathy's able to walk, I might buy some new clothes for myself. Medical expenses. It's been a long, hard row," Kami said.

"I think you look very distinguished. Always in a fresh, clean suit. Coat and tie and shined shoes. How do you get your shoes that shiny?

"And your house is immaculate. Did you clean house? I mean, Kathy, in a wheelchair? How could she?"

"You didn't see the little broom hooked on back? It was photographed in infrared. On all the front pages," Kami joked.

"You are the funniest man I've ever met. You teach mathematics, right? That isn't a very funny subject."

"It can be interesting though. If you have a pen and something to write on I can show you how to make two equal one," Kami said.

"I know that one. You cannot divide by zero, right?" Shirley asked.

"Not one in a hundred of my students can remember that. Do you like math?"

"Sort of. I like things neat and accurate. I worked with my father who was a builder and he taught me how to keep track of everything, including the money. But he retired and I went to college and took some of the hard courses. None of that psychology and political science stuff. I really liked electricity, but I flunked out."

"I can teach you everything about electricity. Starting with the electron. That is in the realm of my understanding. By the way, where is your boyfriend?"

"I'm starved. Look at all that good food. Would you like me to get you a plate?" the red-haired beauty replied.

"Here comes Kathy. Maybe she'd like to join us," Kami said.

"Well, I see you two are getting along. Daddy, I have to go to the meeting soon. Did you give the books back to you-know-who? The ones you told me about on the plane," Kathy asked.

"No. Why would I do that? They were a gift to me and they seem to be working," Kami replied.

"I forgot the name is what I meant. I'm really having a bad day. What do you mean...they're working?" Kathy continued.

"They're called A Course In Miracles. This morning I read a little about Holy Relationships in preparation for my other meeting...and..," Kami said, shifting his eyes towards Shirley.

"Daddy, you're a dirty old man," Kathy said very softly.

"I am supposed to ask if any of the clergy has ever read the books you mentioned," she continued in a normal voice and excused herself after raising her eyebrows at her father.

"What did she mean by that?" Shirley asked. "You are very neat and clean. And you certainly aren't very old."

"Just a family joke," Kami said.

"You know, I've always liked older men. They listen more and they're more interesting. And a lot more honest."

"Oh, really! Let's try some of that food before it's all gone."

"Why don't you save our seats and *I'll* get you a plate. Anything special that *you* like?" Kami asked.

"See? They're a lot more considerate too."

Chapter 25

Kathy rode back to the synagogue with the rabbi who conducted the wedding. He was very pensive and not at ease with her. She expected to talk about the wedding and the ceremony, but the rabbi was very quiet and seemed worried. They went to his office and he introduced her to the other clergy who had been waiting. They were a mixture of clergy from other denominations. There was another rabbi, much older, who took a back seat. When she was seated and made comfortable, the rabbi thanked her for visiting with them.

He began the meeting by asking her if she had read the article by Briggs, the editor who told about his meeting a Catholic priest who seemed to be preaching a new religion. She said she knew Briggs, but had not read the article.

"This priest has been located and is now in Rome. It may be one of the reasons that the Catholics have decided to take a wait-and-see attitude.

"The main reason that we would like to speak to you is that we have been getting a lot of questions from our congregations. Many of our members have already made the *invitation* that you suggested and some strange things are happening. Many marriages are dissolving. Many older couples are back together once more. Many have stopped contributing and are asking questions about where the money for the churches is going. We are receiving a high rate of questions concerning the very basic beliefs of our various religions.

"We were hoping that maybe you could let us know what is going on. What information are you getting from your computer...which is claimed to be the Word of God?" the rabbi concluded.

"The disks are how I communicate. I haven't been told anything about any specific religion. I receive instructions only about what to do regarding Sunday's event.

"By the way, have any of you here made the *invitation* that I talked about and showed you how to do?"

One minister, stating that he was a Jehovah's Witness, raised his hand and said that he had.

"And what happened to you?" Kathy asked.

"I have been in a constant state of anxiety. I am confused, angry, have lost my patience and my wife is threatening to walk out on me. Not exactly the promise you held out at your press conference," he answered.

"If you are having anxiety, you are living in the future. What are your plans for the future?" Kathy remembered one of her lessons.

"My congregation is sending me to the desert to your press conference. They have gone ahead and I'm to catch up. My plane leaves tonight. I missed the earlier flight because of the domestic problems I mentioned," he said.

"Well, then. You'll get your answer on Sunday, won't you? Surely, you can last that long. You couldn't have done anything very wrong or your hell would have been longer, or more intense. Why don't you give your wife some flowers before you go. Better yet, take her with you," Kathy took note of the body language and change of facial expression by some of the others at her last remark.

"Anything else?" Kathy asked.

"Yes. I represent the Islam faith," a very serious and very cold clergyman said. "According to our faith there is only one God. Allah. We have been around a very long time and precede many of the religions that have challenged us. We are still here and our beliefs are stronger than ever. Our position is that you preach blasphemy and that your new religion will fail, like so many others before you. We are not going to the desert. Many of us know the desert already."

"That's not a very good idea. Have you really thought that through? If Allah is God, or if God is Allah, which may well be the case, then He will be talking to the world on Sunday and you'll miss out on hearing Him talk. Or, perhaps you are fearful of meeting Him. If so, what kind of religion are you preaching?

"I'll be real honest. I don't know much about religion as I was in a wheelchair since I was really able to think about things like that. My father was brought up in the Shinto faith, which I think he has

282

abandoned...he never speaks of it. My mother was a Catholic, but she did not take me to church with her and I went to public school.

"My instructions for this meeting were very clear. None of you have anything to fear. As priests, ministers, rabbis, etc., your function is that of a teacher. You are the people who have the call to interpret God's Word and share that with your members. If you don't have the call, perhaps you should find another line of work.

"It's too bad the Catholics are not represented, but I see that there are other Christian faiths here. Jesus was quite clear when He built His "church" upon Peter. He was speaking of Peter's faith and his strong moral character, which was solid as a rock. He wasn't speaking about building a structure out of rock, nor decorating the ceilings with art and lining the floors with marble," Kathy concluded.

"I think all of us here agree with you on that. We all read the Bible," a Baptist minister said.

"I haven't read the Bible, I'll look it up when I have time. Right now, I have to get ready for tomorrow. The President is waiting for me to advise him on how to handle all of the changes for the dignitaries that are coming in. And then, off to New Mexico on Air Force One!

"I think you might be able to answer the rest of your questions for yourselves if you just make a sincere invitation. It can't hurt."

On the way back to the restaurant the rabbi was much more at ease, and opened-up a little. "So, we have nothing to fear? You're quite sure of that?" he asked.

"That's what I hear. Certainly, you're not afraid of the future?" Kathy said.

"I've lost several important members who have made invitations. One did it and told the other and he did it. Both quit their jobs, said they were working too hard. Large contributors. Some others said they made the invitation after hearing Rabinowitz. They were very moved by what he said. I am stumped right now trying to answer one of their questions about 'an eye for an eye'. I've never done anything else except be a rabbi."

"Like I said, I don't know much about the Bible. I do remember 'an eye for an eye'. I would look in the Bible for

283

something after Jesus came along and took away the guilt. Oh, dear. I forgot what I was supposed to ask the other preachers."

"Some of us are preachers, but you told us we were supposed to be teachers," the rabbi said, loosening up a bit more.

"I'm not surprised that the Jehovah's Witness minister was having some domestic problems. I've heard that he has quite a few steady house calls to make each week. When the children are at school and the husband is at work," the rabbi related. "In our position as clergy, we encounter a lot of women who trust us with their deepest secrets and are very vulnerable."

"I hope his wife is forgiving," Kathy said.

"Forgiving! She's for giving out more than pamphlets on the street corners."

"Oh boy, the Holy Spirit's got a tough one. No wonder the preacher didn't get an immediate answer." Kathy said. "I guess I really goofed when I told him to take his wife along with him."

"Maybe he did get an answer and doesn't want to agree to it," the rabbi said.

"You're starting to sound like my computer," Kathy responded and asked, "Have you ever heard of A Course In Miracles? I was supposed to ask everyone that."

"Hmm? Is that a book about psychology or mind-control? The name rings a bell," the rabbi answered.

"Wait a minute! In your office. Behind your desk is a bookcase full of bound books. What is the set of three blue books with gold printing? They caught my eye as we were talking. All the rest on that shelf were one set with red and blue backs," Kathy remembered. She also recalled seeing them in Emily's house.

"Ah. Maybe that *is* A Course In Miracles. It was a gift to me. From the old rabbi who was attending the meeting. Ninety-eight years old now. Very weak and tired. No one pays him much attention these days. He said he couldn't read anymore and gave them to me. I promised to read them to him, but I just never have the time."

"If you read those books to him, you will never have to worry about a job again. You are a very lucky man. You are two days ahead of your colleagues," Kathy said as she was let off at the reception.

"You know, if you're right, next year I could be eating those honey-buns that the Italian bakery sells. I love them for breakfast," the rabbi said as he departed.

She found her father and Shirley sitting where she had left them. They were deeply engrossed in conversation and their empty plates on the floor. She returned the plates to the buffet table after being ignored, and went searching for Victor who she found with Marcie and Mrs. Garcia. She quickly ushered him aside and he saw the cold look she gave to Marcie. He asked her how the meeting went. She replied that it went OK and asked how his conversation with Marcie was going.

Victor said he was glad that Mrs. Garcia (Rosa) was available to talk with. They had a lot in common. She was going to night school to learn computers also. It was impossible for her to learn anything from Larry. He had no patience with her and she could not do the lessons everyday because of the kids, and he finally enrolled her in school. Also, they talked a lot about the different music and styles of dancing between Mexico and the US. They danced once or twice while Marcie watched the kids and she wasn't too happy about it.

And what did he talk to Marcie about? Nothing. He thought she was a spoiled brat. Her parents were rich and sent her to college to get her out of the way. All she talked about was sports and the athletes she went out with. She said she would rather be watching the play-offs on TV. He asked her for a dance one time, but she said her legs hurt from too much time on the Nautilus machine at the hotel.

Her boyfriend couldn't come to the wedding because he was a golf instructor for Japanese tourists in the Philippines.

* * * * *

They treated Larry with respect. The two men apologized and explained that times were tough and they had families to support too. It was hard for Latinos to find good paying jobs in New York these days. They assured him that no harm would come to his wife or kids if he cooperated. He promised he would and got no further information until he was inside the SuperCee twin-engine jet. One well-dressed man checked his identification thoroughly and gave the men a thick envelope and signaled for the doors to close. The engines started. He was led to a lounge and handcuffed to a cocktail table. The plane taxied smoothly. Not a word was said until after the take-off. The handcuffs were removed and the TV was turned on. He was offered a drink from the bar and he asked for a Coke with a lot of ice.

The two male attendants who were watching him got up and left when the well-dressed man returned from somewhere up front in the plane. The man informed Larry that his men had his wife and children in a safe place and that no harm would come to them if he cooperated. Larry said he was told that, but didn't know what they wanted of him. The man said he was needed to decipher the stolen disk and asked him if he knew how to get the disk to do anything. Larry said he needed more information. The man asked if he would like to talk to the computer technician, who had the disk and was sitting, waiting for instructions. Larry said he would help as much as possible. The man left him alone to make the connections with the sophisticated telephone system on board the plane. Larry watched the news on TV and the film clip showing his wife and kids sitting beside Kathy at the wedding!

The man returned and said that he had a secure line into the control room and that he could talk to the computer technician. The man wanted to know if there was any way that the disk could self-destruct. Larry said he didn't know, but thought it would be stupid for God to make a disk that self-destructs when He could just destroy it Himself, any time He wanted to. The man thought a bit, agreed, and relayed the information to Dr. Jeffries. Trying to sound tough, he told Larry, "Any funny business and your family is dead." The man was not used to working at this level of mischief.

Larry and the technician worked by phone until the plane came to a halt. Nothing was accomplished. The computer kept repeating over-and-over, "Yes…he's such a nice man."

Larry was taken from the plane and he recognized his

hometown. He was driven by limousine to SuperCee and taken to the control room. Inside, he remembered some of the people with whom he had worked at meetings. They exchanged pleasantries. He looked the control room over and saw the mainframe that was supporting all of Fenhauser's illegal activities. After an update of what had happened, Larry said he'd give it a try. He started out on a new computer with just DOS and Windows. He typed, "IN GOD WE TRUST," and entered it. The screen lit up and his wife and kids showed up on the film clip of the wedding. His wife waved. The screen went blank and then the caricature appeared and began cheering, "Fenster! Fenster! He's our man. If he can't do it, nobody can!" Ten seconds later a stadium full of people was shown. The camera zoomed into the midfield section and the crowd held up white or blue cards that spelled out "D. FENSE." Then the crowd cheered "D.FENCE! D.FENCE! We want D.FENCE!" Ten seconds later it went back to "Fenster! Fenster!..."

Dr. Jeffries put his fingers in his ears and went to an office to relay the information to his boss.

He came back out and spoke to the well-dressed man. "Go back to New York and change crews. Go to Washington and pick up Mr. Fenhauser. Bring him back here. You better get a full load of gas wherever you can. All the airports are busy with this damned *invitation* thing."

* * * * *

"What d'ya mean, you feel stupid in front of anyone else?" Gordon Briggs was talking on the phone to Lewis.

"OK. C'mon over if you like. Nothing new on TV. Kinda quiet on Good Friday. We don't eat meat on Good Friday, but we've got some terrific brownies."

When he hung up, he told his wife that Lewis was going to come by to practice some of his jokes in front of a live audience. "I kind of like that. Maybe I can give him some pointers. Remember when we did Shakespeare at the arts festival?"

"And you were terrible...with your Irish accent," Mrs. Briggs said.

287

* * * * *

Big man, "Wake up! Someone started a car down there."

Cameraman, "Damn. Gimme some light. The power got disconnected somehow."

Big man, "You ain't got a battery backup?"

Cameraman, "Oh yeah. Got it now. Nothing but headlights. Turning. Lost him."

Big man, "I didn't get diddly. I was looking for the light switch. Nothin' happening here anyway. I asked Hudson about how long we got here and he didn't give me an answer."

Cameraman, "What d'ya think this baby's worth? Complete. Ten grand?"

Big man, "It's worth double that to me when the power cord is plugged in."

Cameraman, "Retail. What do you think this goes for? You ever done retail?"

Big man, "Naw. All I ever done was time. I shoulda' got on the fat-boy program the last time I was in."

Cameraman, "I never done time. So, what's the fat-boy program?"

Big man, "If you're a little overweight, like me. They got a special diet. And an exercise program. Even an instructor. They say it saves the taxpayer money."

Cameraman, "So, what'd you do time for?"

Big man, "Same as this. This guy hires me to keep tabs on his *wife,* he tells me, and we're set up in a van at the address he gives me. She shows up and we got the whole thing on tape; time of entry, when the lights are on and off. The whole thing on tape, waiting for her to leave in the morning.

"Two-o'clock in the morning the cops bust me. Someone in the neighborhood turned me in. I show the police my contract with the guy and he goes to wake up the *wife.* Turns out she's been divorced for over a month and has two restraining orders on her ex. She files charges because she's mad at him and I get time for invasion of privacy.

288

"Get this! She's at her *sister's* house and there ain't even a man living there. First time I ever got stung like that. Got too complacent."

Cameraman, "So, you're sure this ain't illegal, what we're doing here. I got a clean record, man."

Big man, "Yeah, we're OK. Hudson'll have us sprung before they can find a charge sheet.

"My ex sprung me that time. Didn't even wait around to see me get out. I owe her one."

Cameraman, "So, you thinking of making an *invitation* too?"

Big man, "Naw. I heard you gotta' be depressed before it works.

"Right now I got it made.

"We're making big bucks for this job.

"Got a woman and good chow at home.

"I can loose this gut anytime I want to.

"You know, that guy that got me busted. He should try it. Like, man, he just didn't know when to let go.

"That was a good idea you had. Maybe I'll see my ex when this is over and pay her back for springing me. Maybe we can go for a walk."

Chapter 26

It was ten-o'clock on Saturday morning by the time Fenhauser arrived in the SuperCee control room. It was not an easy night. His luxurious company jet had to wait for fuel and in-flight kitchen service was impossible to obtain. He thought that having a woman pilot might be responsible for the lack of service that he was obtaining. The kid she found to ride copilot was useless. Maybe he could fly the airplane in the unlikely event of his ex-heart-throb having a heart attack. He sure didn't know how to talk to the Air Traffic Controllers in getting some priority over the "heavies" that were going long distances.

He was sitting in the jump seat behind the pilots listening to the tower and controllers on the radio. The copilot didn't have an answer when the controller asked him if he could accept a hold-down to twelve thousand feet to Allentown. By the time the pilot explained it to him, the controller lost the option and they had another half-hour delay, burning up expensive fuel in the process. He could have had a good night's sleep if he had known they were going to have all of these ground delays. Instead, he was up at two in the morning, for a chilly helicopter ride to the airport.

The first thing he said to Dr. Jeffries was for him to find a replacement copilot for the return trip home. He had a very important meeting with some visitors and a house full of guests and *had* to be back. He had a foreign ambassador and a finance minister staying with him. Everything was occupied in the Washington area. All because of this *invitation* thing. He hoped this wasn't going to take long.

Dr. Jeffries sent Hudson to take care of the pilot problem and then brought Mr. Fenhauser up-to-date on the disk. He introduced him to Larry and he intuitively shook his hand when he recognized the face. "So, you're the boy-genius that's going to solve this problem for me. You could be a rich man very soon if you can show these guys how to make disks with superconductors. Do you mind if I see the disk again?"

Larry opened the CD drawer and handed him the disk.

Everyone watched as Mr. Fenhauser examined it. Larry saw the monitor message. TYPE IN THE ACCESS CODE. DO NOT ENTER YET.

Larry remembered the code that he obtained from the text-processing disk and let his fingers find the keys.

Fenhauser gave the disk back to him and he replaced it in the computer. "OK, let's see what you can do, now that *I'm* here."

Larry thought quickly. Sure, hit ENTER. He depressed the ENTER key and the screen came to life. "Taaa Daaa. Nothing to it" came from the speakers. A message appeared. DO YOU REMEMBER HOW I GOT'CHA IN THE FIRST PLACE?

"What does that mean?" Dr. Jeffries asked.

"I think it means that I have to type IN GOD WE TRUST and then it will change the color of the disk. That's what happened to the other one," Larry said.

"Yeah. I read about that," Fenhauser said.

"It's been all over TV. Anyone have a problem with that?" Dr. Jeffries asked, looking at his computer chief.

Hearing no response, Larry typed in the command. A very small window appeared with a warning palm and a message saying there was a technical problem. "I'm sorry. That isn't quite correct," a sultry female voice announced over the speakers.

Larry said he thought the computer hard drive had insufficient memory. He explained that when he did this before, he used his personally upgraded computer that had much more memory than any of the ones here except for the main frame. The computer chief verified Larry's reasoning as he was familiar with Larry's computer and had one like it at his house.

Dr. Jeffries was hesitant. He asked Mr. Fenhauser what he thought and he said he was not qualified. Dr. Jeffries asked Larry if he could make the disk do anything else. Larry played with it and it kept displaying error messages to the effect that it could not function in its black condition. If they would just change the color and the internal frequency of the superconductor, it could do anything they wanted.

Dr. Jeffries told Larry to stay away from the computer and requested a meeting with Fenhauser, Hudson, and the computer

chief in one of the private offices. They were in there for about
fifteen minutes and returned. The computer chief asked Larry some
specific questions regarding memory, speed, and other technical
information. Their concern was that they did not want to take a
chance of crashing their mainframe as the disk did to two of the
Pentium PCs. Between the two of them, they devised a system to
prevent that from happening.

Everyone except the computer chief agreed. The chief did not
think it would even work, as it could not get by the access code.
Larry said, "No harm then. Just stick it in the drawer and see what
happens. We eliminate one possibility that way. If it doesn't work,
I can go home and get my computer."

"No. No. No. You're not going anywhere," Hudson said.

Larry took out the disk and handed it to Fenhauser. "It looks
like you're our man."

"I'd like to see something happen here," he said, looking at his
watch. He gave the disk to the computer chief and shrugged his
head to go ahead and try it.

The chief put it in one of the workstations for the mainframe
after typing in some restrictions on the amount of files and bytes that
could be copied. Larry supported the computer chief's reasoning,
and assured everyone that there was no way the mainframe could
get overloaded with the actions that the chief was taking. The
monitor showed that files were being loaded. "Looks like we got a
winner, boss! You're one up on me, Larry. I was sure it wouldn't
work."

The monitor notified them that the installation was complete.
The chief opened the CD drawer and pulled out the shiny *white*
disk. "Yahoo! How about that?" Hudson shouted. He was
ebullient. Everyone in the room was smiling when the chief gave
the disk back to Larry to put back in the PC. Larry was smiling too
as he saw the mainframe lights blinking. He took his time and
started typing in commands. The first question he asked the
computer was, "Where are my wife and kids?"

The computer responded with a high, female falsetto-voice from
the speakers, "Oh, mercy me. In harms way, I would imagine. Mr.

Hudson can be such a nasty man at times." Hudson blushed and looked at Dr. Jeffries.

"Ah, they're OK. Just fine," Jeffries said in a very low voice.

Larry smiled and typed, "What is a superconductor?"

All gathered around, waiting for the answer. The same irritating voice replied, "A superconductor is the guy who lets the old lady ride free. Hee. Hee. Hee."

Dr. Jeffries said to be more specific. "Ask it how you can tell if it is a superconductor."

Larry typed in the question.

"Oh, that's easy. If the old lady is smiling when she gets off the bus, you can be almost sure. If she blows him a kiss, you can be certain," the voice said.

Fenhauser said he was beginning to be annoyed and asked if anyone had thought of some kind of plan. While they were mulling that over the operator of the main frame shouted for Hudson. "Problems! Big time!"

Dr. Jeffries beat Hudson to the workstation where the man was controlling the activities. "What's up? We've got a meeting going on!"

"They've gone out! All of our records for last year and up until today! Wait. I'll see if I can find out where they went," the man said while busily typing in commands. A list of phone-numbers came up on his screen.

"Get me a phone book! I don't recognize any of these numbers. None of these are for our clients," the operator stated.

The computer chief pushed his man aside and commanded the computer to print the list of numbers. "Somebody start checking them out! Somebody call this number and see who answers!" He wrote down the number and handed it to Dr. Jeffries. He went into the conference room and called.

"Hello. You have reached the Philadelphia office of the Internal Revenue Service. Our office hours are eight a.m., Eastern Standard Time until four p.m., Eastern Standard Time. We are open from Monday through Friday. If you wish to continue in English, press one, now...." He jerked the phone-cord from the wall and ran back to the control room.

294

"This one was the IRS office in Fresno! I hung up," someone said.

"This is a fax line, god damn it! Someone get me the number for the main office in Philadelphia. If it's a match, we're dead," the computer chief said. He typed in more commands to see if he could stop the data flow, but he was no match for the computer chips that held the information and were waiting for more data lines to open.

"More trouble. Zurich is sending out account balances in the clear. Look at this! No codes."

"Check the Caymans, Mexico City and our computer in Columbia," Fenhauser instructed. His hands were shaking. He tried a number from the printed list.

"Federal Bureau of Investigation, Agent Matthews speaking. How can I be of assistance to you?" He let the phone drop to the floor and grabbed Dr. Jeffries by his shirt collar.

"Call the airport and have them start the engines. Call me as soon as you get this mess straightened out."

As he was running toward the exit, the computer chief yelled to him that the computer in Columbia had crashed.

No one noticed Hudson collapse. It looked like he was making a call. The phone was still in his hand and he was down on one knee. His requests for help were drowned out by all of the shouting. Larry noticed him and saw that he could not breathe, was having severe chest pains, sweating profusely and trying to vomit. He called nine-one-one, gave them the information, and then tried to comfort Hudson until the ambulance arrived. He stayed on the phone and watched the others react to their fate.

He was alone in the control room with Hudson when he heard the first faint sounds of a siren. It seemed to be coming closer. Hudson was begging Larry not to let him die. "I'm not ready to die. Please, God, help me."

Larry suggested that he make an *invitation*. Hudson said, "Yeah. Yeah. How do I do it? God, this pain is unbearable."

Larry told him to take a deep breath and try to contact the Holy Spirit and tell Him that he didn't want to die. Hudson said he'd try it. The first medical technician to arrive taped a patch over his heart and an oxygen mask over his nose and mouth. He started breathing a little easier.

Larry called Roy and asked him if he could get a message to his wife that he was OK and was there anyone there that could give him a ride. He would bring the disk with him. Badge Number Forty-Three was in the office getting some data for the Assistant DA and offered to give him a ride. Larry could hear the siren over the telephone when he completed his conversation with Roy.

He walked over to the mainframe and verified that all of the records had either been faxed or electronically mailed. He turned on the TV and saw the President greeting Kathy. His wife and children, in the background, were surrounded by nice-looking men in business suits. They looked like they were packing, and very alert.

The Emergency Team moved Hudson on a stretcher, after giving him medication. One of them told Larry that he thought Hudson was going to make it as they got to him in time. Larry told the police officer, who responded with the ambulance that he should inform the District Attorney's Office immediately.

* * * * *

Shirley was supposed to have gone back home on the plane with the rest of the people who attended the wedding. Kami convinced Kathy to take her along on the Air Force transport that was taking off for Washington to meet with the President and help with dignitaries. She told him to check first with Roy to see if he needed her and it was OK with her as long as the Air Force plane had room.

Roy asked him why he was still in New York as he had purchased a ticket for him to Albuquerque and made limo service available to take him to the site. Kami said he wasn't aware of that. Roy asked him if he had read his manual lately and Kami admitted that he hadn't. As a-matter-of-act, he left it at home. He assumed that he was going to accompany Kathy and the President.

Roy informed him that he had agreed to be the MC and that the program was about to start. There were entertainers and celebrities already out there and no Master of Ceremonies. Fortunately, Lewis had received instructions and a manual and was taking his place. Kami said, "Oh, my goodness! He'll never do. He's a reporter!"

"And, you're a physics professor in Washington DC. And he's *there*," Roy said.

"Do you think you could get my manual to me? And also, a set of books that I have in the house. I left them on the shelf by my bed. They are called A Course In Miracles...a set of three books, blue with gold titles. I think I need them."

"How are you going to get to the site?" Roy asked.

"I'll just tag along with Kathy and the President as though that was what I was supposed to be doing."

"I'm sure the military will help me out again. I'll try to get them to you."

There was a young airman in a flying suit waiting to talk to Roy when he hung up the phone. "Have you seen a pair of Vuarnets around the office? One of the Secret Service men thinks he left them in the office."

"And who are you?" Roy asked.

"Airman First Class Eldridge, sir," the young man said.

"That's not what I meant. How did you get here? And where are you going?" Roy asked.

"C-130, sir. We're Reserves...Air National Guard. Came in to pick up some congressmen to go to Washington. Then we're going to Holloman. That's in New Mexico, sir."

"And someone in the White House wants a pair of sunglasses returned, right?"

"Yes, sir."

"You look around in here for them and I'll be right back with some documents that have to go to Washington. You're good at following orders, right?"

"Yes, sir."

Roy left the office to go to the Makino residence for the books.

Emily's brother and niece arrived. He had Emily's set of A Course In Miracles to present to Kathy. His daughter had a bouquet of flowers for her. The airman invited them to wait in Roy's office

297

after he found the sunglasses. Emily's brother put the books on Roy's desk and placed the bouquet of flowers on top.

Roy returned with Kami's set of books and placed them on Kami's manual that was on the desk. Roy listened as everything was explained to him and then he offered that Kathy was not available to receive the items. He didn't expect her back until after the Sunday event.

He saw the niece's liking for the flowers and suggested that she should have them. The girl picked up the flowers and knocked both sets of books onto the floor. The airman was fast. He had them picked up and rearranged in quick order. They were marked Volumes I, II, and, III. He said that he had better be getting back to the plane. Roy gave him instructions and saw that he had all of the items, and then visited with Kathy's friends.

* * * * *

Kathy was really upset with her father. She was being briefed on the plans for the afternoon in Washington by members of the White House Staff. There were so many names and faces to remember. He could be helping her. Instead, he was sitting with Shirley in the back of the plane listening to every word that came out of her mouth and eating everything that the stewards offered, as though that was what he was supposed to be doing.

She wasn't happy with Victor either. He was sitting with a woman reporter and seemed to be deeply engrossed in conversation instead of sitting with the agents and guarding the disk.

And she had done her morning session on the computer. The reporter was a lot older than Victor, she thought, and it was unlikely that anyone was going to rob the disk while they were airborne. She smiled at her jealousy, and returned her attention to the names and faces.

* * * * *

"Go! Go! Go!" Fenhauser shouted to his pilot as he slammed the door shut behind him and turned the large handle.

"Go? Where? I don't have a copilot."

"Lake Placid! You know my summer place. You were up there once. Where the hell is your Space Ace?" Fenhauser asked.

"Probably in the terminal, looking for a ride home. The Director of SuperCee fired him. I sent someone to find him when I got orders to start the engines," the woman said.

"Start taxiing. We have to go *now*. Tell me what I need to do and I can do it. I've flown this plane before," Fenhauser said.

"You're putting me on, right? You probably flew it when it was in the air. Holding it straight and level. There's no way you could land this thing. We have to have a qualified copilot. FAA regulations," she said.

Fenhauser reached in back and pulled a Beretta from its holster. "Taxi. Now!" He pointed the gun at her head.

She released the parking brakes and advanced the throttles. "Put on the headset so you can hear what's going on. We'll never get off the ground. As a- matter-of-fact, the chocks are still in place and that's why we're not moving. The ground crew wants to know what to do."

Fenhauser pushed the throttles forward and told her to shut up and go. He grabbed her headset and threw it behind the seat. She reduced the power after the plane jumped the chocks and she regained control of the plane. He pointed the gun towards the taxiway and told her go that way. "Do you have enough room to take off from here?" he asked her.

She looked at the taxiway. It was clear and there was enough room to take off, but not enough to accelerate and then stop if an engine quit or something. "Yes, but this is crazy. I'll lose my license and you'll go to jail for this. Look at all the people you're putting in jeopardy."

"Shut up and go...now!" Fenhauser said, pointing the gun at her once more.

"OK. Checklist. Flaps, I gotta' put the flaps down. Trim, set for Take-off…" She went through the procedures without the aid of a copilot.

"Annunciator lights...we have a 'door-open' light. Did you throw the handle and put the lever in place?" she asked professionally.

"Go. Now! To hell with the door."

She held the brakes and went up to full power. She released the brakes, accelerated down the taxiway and was airborne quickly. "Get me some charts. What altitude do you want me to fly at? We have no clearance," she said after raising the landing gear and flaps. She reduced power for the climb and turned on the radios and autopilot.

Fenhauser handed her a packet of maps and charts that he found beside his seat. "Is this what you want? How much gas do we have?"

She looked at the maps and said that was what she needed. She said the tanks were full. She said she needed to know what altitude to fly at as they were going to go into the clouds soon. Fenhauser asked if it was clear above the clouds and that they could hide up there if it was. She laughed. She asked him what had happened back at SuperCee.

He told her that his empire had vanished because of the disk. He was going to go to Lake Placid and get his art collection, jewelry and two million in cash that he had kept in a secret room in the basement of the resort for an emergency such as this.

She told him that the plane was being tracked on radar and that he'd never get away with it. As soon as they saw that the plane was heading for Lake Placid, the police would be waiting for them. He pointed the gun at her and asked her how she could stay alive a lot longer. She studied the maps for a long time.

* * * * *

Lewis arrived at Ground Zero wearing a nice suit, carrying his manual and just a small bag of personal items. He met with the contractor to begin the sound system tests. The contractor told him he was expecting a reporter but he looked like a minister. Lewis got up on the stage, found a place to open his manual, and addressed the audience. After introducing himself and telling a few short jokes,

300

he introduced the first group of volunteer singers, who sang Amazing Grace.

The contractor told him, while the group was singing, that he had a great voice, great timing on the jokes and did he learn public speaking in the seminary?

Lewis was perspiring already. He read up on his next lines from the manual. He finally looked out at the crowd. "My God! There must be millions of people out there." He almost choked. However, when the group finished the piece he announced the title of their next one without a trace of stage fright. He asked the contractor if there was some water around and since this was going to go on for eight more hours, could he get some food as he left home without breakfast.

The contractor asked him if he liked "shit-on-a-shingle". He added, "The Army Mess Sergeant makes the best, damned food I've ever eaten. I tried to get the recipe but the sergeant only had it in portions for a hundred men. He didn't think it would taste the same cooked at home. Besides, where would I find de-hydrated onions that gave it that special flavor? They only come in gallon containers.

"They're having beef-stew for dinner. I'll see that you get some." The contractor said you couldn't buy a meal like that for less than twenty bucks at any restaurant and it probably wouldn't taste as good.

* * * * *

Kathy was having a very enjoyable time meeting all of the people and talking to the President. He sure knew what to say to each one and made them feel very comfortable. The aides that kept coming and going, and whispering things to the President were a little annoying but this was how he was kept informed. And, all those cameras and microphones! It sure made people pleasant to talk to. She wondered what some were thinking about while smiling and shaking hands.

She was still upset with her father and was going to tell him about it the first chance she had. She could see him in the TV

301

monitor. He was standing behind them. Now he was holding Shirley's hand and talking to the Cabinet members as though that was what he was supposed to be doing instead of being in New Mexico. Very soon this would be over and she would have an hour or so to freshen up before the plane left for New Mexico. And she was going to get to fly in a helicopter for a change. Maybe she would change her mind about the noise.

* * * * *

The noise of the air escaping through the door seal of SuperCee's jet was irritating. The pilot told Fenhauser that it was also dangerous as the door was closed, but not locked and could open and de-pressurize the airplane at any time. He volunteered to fly the airplane and she could go back and close it properly. "Are you crazy! I'm putting it on autopilot. Don't touch a thing until I get back." She got out of her seat, went to the door, and secured it properly. She asked God to get her safely on the ground at Lake Placid. The noise stopped and the light went out. She returned and strapped herself into the seat once more.

"Have you figured out a way to save your ass yet?" he asked her.

"I think so. Look at the map here a minute. If we head for Lake Erie, there are a lot of cities and airports around there and they won't know where to send anyone. When we get about fifty miles out from the lake, I'll descend as rapidly as I can and go across the Canadian border just above the water. We'll stay north of the lake and then pick up Lake Ontario. We'll turn sharply and cross Watertown. We'll cut through the mountains as close to the road as we can fly. They should lose us on radar. The only problem will be if there are clouds and we have to climb. They'll have us on radar again. Hopefully, there will be some confusion as we cross the borders.

"Yeah. It might just work with a little luck. I'll need you to find the radio frequencies and set the numbers in the little windows here. Go ahead and try one. I can't read the map and fly that close to the ground. This number, here, is the frequency. Dial it in....good.

"What are you going to do after you get your loot? You'll never get out of the mountains, even in your 4 X 4 Jeep that you have there," she asked.

"You're flying me out. I'll tell you where after I make some phone-calls. Can you use the phone system from up here? The secure phone that I have in my office in the rear?" he asked her.

She said that he could and showed him how to use it from the copilot seat.

He began to make long distance phone-calls and slammed the instrument down each time he got through and received the bad news. He told her that the FBI and State Troopers had his estate in Virginia surrounded.

A colleague in New York informed him that the FBI and State Police had placed "Crime Scene" tape around the cemetery in North Carolina and the estates where Jimmy Franklin had visited. The Justice Department had just recalled all of their employees. Both party leaders are due to meet with the Attorney General. The colleague said, "Goodbye. Don't call back."

He called another associate in Nevada. A very clever young man answered the phone, wanting to know who was calling and tried to keep him on the line. He hung up.

"I'll let you know after we take off from Lake Placid," Fenhauser told his pilot. Right now, I want to see what I paid for to send you to flying school. And the favors to get you hired in front of the other guys waiting in line."

"I'm starting my penetration now. You better strap your skinny ass in. It could get bumpy down there," she said.

"Your *what?*" Fenhauser asked.

"Penetration. That's what it's called when you descend like this. Hang on!" She pulled the throttles back, dropped the gear, deployed the spoilers, and pushed the nose of the plane toward the ground. He forgot the chauvinistic idea that had entered his mind when the force of gravity was removed from his buttocks.

She heard his question and it's sexual implication. She thought maybe she could use her former skills to save herself. She was confident she could get the airplane safely on the ground at Lake Placid. After all, they weren't going to shoot the plane out of the sky. All she had to do was fly the airplane, as she had been taught to do. Her thoughts returned to the task at hand as she plummeted through a shallow layer of clouds and saw the dark water of the lake below. She descended lower and lower, slowed to retract the landing gear, and cleaned up the spoilers. She wished she had an altimeter setting. She saw a ship on the water that she could use for a reference and thought she could drop another hundred feet. She put it on autopilot and descended until she was scared, leveled there and engaged altitude control.

Both US and Canadian radar were able to keep the plane on their scopes. Especially since she had turned the transponder to Emergency shortly after take-off. The only thing that was making her nervous was Fenhauser toying with the gun. It could go off and disable an essential part of the plane, like busting the windshield in front of her face at 450 miles per hour! She slowed down to 300 for no apparent reason. She just felt better and the plane was not bouncing so much.

She felt very good when she saw Whiteface Mountain. She prepared the plane for landing and went straight in without a radio call. She taxied to the parking ramp and shut down the engines. There was only one maintenance-man to meet the plane.

An employee of the airport drove out in a marked vehicle with a row of lights on top. Fenhauser pushed the pilot down the stairs in front of him and ushered her into the car. He got in beside her, pointed the gun at the driver, and told him to shut off his radio and drive slowly to the main building. He saw an open gate in the fence and directed the driver to go through. He recognized the road leading into town and told the driver to take it. He gave instructions on how to get to his summer resort. He saw that there were a lot of young kids in town and took some detours. He spotted the Police car with no one in it.

They made the last turn to go up the hill to his luxury resort. With a view of the Lake, six bedrooms, huge living room, complete kitchen and bar facilities, swimming pool, a garage for four cars and a chain-link fence completely securing the property, it could hardly be called just a cabin. The driveway and street were full of cars. Not new ones. He wondered what was going on. He motioned the driver to pull inside the open gates, keeping the gun ready to fire. He saw his caretaker and yelled at him to come to the open window of the car.

"What the hell is going on here? Who are all these goddamned people?"

The caretaker, an older man who was looking for work a few years back had taken the job for a place to stay and enough money to take care of himself and his wife. He apologized when he recognized the owner. He said he had invited his friends and family to see the NBA playoffs on the big-screen TV. They weren't going to hurt anything, just wanted to get together, and since the cabin was never used this time of year, he thought it was all right.

Fenhauser screamed at the man to have the place vacant in two minutes. He shot the gun in the air and told the people to get the hell out of his house. He took a kick at one young lad that was· walking too slowly to suit him. He yelled that if he ever saw one of them around there again he'd have the police on them so fast they wouldn't know what hit them.

He directed the airport official to get out of the car and followed his pilot out her side of the car. He motioned them into the house as the few stragglers swiftly sped by. He pointed the gun at the caretaker and told him to lead the way to the cellar. They went down some stairs to a landing. The walls were made of thick, heavy stone and nicely pointed. Fenhauser placed his hand on a metal plate after dialing a series of numbers onto the keypad. The door lock buzzed and he was able to turn the knob. He motioned all inside to what looked like a vault with an antique table and four chairs. There were paintings on the walls and glass display cases with artwork and sculpture inside. In the center of one wall was a stainless steel door with another keypad and metal plate similar to the main entry. He opened the safe with another combination of numbers and took two satchels of money and jewelry. He stuffed two gold plated pistols in his waistband and a box of cartridges in his coat pocket. He heard a siren in the distance through the open door.

He pushed the pilot out through the door and slammed it shut with the two men inside. He programmed the time delay to maximum. He went out to the airport car and told the pilot to drive. The siren had ceased. He told her to go back to the plane. A police car had stopped one of the fleeing vehicles near the center of town. They drove back to the plane and only the maintenance man was there. He asked where his uncle was, the assistant airport manager. Fenhauser said he had an emergency in town and asked if there was any gas available. The guy said sure, but they would have to pay his uncle first. Fenhauser handed him a bundle of money and told him to start pumping. The man flipped through the bundle of hundred dollar bills and said, "Sure, why not? Lucky you came today. I got off tomorrow, right after the morning flight."

He drove the gas truck to the plane and hooked up the hose. The pilot said she had to turn on the power and open the valves. Fenhauser told her to take care of it. He had second thoughts and went inside the plane with her. He disconnected all of the radio headsets and threw them in the back of the plane. The pilot began to panic. She thought sure she would be safe after landing and that the authorities would catch up with them. But, it was the off-season, the town was very small and the locals were geared for tourists, not highjacked airplanes. It wasn't even highjacked... Fenhauser owned it.

The valves shut down when the tanks were full. Fenhauser took note that all of the tanks were full and told her to start engines. She hesitated and he placed the gun at her head. "Now." She became nervous and forgetful and missed some items on the checklist. The engine did not turn over when she pressed the start button. Fenhauser told her to stop playing games. She was on the verge of tears and realized that she forgot she had no ground power and needed to change the start procedure. She managed that and the first engine began to rotate. It started and she brought it up to idle speed.

"Taxi. Now!" Fenhauser said as he saw some people coming down the stairs of the terminal. The pilot pushed the throttle forward and began to taxi. She was shaking uncontrollably as she tried to start the other engine. "The door's open!" she shouted. She realized that it was a mistake telling him that, as maybe she could have used that as an excuse to abort the take-off and maybe blow a tire. She couldn't think. She didn't have a plan. Fenhauser got out of the copilot seat and closed the door. She taxied automatically and thought, "God, why have You forsaken me? I asked You for help." She closed her eyes and prayed. She heard a voice. "You asked Me to get you to Lake Placid safely, and I did."

Fenhauser returned and pointed to the annunciator panel. "Got it right this time. Let's get this thing in the air."

"Where are we going?" she asked.

"I'll let you know when we get in the air. I have to make some more phone- calls. How many hours can we fly?"

"I don't understand your question. I need to know where we're going and then I'll know how much gas it takes to get there."

"Can we make Cuba?" he asked.

"Yes," she answered.

"Can we make the Caymans?"

"I don't have any charts and we don't have a navigator and I don't know how to operate the system. There's a lot of water out there. I've never been to the Caymans."

Fenhauser saw the flashing lights on the highway that paralleled the airport fence. Two State Police cars. Going to the airport entrance. One more car with lights. Official, but he didn't recognize the markings.

"Get it in the air! Now!" Fenhauser said and pointed the gun at her once more.

She was halfway down the runway with horns sounding in the cockpit. "Flaps! I forgot the flaps!" She took her hand from the throttles and placed the flap lever down. The plane was not flying although she had the nose very high. Then it jumped into the air as the flaps extended beyond the take-off setting. She was able to respond quickly and jerked the landing gear and flap levers to the up position.

"That's what they have copilots for, you idiot!" she screamed at him.

"Take it easy. We got off the ground, didn't we? Go back to Canada and I'll make some phone-calls. It'll be dark soon and they'll have a hard time seeing us."

Chapter 27

The President was delighted with Kathy and as the afternoon wore on, he took a back seat in the conversations and let her do most of the talking. The fact that he had fired his Secretary of State was enough to settle most of the complaints that his visiting dignitaries had. Many even told the President that he might have been too harsh and that he might want to re-consider. After all, the instructions had been sent out early enough for everyone to make a decision. And, again, this was an unusual event. Kathy took responsibility and said that her group was putting on the event and she pressured the President into sponsoring it when she saw that it was getting out of hand. The handshaking ended finally and Kathy had a chance to use her computer to refresh her instructions.

She was invited to a last-minute meeting of the Secret Service, the Military and the President. The Secret Service was dead set against the walk to Ground Zero. The Chief of Staff said that they would help, but that the President's security was not their responsibility. The President's personal advisors had no helpful suggestions. Kathy said that there were already millions of people out there, they were all well behaved, and there had not been one single casualty. If the President does not walk in with some of the other dignitaries, who came from foreign lands, it would indicate he was not safe on his own soil. "Besides, God is the show tomorrow...not the President."

"That's it, then. I'm walking behind Kathy and her father; then the Honor Guard with Starlight Express carrying the UN Flag. The US and Mexican flags side-by-side...that was a nice touch...half of the people out there are from Mexico," the President said.

"My *father!* I'm walking with my *father?* I thought I was supposed to walk with the President and The First Lady!" Kathy exclaimed.

"We don't have a protocol for an event such as this. Perhaps I assumed, incorrectly, that you would want to be with your parents at such a time. Certainly you are the star and need to be in front," one of the White House aides spoke up.

"My *parents?* Did I hear that correctly? My *mother* died in the automobile accident. My *father* is supposed to be out in New Mexico acting as the Master of Ceremonies, but instead, he's hanging out around here with that airhead, eating all of the food!" Kathy complained.

"I should have checked with you sooner, I guess. However, the President said he thought that Kami in the center with you on one arm and Shirley on the other would make a terrific picture. She is really photogenic, don't you think?" the staffer said.

"I'm going to kill him! When this is over, I'm going to kill him!" Kathy said.

"Well, then. That's all settled. Why don't we adjourn and be ready for the helicopter in an hour-and-a-half," the staffer said.

* * * * *

Lewis was developing a style as he went along. He was doing pretty well with the jokes and introducing the entertainment. Now he had to do some improvisation. He wanted to know if there were any people out in the audience who had already made an invitation and, if so, did they wish to come up and relate what happened. He sounded just like the radio evangelist that Victor had imitated when they were trying to get the computer operational.

The first person to come forward was Rosa Sanchez. She asked if she could speak in Spanish and then in English because she wanted to practice her English. Lewis said she could talk in any language as they had translators already broadcasting the show to the world. She said, "English. Espero...no...jo...No... I want to get this right."

Lewis told her to relax and relate her story. She quickly reverted to Spanish and told about how she always wanted to come to America but now the line was closed. She said she advertised for an American husband and her father was angry with her. She started on the journey with a group of students; many turned around and went back home. She continued with a few friends and made

310

her invitation when she was so tired from walking that they had to stop and rest.

Later, as they walked along the highway she tripped and fell. A family from Abilene, Texas was driving their RV to the site, saw her go down, and stopped to give them a ride. Needless to say, their son, a Texas Aggie, was home from school and was along for the ride. They like all of the same things and are going to write to each other. His parents are really nice and they seem to like her a lot. His father owns a construction company and his biggest problem is finding good masons that will take the time to do the job right. Her father is the best mason in his pueblo and has a lot of patience.

She got a long applause. Lewis asked if anyone else had a story to tell.

* * * * *

Air Force One was heading for New Mexico.

Larry caught a ride with the C-130 on its return flight and would be in New Mexico in time for his part in the program.

Fenhauser and his pilot were flying in circles above Pennsylvania. The air traffic controllers had the plane's transponder on radar and were able to divert traffic away from them. The pilot found the flight manual and set the plane up for maximum endurance since she had no destination. She kept busy by writing a list of the violations that she was forced to perform. She was thinking about all of the FAA examiners who would haunt her for the rest of her flying career and the laughing stock she was making for other women who were trying to break into this traditional male job.

Fenhauser made call after call. He originally started for Cuba. When he finally got in touch with his associate there, he was told that if he came anywhere near the country he would be shot out of the air.

His "friend" in Bogota told him he was "dead meat". He was asked, "Do you know how much money is in the pipeline? It is going to disappear. All because you got greedy. You over-extended

311

yourself is what happened. If you had stuck with one thing, like us, we'd all be doing OK."

He finally ran out of calls to make. "Head for Mexico City," he waved the gun as though it were not in his hand and made another call. "Still not available," he said as he placed the phone down. "Because he's still drunk and they can't wake him up."

"What I'm hearing here is that you don't have a friend in the world?" the pilot asked. "What's this all about anyway? Maybe if I knew what was going on, I could help out."

"That god damned disk! It sent all of my financial and business records to the IRS and the FBI," Fenhauser said.

"How could it do that? The disk that was stolen? You stole the disk that is supposed to have God's voice on it?"

"God's voice. Gimme a break. It has *superconductors* in it. Do you know what that disk is worth if we can find out how to make them? Yeah, I stole the disk and I beat the rest of them to the punch. The Japs were willing to put up a lot more money than I paid for it. Even the Russians were after it. I wish to hell I had just sold it to them and doubled my money instead of trusting Jeffries. The whole thing was his fault. I should have shot the son-of-a-bitch back there but I needed someone to call and get the engines started.

"That disk is what did it. I never should have let them put it in the mainframe. I wonder if Hudson was in on it. He could have planned this whole thing. But what's he going to get out of it? That's what I can't figure out. Sure, him and Larry. I remember him covering his butt. 'Oh, no, don't put it in or the computer might crash like the others.' I'd like to cover his butt. With some nine millimeter lead.

"Let me try Mexico again. You know the way don't you?" Fenhauser dialed again.

The pilot waited until he was off the phone. "Still not awake?

"My charts only go to the border. Your friend? Do you think he has some pull with the government? Here's what I'm thinking. Mexico City is a *big* place. I'm sure I can find it at nighttime, like this. See all the cities down there? I don't need a map at this altitude. *If* the weather is clear. That's what worries me. There are a lot of high mountains around Mexico City.

"If your friend has some pull, maybe we can get vectors and the frequencies for the instrument landing systems. If you let me use the radios, I might be able to get us down. If the weather is clear, no problem, I can find the airport. Then what happens?"

"Pull? He *is* the government. A lot of it, anyway. Will he expose himself? That's what worries me. Salinas didn't handle things right. Too many loose ends. Too many loose cannons down there.

"I'm hoping he hasn't been informed of the problem yet. I just want to get on the ground, get a taxi, and get lost." He opened the jewelry case and showed her a pallet of emeralds.

"With these, I can live forever. Look at this one! Five mil if it's worth a penny.

"This is my pride and joy! This, I don't part with!" he said, holding a huge brilliant diamond. "It took a lot of work to get that beauty." He returned it to the case and closed the lid.

He opened the other case and took out five bundles of hundred dollar bills. He put them on the radio console between them. "You get me on the ground and they're yours."

She didn't want any part of it. She was thinking about Mexican jails. She continued flying southwest at maximum endurance, buying time. Fenhauser had no idea that they were not making many miles per gallon over the ground. The prevailing westerly wind aloft had all but ceased. Something was drawing the plane towards New Mexico.

Fenhauser made some more futile calls to other business associates. Many had fled. Many refused to take his call. Some threatened to kill him on sight. Some had already been arrested.

* * * * *

Roy sat peacefully in the OPERATION INVITATION office. His flow charts were completed. He had enough money to clean up the debris, repair the fences and gates, and contractors lined up to do the work. The rainy season was over. He had been worried about damage to the environment and some friends of Kami's at the University volunteered to make an assessment to repair the damage.

He had a meeting with them and he listened as they droned on and on with the cash register ringing. He finally told them, "They picked that place to set off an atomic bomb. The land can wait a year to recover from people peeing on the cactus. For all you know, it might be good for them."

He was sitting at his desk thinking about the meeting. He got up and redlined the last item on his chart. "The plastic and the baby diapers, we pay for. Peeing on the cactus? An act of God. We don't pay.

"Hmmm? Maybe we do."

* * * * *

"There's the Mississippi. We can fly down to New Orleans and follow the coastline. What do you think?" the pilot asked.

"Something I never could figure out. I'd get these guys cold. One favor and then they'd figure out a way to screw me. How do they do it? We had to keep coming up with new ways. That was where Jeffries was good. Figuring out new ways."

"I have no idea what you're talking about. New Orleans or straight ahead?"

"You're call. I was talking about blackmail. They always survived. I can't figure that out."

The plane continued on a heading toward New Mexico.

* * * * *

The procession started late, but that was not a problem as they had about six hours to wait after they got to Ground Zero. There was no lack of entertainers to keep the crowd occupied.

Kathy just said it was time to go and took her father's arm. He was holding a candle but gave it to a bystander. It was awkward to hold the candle with Shirley on his other arm. Everyone must have fallen in behind as there were no instructions to stop and wait. Kathy glanced back several times and all appeared orderly so she kept pace with her father who was speaking to Shirley about nuclear physics, electrons, and stuff like that. The camera flashes were taking their toll on her eyes. Kami complained also. Shirley said she was getting a headache. Kathy looked back at the President and The First Lady and saw that they were wearing tinted glasses. Experience, Kathy thought. The procession with lighted candles was beautiful.

She decided she liked the parade and did a few twirls. She saw the Secret Service men flanking the President and called one of them forward. "See if you can find Victor and get him up here." The man pulled out a radio and spoke into it.

"He'll be right up, mam."

Kathy stopped and turned to the President. "This doesn't feel right to me. Why don't we just all walk together? I haven't had a chance to speak to your wife and this is boring. Is it OK if Victor joins us? He's kind of, my boyfriend."

"Sure. My wife was asking me a lot of questions about you. Now you can tell her in person. You know, you should have gotten some glasses. Don't you have a headache from the flash bulbs? I'll see if someone can find you a pair," the President said, motioning for one of his aides.

"Get some for Shirley too. She already has a headache. I can't imagine why!"

Just then Victor showed up and joined the group. He was introduced to the First Lady. She said she had heard a lot of good things about him and wished him luck on his skating project. Kathy raised her eyebrows.

Before they resumed the procession, four Military Policemen arrived escorting a young airman who had some books to deliver to Professor Makino. He said he got them in exchange for sunglasses. Kami asked if he still had the glasses and the young man pulled them from a zippered pocket in his flying suit. Kami gave them to Shirley.

One of the Military Policemen was trying to catch his breath. Apparently, they had been running for some time to catch up with Kami. "Anybody here smoke?" he asked the crowd. A hand went up and the sergeant threw him an open pack of cigarettes.

"That's it! I quit. Tomorrow I lose this gut."

He was telling his buddies that he never should have started lifting weights. He did it to look good. He bulked up and then when the family came along he stopped. Tomorrow he was going to the gym and start playing basketball and maybe do some running or swimming. Yeah, he'd take the kids to the pool.

"You're working tomorrow," a buddy said.

"Tomorrow, I'm running. I'll take the kids to the pool when I get home. Hey, I'm serious. I'll give you twenty-five bucks if I smoke another cigarette. This little jog made a believer out of me."

Kathy overheard him talking and jokingly asked if he had made an invitation lately.

"As a matter-of-fact, I did. Had nothing to do with this though. Me and the missus having a go at each other."

By the time the procession had gone a hundred yards, Kami and Shirley were walking out in front, with a foursome behind. Victor and the President were talking about basketball and Kathy asked the First Lady, "What did Victor tell you about a skating project?"

"I heard this from one of the reporters. Victor loves to roller-skate and he wants to open a skating rink and teach roller dancing. It's becoming quite popular."

* * * * *

"Anyone else with a story to tell? Now's your chance to tell the world. Don't be nervous, we're all friendly people here. We want to hear what you have to say. OK. Miss?" Lewis looked at the card one of the volunteers handed him.

"Miss Julie Patterson. A nice round of applause, please." He handed her the mike and told her to relax. Julie had a very pretty face but it was obvious from her pear-shaped figure that she didn't spend much time doing anything physical.

"I'm a student. Actually, I'm more than that. I'm a Ph.D. I study religion. I want to refute some of what I've been hearing in the news and here tonight about A Course In Miracles. I have A Course In Miracles in my library and have read the entire text. It is very interesting and I agree with most of what is written. However, it has not changed my life or any of the views that I hold on the

316

subject. I certainly have not experienced any miracles as a result of reading it.

"I'm extremely happy for the gentleman who was up here earlier and told you how A Course In Miracles resolved his business problem. But, as many of you in business know, all he did was use common sense. The fact that a friend of his knew the tax code wasn't a miracle. These things happen at business lunches all the time."

"Interesting. Have you made an *invitation*? If so, tell us about that," Lewis announced to the crowd.

"No. I haven't. Perhaps at some time in the future. I was impressed with what I read in the medical report when Kathy was examined. My life has been rather pleasant, my parents have enough money to support my education, and I have a very supportive relationship."

"OK. We have another point of view. Thank you.

"Wait a minute! I see a hand up. Someone wants to ask you a question." Lewis motioned the person to come forward and ask the question.

A very attractive lady in her fifties, looking like she was in her thirties, and dressed like she was in her twenties, took the mike.

"The Course worked for me. I used to be a hundred-and-ninety pounds!" she said enthusiastically, as she turned full circle to show off her figure. "I do my lessons every day. You said you *read* the text. Are you doing the lessons? And the second question, you are still studying and you're what, thirty? Have you found your purpose in life?"

"No, I haven't done the lessons. It seemed like a waste of time after I read the text. Like I said, I read the text and I agree with most of it. Some of it is very vague."

"And your purpose?" the woman asked.

"I suppose I'll get a job and try to help people solve their problems. I hold a degree in Psychology. I would like to be a minister, but I haven't found a religion that I really believe in."

"Why don't you start the lessons, read the teachers manual and write to me when you have a chance. I live in Phoenix and maybe we can get together. Where do you live?"

"I'm from Phoenix also."

"C'mon. Let's exchange phone-numbers. I know a great restaurant that has a low-cal menu." The ladies left the stage holding hands while the audience clapped theirs.

"Thank you ladies for sharing your experiences with us.

"If you will all look towards the east, you'll see the procession making it's way in. Beautiful isn't it?

"And now, I have some great news for those of you who are bothered by the noise and exhaust from the generators. We are going to take this opportunity to shut down the sound and light systems.

"The utility company has brought in power lines and switchgear, and is going to provide the electricity free. They need about five or ten minutes to make the transfer.

"When we come back on, we will be on one hundred percent nuclear power. No more coal or oil will be needed to produce the energy. No oil spills or mine cave-ins to worry about either.

"So let's take this opportunity to enjoy the procession and take a few minutes to reflect on how far we have come in our lifetime."

Lewis signaled that he was finished. The lights went out and the generators silenced.

The contractor offered him a tray of food. "Best damned beef-stew I ever ate. The Mess Sergeant is retiring in another year. He's coming to work for me. I never thought of it before, but they have food at all the events that I set up for. He's an expert at working in mobile kitchens. His food is cheap to make. We'll make a fortune. Do you know how much they get for a hot dog at a Rock concert? I can put together a package deal that even Roy would have to buy."

* * * * *

It was after midnight when Fenhauser got the call from Mexico. It was the secretary for the man he was trying to contact. Her English was not perfect, but he understood enough to know that the man he wanted to talk to was up in the mountains and his portable phone was not answering. She said men were out looking for him in the dark as there were many important calls coming in.

318

Fenhauser gave her his number and told her to disregard all of the other calls as he had taken care of the problem. When they found the man to give him his number only. She said she understood.

"All right! Mexico City and step on it!" he told the pilot.

Stupid, she was not. She heard the parts of conversation with the lies in it. She turned the plane south and was sure that Brownsville, Texas was causing the light that made its way through the clouds below.

"Step on it!" Fenhauser told her again. "How fast will this thing go?" he asked while waving the gun.

"Listen to me for a minute. If we go faster, we use more gas. I think we can just make it. If you hadn't fired the copilot, none of this would have happened. If you had another person to help you, you could have had twice as much money. How much did you leave back there in Lake Placid?"

"Shut up and fly the plane. I have to think of what to say." Fenhauser leaned back in the copilot seat and closed his eyes.

The pilot checked a chart and found the frequency for Brownsville VOR. She dialed the numbers into the equipment. Fenhauser saw her hand move and shot the radio.

"What are you doing? Are you crazy? That was our navigation radio. I can't talk to anyone on that!"

* * * * *

The contractor told Lewis that they were all set to go with the power. Lewis looked at the procession. "Beautiful, isn't it? Can you leave the lights off until everyone is in and seated? I don't want to break the mood. Maybe another fifteen minutes. Man, my belly's full. You were right. That is the best beef-stew I've ever eaten."

"The serge can put that out for less than a buck. Can you believe that stew comes out of a can!

"You got a visitor. Let me know when you want lights. The sound is all set to go."

The cameras that were up on towers did a magnificent job of recording the procession. The announcers and commentators

319

reflected on the event and a lot of people at home in the Western Hemisphere went to sleep. The churches in Europe were packed to capacity, as the sun was high above the horizon there.

Kathy and the President sat next to each other with the First Lady on the other side of him. It felt good to sit down and take a rest. Most of the candles had burned out. The lighted ones were used to find seats. There were plenty of ushers, military men in their dress uniforms. They seemed well informed and directed everyone to the sections reserved for them.

Lewis sensed that it was time and signaled for the lights. He had to laugh at the joke that was prescribed in his manual and went over again the gesture he had to make at the end. Timing had to be just right. He was at the center of the stage when the lights came on.

"Ladies and gentlemen! Please. Por favor.

"Ladies and gentlemen, I have some great news to announce.

"Many of you may have heard about the disk that was stolen and the man who was kidnapped to make it operate. Larry Garcia. A close friend of Kathy and her father, Professor Makino.

"I'll tell you, miracles never cease on this show. Please. Let's all stand up and give Larry a big hand."

Larry walked to the center of the stage amidst a thundering ovation, waving the disk over his head.

Lewis called for quiet.

"Larry is shy and wants his wife and family to know that he is safe and sound. If they are out there anywhere, come on up.

There was movement in the front as Mrs. Garcia was located. Suddenly, there was a flash of light and a fat man in one of the contractor's uniforms began to float in the air. He dropped the tools that he was using to repair a speaker and then shot off like a noiseless rocket. He disappeared overhead.

"I don't know what that was all about folks. Maybe I'll get an answer from someone up here," Lewis said as he greeted Mrs. Garcia.

After giving his wife a warm kiss and a big hug, Larry waved the disk again and said he would go to work on the computer, as that was his job. Perhaps the answer was on the disk.

His wife returned to the audience. Larry inserted the disk and typed: IN GOD WE TRUST and entered it. The printer operated. Larry handed Lewis a paper.

"Folks, you won't believe this. Kathy, I think we have a show," Lewis said after reading the paper that he was given.

"Let me read this:

"Cecil B. DeMille is directing tomorrow's activities. The man you just saw was Alfred Hitchcock, who also wanted to direct it. Peter took roll call and found that Alfred was missing. Peter located him in the crowd posing as a sound technician and brought him back home."

Lewis had enough entertainers on hand to last a week. At three in the morning, he sensed it was time to close. He wanted to get in his joke before letting Whitney Houston set the tone.

"There were these two guys, Patty and Tom. They were in the pub, well into their beers, when Patty decided it was time to go home. He took the shortcut through the cemetery and wouldn't you know it, he fell into an open grave that the workers had prepared for the next day.

"He tried everything he could to get out. He was finally exhausted and sat down in a corner to wait 'til mornin'.

"Well, wouldn't you know it? Along comes Tom, and down he goes. Tom, being a bit younger, didn't give up so easily. He dug his toes in the dirt on the walls, stretched up and almost made it a couple of times, but he lost his grip and came tumbling back down. He tried again-and-again to get out, but he couldn't. In desperation, Tom made an *invitation*...

"Patty saw the predicament his friend was in and tapped him on the shoulder and said, 'Tom, you can't get out.'"

And then Lewis made a sweeping gesture with his arm, took a big jump and said, "But, he did!"

There was polite laughter.

Lewis introduced Whitney Houston to sing the "Ave Maria" and set the tone for the wait until morning.

"Your timing was way off. You need to work on that one a little more. The Irish accent. That was good," the contractor told Lewis.

321

* * * * *

The phone rang. Fenhauser picked it up and his hand was shaking. "Fenhauser here. Is that you, Juan?"

"Si, gringo. Where are you?"

"I'm flying down to explain. Everything is taken care of. A little damage, but we can fix everything.

"So, how are you? I heard you got lost up in the mountains. I was worried about you. That's why I headed right down."

"You fixed everything? Tell me how you fixed everything."

"Well, ah, exactly what kind of problems are you referring to? What have you heard?"

"I've got a war going on here. You tell me how you fixed it. Go on, I want to hear. You're coming here? I want to meet you personally. I'm going to kill you personally. Like my son, killed on the way here to tell me the news of this disaster.

"I want to know one thing. What is it with the disk? I don't understand that part. How could you be that damned stupid?

"Please come down. I want to be the one to put the bullet between your eyes." The man was crying when he let the phone fall from his hand.

Fenhauser looked out the window.

"We can't go to Mexico. One last chance. Head for Vegas."

"I don't think we have fuel to make Vegas. We're clear down here over the Gulf. Vegas is way over here," the pilot said pointing at the chart in the dim light.

Fenhauser pushed the chart away with the gun and told her simply, "Vegas."

She turned north, hoping to get across the border into US airspace and find a place to land. She knew she couldn't make Vegas and stayed at maximum endurance airspeed. All she had was time and that was running out.

It was impossible to keep the news coverage under control. A highjacked airplane! A dispatch of Federal Agents to the Lake Placid airport. A missing airport manager. A smiling copilot who thanked his lucky stars that he decided to make an invitation.

322

Especially when he saw pictures of the airplane taken by Air Force fighters. It was on TV when he got home and he called in to the FAA to tell them his story.

Some channels whose management steered clear of the Kathy story or had contracts to fulfill, were thankful that they had people for coverage of the event. The NBA games were constantly being interrupted for updates. The interview with the maintenance man at Lake Placid was particularly humorous. The Canadians kept switching channels back and forth all evening.

The Chief of Staff had everything under control. He had spoken to the FBI Director and had his fighters stay well back, out of sight. They decided to let the plane and its passenger lead them to a destination. They had not yet figured out a way to break the code on the telephone transmissions that were coming from the plane. It was recorded, but not yet transformed into something of use. It was just a matter of time and the speed of the computers. Officials of the Mexican government were well informed. They had every possible destination alerted and troops in place. They were instructed not to shoot. The passenger was positively identified and wanted alive. The pilot was performing under duress.

* * * * *

It was peaceful at Ground Zero. The lights were turned down. Some were asleep. Some were awake and engrossed in their thoughts. Some were talking to their companions or friends that they had made. Even the American men were peeing on the cactus rather than walking to the portable latrines. The American women walked the extra mile. The Mexican women knew how to pee. They made a hole in the sand with their foot, did their thing, and kicked some sand over it.

CHAPTER 28

"I can't hold it any longer. I have to pee. *Now*!

"Don't touch *anything* until I get back. The autopilot is headed for Vegas," the pilot said and got up to relieve herself in the plush lavatory in the rear of the plane. On the return walk she saw the TV and turned it on. She watched in awe. She saw the pictures of her plane and the commentator describing the flight path she had taken so far. She looked out one of the side windows and saw the lights of the fighter that was flying *very* close formation, probably because they had been in and out of the clouds and he didn't want to lose her, even momentarily. She waved, and then thought that was stupid. However, the fighter pilot waved back. She just couldn't see him in the darkened cockpit.

She looked through the basket of fruit that was on the galley counter, and didn't see anything she liked. She found some apple juice and drank that. As she walked past the TV to go forward to the cockpit, the commentator was announcing to the world that one person, believed to be the female pilot, had just waved to the pilot of the chase plane.

In the Pentagon, the Air Force Commander was explaining to the Army Chief of Staff why the pilot was in that close. The Chief of Staff pulled rank and told him to move his "cowboy" back. Waco, Texas was still on his mind.

When she got back into the pilot seat, she told Fenhauser she had some rather bad news for him. "Such as?" he asked.

"It's better you go find out for yourself. You're going to Class 26 your pants and I don't want the stink up here. Go watch TV. I'm turning for the nearest way to get back to the US airspace and find a place to put us down. We don't have gas to get to Vegas anyway."

Fenhauser went back to relieve himself also and glanced at the TV on the way back to the cockpit. He made himself a stiff drink at the bar and sat down to watch the live coverage of his misadventure. A Justice Department spokesman was telling about the files of information that they been receiving all day that had yet to be verified, but implicated many "known criminals", and high ranking government officials. No names or titles were announced.

That was followed by pictures of a limousine shot full of holes, several of the bullets passing through the body of the passenger, who was believed to be a major distributor of drugs. The commentator said this may be related to the SuperCee disclosure. TV footage showed the outside of the SuperCee building.

A still picture was shown of Mr. Hudson being placed in an ambulance. There was TV coverage of the control room inside SuperCee. It was complete with pictures of the computer that reportedly sent the information to the various financial and law enforcement agencies. Men in business suits were putting files in cartons. The chief computer operator was standing behind a man in a business suit who was operating the computer. It looked like the man standing was handcuffed to a uniformed police officer.

There was TV footage of Larry, waving the disk on stage at Ground Zero.

The TV hurled glass particles throughout the passenger section of the plane as the 9-millimeter bullet penetrated it.

The pilot heard the explosion, but did not panic. She put the chart down and looked back to see Fenhauser coming forward. He returned to the copilot seat. He was quiet.

She had it all figured out finally. She would just stay on this heading until she saw something she recognized; a large city or even some airport lights. She checked the time and fuel remaining as accurately as she could. She wanted to hold off until daylight and was sure she could do it. She just had to be near an airport when the time came, as the plane was going to eat up fuel rapidly at the lower altitude. She wished that the chase plane would come up and direct her and for the life of her, she could not remember the signals to communicate with a chase plane. She heard of them and read about them one time, but, at-the-moment, couldn't remember them or where to look to find them.

She kept reviewing in her mind all of the different options she had. She knew she would see some lights soon. She was glad that Fenhauser wasn't talking. If he'll just sit like that until they were safely on the ground.......

The sun's first light appeared in the east. At thirty-five thousand feet, she saw it before the people in the desert. She saw lights and a huge glow ahead and   eased the throttles back. Fenhauser did not move. She wished she had a navigation radio. She eased the throttles back a little further and Fenhauser gazed into the barrel of his Beretta.

Without the engine noise, it was very serene in the plane. The pilot was pleased with her performance. She knew she was going to get the plane on the ground safely and would probably get a commendation, rather than jail or a reprimand. She was even thinking she might be able to sell her story.

Her mind returned to flying as she noticed the airspeed was a little too low. She wanted to get across the line and then she remembered some trivia she once heard. New Mexico is the highest State in the Union! Daylight. She wanted daylight. She reduced the airspeed and added a touch of throttle for no apparent reason. Why is the guy just hanging back there instead of leading me down? He saw me wave. She thought of asking Fenhauser if she could use the radio. No. As long as he just sat there, she was safe. There was no telling what he was going to do.

Chapter 29

Conclusion

The first direct rays of the sun appeared on the horizon and a hush fell over the assembled mass. Kathy walked to the center of the stage and waited. A few younger members of the assembly began a count down, but when no one joined in, they too, fell silent with the others. The sun appeared to burn a hole on the horizon of the desert as it rose slowly in the east. When it was in full view, Kathy pointed to Larry at the computer, and he pressed ENTER.

Zamfir's rendition of "The Lonely Shepherd" filled the desert air. At the conclusion a suave, baritone voice said, "That's my favorite piece of music." God's voice was heard by all who made the effort to listen.

"Thank you for inviting Me here today. I am your Creator." There was a mixture of emotions throughout the crowd as God paused.

"You have nothing to fear from Me. I am here today because I love you." There was finally complete silence as God paused once more.

"I chose this time because you now have the ability to make My voice heard around the world and because you have finally learned the value of peace.

"I chose this place because it was here that you proved the power of the atom. Knowing that there existed great power was not enough. The proof of that knowledge occurred here. Knowing and not acting on that knowledge would have resulted in nothing. The action that took place here resulted in the single most significant saving of lives in the history of this project, which you have named 'Earth'.

"One man looked at the sun and using the free will that I gave him, figured it out. In 1905, that man knew and he wrote the Theory of Relativity. Forty years later the world knew, although only the students of that one man understood the theory. And now, that knowledge is used to make earth a better place.

"Before the action that took place here, there were many beliefs regarding the sun. Some even believed the sun was Me. I'm glad they were wrong because it's too hot there for Me.

"When I hear about fish flopping up on the beach and evolving into men and women, I have to laugh. That *theory* has been around a long time. Many choose to believe that it actually happened in spite of the obvious failure to observe one instance of it's ever occurring, even after exposing the most basic species to the limits of their existence.

"Almost everyone has had the opportunity to observe the sun and feel its warmth and it's energy and figure it out. One man finally did. Because the power is so great, you put strong controls and limits on its use.

"Looking beyond that, everyone has the ability and the opportunity to look within himself. Enormous power is there, waiting to be used. You have all felt it. You know it is there. It is just a little stronger than your ego, which I also gave you. Because the power is so enormous, I put a condition on its use. You must invite Me before I can enter.

Many years ago one man, created exactly as each one of you, figured it out and acted on that knowledge. As He told you, the power that He possessed, came from Me. His name was Jesus and He removed some of the guilt that had grown too strong. If there were *no* guilt, you would slaughter each other in a very short period-of-time, and that would be the end of this project. In other parts of the earth, and at different times, others have figured it out and balanced the forces in different manners by using their free will.

"Many of you here today have figured it out. Many haven't.

"Some have figured it out at one time or another and then forgotten.

"Some have figured it out and not acted on that knowledge.

"Some have figured it out but are not willing to pay the price.

"Some are content with having figured it out and do not reach out to teach others.

(Pause)

"Let us start then, at the beginning.

"I created Adam, Eve, and others like them in your present form. I gave them knowledge freely and would never put my children in a position where they could destroy themselves. If I had forbidden them to eat of the tree of knowledge, the fruit could not have been eaten. Some of my other creations made wrong choices and perished along the way. Separated from other groups they took on different ideas and beliefs. Today, you accept language differences as normal and have made great strides to overcome the differences. Why is it so hard to accept that people, separated from each other, would develop different beliefs?

"Next. The so-called Ten Commandments. If I commanded them, they could not be disobeyed. I gave your ancestors free will, but it grew a little heavy on the side of guilt for those living in the Western Civilization. Jesus figured that out, made the correction and I think He got it just right. That is why you don't see them mentioned in the Bible after Jesus came along.

"The first 'commandment' is irrelevant. There *is* no other God to put before Me. Some of My creations who are now with Me think Moses started a fire using a marijuana plant and inhaled some of the smoke. The fact is, he got them right. But egos chiseled away at them over the years to suit their own purposes.

"For example, I think the first 'commandment' was introduced to create fear of Me. That fear could then be used to induce others to make changes beneficial to the author. Before this day is over, you will see that there is nothing to fear from Me. That is, if My creations that I selected to enlighten you make the decisions that I expect of them.

(Pause)

"Because of Kathy's miracle, you know who I am. I've told you about Jesus and others like Him. Each one of you has the same ability to use My power. The third part of the team is the Holy Spirit who is now waiting for your invitation. She wants to discuss

331

your ideas with you and then, when you are both in agreement, to put Me to work. A little clue here. If you make a sincere plea to the Holy Spirit, I *have* to help you. That's My job.

"The Holy Spirit will never ask for more than you are capable of doing. She will always provide more than you agree to. Actually, She's a softie, so you have no reason to fear Her either.

"Let's take a break here and allow all of that sink in.

" Most of you saw or heard about what happened earlier with Alfred. I hope the rest of My presentation goes OK. I chose Cecil B. DeMille to direct today's show. I was impressed with the work he did while he was down there.

"Henny Youngman wanted to write the script, but I gave it to a committee of Matthew, Mark, Luke, and John. I used William Shakespeare as the tiebreaker.

"No one could get a consensus for the music. Louis, Irving, Johann, Gregory, Nat, Peter. So many to choose from, so much talent, and they all wanted to participate. I finally made the choice Myself.

"By the way, the best waltz has not yet been composed.

"OK. Back to work.

"So, until you make that invitation, or if you've forgotten and find yourself with a new set of problems, I offer these *suggestions* to make your life more enjoyable:

"One. Resolve your differences through arbitration and negotiation. Deal with facts. The more knowledge and facts that you have at your disposal, the greater your chances of getting what you think will make you happy.

"Two. Earn your livelihood through intelligent use of your mind and the talents that I gave you.

"Let Me tell you a bit about how that works. This was one of the easiest programs to install and it never fails. If you steal something or cheat someone, you *automatically* miss an opportunity to earn something of **equal** value.

"If you give something to another, you *automatically* receive something of equal or **greater** value. That way, you always create more than you started out with.

"Three. Tell the truth in all matters. If you find that difficult it is because of the society that egos have created. Maybe you should examine that.

"Four. Keep your promises.

"Five. Develop holy relationships. Turn them over to the Holy Spirit to use for Her purposes. Remember that sex is for mutual satisfaction.

"Six. Live in the present, not the past or the future. As simple and as logical as that seems to most of you, Sigmund was not able to figure it out.

"Seven. Bring children into the world when you have the resources to nourish, educate, and love them. Remember that you must take responsibility for all of your decisions.

"Eight. If you disable the ego part of your brain, you cannot communicate with the Holy Spirit. If you cannot communicate with Her, your chances of finding solutions are confined to the remaining capabilities of your ego system, hardly an intelligent choice. I'm talking 'drugs' here.

"Nine. Invest in the poor. There is enough of everything for everyone.

"Hmm. That's only nine. Ten is a good number. I like ten. That's why I gave you ten fingers and ten toes.

"I got it! Ten. Develop a sense of humor.

"I always thought Jesus was way too serious. But then, He figured out what they were going to do to Him."

"Just a minute. Cecil, what is it?

"Yes, He can say a few words at the end. Check with Allah again and find out what He wants to do. He told me earlier that He wanted to watch the camel races. Confucius and Buddah are going to be tied up all day with orientations. I can't break now because the plane is in the right position.

"While I've got you, it would be nice if someone up here gave Allah a clue. No matter which camel He bets on, it's going to walk home.

(Pause)

"The next part of the program deals with Forgiveness.

333

"One of My creations has chosen this time and place to demonstrate how it works. He is a man you will be hearing a lot about and seeing on TV. He was one of the most powerful men in the world until he chose to steal the disk. He has never made an invitation. He has enjoyed a moderately good life up until now, but he has never been very happy for very long. He hasn't a friend on earth. He's never known peace. He's spent most of his life living in the future in order to avoid the consequences of his mistakes in the past. He is presently in hell, a condition entirely of his own making.

"The other participant is a woman who is the pilot of his plane. She has had some good times and some bad times and I have helped her before when she asked. I haven't heard from her since she asked for help to get her pilot's license. Earlier today, she asked to get on the ground safely at Lake Placid. She did a great job of flying and thought she could handle the situation. Then the man decided to blame the disk instead of himself for his problems. At this moment she has a gun pointed at her head and is having a bad day.

"If you will look to the south, you will see that the plane is approaching at a high rate of speed. The pilot has been ordered to crash into the stage in the center of this group to destroy the disk that he feels is responsible for his discomfort. Please do not be afraid. I know the pilot well and I know she'll do the right thing.

"Kathy, please show your courage and stand in the middle of the stage.

"Jerry! Jerry Lewis! Don't taunt him like that. Put the disk down, return to your seat and control your ego. Most of the people here did not think that was funny because they didn't know it was a CD of Dean Martin favorites.

"Cecil. Have Peter put more guards on the gate...and don't let Elvis's image out of your sight for one second.

"The plane is now over the edge of the crowd, aimed at the center.

"The pilot sees the stage. She sees Kathy.

"She pulls the plane up.

"The man fires the gun and the plane is out of control. It is climbing to the north, and no longer a danger to anyone here.

"The pilot no longer has a functioning body and it falls forward onto the control column. The plane is diving rapidly.

"The man tries to shoot himself, but the negative G-forces have thrown him out of his seat and his head is pressed against the top of the cockpit.

"The pilot is free of her body and I forgive her for her mistakes. She can see the plane crash into the desert.

"The man is now free of his body and I forgive him for his mistakes.

"Now their spirits stand in front of all those who have arrived before and they are invited to join them and watch the rest of the show.

"Ah, just a minute. We seem to have another problem up here.

(Pause)

"OK. It seems that more than half wants to do a re-run of the plane crash.

(Pause)

"No. I'm a merciful God. I know he made a lot of incorrect choices, and she had plenty of chances to make another invitation, but I'm not going to put them through that again.

"Oh, you're going to use real dummies? OK, you should have told Me that.

"OK. I'll put the plane back. There. How's that?

"Bigger? So everyone can see?"

A huge replica of the SuperCee jet hung motionless over the crowd.

"Cut off the skin? Oh, so the people can see the dummies. Got it."

God removed the metal covering the cockpit section of the aircraft. Ralph was sitting in the pilot seat wearing wings on his bus driver uniform. Norton was sitting in the copilot seat wearing his vest and waving a gun around.

335

"Not these dummies!

"Peter. Were you in on this?"

The plane and crew disappeared.

"I'm sorry folks. You don't know what I go through up here. Jesus is going to have a talk with them before this day is over. He wants to say a few words to you also.

(Pause)

"Now that you know how it works, you must turn that knowledge into action. You must begin with the invitation, reach agreement with the Holy Spirit, and turn the problem over to Me to solve. When you are confident and have faith that it works, you must then teach others so that the knowledge isn't lost or forgotten. When you all figure it out, Heaven and Camelot will be one once more.

"William, that's corny. 'Heaven and Earth' has a much better ring to it.

(Pause)

"And now for the good news.

"It looks like you are over the hump. Someone has figured out how this all works and has written down the instructions so that everyone can learn the 'How To'. Knowing that the instructions exist is not enough. Find them and act on them and let's wrap up this project so you can all see what I've got happening on some of My other projects.

"I have one going now that I'm really proud of. It's too far away for any of you to ever get there. Besides, you ought to spend a little more time and effort on the things I mentioned earlier.

"I used a smaller mass resulting in less gravity, added some more oxygen to the air, and used your forms. I have guys who can jump eight feet off the floor and can run all day without getting winded. Most of the spirits up here are watching them play now. I know, we still have the same problem with officiating. I tried

336

calling one game Myself, but it got out of hand and no one had any fun.

"I look forward to visiting each of you in person. The Holy Spirit will bring your agreement to Me.

"OK, Jesus wants to say a few words now."

* * * * *

"Hi. I'm Jesus. I'm feeling much better." He sounded a lot like Robert Kennedy.

"I'd like to congratulate you also on how far you've come. You know, it wasn't such a nice place to live when I was growing up. Everyone felt guilty all the time, and was very defensive. You couldn't have any fun without breaking some law. You were constantly being judged and judging everyone else. It was very stressful. Anyway, I hope I solved all that.

"One word of advice to those of you who are wasting your life by clinging to the old rugged cross. Been there, done that, so you don't have to. Make the invitation and invite My Father into your life. Until you do, of course, you are free to crucify yourself as often as you like.

"Speaking of My Father, I know He's still listening.

"Dad...Cecil said *real* dummies!

"GOTCHA!"

* * * * *

Kathy remained standing in the center of the stage. Larry brought her a printed message from the computer. She read it and then took the mike.

"God thanks you all for showing up here today and the people at home for tuning in to hear Him speak. He said He was sorry for the interruptions, but Cecil thought He could pull it off without a rehearsal.

"He thought it would be better if we closed the show with a personal story to tell and reminded me of a conversation that I had with my father.

"We were on our way to Washington to meet the President and every little thing was upsetting me. I was upset with the press, with the Governor who was there to accompany me, the airline people, everyone.

"My father asked me if I had done my daily lesson as I promised and I had to confess that I hadn't. The moral of the story is that if you make an invitation every day, you probably won't have any bad ones.

"God just said that, didn't He? *Keep your promises.*

"And now, my father has something to say."

* * * * *

"Thank you.

"As a professional educator, I listened to the program today with interest.

"It occurred to me as God spoke that He was saying the same things that I discovered while doing A Course In Miracles. I don't know who wrote it, but I know from experience that it works. And that's what life is; an experience.

"This Course should be in the hands of every educator, priest, minister, doctor, counselor, lawyer, judge, or anyone interested in solving problems, which includes all of us, I guess.

"For those amongst us who can remember everything that was said here today I suggest you put that into action. For those who can't remember or can't figure it out, I suggest getting your hands on the Course and then doing it everyday and not let it sit on the shelf for years like I did. I wasted about eight years of my life by not asking the right question and that is covered in the Course. Lesson number 71.

"Some of you may have seen the TV coverage of the procession and noticed a young Airman in uniform deliver a set of books to me. This set that I'm holding in my hand. This is A Course In Miracles. One of these books is not mine. The Workbook belonged to Emily Mullin, Kathy's physical therapist and her best friend.

"The set was intended to be a gift for Kathy. Emily's brother noticed that Kathy showed an interest in them. Somehow, I

338

received this one by mistake. It is her Workbook. It is full of Emily's notes.

"One note, about half way through, indicated that Emily offered her life to God if Kathy could walk and lead a normal life. Apparently, Emily and the Holy Spirit came to agreement and Emily was willing to pay the price.

"I suggest we all meet here next year and see how much farther we have come towards turning this place into *Camelot.*

"God was right. *Heaven* does sound much better."

End

Appendix

HOW TO MAKE AN INVITATION

By their very nature, books and courses of instruction are linear. They have a beginning and an ending. Such is the case with A Course In Miracles, with a significant distinction that, in each particular person's situation they will be guided to the area of interest to resolve their problem in the most complete and timely manner.

There is no substitute for doing the entire Course in order to gain the maximum benefit, however, many people delay in taking corrective action for their problems until they are well into a crisis stage and no other remedies are presented by their ego. Because you have free will, this should not cause you to feel guilty, unworthy or possessing of bad luck. If you find yourself at this stage, consider yourself completely normal, and that you are going to benefit from other's experiences by taking a short-cut that is going to offer immediate and lasting relief.

Because relaxation and visualization techniques work for many people, you may have heard of them. The lessons presented in A Course In Miracles work **all** of the time, for **everyone.** The problem is: Do you have enough time to learn them before the consequences of your situation take effect? The answer is an overwhelming, "YES". If you have one breath of life left in your body, you can, like the fictitious Mr. Hudson you just read about, make an invitation. I recommend that you not wait until reaching that stage and begin immediately.

In the techniques that follow you are actually going to meet your Creator. This should cause no fear. Nor should you be overcome by awe or anxiety. Peace is the overwhelming experience to anticipate. You are about to receive the gifts that will make you happy.

* * * * *

General Information

Only your mind is necessary to make an invitation. Because your mind lives in a body, which functions in a physical world, the following suggestions are offered to minimize disruptions and distractions and to allow you the optimum conditions to achieve your goal:

1. Select a time and place where you can be alone and feel secure.
2. Hearing the words of a close, trusted friend will greatly increase your chances of getting through. Lacking this relationship, I recommend taping the exercises and listening to them. As a last resort, read them, commit the major parts to memory, and then, just do it.
3. Soft music helps many people. Select pieces that are inspirational to you. Keep the volume low and concentrate on the lesson.
4. Best results are obtained in a prone position on a comfortable surface.
5. Select a location that is neither too hot nor too cold.
6. Wear comfortable, loose clothing.
7. For many people, a pleasant fragrance, such as a bouquet of flowers, is helpful.

* * * * *

Important Note

One part of your mind (your ego) does not want you to do this exercise. It is offering other suggestions, making excuses, reminding you of things that you may have overlooked, etc. You may be experiencing that now.

Here is how to deal with it: Say, "Shut up and go to hell. I am going to solve this problem." Go ahead and say that now if you are being bothered. It is OK to say *hell* in this case as the ego is already there and you won't cause any harm. If you have led a sheltered life and find this a little strong you might say, instead, "Please allow me

some privacy, I have to take care of some rather urgent business."
Just don't give in and give up.

* * * * *

First Attempt (Unassisted)

"God goes with me wherever I go."[1]

This idea will eventually overcome completely the sense of loneliness and abandonment all the separated ones experience. Depression is an inevitable consequence of separation. So are anxiety, worry, a deep sense of helplessness, misery, suffering and intense fear of loss.

The separated ones have invented many "cures" for what they believe to be "the ills of the world." But the one thing they do not do is to question the reality of the problem. Yet its effects cannot be cured because the problem is not real. The idea for today has the power to end all this foolishness forever. And foolishness it is, despite the serious and tragic forms it may take.

Deep within you is everything that is perfect, ready to radiate through you and out into the world. It will cure all sorrow and pain and fear and loss because it will heal the mind that thought these things were real, and suffered out of its allegiance to them.

You can never be deprived of your perfect holiness because its Source goes with you wherever you go. You can never suffer because the Source of all joy goes with you wherever you go. You can never be alone because the Source of all life goes with you wherever you go. Nothing can destroy your peace of mind because God goes with you wherever you go.

We understand that you do not believe all this. How could you, when the truth is hidden deep within, under a heavy cloud of insane thoughts, dense and obscuring, yet representing all you see? *Today,*

---

[1] *Lesson #41. A Course In Miracles. Slightly edited for first time students who would be distracted by instructions for those who started at the beginning of the Course.*

343

we will make our first real attempt to get past this dark and heavy cloud, and to go through it to the light beyond.

Make no effort to think of anything. Try, instead, to get a sense of turning inward, past all the idle thoughts of the world. Try to enter very deeply into your own mind, keeping it clear of any thoughts that might divert your attention.

From time to time, you may repeat the idea if you find it helpful. But most of all, try to sink down and inward, away from the world and all the foolish thoughts of the world. You are trying to reach past all these things. You are trying to leave appearances and approach reality.

It is quite possible to reach God. In fact it is very easy, because it is the most natural thing in the world. You might even say it is the only natural thing in the world. The way will open, if you believe that it is possible. This exercise can bring very startling results even the first time it is attempted, and sooner or later it is always successful. It will never fail completely, and instant success is possible.

Throughout the day use today's idea often, repeating it very slowly, preferably with eyes closed. Think of what you are saying; what the words mean. Concentrate on the holiness that they imply about you; on the unfailing companionship that is yours; on the complete protection that surrounds you.

You can indeed afford to laugh at fear thoughts, remembering that God goes with you wherever you go.

* * * * *

Second Attempt (Unassisted)

Read again Lesson #41. (Close your eyes and think about it for a moment when any of the ideas presented seems to fit your situation.)

* * * * *

344

Hi! I'm Dave. I hope you got a few good laughs out of my book. Now we have some serious work to do.

I am going to be your guide for this lesson. Very few people get the message the first time. Some of us are just stubborn and many of us have our minds already made up. That's OK, but there is no substitute for truth. Truth will make this plain to you as you are brought into the place where you must meet with truth. That is my job, to lead you to God where He and His Son await you. With gentle understanding, I will lead you nowhere else. Where God is, there you are. Such is the truth.

(Close your eyes and think about that. You are going to be led to God.)

It is a journey that I have made many times before. As your guide, I can only accompany you. I will be with you at all times. I will tell you what lies ahead and explain your options. I will be asking for your decisions and you need only say "Yes" or "No". You may stop the journey at any time and return to your present state. There is no harm that can befall you on this journey. You can only profit. I will not be in front of you nor behind you. I will not pull you nor push you. I will only be at your side. Today's voyage will take about thirty minutes, so check the stove and turn on your answering machine. Better still, take the phone off the hook. Nothing is more important than this. Reaffirm with your ego that **you** are in charge.

(Close your eyes, take a deep, comfortable breath and clear your mind.)

If you are ready, we'll begin.

You know that there is something inside of you giving advice, creating feelings and controlling your behavior at times. It has been called many things: soul, spirit, "the real you", etc.

We know that there is great power available in this part of the mind. The problem we face is how do we get to use it. Today, I will give you the answer and then you will have the opportunity to experience it.

The answer is that you must have God's approval before putting it to use. This is to prevent abuse of the power either by design or because of insufficient information on your part. Only good things will be approved.

How do you obtain permission?

Communication with God is achieved through the Holy Spirit. The Holy Spirit does not initiate communication, but **must respond** to your sincere invitation. When the means of communication have been established, conduct your business. You will never be asked to do more than you are capable of and you will always receive more than you ask for.

(Close your eyes and think about that. The Holy Spirit **must respond** to your invitation. Have no thought of rejection.)

Let's take the first step together now.

Visualize the color red. Picture before you a beautiful, red, ripe apple.

Allow yourself to relax. Begin with your facial muscles. Now, slowly let the color red come down over you and relax the back of your neck and your shoulders.

Continue bringing the color red, slowly down your body, relaxing each muscle as you go. Relax your arms and hands. Remove all feeling from your fingers.

Whenever we think of the color red, it will relax us and bring peace.

(Close your eyes, visualize red and feel its relaxation.)

Now change the color to orange. Picture in your mind a sweet, ripe, juicy orange. Think of peace and beauty. Relax the rest of your body. Bring the color orange over the rest of your body. Relax your legs and the bottom of your feet.

(Close your eyes, visualize orange and notice the relaxation.)

To continue our journey we must leave our bodies behind. It will perform perfectly by itself until we return. Notice that your breathing continues without your mindful attention. All of your organs are functioning perfectly. We are directing our thoughts inwardly and leaving our bodies safe and secure. No harm will come to them.

As we think of the color orange, we become completely relaxed and secure. Our body is operating unattended as it does when we are sleeping. We are conscious only of our spirit, which we keep

346

housed in this body. We are completely relaxed, at peace, and have completed our first step on this journey.

(Close your eyes and think of this. No harm has come to you, nor is it likely to.)

Ready for the next step?

Think of the color yellow. See that firm, yellow lemon before you. This is the color of caution. Should we go ahead or should we return. If we go ahead we will experience joy. You will never be unable to face life's problems. You will never again be fearful and you will never again be alone. We can go back. It is up to you. Your body is relaxed, it is functioning perfectly and we are at peace.

(Close your eyes and think of yellow for a moment.)

Let us proceed to the next color, which is green. Here is where I spent most of my youth. On the fields, playing baseball, football and later on, golf. Green was a happy time for me. I hope it was for you also.

Think of green and the happiest time you ever had. Was it on a grassy knoll overlooking the sea? Perhaps under a big, green tree? Choose your favorite green place and lead me to it now.

I am at your side as we approach this lovely spot you have selected. Let us sit here for just a moment and enjoy this lovely green and be thankful for it. Our bodies are functioning perfectly and we are at peace.

(Close your eyes, think of green and remember all the good things associated with this color. Take a few moments here to relax and enjoy.)

Let's move on now as we have work to do.

Visualize the color, blue. Think of "blue-collar", as this is where we are going to work. You are going to build your office here.

There are no restrictions on what you may build. Take a moment and think of what you will need for your office. You will need a comfortable chair for yourself, and some for guests. You need a desk. You can have as many telephones, computers, fax machines, books, etc. as you like. There are no limits. If you wish, you can have an elevator to bring anyone you want to see into your office.

I want you to create a room on one side with a locked door. Only you can open it. The room can be any size you wish, but it can have no windows or other openings. In the center place a small table with one light shining on it. Nothing more.

Take a few moments and build your office or workshop. I will return to the green area and leave you alone to finish your project.

(Close your eyes, visualize blue and then take some time to build your workspace. For now, just the essentials.)

Let us take a moment to go back and check on our bodies. We will find that everything is functioning peacefully and normally without our attention.

(Close your eyes and think about that. If there is any discomfort, adjust that now.)

Remember that red is to relax; orange brings you peace. Think of yellow and acknowledge that no harm has come to you. Think of green and the joy it brings. Blue is for work and your workshop.

(Close your eyes; go through the colors and return to your workshop where we left off.)

We are standing just outside your workshop. I would like to come in and visit with you, but we can do that at another time. Today, we have an important mission.

Before you enter your workshop visualize the color purple and associate that with people. It would be very lonely here without people. Perhaps that is why God made us. Perhaps He was lonely.

I will wait outside while you go into your workshop and try to contact people. You have your television, telephone, your elevator. Sit at your desk and try to make contact with anyone you wish. Perhaps a close friend or confidant. Living or deceased…it makes no difference, as the spirit lives eternally.

(Close your eyes and select a person that you would like to have visit you. Use your tools to assist you in bringing that person to you. Many people have success using the elevator.)

If you had success with that exercise, the next step is assured.

Your workshop is a holy place where only good things are done. I want you now to think of the color white. A clear, pure brilliant white. This light is you. Look around you now and see if you have been carrying around any slime or scales or dirt. If so

348

discard them now and let your pure light shine before you re-enter your workshop.

(Close your eyes and leave all your useless baggage outside. Enter and sit at your desk and look at all that you have created. Here you can work in peace and quiet, quite removed from the problems that surround your body. Take a moment or two to reflect on this.)

You can still hear my voice although I may not enter your private space. It is now time to meet with truth.

There is no substitute for truth. Truth will make this plain to you as you are brought into the place where you must meet with the truth. And there you will be led, with gentle understanding, which can lead you nowhere else. Where God is, there you are. Such is the truth.

Remember the room you built adjacent to your office. If you haven't completed it do so now. One door, one table in the center. No one else may enter.

(Close your eyes and finish the room if you have not done so before. Visualize every detail. Take a moment or two to make sure everything is perfect before continuing.)

Approach the door now. This is the room of Truth. There is now an object on the table. Please enter the room and close the door behind you. If you wish to communicate with God you need only invite the Holy Spirit into your room of truth. Do that and you will know the truth.

When you have done that and made contact, the Holy Spirit will ask you what you want and will offer advice. Remember that God has to give you what you and the Holy Spirit agree to; so do not settle for less.

I will now leave you alone and wait to hear from you.

(Close your eyes and complete the exercise.)

* * * * *

First Attempt (Assisted)

The person that you select to assist you should have one or more positive characteristics, someone who always seems happy and doesn't cause problems, someone that you would like as a friend, perhaps a friend already. If no one like that is available, choose someone who has at least one thing that you like about the person, even if it is only that they are physically attractive or have some smarts. That one thing will do.

Instructions for assistant:

1. Depending on your qualifications, you are filling the role of Teacher, Guide, Companion, Healer or just a Friend. Whatever role you choose will be the right one. Accept the responsibilities that accompany the role you will take.
2. Read the entire Appendix to inform yourself about what you are attempting to achieve.
3. When you have done that, complete as many of the General Information items that you can reasonably accomplish.
4. Read the text exactly as written. Speak slowly and pause after each sentence. Pause longer after each paragraph. Keep the pace uniform. If a particular passage has meaning for you, it may not have any meaning for someone else, so, do not let yourself be tempted to emphasize or diminish certain contents of the exercise.
5. Refrain from answering questions or injecting your own comments into the lesson. There will be plenty of time for that afterwards.
6. Don't worry if you are feeling uncomfortable…that is **your** ego telling you that if this works, **you** might try it, and then **it** will be out of a job.
7. Don't worry about making mistakes. Just do it.

Go ahead now and begin reading Lesson #41, "God goes with me wherever I go."

* * * * *

Second Attempt (Assisted)

Again, choose your assistant with care. Don't blame your assistant because you failed to get through the first time. **Sooner or later, it is always successful.**

Instructions for Assistant:

1. This exercise will require a bit more input from you. You need to make some changes to the text for the second attempt that are appropriate for your relationship with the subject.
2. With a piece of paper and something to write with, review the second lesson and make notes.
3. The introduction, "Hi, I'm Dave, etc. needs to be changed since **you** are going to be taking my place. Decide what you are going to start off saying and put it on your note-paper.
4. If this is your first time, don't say it is, "a journey that I have made many times before." Change anything in this part that is incorrect about you and replace it with factual information concerning yourself.
5. When we get to the color green, change this personal information about me to personal information about you.
6. Make all of the corrections before you begin and have them available to insert at the proper time.
7. Your sense of timing is important. Observe your subject as you are speaking and pause long enough for them to complete their thoughts. It is better to fail on the long side than to cut them off in the midst of thought. If you can develop a method of facial or hand-signals that the subject is ready to continue, by all means, do so.
8. Again, I want to caution you about **your** ego. It wants you to fail. It is going to offer you advice and suggestions that will be counter-productive. It will be most active during the pauses. To defeat it, read ahead in the text, prepare

yourself for what you are going to say next. Inject nothing new. Stay with the script.

Go ahead now and begin reading Lesson #41, "God goes with me wherever I go." Then begin with the introduction you have made on your notes and complete the second exercise.

* * * * *

Notes and Comments

1. It is not necessary to read Lesson #41 prior to any subsequent attempts. Your ego already has received the message and has been unable to defeat the ideas presented.
2. This is not a permanent solution for all of the challenges that life presents. It **is not a replacement** for the entire Course In Miracles. It is only the beginning.
3. With practice, you should be able to move quickly to your workshop. Don't forget to wipe your feet before entering...go all the way to the color white.
4. I, frankly, do not know at what age children ought to be exposed or encouraged to participate. I do know that less harm can come to them via this type of activity versus some of the TV programs that they watch, books that they read, and computer-aided atrocities that they regularly spend huge amounts of money to participate in.
5. This can be tried at home. If you are feeling a bit frisky, you might want to try some of the things God did in the Conclusion to my book. A person more intelligent than me would probably reserve the use of that power for matters of more immediate concern, such as solving problems in a relationship, money or career problems, health problems etc.
6. People who worry about earthquakes die all tensed up. I you do not make the invitation the same thing will probably happen to you, just as it did to Fenhauser...GOTCHA!

Dear Reader,

Thank you for buying *The Invitation*. I have witnessed some significant 'miraculous' recoveries from illnesses and other problems that we humans are faced with on this project. As A Teacher of A Course In Miracles, I try to keep an open-mind and learn from the experiences of others. Toward that end, I would appreciate any feedback from my readers; especially from the results of the exercise outlined in the Appendix.

Please send the results of your experience to me at this address:

The Invitation
12225 North 25th Place
Phoenix, AZ 85032

Your name, address, etc. need not be included. If they are, I guarantee your complete confidence and that's a promise.

Sincerely,
Dave Lucas

353

Coming soon!

VICE OF FOOLS

BY

Dave Lucas

Of all the causes which conspire to blind
Man's erring judgment, and misguide the mind
What the weak head with strongest bias rules.
Is Pride, the never failing vice of fools.

Pope, Essay on Criticism, II

Pride, often considered a virtue, is dissected in this entertaining story involving murder, adventure, and romance. Military and aviation buffs will appreciate the setting while women will enjoy the romance. Both will enjoy the story. A must read for anyone interested in how the Cold War was won.

About the Author

A graduate of Chaminade, a Marianist school in Mineola, New York, Dave Lucas learned the basics of journalism that served him well throughout two very high-tech careers. At age 20 he earned his "wings" as a USAF pilot. At age 26 he found himself commander of a nuclear bomber in the U.S. Air Force Strategic Air Command. He later served as a Maintenance Squadron Commander and Quality Control Officer.

Retiring from the military, he was a successful building engineer in Berkeley, California. Twenty-two years in Berkeley provided a wealth of examples of wrong choices. Having made more than a couple himself, he found solutions in *A Course in Miracles* and became a dedicated student.

He is now fully retired, lives in Puerto Vallarta, Mexico and spends every opportunity implementing the lessons to help other people as a teacher. He has accomplished some rather significant "miraculous recoveries" using the technique described in the book.